Endorsements for *Tears of a Dragon*

Tears of a Dragon was absolutely riveting. I honestly couldn't put it down. This series has inspired me, driven me to be a better man. I've always identified with Billy, but for him to ask in this book, "How far do I really trust God?" and answer, both as a man orsf faith and a hero, was the ultimate way to end this story. If you pass *Tears of a Dragon* by, you will miss something special.

—**Chris Shupe** (Age 24)

This is an extremely powerful and life-changing novel, surpassing all the others in the series. The mysteries and prophecies were astounding. How Mr. Davis has intertwined God and spiritual truths in this book is amazing. I could read it at least five times over and find something new each time. These books have touched and changed many lives, including mine, making me want to grow closer to God and increase my faith. I thank God for giving the inspiration and Mr. Davis for creating these magnificent books. I pray that these books go forth and change lives just as they have changed mine.

—**Alyssa Smith** (Age 14)

Tears of a Dragon is a stunning conclusion to the series! I loved it! It was the epitome of a grand archetypal battle: ultimately what is torn asunder will be put right. And the ending was precious. Absolutely precious!

—**Lynne Stephenson** (Age 21)

I loved *Tears of a Dragon*! I tried to decide on my favorite character, but I love them all. I believe the *Dragons in our Midst* series is an answer to the prayers of moms, dads, extended family, educators, the Christian community, and especially grandmothers like me who share a passion for Christ and want to pass it on to our youth.

I am thrilled to recommend Bryan Davis's books as I speak to groups around the country. It is exciting to see the way parents and young readers respond after reading the first book. Adults who think these books are just for children are missing a treat!

—**Shelby S. Parris** (Grandmother of 6)

WOW! *Tears of a Dragon* is so good! Now, books from other series seem boring by comparison. The *Dragons in our Midst* series is THE greatest EVER, and *Tears of a Dragon* is my favorite!

—**Rachel Brown** (Age 11)

Tears of a Dragon rocks! While I read it, I felt what Billy and Bonnie went through. It's like I was in the story throughout the whole book.

—**Kelsey Marsh** (Age 12)

I really enjoyed *Tears of a Dragon* because it had a lot of action, entwined with mythology that taught me about the past. My favorite part was the ending when everyone made a very important decision based on what was in their hearts.

—**Kevin Kenel** (Age 14)

I love this book! In fact, this is my favorite book in the *Dragons in our Midst* series. It was so cool how the story ended. Once again, Walter and Larry crack hilarious jokes.

—**Nic Laudadio** (Age 13)

Move over Harry Potter! Here comes *Dragons in our Midst*. This adventurous story keeps the pages turning. I love dragons, and this fantasy series contains the most realistic dragon characters that I have ever read. I love how they are an intelligent species similar to humans rather than dumb animals, which would not do justice to their magnificence. I love these books and the author, and I hope there are many more.

—**Joshua DeMarco** (Age 11)

Tears of a Dragon has a way of gripping readers and holding them in suspense, and you NEVER want to put it down. I read this over the summer and it's a good thing, because I would not have stopped to go to school. I love how Mr. Davis is able to incorporate God into the story and make it upbeat and a thriller. The characters are realistic, and the reader comes to love them all in their own special ways. To anyone who loves to read fantasy like I do—keep with Mr. Davis; his books are the best!

—**Jenna DeMarco** (Age 15)

Tears of a Dragon hits the top. It has action, romance, and everything else I can think of. I love it!

—**Stephanie Coe** (Age 9)

The *Dragons in our Midst* books have more suspense than all the Harry Potter books combined! It's an awesome series!

—**Jared Wood** (Age 17)

Tears of a Dragon

Bryan Davis

LIVING INK BOOKS™
Writing Worth Reading™

Tears of a Dragon
Copyright © 2005 by Bryan Davis
Published by AMG Publishers
6815 Shallowford Rd.
Chattanooga, Tennessee 37421

All rights reserved. Except for brief quotations in printed reviews, no part of
this publication may be reproduced, stored in a retrieval system or transmit-
ted in any form or by any means (printed, written, photocopied, visual elec-
tronic, audio, or otherwise) without the prior permission of the publisher.

All Scripture quotations, unless otherwise noted, are taken from the
NEW AMERICAN STANDARD BIBLE, Copyright © 1960, 1962,
1963, 1968, 1971, 1972, 1973, 1975, 1977 by The Lockman Foundation.
Used by permission. All rights reserved.

ISBN: 0-89957-173-5

First printing—October 2005

Cover designed by Daryle Beam, Market Street Design, Inc., Chattanooga,
    Tennessee
Interior design and typesetting by Reider Publishing Services, West
    Hollywood, California
Edited and proofread by Becky Miller, Susie Davis, Sharon Neal, Rick Steele,
    and Dan Penwell

Printed in the United States of America
17 16 15 14 13 12 –W– 14 13 12 11 10

Library of Congress Cataloging-in-Publication Data

Davis, Bryan, 1958-
    Tears of a dragon / by Bryan Davis.
        p. cm. — (Dragons in our midst ; bk. 4)
    Summary: Ashley and Billy, aided by the dragons, their friends,
and a powerful, ancient book, each take courageous steps to rescue
loved ones from Morgan Le Faye and her demonic Watchers.
        ISBN-13: 978-0-89957-173-7 (pbk. : alk. paper)
        ISBN-10: 0-89957-173-5 (pbk. : alk. paper)
        [1. Dragons—Fiction. 2. Demonology—Fiction. 3. Knights and
knighthood—Fiction. 4. Christian life—Fiction. 5. Supernatural—
Fiction.] I. Title. II. Series: Davis, Bryan, 1958- Dragons in our midst ; bk. 4.
PZ7.B285557Tea 2005
[Fic]—dc22   2005023905

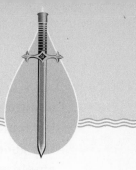

Recap of *Raising Dragons, The Candlestone,* and *Circles of Seven*

As the group huddled around the campfire, Bonnie opened a notebook on her lap and withdrew a Papermate from its coil binding. She and Professor Hamilton would soon be leaving for Baltimore, so she had a few minutes to add to her journal. The professor had suggested that she write something for Sir Barlow to read in the hospital, maybe something about their adventures since he probably didn't know all the details.

Bonnie decided to write a letter to fill him in. She kicked a marshmallow-roasting stick away from the fire. Where should she start? Ah! She lifted a finger in the air. With the dragons!

> To my friend and brave knight, Sir Barlow,
>
> Back in the sixth century, as you know, hundreds of fire-breathing dragons ruled the skies. The people of Camelot feared these beautiful creatures, because many of them would steal from humans and burn their houses down. A few even consumed the humans themselves, a crime that prompted King Arthur and his noble knights to try to eliminate dragons from the kingdom.
>
> So King Arthur told Sir Devin and the other dragon slayers to kill all the dragons, but the king was

unaware that some of the dragons did not take part in the murder or thievery. Merlin, therefore, prayed for the good dragons to be transformed into humans, shielding them from the slayers. Since the dragon-humans retained a genetic predisposition toward long life, they were able to live for centuries. A few of them gave birth to children and passed dragon traits to them. For example, Billy Bannister is able to breathe fire, and I, Bonnie Silver, have dragon wings.

Sir Devin survived through the centuries using the healing photoreceptors in dragon blood in combination with a candlestone, a gem that absorbs light. It weakens a dragon but provides power for Devin, who killed all the known dragon-humans except for one, Billy's father, Jared, who was known as Clefspeare. After Devin supposedly killed my mother, Irene, who was called Hartanna as a dragon, I escaped Montana and found Billy in West Virginia. Then Devin, disguised as our school's principal, found out that Billy had a dragon father and tried to kill both Billy and me.

Billy's father transformed back into a dragon, and we all escaped Devin when I disintegrated him with Excalibur. Then my father found me and claimed my mother was still alive, so I went home with him to Montana.

When Walter, Professor Hamilton, and Billy followed us, they found Excalibur, but it took awhile for Billy to learn to use its laser beam to transluminate people, a process that changes matter into light energy, which disperses if it isn't trapped in a candlestone or something else that can hold it in place.

Speaking of the candlestone, my father told me that he transluminated my mother and stored her in the candlestone until he could find a way to heal her, so I had to go in and get her out. That's where Ashley, my father's lab assistant, comes in. She invented the machinery to transform me into light energy so I could dive into the candlestone and pull my mother out. Then my mother and I were supposed to travel into a restoration dome, a tall glass cylinder that would transform us back to our physical forms.

When I dove into the candlestone, I discovered that Devin was really trapped there instead of my mother, and I got trapped myself. It turns out that my father had been experimenting with dragon blood, trying to make people live longer, and he needed the candlestone empty to make it work. He adopted some runaways—Karen, Rebecca, Stacey, and Pebbles—and used them in his experiments. Eventually, the girls escaped and were taken in by Billy's mother. Ashley, who is a super genius because she's also a daughter of a dragon, calls those girls her sisters.

Finally, Billy came into the candlestone to rescue me, and he found some knights from King Arthur's time. (One of them, of course, was you, Sir Barlow, and I still laugh when I remember you thinking I was an ape!) Well, Billy was able to get everyone out, including, unfortunately, Devin, who became a half-restored, energy monster and killed my father. Billy slashed through Devin with Excalibur's beam and turned him into a formless spirit that escaped to his mistress, the dark sorceress, Morgan Le Faye. Morgan had been in charge of the dragon slayers all along. She wanted to kill all the dragons so she could set free the most powerful demons in the world, the Watchers, from the lowest pit of Hades.

I'm sorry, Sir Barlow. I'm getting ahead of myself. Regarding the trip to Hades, Billy first went to England with the professor, because they found out that Billy is an heir to King Arthur. In order for him to be initiated as the rightful king, Sir Patrick said he had to go into a place called the circles of seven to rescue prisoners. It turned out that this place was actually Hades, and Morgan had trapped Patrick's daughter, Shiloh, there.

The other prisoners in that place were the spirits of the dragons turned humans that the slayers had murdered over the centuries. Morgan's henchmen were able to get Billy's father, Clefspeare, to enter the circles, but once there, the spirit of Devin took over the dragon's body, and Clefspeare's spirit was cast into the abyss with the Watchers. Billy revived the dragon prisoners and got them and Shiloh out, but in the process, he also released the Watchers.

The dragons escaped from Hades through a portal in Glastonbury, England. They were real, fire-breathing dragons, and the media covered the whole event, including getting pictures of me with my dragon wings. And since the demons escaped as well, the entire world was suddenly plunged into peril. Because of the danger and the media exposure, we all had to escape and camp out here in the middle of nowhere in West Virginia.

But even now we're in danger. The Watchers are fallen angels with tremendous power who could probably find us easily. They fear only dragons, the creatures who defeated them millennia ago. Morgan knows she has to defeat the dragons before she can use the Watchers to dominate the world. The greatest mystery for us is what happened to the spirit of Billy's father.

We have one clue. Shiloh had a pendant with a centrally mounted rubellite, the gem of dragons. When she emerged from the circles of seven, the gem pulsed with a red light. We don't know what it means, but Billy has it now, and we're trying to figure out the puzzle.

Professor Hamilton rose to his feet. "Miss Silver. Are you ready to go?"

Bonnie lifted a finger again. "One second." She scribbled her ending.

> I have to go now, Sir Barlow. I'll be delivering this letter, and some blood for your healing, in a little while. May God speed your recovery.
>
> Love,
> Bonnie Silver

Bonnie pushed her pen back into the coils. "I think I got it all, Professor, but it's a long story. I think someone could write a whole book series about what's happened to us."

"Maybe someone will," the professor said, helping her to her feet. "Maybe someone will."

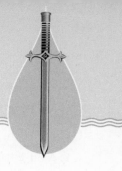

CONTENTS

CONTENTS

A boy dreams with a sword in his hand. A girl gives him reason to draw it from its scabbard, and she infuses him with the power to charge into battle.

This book is for every boy, even those who are now wrinkled and gray, who feels his heart race and his spine tingle every time a sword is drawn to conquer an enemy. Although many of us often feel weak, when our women and children are in danger, we transform into mighty warriors.

This book is for every girl, even those who have given birth to boys and girls of their own, who feels her heart swell when she mends up her wounded man and sends him back out, fully charged and ready to battle for the sake of righteousness. Without you, our swords would rust in their scabbards.

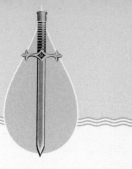

ACKNOWLEDGMENTS

I would like to depart from the usual format of acknowledgments and just say thank you again to everyone I mentioned in the first three books.

For this book, the final installment of *Dragons in our Midst*, I want to set aside this section exclusively for my wonderful life mate, Susie.

My wife, my love, without you, I could never have written this series of books. You have faithfully stood by me, correcting hundreds of errors as you read the manuscripts over and over again. Your dedication is unmatched. Your patience is unparalleled. Your love is unfathomable.

MERLIN'S PROMISE

When dragons flew in days of old
With flashing scales and flame,
They soared in scarlet droves of fear
With hearts no man could tame.

The Watchers sang a siren's chant,
Seducing tickled ears,
Ensnaring girls with heads laid bare
And dragons far and near.

While most fell prey to Satan's song,
A few held fast their birth
And worshipped God's created realm,
Religion of the earth.

Content to suffer wrapped in chains,
A dragon leaves the skies.
Content to bleed for souls unknown,
A dragon bows and dies.

But can such faith repel the wrath
When evil is reborn?
Can sacrifice alone endure
When scaly hearts are torn?

A warrior comes with sword and shield,
With truth and faith in hand,
Exposing lies and cutting through
The darkness in the land.

Has eye not seen, has ear not heard,
The love that sets men free?
From scales to flesh he softens hearts;
From red to white he bleeds.

And when the warrior rests his blade,
With virgin bride he kneels.
The dragons fade from scales to dust
And bless the golden seal.

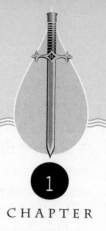

FAMA REGIS

Bonnie leaned against the bedrail and clutched Sir Barlow's burly hand. "I'm glad you're feeling better."

Barlow smiled, lifting his mustache. His dark eyes sparkled. "Yes, Miss. Thanks to an infusion of your blood, I am as fit as a fiddle." The knight's brow furrowed under thick strands of unkempt hair. "That is the correct idiom, isn't it?"

Bonnie tightened her grip on Barlow's hand and laughed. "That's the perfect idiom for a true gentleman!"

Barlow's smile broadened, revealing a chipped front tooth among a half-dozen yellowed incisors.

A new voice filled the room, strong and cheerful. "Indeed it is the correct idiom. A fine violin well played is fit for heaven itself."

Bonnie spun toward the sound. Professor Hamilton, her teacher and friend, ambled into the hospital room, unbuttoning his black trench coat. She glanced at a clock on the wall. "Did you run into trouble somewhere?"

"Only minor annoyances." The professor clipped a cell phone to his belt and leaned a wet umbrella against the wall. "I'm afraid the foul weather has caused the entire populace to forget customary manners. There seems to be a general uneasiness, an underlying anxiety weighing down every man, woman, and child." He pulled a wrapped sandwich from his coat pocket and handed it to Bonnie. "The restaurant queue seemed interminable, and several pushy fellows insisted on . . . ahem . . . butting into the line." The professor nodded at Barlow. "I could have used the services of a battle-trained warrior." He withdrew another sandwich from his opposite pocket. "This is for you, but Dr. Kaplan said you must maintain the hospital diet until tonight, so I'll save it. Was your noontime meal sufficient?"

Barlow mumbled something unintelligible under his breath, then added in a louder voice, "A ghost couldn't survive eating the paltry servings here."

Bonnie put her sandwich in the side pocket of her backpack. "I'll go outside to eat this later. No use torturing our good knight." She hitched up her pack to make her hidden dragon wings more comfortable. "Did Sir Patrick have any news?"

"Quite a bit." The professor ran his hand through his unruly white hair. "It seems that the Great Key, as he calls it, is now in William's possession. Apparently Shiloh gave it to him last night at the campfire."

Bonnie caressed a colorful string of beads around her neck. "The pendant with the rubellite? How is that a key?"

"Patrick says he will tell us more when he comes." The professor squinted at the intravenous tube stretching from a dangling plastic bag to Barlow's arm, then pulled a pair of spectacles from his shirt pocket. "He did tell me that Merlin called it the Great Key in a prophecy, indicating that it would be crucial should the Watchers ever emerge from their prison." He slipped the glasses on

2

and read the label on the IV bag. "Patrick confirmed our thoughts, that we should locate the king's chronicles. The book will help us unlock the mystery of the key." He lowered his head and sighed.

Bonnie tried to make eye contact with the professor. "Is something wrong with Sir Barlow's IV?"

The professor's gentle smile quivered. "No, no. That's not it at all." He slid his hands into his pockets. "It just reminded me of days long past when I spent many hours coaxing instruments like these to work just a little bit better." Drooping his head, he pushed an electrical cord under the bed with his foot. "Those were times of shadows, the darkest days of my life."

Bonnie took a step closer. "Do you mind telling me what happened?"

"Oh, no. Not at all." The professor pulled a wallet from his back pocket and fished out a locket-sized photo from inside. He bent over and showed it to her.

Bonnie studied the photo, a black-and-white picture of a man in a tuxedo and a woman in a wedding gown. She felt the joy of the smiling faces and the oneness of the clasped hands. "She's beautiful, Professor. You look very happy."

"Yes, we both were." He returned the photo to his wallet and straightened. "It has been more than twenty years since she passed away."

"I knew she died, but I didn't know when." She took the professor's hand in hers, trying again to catch his faraway gaze. "It must have been very sad for you."

The professor finally looked down at her and smiled, but it was a sad smile. "Indeed. She was the light of my life. We were as close as two people can be, one mind, one spirit. Our daughter, Elizabeth, was about to be married, and the evening before the wedding, we attended the rehearsal dinner, a beautiful affair at a posh restaurant—white tablecloths, crystal, silver, fine

3

china—all the trimmings of an elegant feast. Later that night, my wife became deathly ill—food poisoning of some sort—and she had to go to the hospital. She insisted that the wedding go on as planned, and since one of my students, Carl Foley, whom you know, of course, as Walter's father, volunteered to stay with her, we decided to set up a live video feed to the room so she could attend the ceremony from her hospital bed."

"Then she got to see the wedding?"

"Yes, but by the time I returned to her side, she had worsened. The doctors had no explanation, but it was as if she were drifting away; her mind was leaving her body. She would cry out, 'Help me! I'm falling!' though she lay securely in bed. As you can imagine, I was beside myself, but God did not answer my prayers according to my desires." He straightened the intravenous tube, his bottom lip quivering as his voice began to crack. "She . . ." He swallowed and wiped a tear. "She passed away that very night."

Bonnie slid her hand around his elbow and leaned her head against his arm. "I'm so sorry, Professor."

He leaned over and kissed Bonnie gently on the top of her head. "As were many others, little angel. It was such a lovely funeral with hundreds of gracious mourners. And so many people brought flowers! We both loved our flower garden, so I made sure I flooded the funeral home with her favorite, the carnation, and I added Easter lilies, of course, but the guests brought dozens and dozens of bouquets and laid them against the casket. And, strangely enough, people also brought dresses and skirts my wife had made for their daughters." He laughed under his breath, his eyes glistening. "She couldn't bear to make pants for them. She believed young ladies should look like young ladies. In any case, the visitors expressed their thankfulness for my wife's skill and generosity in sharing her love with so many friends and neighbors. It was as if the story of Dorcas in the book of Acts were being replayed at the funeral." A new tear made its way down the sage's wrinkled cheek, and his voice pitched up ever so slightly. "But there was no apostle Peter to come and awaken my precious one from sleep." The professor raised his hand and bit his knuckle, closing his eyes as his body heaved with stifled sobs.

Bonnie wrapped her arms around his waist and held him close. She glanced at Sir Barlow. Tears streamed down the knight's face, too.

After a long pause, the professor spoke again, his voice now much stronger. "So I will have to go to her when I finish my course here on earth, and I look forward to that day with great anticipation."

Bonnie gave him a strong hug. "I know you miss her, but I hope your course isn't finished for a long time." She pulled away, looking up at the professor with the brightest smile she could muster. "So she was a seamstress? What a wonderful gift!"

"Yes. What she could do with a needle and thread!" He sighed again, his lips tightening. "But that is in the past, and there are new dark days to deal with, I'm afraid." He strolled to the window, sliding his hands into his pockets again as he gazed at the wet landscape through the foggy glass. Raindrops pelted the windowpane, sounding like a hundred soft fingers tapping for permission to enter. "I am concerned for Patrick. He seems weak . . . exhausted." He withdrew one hand and sketched a square on the condensation. "He is many centuries old, even older than I knew. And now, being fully human, he will certainly die. I fear his days are coming to a close."

He wiped away the condensation with his sleeve. "And Patrick informed me that this is no ordinary weather event. These monsoon conditions are spreading over the entire North

5

American continent, and a similar phenomenon is beginning in Europe. While I was walking in the downpour, it seemed that each drop emitted a popping noise as it struck the sidewalk, much like the sputter of a droplet on a hot fryer, yet so faint that I doubt I would have noticed if I had not leaned over to pluck a quarter from the walk. With thousands of droplets popping, it reminded me of Rice Krispies in a bowl of milk."

"Do you think that's what's making people so irritable and jumpy?" Bonnie asked.

"Very possibly. If this is demonic work, stirring fear in the hearts of people would certainly fit their modus operandi, but there may be more substance to this rain than simple fear mongering."

Barlow sat up in bed and threw off his sheets. "There is no time to lose." He stripped the tape that held his IV tube in place. "Those scoundrels from the abyss are a step ahead of us. We must summon my knights to battle!"

Bonnie wrapped her fingers around Barlow's wrist. "Wait! The nurse will do that."

The professor jumped to the bedside and grasped Barlow's shoulder. "Patience, my good fellow. Dr. Kaplan has already ordered your discharge. We will get you out of here as soon as possible."

Barlow laid his hand over Bonnie's, an apologetic look on his face. "I'm sorry for my outburst, Miss, but I'm anxious to lead my men into battle against the demons."

Bonnie gently fastened the tape back on Barlow's arm. "It won't be long now. If we can get you out of here soon enough, we can all go and get Sir Patrick and your knights at the airport."

"That reminds me," the professor said. "We couldn't possibly carry everyone in my car, so I called Marilyn this morning and asked her to fly here and ferry some of us back to West Virginia."

Bonnie straightened the IV tube and draped it around the bed. "Did you ask Billy to search for King Arthur's book?"

The professor patted her on the shoulder. "Yes. He said he would search for it right away."

"Right away? In this downpour?"

"Yes. With the Watchers on the move, we must act quickly. If they are able to manipulate the weather, the magnitude of the disasters they can wreak is incalculable." He ran his finger along the IV tube and sighed, his eyes wet with new tears. "Are you ready to face more danger, Miss Silver?"

Warmth surged through Bonnie's body, as if an oven-heated blanket wrapped around her and chased away the autumn chill. She gazed at her teacher. If only there were some way she could give him a glimpse of all the wonder she had seen in heaven after dying in the sixth circle. What earthly words could possibly express the joy of perfect bliss? "Professor, I have been in the arms of my Lord in heaven, and I saw a reflection of my face in his laughing eyes." She felt her own tears welling up as she folded her hands at her waist. "I've never been more ready in all my life."

7

B illy tiptoed across the rocky cave floor, guiding Excalibur with both hands. The sword's energy pierced the darkness and spread out into a glowing sphere, surrounding him in a wash of alabaster light. As he glided under the bright shroud, the cave's shifting air penetrated his skin like the grip of a life-devouring phantom.

The professor's call had already delivered a numbing bite to his senses. "Locate *Fama Regis*," he had said. "And guard the pendant well. The fate of the entire world could hang in the balance."

Billy shivered hard. His journey to the dragon's den had begun under gloomy skies that quickly deteriorated into a torrential downpour. Now, in the cave's cool draft, his wet clothes sapped his body heat. He freed one hand and blew a stream of superheated breath on his fingers, making them toasty warm in seconds.

As he advanced deeper into the expansive cavity, a hint of danger pricked his mind, prompting him to creep more slowly, one gentle step after another. A trickle of water echoed nearby. That was new. Clefspeare's cave had always been perfectly dry before. But now a steady plink, plink, plink troubled the silence, slowly escalating in frequency. The sound racked his nerves. He couldn't see any water yet, but those drips had to collect somewhere, and that meant trouble. If a growing pool reached the ancient book . . .

He stopped and sniffed the damp air. After his experiences with scentsers in the circles of seven, he vowed never to let one of those mind-altering odors sneak up on him again. This was no time to get waylaid by sleepiness or anger, or even worse, fits of laughter. The needle on his danger meter pushed toward the yellow-alert zone, but he had no way to tell who, or what, might be lurking in the shadows. It was time for silence.

He dimmed the sword's glow and crept forward again, mentally shushing the crunching pebbles under his hiking boots. At the back of the cave, the walls came together in a crease. A collection of marble-sized stones lay in a pile where the corner met the floor. Billy crouched, picked up one of the stones, and brought it close to the sword. Its polished facets shimmered red, sending streaks of crimson across his fingers. A laser-like beam shot toward an octagonal pendant dangling from a chain around his neck. The gem in the pendant's center seemed to answer the stone's red aura, pulsing vibrantly with its own shade of crimson like the heart of a ready warrior.

"Yo! Billy!"

Billy dropped the gem and jumped to his feet. He extended Excalibur and brightened its glow. "Walter? Is that you?"

"Who else?" Walter stepped into the sword's corona. "Thanks for the light. It would've been hard to find you without that overgrown mosquito zapper." He extended a dripping umbrella. "It's pouring out there. I thought you might want this." He pulled down the hood of his olive drab rain slicker. "Something wrong?"

Billy tucked the pendant under his shirt and took the umbrella. "My danger alarm's working overtime, so you kind of spooked me. But it couldn't be you setting it off; you're not dangerous."

"Who says so?" Walter unbuttoned the front of his raincoat. "I'll bet Devin thinks I'm dangerous by now, sitting in that candlestone with nothing to do but twiddle his claws."

Billy poked his friend's lean belly with the umbrella and grinned. "You're only dangerous at the buffet line." He propped the sword against his shoulder and tilted his head upward. "I hear water dripping, and it's getting louder."

"No wonder. It's raining so hard out there I had to ask directions from a fish." Walter glanced all around the dim chamber. "The cave probably has a leak somewhere."

"Yeah, could be." Billy tapped the floor with the umbrella, shaking out a spray of droplets. "I thought you were staying with the womenfolk. That's more important than keeping me dry."

"Your mom decided there was enough room for everyone to head for Baltimore." Walter began counting on his fingers. "Prof will drive back with Barlow, Fiske, Standish, and Woodrow, and your mom will fly back with Bonnie, Ashley, Karen, Shiloh, Patrick, Newman, and Edmund." He shrugged his shoulders.

9

"Sounded like a boring trip, and besides, Karen stays glued to me like old chewing gum, so I decided to hike up here where the action is."

"It's dull as dirt here," Billy said. "I was hoping the dragons would fly in. That'll stir things up."

"Yeah. Ashley said they could get here today if they hurried. I told her we'd go dragon riding as soon as they finish off the Watchers, but who knows how long that'll take." Walter bent down and kicked some loose gravel. "Any luck finding the book?"

Billy pushed the top of the pile of stones with the umbrella tip. "Not yet. I thought Dad would've hidden it in his cave, but all I've found is this pile of gems."

"Gems? Cool!" Walter held up a black square of leather. "If you cash those in, I guess you won't be needing this."

"My wallet?" Billy took it and stuffed it in his back pocket.

"Yeah. Your mom put some money in there in case you needed it." Walter shoved the pile of gems with his shoe, then knelt and leaned close. "Well, Sherlock, I guess you didn't look right under your nose."

Billy lowered the sword, lighting up the stones. An old leather binding protruded from the toppled pile. "I didn't have a chance," he said, dropping the umbrella and grabbing the book. "You sneaked up on me before I could." He blew a coat of sand from the cover.

Walter stood again and craned his neck to read the raised script. "What does *Fama Regis* mean?"

"The acts of the king, or something like that. It was written by Arthur's scribe." Billy opened the heavy cover. "Believe it or not, the scribe was Palin for a while." He flipped through several pages of thick parchment. "And he drew some awesome pictures. Take a look." He gave the book to Walter and held Excalibur close. In a drawing, a knight draped in chain mail raised his sword and shield against a lunging dragon. The dragon blasted the shield with a tsunami of flames, its wings fully extended in battle. A young lady dressed in silky white stood close by, her delicate hands covering her ivory cheeks.

Billy tapped on the parchment. "Let's get this to camp. Maybe when Prof gets back we'll find some clues and—" He spun around, pointing Excalibur toward the cave entrance.

Walter slapped the book closed and whispered. "What's up? Danger getting close?"

"Big time." He lit up Excalibur like a blazing torch and nodded toward the entrance. "Come on. I'm tired of waiting for danger to sneak up on me. Let's give our visitor a greeting he'll never forget."

Billy charged ahead, Excalibur's beacon leading the way. As they neared the entrance, muted daylight mixed into the darkness, brightening with every step. Billy halted at the archway and glanced all around, sniffing, listening. Walter skidded to a stop at his side. A curtain of rainwater cascaded from the top of the entry arch, pelting the ground and streaming down the slope, away from the cave. Billy whispered, "You smell something?"

Walter wrinkled his nose. "Yeah. Smells like a wet dog."

A twangy voice rose in the distance. "Now, Hambone, ain't nuthin' to be skeered of in that cave. Do you want to get colder 'n a nekkid rat in Alaska?" A skinny, long-legged man pushed through a thicket, a shotgun poised on his shoulder and an old hound trailing behind on a leash.

Billy laughed. "It's just Arlo Hatfield!"

Walter tucked *Fama Regis* under his coat and fastened the buttons. "Cool! I've been wanting to meet him."

11

"Danger's still close," Billy whispered, "but I don't want to explain Excalibur to Arlo." He thrust the sword into his back scabbard and waved at the old hillbilly. "Pssst! Arlo! Get in here, quick!"

Arlo tightened his grip on his gun for a second, but when his gaze found its way to the cave entrance, he relaxed. He spat out a stream of tobacco juice and stepped up his pace. "C'mon, Hambone. Looks like we'll have comp'ny."

The blue tick hound hesitated, prompting Arlo to pull him along. "What's wrong with you today? Ain't you got a lick o' sense? You remember Billy, donchoo? The boy what lost his pa?"

Arlo jerked Hambone's leash, nearly dragging him forward. He gawked at Billy, water streaming from the bill of his baseball cap. "Whatchoo doin' here?"

Billy gestured for Arlo to come inside. He stooped and petted Hambone, still whispering. "I was looking for something that belonged to my . . . uh . . . my pa." As he stroked the dog's ears, his pendant fell outside his shirt again and dangled on its chain. "Why are you here?"

"Hambone and me were out huntin' squirrels near the crick when the rain commenced to gettin' mighty fierce. I remembered the cave up here, so we came lookin' fer it. But Hambone's actin' awful queer, like he's skeered of somethin'."

Billy stood again. "Maybe the weather has him spooked. I haven't seen it rain like this in . . . in a coon's age."

Arlo scratched his head through his cap. "Could be. But I don't rightly know how long a coon lives." He reached out and slipped his fingers behind Billy's pendant. "Now here's a purty thang. It's flashin' like a radio tower light. Where'd you git it?"

Billy's danger sensation suddenly jumped to red alert, a thousand needles pricking his skin. The pendant's glow washed over the hillbilly's face like a pulsing laser. His wrinkled skin seemed to melt, rivulets of flesh pouring down like bloody sweat until a new face appeared, a shining, ghostly visage with cruel red eyes.

Billy jumped back and yanked out Excalibur. Walter leaped at Arlo and twisted the shotgun from his grip, giving the hillbilly a hefty shove as it pulled away. Arlo stumbled back into the downpour, leaving Hambone in the cave. As water splashed on his head, the hillbilly's face reappeared as if painted on his skin by the windswept rain.

Excalibur's beam shot out from the tip and waved over Arlo's head. "I don't know who or what you are," Billy shouted, "but if you take one step, I'll zap you to kingdom come."

A glowing foot stepped forward, leaving Arlo's foot behind. Then, an entire body emerged from the hillbilly, a nine-foot-tall goliath of a man dressed in brilliant silver mail. Arlo's body collapsed behind him, motionless.

"Go ahead and strike!" the man shouted. "I've already been to kingdom come."

Billy tightened his grip and whispered to Walter, "I hate it when someone dares me to strike. It usually means it won't work."

Walter broke open the shotgun barrel and peered inside. "No shells." He tossed the gun on the ground. "You got any fire-breathing ammo?"

"Yep. It's been brewing in my belly for a while."

"Then let's fry this pig and start makin' bacon."

Billy dimmed his sword and launched a torrent of fire at the creature, splattering his shining body with biting orange flames. The man swelled in size, growing to at least twelve feet tall. Plumes of steam shot into the air as sheets of rain cooled the inferno.

Walter grabbed Hambone's leash and backed away. "So much for that idea."

"No! Wait!" Billy pointed with Excalibur. "Something's up!"

The humanoid creature stumbled on shaky legs, smoke rising from his scorched torso. He dropped to his knees and spread his arms wide. He shouted, "Be closed!"

A rolling wave of darkness flew from the creature's hands. It splashed against the cave entrance and spread out, laying a sooty coat over the archway.

Billy lit up Excalibur again and swiped the beam against the black curtain. It tore across the expanse, and sparks of light ate away the darkness like buzzing termites.

"He doesn't like the fire!" Walter shouted. "Hit him again!"

Billy launched another fiery salvo, but it bounced off the entrance and shot just past his head toward the inner recesses of the cave. Hambone whined a mournful lament.

Walter hovered his hand over the archway. "A force field?" He kicked at the base of the field, sending out a splash of sparks. "Owww!" he yelled, jumping on one foot. "These things are such a pain!"

The shining creature stood and laughed. "That should keep you in there long enough."

"Long enough for what?" Billy yelled.

"You'll soon find out." An evil smile grew on his face. He opened his enormous palm to the sky, allowing the rain to pool and drip over the sides. "These waters are courtesy of my lord, the prince of the power of the air. He sends his greetings, young king, and hopes you will enjoy a refreshing swim."

Walter slung a baseball-sized rock at the force field, but it ricocheted harmlessly back. "You're a big talker for someone who's scared of a couple of kids and a hound dog!"

A pair of wings sprouted from the back of the creature. "We are wise enough to know our weaknesses. Why battle against your strengths?" He laughed and launched into the air, disappearing from sight.

14

"Coward!" Walter shouted. "Come back and fight like a . . ." His voice trailed off to a whisper. "Like a man . . . I guess."

Billy gazed at the hillbilly's body on the ground outside. Rain poured over the still form without mercy. "I sure hope Arlo's okay." He touched the field with Excalibur's tip. The contact point sizzled and threw the blade back. "The blade won't pierce it." He summoned the beam and let it slowly approach the field. As soon as it brushed the surface, the beam angled away as if bouncing off a mirror. He doused the light. "It must not be like the portals in the circles. The beam doesn't faze it either."

"It's not soundproof," Walter noted. "We heard that ghost creature, and I still hear the storm."

Billy turned slowly toward the back of the cave. "I hear something else."

"The dripping sound again?"

"More like gushing now."

Hambone let out a howl. A stream of shallow water had pooled all around, lapping against the dog's paws. It flowed to the cave entrance and stopped at the force field, unable to drain through the exit.

"We'd better think fast!" Walter shouted. "Can that beam of yours go through rocks?"

"It only transluminates organic stuff!" Billy lit up Excalibur again. "But it's worth a try."

The beam drilled into the ceiling as if trying to bore a hole through the solid stone above their heads. Steam poured from the contact point, masking his efforts.

Walter grimaced as sparkling light rained on his head. "Is it working?"

Billy moved the beam, dimming it slightly. The steam dispersed, revealing solid rock, clean and shiny, as if polished by a buffing brush. "No. Not even a dent."

15

"And the floor's hard as concrete, so we can't dig under the field." Walter marched in place, sloshing in the calf-deep water. "I'm running out of ideas. You got any?"

Billy grabbed Hambone's leash from Walter, yelling to compete with the sound of rushing water. "Just keep *Fama Regis* dry." He waded toward the back of the cave. "Hambone and I will try to find the source. Maybe we can block it up somehow. See if you can find a big, loose rock."

"I'm right behind you." Walter dragged his feet through the knee-deep water. "Maybe I can kick up a rock while I'm walking."

Lifting his legs high, Billy trudged into the darkness, lighting his way with Excalibur. When he reached the rear wall, cold mist sprayed his face. Water rose past his thighs, and Hambone paddled frantically to keep his head above the surface.

Walter shouted over the din. "Sounds like it's coming from the ceiling." He lifted a rock the size of two fists. "This is the best I could do."

Billy raised his sword, guiding the glow upward. Torrents of water gushed from a back corner and plunged into the flood. "I can't hold the sword and try to plug it at the same time."

Walter handed *Fama Regis* to Billy. "Don't worry. I can handle it." He clambered up the wall, clutching stony projections with his free hand. As he pushed the rock into the gaping hole, the fountain split into dozens of fingers and splashed across his face. The stream slowed for a second, then spat out the rock like a shot from a rifle. "There's no way!" he shouted. "It's too fast!"

Walter jumped, splashing down into waist-deep water. He took *Fama Regis* back and held it high. "I say we try the entrance again!"

"Yeah. We're not doing any good back here." Billy scooped up Hambone under one arm. "C'mon, boy. You're getting tired."

They forged ahead into the more illuminated part of the cave, reaching the archway once again. Billy lifted Hambone over a wall protrusion and set him down on a ledge just above the flood. The water now crested at the bottom of the pendant as it dangled over Billy's chest. "I'm going to try Excalibur," he yelled, "and a blast of fire at the same time."

Walter balled one hand into a fist. "Give it all you've got!" He rested the book on top of his head. "Even a little hole might keep the water from rising."

Billy charged up the sword's energy, making it so bright he couldn't keep his eyes on the blade. He slashed the beam against the entry and launched a ferocious salvo of fire. The flames bombarded the field, spreading out over the entry space, making ripples of orange along the plane. The laser beam bounced off the field again and struck the water, lighting up the surface with dancing sparks of white.

"Turn it off!" Walter yelled. "The water's like electrified ice!"

Billy shut down the sword and stopped the flames. The force field shimmered like a disturbed pool, then turned crystal clear again. With water rising to his armpits, he resheathed Excalibur and lifted his elbows over the dying sparks. "Got any new ideas?"

"Just one." Walter placed the book on Billy's head, and Billy instinctively grabbed it. Walter stepped toward the force field, took a deep breath, and leaped into it. A tremendous explosion of sparks sent him flying back through the water, like a torpedo shooting through the depths. When he stopped, he lay floating on the surface, facedown and motionless.

Billy lunged for him and screamed. "Walter!"

THE GREAT KEY

B onnie lay on her side in the back of Professor Hamilton's station wagon, a downy blue blanket draped over her body. She had been up most of the night during the drive to Baltimore, so she hoped the short trip from Johns Hopkins Hospital to the Baltimore/Washington International Airport might allow her a few winks of sleep. With the downpour continuing, traffic on the expressway crept along like a traveling ant colony, bumper to bumper in a methodical roll. Bonnie yawned. All the better. More time to sleep.

As she gazed at the gray skies, her heavy eyelids blinking more and more frequently, a billboard caught her attention. Could it be? She rubbed her eyes and looked again. It was a picture of her! A huge reproduction of the TV shot at the Glastonbury tor with her wings exposed! What did the billboard say? Bonnie propped up on her elbow and read the six-foot-tall words. "Help us find the dragon girl. One million dollar reward for an exclusive interview."

Bonnie pulled the blanket over her head. Now everyone would be looking for her! She squeezed her eyes shut, trying to block out horrifying thoughts of being paraded around as a media freak, tabloid covers blaring "Bat Creature from Mars" or "Dragon Girl Prophesies Doom." Of course, there would have to be the obligatory Elvis article. What would that headline be? "Dragon Girl Marries Elvis"? They'd undoubtedly dummy up a picture with her alongside the music star, maybe with her wing draped over the shoulder of his sequined white suit. Bonnie muffled a giggle. Okay, she could deal with this. She would just have to stay hidden. She yawned again, her body and mind aching for a long nap. And sleep.

Bonnie tucked the blanket tightly, trying to tune out the world, but the conversation between the professor and Sir Barlow in the front seat drifted back to her.

Even whispering, Barlow trumpeted like a barker from a bad car commercial. "So will the young miss marry William?"

The professor's voice, barely audible as it competed with the pounding rain and surrounding car engines, rose and fell. "Merlin's prophecy seems to indicate that they will eventually wed, and I get this strange feeling that Merlin himself is speaking to me in my dreams, even though he no longer resides in my body. Just a fortnight ago, I dreamed that I saw him through a pulsing red window. At least I assume it was he, for the image was my own, as if I were gazing into a mirror shrouded in the glow of a scarlet beacon. He said, 'Young Arthur must concentrate on one goal alone, finding his father. All other goals pale in comparison.'"

"Even compared to stopping the Watchers?"

"Yes, and I believe I have deduced the reason. With the release of the Watchers, the fate of the world stands on a razor's edge. They have only one enemy that can defeat them—dragons.

Since Devin would be in dragon form himself, Morgan is sure to try to free him from the candlestone. He could counter the other dragons while the Watchers fulfill their purposes."

"Their purposes?"

"World domination might be one, I suppose. Yet, I wonder if their purposes are subtler than that. We shall see. In any case, I advised Carl to remove the candlestone from his office. The demons are sure to look for it there."

A long pause ensued, each man sighing, then the professor continued. "Somehow we must restore William's father. It's our only hope."

Barlow coughed a fake sort of cough. "Well, that's a fine proposition. Our only hope is to locate and rescue a man who has no body."

"I concede it does seem hopeless, yet we have no choice but to try. I believe that William's fate is tied to his father's, and now that he carries the Great Key, perhaps he will find the guidance he needs to restore the man, or the dragon, he once admired with all his heart."

"But the scoundrel Devin holds the dragon's body. Which one would William restore? The man or the dragon?"

The professor yawned in the same way Bonnie had—understandable since he had driven most of the night. "Indeed," he replied. "The man or the dragon? I wish I knew. But getting back to your first question, William would be best advised to concentrate on his objective. His teamwork with Miss Silver has always been a boon, but I think this final quest is one William might do well to make alone. Any distraction could be costly, including, and perhaps especially, the lovely Miss Silver."

Tears welled in Bonnie's eyes. Nausea boiled in her stomach. She bit her lip, trying not to sob. She had considered herself once before as a possible distraction, though she had later dismissed it as self-absorbed nonsense. Who could be distracted by a freakish girl like her? But now, after her experience in the sixth circle, she understood so much more. Someone like Billy really could love her, just the way she was. And the professor was right; they did make a great team.

But hadn't Billy proven now that he was strong on his own? Shouldn't he make the journey to find his father without her? She had no part in the matter, so maybe it was time for her to step aside and stay out of it. Maybe it was time to let the boy become a man. Bonnie clutched the blanket to her. At the end of Billy's journey, when he became a knight in shining armor, would he still want a dragon girl at his side?

Hundreds of people jammed the airport terminal, hustling from ticket counters to security checkpoints, scrambling up and down escalators, gazing at arrival and departure monitors, sometimes cursing when 'Flight Canceled' flashed on the screen or the departure time numerals changed by two hours.

The nasty weather seemed to have everyone on edge, especially Bonnie. She pulled her sweatshirt hood as far over her eyes as she could and kept her head down as she followed Professor Hamilton to the rendezvous point. Sir Patrick and the other knights had planned to arrive on a British Airways flight at about three o'clock, so Professor Hamilton asked Mrs. Bannister and her company—Ashley, Karen, and Shiloh—to fly in on *Merlin II*, the Bannister's airplane, at about the same time. But the international flight had been delayed by the weather, and who could tell what the storms might do to the little private plane?

The professor slowed. Bonnie lifted her head and scanned the crowded terminal. A familiar face appeared above a woman's shoulder. Ashley! Bonnie tugged the professor down to whispering level. "I see Ashley. Be right back." With her hands stuffed in her sweatshirt pockets, she scooted toward the eighteen-year-old genius, the brains behind all the gizmos that had allowed her to dive into and return from the candlestone. Ashley strolled from a vending machine area, smiling as she read what looked like a greeting card, her brown hair falling into her eyes.

Bonnie sidled up to her, whispering. "Ashley. It's me."

Ashley threw her arm around Bonnie's shoulders and guided her to a more secluded spot, leaning over slightly to talk eye to eye, her voice low. "Where's Prof?"

Bonnie gestured with her head. "Over there, where the passengers come out." She nodded toward the card in Ashley's hand. "Whatcha got there?"

Ashley held up the card and chuckled. "It's from Pebbles. Mrs. Bannister stopped in Castlewood and picked up the mail."

"And you didn't read it until just now?"

"Right. I've been learning to fly the plane." Ashley opened the card and read out loud. "Dear Alberta."

"Alberta? Oh, yeah. Alberta Einstein."

"Right." Ashley cleared her throat and continued reading. "Dear Alberta. I miss you. Ever since you sent Beck and Stacey away with Gandalf, I've been real lonely. I know you're just trying to keep us safe, but I don't have anyone to play with. I hope you and Red are having fun, and I hope you find your mother. Please try to remember all your adventures so you can tell me about them when you come home. Soon, right? Did I mention that I miss you?" Ashley hesitated, and with a cracking voice finished with, "Love, Pebbles."

Bonnie pinched the edge of the card. "Wow! I didn't know Pebbles was old enough to write like that."

Ashley sniffed and showed Bonnie the drawing on the front, a dragon picking daisies. "She's a smart one, but she probably

23

dictated it to Mrs. Foley." She flipped the envelope to the address side. "Cumberland postmark. I guess Mr. Foley has them hiding in Western Maryland."

"Probably." Bonnie tried to read Ashley's weary eyes. "Pebbles mentioned finding your mother. Do you still think she's one of the dragons we rescued from the circles?"

"She has to be," she said, putting the card back into the envelope, "and I'm pretty sure which one she is."

"The healer?"

"That's my guess." Ashley slid the envelope into her jeans' back pocket. "The dragons are on their way, and they know where to meet us, so I'll get to see her soon."

Bonnie glanced around the area, trying to spot the others. "So where are Mrs. B and Shiloh and Karen?"

Ashley pointed her thumb over her shoulder. "They're waiting in the plane at the air cargo gates. When Sir Patrick and the knights show up, we'll all head back to West Virginia." She bent closer and whispered, "Have you seen all the ads offering money for an interview with you?"

"I saw a billboard."

"Well, they're on TV and radio and in all the newspapers." Ashley pulled Bonnie's hood down farther over her eyes. "Just be careful. You lead the way to Prof, and I'll kind of hover nearby."

Ducking through a swarm of scurrying legs and feet, Bonnie wove her way in and out of the bustling crowd to the place where she'd left Professor Hamilton and Barlow. Finding both still waiting at the security checkpoint, she squeezed in between them. With her gaze riveted on the floor, she flattened her voice into a mock monotone. "Secret Agent B. Silver reporting. I have located super genius, Ashley Stalworth. What is my next assignment?"

Her head pressed against Professor Hamilton's shoulder, allowing her to feel the tiny tremors of his silent laughter. He patted her head lovingly. "I think Walter's humor is rubbing off on you."

The professor's cell phone chimed the opening notes of Beethoven's fifth symphony. "Want me to get it?" Bonnie asked.

The professor glanced down at his hip. "Very well."

Bonnie unhooked the phone and flipped it open. The caller ID said, "Carl Foley," so she decided to have a little fun with Walter's dad. "Hello. Professor Hamilton's new personal assistant speaking."

"Bonnie? Is that you?"

He sounded a bit agitated, so she dropped her game. "Hi, Mr. Foley. Yes, it's me."

"I assume you're with Prof. Are you at BWI yet?"

"Uh huh. Just got here a little while ago."

"Good. You know Walter's sister Shelly, right?"

Bonnie noticed a man staring at her. She turned and lowered her head. "I've never met her. I wore her coat once, though."

"She was supposed to fly home from Boston tomorrow, but she got worried about the weather. If this rain keeps up, they might cancel everything, so she's flying to BWI right now. Think you guys can give her a lift to the campsite?"

Bonnie glanced up. A middle-aged woman nudged the man next to her and gestured toward Bonnie with her head, whispering.

Bonnie turned again. It seemed no angle was safe.

"Bonnie, did you hear me?"

"Oh, sorry, Mr. Foley." She cleared her throat. "I'm sure there'll be room on the plane."

"Great. She's coming in on AirTran. I think it will be the only flight from Boston."

"We'll just check the monitors," Bonnie said. "No problem."

"Thanks a million. I'll meet you at the campsite."

Bonnie reclipped the phone and relayed the message to the professor. He just nodded his approval and kept his eyes fixed on the passageway to the concourse gates. With flight information monitors flashing all around, he wouldn't have any trouble finding Shelly's gate, so Bonnie kept her head low.

As they waited, Bonnie felt hundreds of eyes gawking at her, though she couldn't see any of them. The sound of a woman clearing her throat prompted Bonnie to tip her head back up. A lady had stopped in front of the professor. "Don't I know you from somewhere?" Her British accent was thicker than Prof's.

"I don't know, Madam," he replied. "I don't recognize you."

"Well, then, some relation who looks like you, I suppose."

"Yes, Madam. That must be it."

A British accent. Maybe the British Airways flight had arrived. The professor had also been on television in England when the whole world saw him with the dragon girl, so it's no wonder he looked familiar.

Bonnie peeked up. Dozens of passengers were making their way into the terminal, but it wouldn't be hard to spot Sir Patrick and his crew.

"I see them," Barlow whispered. "Act natural."

Bonnie dared to peek again. Yep. There they were. Sirs Edmund and Newman in the front, looking like two buddies on holiday; Woodrow, Fiske, and Standish behind them, examining a brochure of some kind; and Sir Patrick bringing up the rear, tapping a long white cane on the floor.

"Hmmm," Professor Hamilton murmured. "Obviously, Patrick has already instructed his company to act circumspectly, and his cane is part of the ruse."

Sir Patrick walked directly up to the professor, pressed something into his hand while whispering in his ear, then walked away without his cane. Leaning close to Bonnie, the professor handed her the cane, then slipped a pair of dark glasses over her eyes. "You're a blind girl now," he whispered. "Patrick's idea. And he said to keep your hood low over your brow."

The professor gazed at the flight arrivals monitor. "Barlow, follow their lead to the baggage claim area. Miss Silver and I will try to find Miss Foley at concourse D. We will all meet back at this spot and reconfigure our travel arrangements."

Bonnie felt the professor's arm around her shoulder as he guided her down the wide, terrazzo hallway. She glanced back and saw that Ashley had decided to stay close to Barlow and company, peeking over the card she had received from Pebbles while the others bustled toward baggage claim.

"Don't look around," the professor said softly. "You're blind, remember?"

Bonnie hovered the cane in front of her. "Should I tap it or something?"

"There is no need. I'm guiding you."

Although Bonnie had to march quickly to keep up with the professor's long strides, she enjoyed the secure embrace of his steady arm. She had learned to completely trust this amazing gentleman, his wisdom, his spiritual strength, and his physical stamina. Even if she really were blind, she would go wherever he guided, no questions asked. They had been through so much together, he was like a grandfather she had known all her life.

The professor pulled Bonnie to a stop, and his warm breath brushed her ear. "We've arrived, Miss Silver. Do you know what Miss Foley looks like?"

She kept her gaze straight ahead. "I saw pictures of her at their house, but I don't know how old they were. She's real pretty—shoulder-length blond hair, blue eyes, dimples when she smiles. In the family shot, she was the same height as Walter,

27

and she's kind of thin like he is. But I can see through these glasses. I'll help you find her."

"As long as you keep your head still. Otherwise you won't appear to be blind."

"Sure, I'll just—"

"Enough talking," he said, taking her hand. "Squeeze twice if you see her."

For the next twenty minutes or so, Bonnie surveyed the crowds of people streaming in from the arriving flights. Quite a few looked sort of like Shelly, and she worried that the dark glasses might skew her vision too much. Several onlookers held signs with people's names on them, obviously searching for someone they wouldn't recognize. A "Shelly Foley" sign would make it all so easy, but would it draw too much attention?

Bonnie read some of the signs to herself, *Alf Mortenson, James Ricardo, Juanita Ames,* wondering about the person represented by each one, where they were coming from, where they were going. *Sam Hutchinson, Bill Marks, Shelly Foley.* Bonnie stiffened. *Shelly Foley!* She squeezed the professor's hand twice.

He leaned down. "Where is she?"

Bonnie whispered hoarsely. "Look at the sign to your right, about twenty feet away. The guy with the curly blond hair."

A young man held the sign, so stunningly handsome he seemed unearthly. Bonnie distrusted him immediately. "He's up to no good. I can feel it."

"And I concur." The professor placed his arm around her shoulder. "Let's see what his intentions are."

They crept toward the man, Bonnie with her cane in front, but just before they came within speaking distance, a young woman broke free from the crowd. "You looking for me?" she asked the man.

The young man's bright eyes gleamed as he flashed a million-dollar smile. "Shelly Foley?"

She nodded. "That's me."

Bonnie looked her over. She certainly resembled Shelly, but Bonnie had never seen a photo of her dressed so . . . casually—an unzipped sweatshirt revealing a tight Harvard top that didn't quite reach her low-slung jeans.

Bonnie kept her chin tucked close to her chest. With the hood draped over her brow and the shades over her eyes, she doubted that Shelly would guess who she was.

Professor Hamilton strode forward, leaving Bonnie behind. "Excuse me! Miss Foley! I was summoned by your father to pick you up."

Shelly pulled her head back, staring at the professor suspiciously. "Who are you?"

He dipped his head in a quick bow. "I am Charles Hamilton, your father's professor and mentor from Oxford and your brother's homeschool teacher. Surely they have mentioned me to you."

"Of course he's talked about the Prof," she replied, her brow furrowing, "but I've never seen a picture, so I don't—"

"Perhaps I can explain, Mr. Hamilton." The young man placed a hand behind the professor's shoulder. "I'm Christopher Hawkins with Freestate Limousine Services. Shelly's father called and asked us to pick her up. He was concerned that you wouldn't be able to find her, so he made a reservation for her just in case." He flashed his smile again. "Sounds like a good father to me."

"Carl is a devoted father, to be sure." The professor's voice grew just a bit more aggressive. "But we have found her, so your services will not be necessary."

Christopher stepped back. "Of course. As you wish."

"Wait a minute," Shelly said, grabbing the placard. "Does my father have to pay for the limo anyway?" Her gaze seemed locked on the company logo at the bottom of the sign, a black stretch limousine with a long-legged woman stepping into the back.

Christopher folded his hands behind him. "Not the full fare for a ride to West Virginia, but there is a cancellation fee."

Shelly pointed the placard at the professor. "What are you driving?"

Professor Hamilton shifted from one foot to the other. "A, er, a Chevrolet station wagon."

Shelly nodded toward Bonnie. "With the blind girl?"

The professor stepped back and pulled Bonnie alongside him. "No. I will be with at least three other men, and she wishes to fly with her friends in a Cessna, so you have the option to go with her. Mrs. Bannister is an excellent pilot, and—"

Shelly leaned back, waving her hand. "Oh, no! I'm not flying again in this storm. We bounced around like a pinball, and that was in a jumbo jet."

Christopher took the sign and folded it slowly, keeping his eyes on his hands. "My limousine has a DVD player, snacks and drinks, and a guaranteed smooth ride."

Bonnie wrinkled her nose. Smooth was right. Too smooth.

The professor unclipped his cell phone. "I'll see what your father wants you to do."

"What *he* wants me to do?" Shelly said, scowling. With her voice rising, several passersby turned their heads. "Look, I can make this decision myself. If Dad wants me to pay him back for the ride, I will, but I'm not flying, and I'll take a limo over a station wagon crowded with a bunch of men I don't know, anytime." She curled her arm. "Lead the way, Christopher."

Christopher flashed his brilliant smile again, took Shelly's arm, and led her away.

Bonnie grabbed the professor's sweater and jerked hard. "Call her dad! Quick!"

"Again, I concur." He pressed a speed dial button and held the cell phone to his ear, waiting for an answer.

Bonnie chewed on her lip. It was taking too long. She tried to follow the pair with her eyes, but they disappeared into the crowd. The creep was getting away.

The professor's brow lifted. "Carl. It's Charles. Did you send a limo service for your daughter? . . . You didn't? Hold on!" He pressed the phone into Bonnie's hand. "Talk to him!" The professor dashed down the airport corridor, running faster than she imagined he could, dodging people with amazing agility. Just a few seconds later, he returned, his hands raised in frustration as he stood on tiptoes scanning the heads in the crowd.

Bonnie lifted the phone, her hands trembling. "Uh, Mr. Foley. Bonnie again. I think we have bad news . . ."

31

Billy threw the book onto the ledge with Hambone and splashed toward Walter. He jerked his friend's body upright, lifting his face above the water. His head lolled to one side, his cheeks ghostly white. Billy grabbed his forearms and spun him around, screaming. "Walter!" Sparks of fire spat out with his words. "Say something! Anything!"

No response.

Billy shivered so hard, the water around him rippled. He pulled Walter into a bear hug, holding his head near his ear. A gentle stream of air from Walter's half-open mouth grazed his lobe. "Thank God!" Billy said.

Towing Walter's inert body on the surface of the rising water, Billy sloshed to Hambone's ledge and heaved his friend onto the flat protrusion, then rolled him next to the dog. With a quick lunge, he hoisted himself up, ducking to keep his head, and Excalibur's hilt, from hitting the ceiling of the rocky cleft.

He squatted, his eyes darting to take in the scene. With water inching up the walls, the entire cave would be full in no time. The entrance seemed impenetrable, unyielding. Tiny wrinkles of energy undulated across the field as the wall of water pressed against it, but the barrier held fast.

The water rose over Billy's ledge and streamed around his boots and Walter's limp body. Billy grabbed up *Fama Regis* and laid it across his thighs. Hambone whined and licked Billy's face. "Cool it," he said, pushing the dog away. "I'm trying to think." As he squatted, Shiloh's pendant dangled over the book's gray cover, its pulsing rubellite casting scarlet beacon signals over the ornate black letters.

Billy gazed at the title absent-mindedly and murmured the words. "*Fama Regis.*" He opened the book to the first page, a thick yellowed parchment with two words emblazoned at the top that looked vaguely like "*Fama Regis,*" perhaps archaic English runes that had perished from use before the pages were bound. Underneath the title, a fabulous sketch spread across the page, a warrior holding a sword high over his head while hundreds of enemies swarmed in all directions, swords and bows in full attack positions. Light flashed from the sword, streaming around the warrior's body and creating a dome all around.

With water now lapping at his ankles, Billy pulled the book close to his eyes and stared at the ancient drawing. Dozens of arrows lay at the base of the dome, some twisted or broken, as if mangled when they struck the sword's glowing field. He laid his hand on the page. A photo-umbrella!

He slapped the book shut and yanked out Excalibur. After scooting close to Walter and Hambone, he summoned the beam and waved it, as if trying to paint the entrance to their alcove with Excalibur's radiance. Within seconds the beam appeared to solidify into a luminescent wall, and the rising tide began crawling up the outside of the barrier of light.

Billy blew out a long breath. "Safe. At least for now." He moved the blade slowly back and forth, biting his lip until it hurt. Would it hold when the water had nowhere else to go? Was there any other way to use Excalibur to get out of this mess?

Keeping one hand on the sword's hilt, he laid the book on his lap and flipped it open again to the drawing, his eyes darting across the page. Under the drawing, a smudged caption drew a line of tiny, unintelligible runes that flashed black and red under the glow of Billy's strobing pendant.

Walter labored through convulsive breaths as he lay next to Hambone. The aging hound whined again, his sad red eyes staring into Billy's.

Billy groaned. "Give me a break! I'm working on it!" As the water crept toward the ceiling, he turned the page, finding dozens of lines of careful script, most of the letters containing a straight, vertical line with oddly angled appendages. Billy tilted his head upward. "Dad!" he called, his voice drowning in the tumult, "you know how to translate this stuff. Where are you when I need you?"

As the sword's light cast a ghostly radiance across the parchment, the rubellite's incessant pulse mixed in a bloody hue, outlining the runes with scarlet shadows. With each red flash, the characters seemed to morph, appearing ancient under one shade of crimson, then reappearing in a translated form during the next brief flash. After that, they alternated between old and new, the translated text becoming more readable with every pulse.

During each flash of intelligible words, Billy read quickly, then waited for the next flash.

"A warrior craves the power of light."

A drop fell onto the page. Was the dome springing a leak?

"Yet strength alone will not avail."

The water rose to within inches of the rocks above.

"For keys to mysteries hide from men."

33

Billy tightened his grip on Excalibur, willing it to hold back the flood.

"Who think their eyes can pierce the veil."

The morphed words suddenly remained intact, as if solidifying in their new forms. He read faster.

A dragon's key unlocks the truth
Of light's redeeming power to save.
Its eye transforms the red to white;
It finds the lost, makes wise the knave.

For light explores the darkened heart,
Igniting souls with probing flames.
It cuts and burns away the chaff—
The flesh of dragons, knights, and dames.

The way of darkness traps and keeps
Its captives naked, cold, and blind,
But light revealing words of truth
Will open doors that snare and bind.

Billy gripped the pendant. "This must be the key!" He glanced around. His photo-umbrella shrank under the strain of the pressing water. The edge of the dome of light no longer covered Walter's lower body, leaving his legs out in the water. Hambone, sitting with a forepaw propped on Walter's chest, sniffed the unconscious boy's head and licked his ear.

Billy pushed Excalibur into Walter's hands and intertwined his fingers around the hilt. It held fast, and the photo-umbrella continued to glow, but it shrank more quickly. He grabbed Hambone's collar and pulled him close. "Listen," he said, staring earnestly into the old hound's sad eyes. "Stay with Walter, no matter what."

He closed the book and tucked it tightly under his coat before taking a deep breath and plunging through the dome of light. Keeping his eyes open, he swam frantically for the entrance, following the dim light that seeped through the force field. He let out some air, allowing his body to sink until his feet touched the cave floor. Struggling to stand in the midst of the flood, he held out the flashing pendant, guiding the jewel's glow closer and closer to the barrier. Its crimson light flashed a vague, wide circle on the surface of the field, narrowing to a disc and then to a pinpoint as he continued to guide it forward.

His lungs begging for breath, Billy waited, praying for a miracle. Could this little light possibly cut through what Excalibur couldn't even dent? The red point reminded him of the communication laser that Dr. Conner shot into the candle-stone, filling the gem with crimson, like a crystal scarab engorged with blood.

The pinpoint grew. Like tiny capillaries branching out from an artery, red light trickled from the point, making the force field look like a huge bloodshot eye. Billy's lungs felt like they were about to collapse. He had to breathe! Now!

The red focal point continued to expand. Water spilled outside, a miniscule leak in the massive dike. Billy felt faint, his heart pounding. His chest tried to heave in a breath, but he pinched his nose and squeezed his lips together. Both arms trembled. Could he keep the pendant in place long enough?

With the outlet hole slowly growing, darkness began flooding his mind. His arms and legs went numb, and the burning pain in his lungs vanished. An awareness of floating overtook all other sensations, but it was short-lived. A new pain ripped through his body as he felt himself tumbling across rough ground. He thrust out his arm and grabbed something that felt like a tree root. A river of water rushed by, and heavy rain pelted his face, but he held on.

35

Dirty water and debris gushed from the cave. Billy struggled to his feet and stood in the calf-deep wash, clutching his knees and coughing violently. He spat out a mouthful of water, then a plume of steam. As he gasped for breath, his lungs gurgled, forcing him to cough again. After three cycles of coughing and gasping, he finally straightened his body and drew in a deep, cleansing breath, then swiveled his head, searching for any sign of Walter and Hambone.

He spotted something moving near the cave entrance and dashed toward it. Hambone paddled furiously across the raging current. Clutching Walter's coat in his teeth, the dog barely kept the boy's head above water. Billy waded through the flow, yanked Walter upright, and hugged his drenched body. Hambone, now free of his burden, swam easily to the side of the river and shook a spray of droplets from his coat.

36

Billy trudged out of the current and laid Walter gently on the leaf-matted slope next to his canine rescuer. As the downpour sprayed Walter's forehead, Billy patted his friend's cheeks with his frigid hands. "C'mon buddy! Wake up!"

Gaunt and pale, Walter coughed and spat out a stream of thin saliva. Sitting up slowly, he wagged his head back and forth before looking up at Billy. With a feeble grin and a trembling voice, he said, "I dreamed I was surfing in a washing machine."

"Pretty close," Billy said, bracing Walter's back. "That rinse cycle was nearly a killer."

Walter rubbed his neck. "And a long-sleeved shirt with sharp teeth grabbed me and wouldn't let go!"

Billy scratched Hambone's floppy ear and laughed. "And it's a good thing, or you'd be all washed up!"

Walter bent his neck from side to side, grimacing as loud pops sounded from his vertebrae. He motioned for Billy to let him lie down. Once his head rested on the ground again, he took a deep breath, his eyes closed. "So what now? Chase that Watcher creep?"

Billy unfastened his coat and pulled out *Fama Regis*. Water had drenched the cover, but the inner pages seemed dry enough. "We have to find Arlo and see if he survived, and Excalibur's still gotta be around here somewhere." He tucked the book under his coat again. "I put it in your hands to keep a dome around you, but I guess you let it go."

Walter flashed a weak smile. "I guess it was the beach umbrella I was holding in my dream. I couldn't surf with it, so I dropped it in the spin cycle."

Billy stepped back into the flow of water, now abating to a gentle stream. "After we find them, we have to figure out a way to contact Mom and Prof."

Walter shivered in the cool breeze, his eyes still closed. "Give me a minute, and I'll help. My arms and legs are tingling."

"Hey! Maybe Arlo carries a cell phone with him."

"Yeah, right," Walter said, a broad smile spreading across his wincing face. "The hillbilly wireless network." He put an imaginary phone to his ear, his voice still quiet and pained. "Izzat yew, Agnes? Lemme talk at my hound dawg fer a min-nit. I want to—"

"That's purty close," a voice interrupted.

Billy spun around. Arlo, drenched and dirty, held out a cell phone. "My sister's named Agnes, but I don't never call Hambone on a cell phone." The old hillbilly grinned. "He uses e-mail."

37

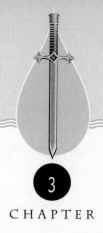

A New Hostiam

Shelly gasped at the amazing sights hundreds of feet below—fields and farms laid out in green and brown checkerboards, highways and rivers lining the mountain creases like gray and blue ribbons decorating a royal garden, tiny houses with even tinier people rushing in and out pointing at the sky.

Shelly laughed at their antics. No wonder they were frightened! Her smooth limo ride had turned into a flight in the arms of an angel! Here she was, soaring through the air, embraced by powerful, yet tender arms and shielded from the driving rain by a shimmering, transparent dome. The angel, gently gliding under wings of gold, his chiseled bronze face smiling under flowing blond hair, was more than a dream come true. He was heaven on earth.

"Fear not," the angel whispered in her ear. "We will now descend quickly."

Shelly suddenly felt weightless, the ground rushing up toward her as though a movie camera were zooming in on a grassy field below. Excitement shook her body and snatched her breath away. Then, the soles of her shoes pressed against soft earth, saturated grass and mud with puddles all around. She pushed her hair out of her eyes and tried to settle her feet, but, still feeling the effects of the weightless plunge, she wobbled until the angel caught her and set her upright. The gentle touch of the radiant man sent new chills of delight racing across her skin. She rubbed away the goose bumps and sighed. A real angel had flown her to a secret hideaway! What would be next?

The angel led her into a thick forest, his soft, deep voice rumbling. "Take heed, fair maiden. The trail is dark, and the mud is slick."

The two sloshed through the dim woods, the angel keeping one hand on her shoulder. His grip was soft, caressing, like a kindly grandfather's guiding hand. They rounded a large boulder and approached a sturdy looking cabin with stacked, hewn logs and draped windows. The scent of burning wood mixed with the musty smell of damp earth, and clouds of bluish gray puffed from a brick chimney atop the sloped, cedar roof. As they drew close, an ebony door opened by itself, its hinges silent in the drum of vertical sheets of rain. The angel motioned for her to enter.

Shelly stepped up to the threshold, noting an odd design burned into the lintel. No larger than an old silver dollar, it looked like a compass with a circle at the end of each directional point. Inside, the smell of wood grew stronger, pungent, a sickeningly sweet incense injected into the smoke. The malodorous vapor hung from the low, plastered ceiling like a translucent theatre curtain that had just been raised for a performance. A steady drip from a crack in the gray plaster disclosed a leaking roof, each dime-sized drop adding to a growing puddle on the polished wood floor.

The fireplace, its flames greenish-orange, infused the cabin with stifling heat. In front of the hearth sat a low, stone table, perhaps a pedestal for the flaming crystal ball that perched on its marble top. A woman sat on a swivel chair, her hands hovering over the blazing crystal as if warming her bony fingers in the ball's rippled aura. Shelly could only see the side of the woman's wrinkled face, deeply creased and cracking, yet somehow still beautiful, like an antique sculpture that needed buffing.

A huge, multicolored dog lay curled at the woman's feet, its triangular ears perking and its black eyes shining. Shelly tiptoed closer. A strange light emanated from the dog's coat, waves of color washing through a yellowish glow. A low growl rumbled from its throat.

Shelly halted and wiped her sweaty palms on her jeans. The air in the cabin was too stifling, the situation too strange, even scary. While the angel helped her slip off her sweatshirt, the dog let out another growl. Its bared teeth didn't impress her as a smile of greeting.

The woman turned her chair and tapped the dog on its head. "Quiet, Iridian!" Shelly jumped back a step. The woman's sharp voice sounded like a firecracker, belying her apparent age. Dry, wrinkled skin hung over her skull like a rotting mask, a deep scar blistering one cheek, but her eyes blazed red, alive with vibrant energy and ancient wisdom. Shelly trembled.

The angel whispered, "Drop to one knee when I address her." He stepped in front of the woman and bowed his head, speaking in a deep, echoing voice. "I have found her, Morgan. Your hostiam has come."

Shelly lowered her body and planted one knee on the wood floor, her jeans slipping an inch on its wet surface. She noticed that the angel didn't bow, and his gaze seemed fastened on her instead of Morgan, his eyes moving slowly as though surveying every inch of her body. She wished she had her sweatshirt to cover her bare arms.

The old woman spoke again, croaking like a deep-throated bird. "Shelly, my dear, it's so nice of you to come. I am Morgan, and I am acquainted with your brother, Walter."

The angel's strong hand pulled Shelly back to her feet, his palm lingering in hers before he let go. She felt the angel's gaze still locked on her. She didn't know what else to do, so she gave Morgan a clumsy bow. "Uh, glad to meet you."

Morgan slowly turned her head, eyeing the angel carefully. "Did you find the genealogy?"

"In an ancient vault in the Glastonbury abbey." The angel's deep voice sent a quiver through the floor and into Shelly's legs, but she resisted the urge to look at him. "She is an heir, as you suspected," the angel continued. "Though I doubt anyone in her family knows the truth. Those documents had not seen the light of day in centuries."

42

Morgan's purple lips spread into a thin smile. "And who is her guardian?"

"There is none. She has left her home and is of legal age, and she has already proven that she speaks for herself."

Morgan's eyebrows lifted. "I see," she said, stretching out her words. "And the candlestone?"

"We could not find it." The angel's voice vibrated as it deepened to an angry tone. "I assume the father hid it elsewhere. I could have killed him, but I feared the secret would die with him."

Morgan glanced away, waving her hand. "Don't worry. I have another candlestone that will help me capture the one we want."

"We did find the clothing you requested."

Morgan's eyes jerked back toward the angel. "Shiloh's dress? And the analysis?"

The angel's voice returned to normal. "Some interesting results, but not what you were hoping for. We found blood, skin, and hair samples that revealed an unusually high concentration of cyanide."

"Cyanide?" Morgan's eyes narrowed to red slivers. "But that would kill her, not keep her alive."

"Exactly my thinking, but the secret to her youthfulness is unimportant now that you have a hostiam. You will live on."

"Indeed." Morgan pushed out of her seat, her skeletal arms trembling. As she stabilized her body, her weak smile contracted. "Shelly, I assume Samyaza has told you about my offer."

Shelly nodded, now feeling a shiver in spite of the oven-like heat. "But how is it possible?" She watched Samyaza out of the corner of her eye. He was still looking at her. "I mean, I believe in angels and all that, but how can I bring peace to the world? I'm just a girl." Samyaza's continued stare sent prickles crawling across her exposed waist. She pulled the hem of her shirt down.

Morgan reached up and set her hand on Samyaza's cheek, turning his face away from Shelly. "Patience, my love. Our time will soon come."

Morgan moved her hand from Samyaza's cheek to Shelly's. "You are a blossoming flower, and, as you can see, I have angels who do what I ask." Morgan spread out her hands, and her crystal ball materialized, hovering above her palms. Within the sphere, a battle scene appeared, two ancient armies clashing in a field, a young woman in the midst of the fray, mounted on a battle horse and shouting out commands. "Joan of Arc was younger than you," Morgan continued, "yet she led an army and conquered a nation. She had the innocence of youth, a heavenly fairness of face, and the ability to converse with angels."

Morgan pressed her hands together, and the sphere vanished, instantly reappearing on the pedestal. "You lack only the last of these, and with my indwelling presence, you will learn to command the most powerful angels in the universe." She extended her arm and let the steady drip from the ceiling collect in her palm. "The difference is that you will not have to go to war to assert your will. With angels standing all around you, the media will fall all over themselves to hail you as a world leader, Joan of Arc reborn, finally receiving the accolades she deserves." Morgan tilted her hand, spilling the water, now thick and red. "When all nations rally to our cause, we will establish peace in the world without spilling a single drop of blood." She took Shelly's hand in hers. "Are you willing?"

Shelly recoiled at first, wondering about the bloody liquid on the old woman's skin, but Morgan held firm. Her touch sent a calming warmth throughout Shelly's body. Her shivers vanished. The incense now smelled pleasing. No, better than that. Heavenly. She looked up at Samyaza again. His eyes met hers. She no longer cared that his gaze lingered. In fact, she wanted him to keep looking. How often did a girl get this kind of opportunity, to be eyed by an angel?

As long as she could remember, she'd dreamed of angels, wanting more than anything to see one, and now, with just one word, she could have them always at her side. And not only that, she could realize her desire to bring peace to a world of conflict and turmoil. The new Joan of Arc? Why not? Nothing made more sense.

Still, nagging thoughts scraped her conscience. She pulled away from Morgan and crossed her arms over her chest. "How do we know the governments will go along? I mean, they've never agreed on much of anything before."

"An excellent question, my dear." Morgan rubbed her hands together, creating a thin layer of red powder on one palm. She swept her hand through the air as if to toss the particles away, and a line of red flew toward the fire, igniting a flashing green flame. Clapping her hands together, she let the remaining residue fall to the floor. "Samyaza, is the president on board with our plan?"

The odor of incense grew stronger, even sweeter than before. The angel's voice seemed more commanding, like the greatest hero in a conquering army.

"Without question. He has already implemented the first step. The skies and roads will soon be clear."

"And Congress?" Morgan continued.

The angel smirked. "It seems that there's a fire sale on souls in Washington. I've never seen so many bargains."

The room grew hotter, and now Shelly was glad to have bare arms and shoulders. She felt unashamed and free, ready to do anything Morgan and Samyaza asked.

Morgan took Shelly's hand again and pulled her close, almost nose to nose. Morgan's breath smelled much like the incense, except older somehow. "You see, Shelly?" Morgan whispered, laying her palm over Shelly's heart, just above the *V* in Harvard. "Everything is in place. All that is left to do is to allow me to enter your body. When I enter, you will feel a sudden surge of cold, then a warming sensation as my presence begins coursing through your veins. Then my mind will enter yours, and we will cohabit as twin sisters in a common womb, speaking to each other mind to mind. Other than the first wave of cold, the process is simple and painless. I just need your permission."

Shelly's gaze locked onto Morgan's crackling red eyes. What would it feel like to have another person, someone this powerful, living inside? "Will you take complete control of me," she asked, "or will I be able to think my own thoughts?"

Morgan's smile widened, seeming to crack her wrinkled face into two pieces. "As long as you follow my plan, I will allow you complete control. I will be able to read your thoughts, and you will hear me speak to your mind whenever you need

45

instructions." Morgan spread out her fingers, pressing her palm more firmly. "It will take a great amount of courage for you to allow this invasion of your soul, but your passion for world peace and security, I'm sure, will overcome your fears."

Morgan's touch sent a surge of new warmth into Shelly's bones. If Morgan lived within her, would she always feel like this? She looked up again at Samyaza's beautiful, wondrous face, an ageless face that radiated wisdom, strength, and courage. Surely he had the power to do whatever Morgan might bid him to do. After all, he was an angel, so the plan had to work! There could be no other answer! Finally, she let out a long sigh and nodded. "Yes. I'll do it."

The professor kept one hand on the steering wheel while using the other to hold his phone. "Yes, William. The Watchers probably know the campsite's location, so there's no use returning to it and risking an unnecessary confrontation. . . . Yes. I think you should try to get to the airstrip before your mother arrives. She and her passengers may need you there to protect them." The professor turned the windshield wipers to the fastest setting. "Flooding? Yes. The roads may not be passable, but we'll figure out a way to join you even if we have to build an ark. . . . No. No news from the dragons. I expect that our winged friends will arrive at night to maintain secrecy. . . . Good point. With clouds covering most of the world, they might come at any time. . . . Why am I repeating your words? Because Barlow's mustache is tickling my neck at this very moment. He's trying to listen, and I want him to relax."

Barlow leaned back in his seat. "Terribly sorry."

A crack of thunder rattled the car. "I had better concentrate on my driving, William. Traffic is practically nonexistent, but the wind is whipping us around. Yet, if all goes well, I expect to be at camp by nightfall." He set the phone on a dashboard clip and checked the clock. "Ten minutes after." He tapped the radio button. "The president's address has probably already started."

Static crackled from the speakers, but a voice managed to overcome the noise. "—given the crisis at hand. Therefore, Congress has voted to give me emergency powers to temporarily limit selected privileges in order to track down the source of this disaster and ensure security for all citizens. Our scientists have assured me that this weather phenomenon is not of natural origin, and we are tracing a line of evidence that will soon pinpoint the culprit." There was a long, static-filled pause, followed by the sound of shuffling papers. "Because of the need to clear the already flooded highways for emergency transports, I am ordering all nonemergency vehicles off public roads. All private transportation is suspended on ground and in the air. I am sorry for having to take such drastic action, but we must maintain the safety and security of our people."

Professor Hamilton turned off the radio. "Very interesting."

"Does that mean we're illegal?" Barlow asked. "I mean, we're on public roads, correct?"

"Technically, I suppose we are driving illegally, but I doubt that a police officer would fine us for violating an order that was implemented less than a minute ago."

Woodrow, sitting in the front passenger's seat, pointed ahead. "By Jove! Is that a hitchhiker? In this weather?"

Barlow leaned forward again. "It's a young woman! Not much older than a teenager, I would guess."

Professor Hamilton passed the hitchhiker and pulled the car to the side of the road. He opened the window and leaned out into the driving rain. The girl kept her head down as she approached, her pace slowing. "Excuse me!" he yelled. "Would you like a ride?"

47

The girl lifted her head, then jogged up to the car, but she stayed a few steps away from the window. Her voice sounded weak and faraway in the downpour. "A ride?" She peered into the back window at the four men, wrapped her arms around herself, and shivered. "I . . . I don't think so."

Barlow opened his window, and the girl stepped farther away. He pushed his head through the opening and looked back. "I assure you," he said, water already dripping from his mustache, "on my honor as Sir Barlow, Lord of Hickling Manor, no harm will befall you."

The girl laughed. "I've heard pretty speeches like that before, Sir Whatever. Lord or no lord, I'm not getting in a car with a bunch of strange men."

The professor opened his door and stepped out into the swirling sheets of rain. The girl stepped back again. "Please don't run," he said, holding up his hand. "I'll stand right here." The rain quickly matted down his wild hair and streamed down his face as he studied the girl. Dressed only in blue jeans and a thin, wet tank top, she had to be cold in this cruel late-autumn storm. "You look very familiar to me," he went on. "Miss Foley?"

The girl rubbed her bare arms, hesitating for a moment. "The professor guy?"

"Yes!" he said, "please come in out of the rain. We were just on our way to meet Walter."

Shelly jumped into the car, slid to the middle of the front bench, and clenched her fists. "I couldn't believe that Christopher creep! He just dropped me off in the middle of nowhere!"

The professor sat beside her and mopped back his wet hair. "I called your father, and he said he never hired a limousine service."

Shelly rubbed the goose bumps on her upper arms. "I figured that out a little too late. Apparently he was working for someone named Morgan, and I said, 'Either take me home to my father, or you'll wish you had.' So he said something about me giving my permission to host someone, and I said, 'No way!' even though I didn't understand a word of it. Then, he got real mad and just dropped me off." She scooted closer to Professor Hamilton, pulling her wet, stringy hair away from Woodrow. "Sorry. I didn't mean to get you wet."

"Quite all right, Miss." Woodrow pulled his sweatshirt over his head and draped it over Shelly's shoulders. "I am Sir Woodrow, at your service."

The professor rolled his window back up and shifted the car into gear. "And we have Sirs Barlow, Fiske, and Standish in the backseat. Has Walter told you about our knights?"

"Yeah. I remember Barlow's name now." She deepened her voice. "Death to all who dare enter heaven naked." She winked at the burly knight. "Right, Sir Barlow?"

Barlow's face turned pink. "Yes, yes. I did say that. I was hoping to frighten one of the traitors."

The professor eased the car back onto the highway and accelerated slowly. "If you know that much, then I assume you heard about the dragons and what happened in England."

"You bet! And Billy's fire breathing and Bonnie's wings. After Bonnie got plastered all over the news, Walter decided to tell me everything."

The professor slowed the car at the bottom of a hill, easing the wheels into a stream that crossed the highway. "You mentioned the word 'host.' Did the driver say something about a hostiam?"

"Yeah!" Shelly raised a finger. "That was the word!"

"And since you didn't give your permission," the professor continued, "Morgan couldn't use you."

Shelly wrapped the arms of the sweatshirt around her. "Sounds like you were listening in. How'd you know all that?"

49

With the water rushing as high as the tops of the tires, the professor gunned the engine and plowed through the stream. "It's part of the England story. I suppose it was too esoteric for Walter to tell you about it."

"I guess so." She patted a cell phone on her belt. "Anyway, I couldn't get a signal out here in the boonies to call Dad, so I started hoofing it. I figured I'd find a place to call from eventually."

"We must be out of range now." The professor checked his own phone. No signal. "Well, I think it's providential that we found you, but with the rivers rising it may take another measure of supernatural help to get us where we're going, especially since we don't know our destination. Finding the airstrip may be easy enough, but we cannot stay there, nor can we safely return to our old campsite."

Shelly kept her gaze down as she drummed her fingers on the knees of her soaked jeans. "Oh, I think we'll get all the help we need."

"You do?" The professor turned the defroster up a notch. "I take it, then, that you are a believer?"

"Well . . ." Her eyes stayed low for a moment before finally looking up at him, her eyelashes batting. "I do believe in supernatural intervention."

"Good. William's mother and her passengers are flying through this storm, so they'll need all the help from above they can get."

Shelly patted the professor's shoulder. "Don't worry. I'm sure they'll get it."

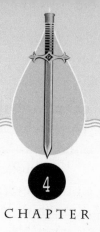

4

BATTLE IN THE SKY

Merlin II's propeller droned a lullaby in Bonnie's ears, a peaceful, soothing hum that seemed to weigh down her eyelids. Although she wanted to obey the hypnotizing buzz and drift off to sleep, the plane kept bucking in the storm-swept air, jolting her body. During the hour since takeoff from Baltimore, the passengers had remained fairly quiet. From time to time, Marilyn announced an update from her pilot's seat—altitude, weather conditions, and best of all, estimated minutes to arrival at the mountain airstrip in West Virginia. Ashley, seated in the copilot's chair, also interrupted the silence, asking frequent questions about the instrument panel and talking to Larry, her supercomputer, through her tooth transmitter.

Giving up on the idea of curling up into a little ball and snoozing in the back of the plane, Bonnie busied herself with a new variation of Cat's Cradle with her cousin, Shiloh. A few more minutes of forcing herself to stay awake wouldn't matter too much. She planned to take a long nap at their wilderness camp. With the constant rain beating down, it would be cold and wet, but at least the solid ground wouldn't shake her out of a snooze.

She pushed her fingers into the string pattern, a patchwork of triangles stretching from one of Shiloh's hands to the other. "Like this?" Bonnie asked, twisting in her aisle seat to get more comfortable.

Shiloh, seated next to the window, kept the string taut. As she answered, her gentle British accent sounded like a melody. "You got it. Now push up and spread your hands apart." A gust buffeted the plane, making Shiloh's hands bounce.

Bonnie took the string "cradle" into her hands but kept her eyes on Shiloh, her virtual twin. Although she was actually a fifty-five-year-old woman, she looked and acted like a teenager, as if her imprisonment in the circles of seven had frozen her in time. But her youthful manner wasn't really a surprise. She had wandered for forty years in a deserted town, seeing only silent ghosts wandering from place to place, ignoring her as she begged them to play games of marbles or hide and seek to pass the time. Since she had no one to interact with, she couldn't really grow up. It was a miracle she hadn't gone stark raving mad!

Sitting near Shiloh, Bonnie felt at peace. Most people grabbed an armrest or laughed nervously when an airplane gave a sudden jolt, but Shiloh never flinched. She seemed immune to fear and doubt, perhaps because she had witnessed God's protective hand through a generation of torture. Refusing Morgan's luxurious banquet, she settled for a plant that grew miraculously, exactly when she needed it, in the spilled water of a pitcher pump. The bud at the top of the stalk held a sweet-tasting white bulb that turned horribly bitter in her stomach, but a daily ration of it kept her alive for decades.

Behind Shiloh, Sir Newman cleared his throat and extended his hands. "Miss Silver, I think I have divined how this game works. May I try the next step?"

Sir Edmund set a copy of *The Art of War* on his lap and nudged Sir Newman in the ribs. "Another intellectual pursuit, my friend?"

Bonnie smiled and let Newman work his fingers into the string. Ever since they had escaped from the candlestone, the knights had been learning about their new world, voraciously reading every book from *Sense and Sensibility* to *Superman* and enthusiastically engaging in every new activity from hot-air balloons to hopscotch. Fifteen centuries inside the crystalline prison had stirred up an insatiable appetite for knowledge.

Marilyn's voice sounded from the cockpit. "Now take us down a hundred feet."

Bonnie swung her head around. As rain pelted the windshield, Billy's mom pointed at a gauge on the panel. Ashley nodded, her headset and extended microphone bouncing up and down as she pushed the control yoke. "Is that smooth enough?"

Marilyn, a matching headset pressing down her shoulder-length brown hair, hovered her hands over her own control yoke, allowing it to shift along with Ashley's maneuver. "Perfect. I should've known you'd learn fast. You could probably fly this bird already." She pressed a button on a colorful screen in the middle of the dashboard. "The only thing I haven't taught you is how to use the GPS, but you can see the airstrip on the map. It won't be long now."

Karen's red head bobbed up from behind the pilot's seat, her face tinted green. "Thank God!" She sat back and tightened her seatbelt. "Let's get this bucking bronco on the ground before I run out of barf bags."

Sir Patrick unbuckled his seatbelt and grasped Karen's seat. He ripped open a small foil pouch, took out a pill, and reached it forward. "Better take another one," he said softly.

As Karen took the pill with a swig of water, Patrick glanced at Shiloh and Bonnie. He smiled, the crow's-feet around his eyes more pronounced than Bonnie remembered. When they met in England, he seemed heartier, livelier.

Patrick locked his gaze on Shiloh, his eyes adoring. After losing his daughter for forty years, it seemed that he wanted to drink in every second of her presence. He patted Karen on the shoulder and leaned back in his seat.

Marilyn gave one of the gauges a light tap on its glass surface. "Now take a peek at the altimeter every few seconds while we're descending and I'll show you—"

A flash of light zoomed past the right side of the plane, too fast to tell what it was. The plane suddenly rocked to the left, tipping its wing nearly straight up. Marilyn snatched her yoke and corrected, throwing *Merlin II* to the right, then back to the left again before stabilizing.

Marilyn barked into her microphone. "Security breach? What are you talking about?"

Ashley pressed her hands over the headset earpieces. "Restricted airspace? How could we be in restricted airspace?"

Bonnie leaned forward. It was torture not knowing what the two pilots were hearing.

Marilyn gripped the control yoke with both hands and shouted, "This is Cesna N885PE calling Elkins/Randolph County air control. We are not in restricted airspace. We're over the West Virginia mountains, for crying out loud! Call off the escort jet!"

Marilyn banked the plane hard to the left. Bonnie felt her body press against the seat as if she had gained fifty pounds.

Marilyn's face twisted with anger. "We will not proceed to Elkins airport or any other airport!"

Ashley kept her hands over her ears, her eyes growing wider.

Marilyn's eyebrows shot upward. "Shoot us down! Are you nuts? We're not commercial or military, and there are children on board!"

Marilyn nodded several times, then sighed. "Two miles south of Elkins, runway thirty-two, fourteen. Roger. I copy." She threw off her headset. "This can't be for real! Someone's after Bonnie. I'm sure of it."

Ashley spun around. "Karen! Fire up the handheld and send Larry our coordinates! Maybe he can figure out a way to confuse the jets."

Karen, holding her fingers over her puckered lips, rummaged through a duffle bag behind the pilot's seat. She gasped. "Busting . . . into radar systems . . . might take a while." She withdrew Ashley's palmtop computer from the bag. The plane suddenly dropped a dozen feet before catching itself. Karen clutched her stomach and tossed the computer forward. "You talk to him. I think I'm going to hurl."

Ashley snagged the computer out of the air and yelled into it. "Larry! You got our location and those airstrip coordinates I told you about?"

"Of course."

"Do you have any way of finding jets in the area and calling them off?"

"Give me two seconds."

Bonnie slipped her hand into Shiloh's and clutched it tightly as the plane continued to dance in the wind.

"I hacked into a network of local radar sites, but I can't send commands."

"How many jets are we dealing with?"

"Exactly zero."

"Zero? What are you talking about?"

"Zero as in zilch, nil, nada, the absence of any quantity. Simply put, there are no jets."

Sir Patrick squeezed into the cockpit and reached for Marilyn's headset. "May I?"

She nodded. "Go for it."

Patrick pushed the set over his head and barked into the microphone. "Listen, you demonic scoundrel! It doesn't take a dragon to figure out who you are. We're not the gullible fools you're accustomed to dealing with, so just get lost. We're not landing."

A voice answered, reverberating through the cabin, penetrating it from the outside. "Perhaps a more direct form of persuasion will convince you otherwise."

The flash of light zoomed by again. Shiloh pressed her nose against the glass. "I saw it! It had white armor and huge, powerful wings, like a warrior angel!"

Patrick slipped the headset off, his gaze upward as though he were trying to see through the ceiling. Newman wadded the string in his hands and peered out the window, his eyes searching all around. "One of those demon creatures, I'll wager. One of the Watchers."

More flashes of light zipped past the front of the plane. Ashley followed them with her finger. "I see two! No, three! They're zooming all around!"

A loud, metallic thump sounded. *Merlin II* rocked to the side again. Karen, her face now white, grabbed her seatbelt and cried out, "I saw one bump the plane! They're trying to make us crash!"

Bonnie closed her eyes, praying with all her might. They needed help, and fast! Another bump snapped her eyes open again. A face appeared at her window, its eyes seemingly on fire, staring at her. It seemed to snarl, showing a set of upper fangs, then, with slow, deliberate strokes, it licked its lips with a long, black tongue.

Bonnie jerked her head away, a wave of nausea erupting in her stomach. Sir Patrick leaped up and pushed his way in front of Bonnie and Shiloh. He pulled both girls close to his chest, his arms over their heads. "Whatever you do, don't look them in the eye. It will flame their passions."

"Look!" Marilyn shouted. "A dragon! Bonnie, is that your mother?"

Bonnie turned toward the window. The evil face had disappeared. She leaned under Patrick's arms and peeked through the rain-streaked glass, catching sight of the awesome creature, its leathery wings beating against the storm. "I see the dragon, but it's not Hartanna. I don't know who she is." The dragon spewed a stream of bright orange flame.

Sir Edmund unbuckled his belt and lumbered to the front of the plane, leaning into the cockpit and balancing his body against the rough ride. He squeezed between Marilyn and Ashley and gazed out the windshield. "I see her. It's Thigocia! I would recognize her anywhere! She's a war dragon, the second best I've ever seen. As a teenager, I rode her in the Weary Hill Assault, back when dragons and humans were still allies. Newman rode in the battle as well."

"So did the dragons always carry riders into battle?" Bonnie asked.

"Usually, yes. Dragons are fiercely independent, so they are not adept at organizing their attacks or defenses." Another jolt shook the plane, and Edmund braced himself against the co-pilot's seat. "When trained knights ride them, shouting maneuvers in their ears and whistling to each other, they all work together in magnificent array." He pointed out the side window. "Look. There are at least three other dragons out there, and the

57

TEARS OF A DRAGON

Watchers are grouping at a lower elevation to the right. The dragons need to make a thirty-degree bank and engage head-on, or the Watchers will be able to attack with their darkness spells."

Ashley grimaced. "Darkness spells?"

"It's a legend Thigocia told me about, but there's no time to explain. She needs my help, so I must get her attention." Edmund waved his hand in front of the windshield. "If she doesn't know I'm coming, she won't be ready to catch me."

Bonnie peeled off her backpack straps. "I'll carry you to her!"

The plane suddenly dipped. Edmund grabbed the copilot's chair again and spread his feet to balance. "Young Miss, it's too dangerous. I dare not ask you!"

Patrick backed into the aisle, and Shiloh pulled the pack away from Bonnie's collapsed wings. Bonnie unfurled them as far as she could in the cramped quarters. "You didn't ask me." She pulled the sleeves of her sweatshirt down to her wrists and firmed her chin. "I've carried you before. I can do it again."

Edmund's lips thinned out over his angular face. "Very well, maiden. I should have learned by now that you are brave beyond words." He pointed a finger at her. "But you must promise to steer clear of the battle once you have released me. You have no weapons."

Bonnie gave a quick nod. "I promise. I'll land right away."

"I'll move closer to the dragons," Marilyn said as she pulled the throttle back and banked to the right. "Bonnie, how will you find the airstrip once you're on the ground? You can't wander in the wilderness by yourself."

Ashley tucked her miniature computer in the waistband of Bonnie's jeans. "Larry can track the magnetic reckoning chip in this unit. He won't let her get lost." She flipped a switch on top. "Just talk right into it. Larry will be listening."

Marilyn kept her hand on the throttle. "Ashley, strap back in. As soon as they're out, I'm going to get us down as fast as possible. With the cargo door open, it'll be a lot rougher."

"A lot rougher?" Karen moaned, closing her eyes. "Tell me when it's over!"

Edmund clapped his hand on Newman's shoulder. "Will you join me?"

Newman unbuckled his belt. "Just say the word!"

"One minute after you see me straddle Thigocia, you must jump. I'll make sure one of the dragons is ready to catch you. We will use the Weary Hill strategy in battle."

Newman's eyes brightened, his wispy mustache twitching above a big, toothy grin. "Brilliant!"

Bonnie scooted over to the cargo hatch on the left side of the rear of the plane, folding in her wings and keeping her head low. The hatch was divided into two sections. The upper half had hinges at the top so that it would swing up and out, while the lower half had hinges on the right designed to make it swing toward the front of the plane. She found the upper lever, and Edmund helped her push the door open.

Wind and rain poured through, beating their faces with violent, wet slaps. The buzz of the propeller drilled into her ears. The plane rode up and down on the wind like a buoy on the high seas.

Edmund tried to open the lower half of the door, but the rushing air pinned it closed. "We'll have to climb over it," he shouted.

"No problem," Bonnie said, tying her hood in place. "You ready?"

Edmund took a deep breath. "Let's go!"

Bonnie pulled her wings in tightly as they lifted their legs over the lower door. Once they were both seated on the top edge, she wrapped her arms around Sir Edmund's waist and

59

pressed her chest against his back. She held her breath as they tipped over the side and fell into the empty gray air.

B illy handed Arlo his cell phone, but paused, squinting at him. "How do I know you're not possessed by a Watcher again?"

"A What-cher?"

Billy waved toward the valley. "When you were hunting down there, did you see a bright, angel-like creature just before the storm hit?"

"Shore did. I thought it was a ET of some kine. Nearly spooked the bones right outta me. But I don't 'member nuthin' after that,"—he nodded toward a clump of trees—"until I found myself layin' in the mud over thar."

Billy felt no danger, but he raised his pendant and cast its light on Arlo's face. No change.

Arlo smiled a gap-toothed grin. "Is that a ruby?"

Billy tucked the pendant under his shirt. "Close. A rubellite." He reached down to help Walter up. "C'mon, lazybones, let's see if you can walk. I couldn't get anyone on the phone, so we have to get going."

Walter grasped Billy's wrist, pain contorting his face. His grip slid away, and he clutched his chest. "Something's wrong," Walter said, his eyes barely visible through his grimace. "I can't move my legs, and my heart's doing jumping jacks."

Billy dropped to his knees. "Okay! Just relax! We'll think of something." He looked up at Arlo and shouted louder than he intended. "Any ideas?"

Arlo squatted at Walter's side. "That heart jumpin' happened to me when lightnin' struck me right in the noggin. Purt near killed me and addled my brain. I was nuttier 'n squirrel scat for a week." He grabbed Walter's wrists and pulled. "Help me hoist 'im over my shoulder. The sooner we get some help, the better."

Billy helped raise Walter to his feet. "Hear that, Walter? We're going to get you to a doctor."

No answer. Walter's eyes had closed, and his limbs hung loose. Billy gulped through a tightening throat, steadying his best friend's body while Arlo pushed his shoulder under Walter's waist.

The old hillbilly lifted Walter as easily as he would a burlap bag of peanuts. "You ready to go?"

"I'll catch up with you." Billy glanced around frantically, shivering hard. "I just have to find my sword."

"Suits me." Arlo set out across the mud-slicked hill, Hambone sniffing the trail ahead of him.

Billy hustled toward the cave, his eyes darting back and forth. Excalibur had to be around somewhere. As his own heart raced, Billy thought about Walter and his collision with the force field. Bonnie had done the same thing back in the circles, and her heart went kind of crazy. Then she died.

Billy swiped dripping water from his eyes with the back of his hand. He had to find the sword, and fast. He dashed into the cave and saw a glimmer at the base of their refuge ledge. Ah! There it was! He snatched it up and thrust it into his back scabbard, taking off at a trot. Fortunately, with such a heavy burden, Arlo was only a hundred yards or so down the slope.

Billy shielded his face while searching the skies. The gray canopy seemed forbidding, almost unearthly. Even the raindrops felt funny, tickling his cheeks, as though his inner danger sensation had crawled out onto his skin. Maybe it was like acid rain, just enough impurities in the water to produce a miniscule chemical reaction.

A streak of light flashed overhead and vanished. What could that have been? A weird kind of lightning? He lowered his head and picked up his pace. It was time to really get moving!

61

Hurricane-like winds seized Bonnie's wings and threw her body against the rear fuselage. Her head banged against the tail section. Sharp pain jolted her spine, and Edmund nearly slipped through her arms. Darkness flooded her eyes as she plummeted through the whipping storm. Fighting gale and gravity and battling to stay conscious, she redoubled her grip on Edmund. Through bleary vision and blinding rain, she spotted a dragon diving to meet her. The huge creature glided underneath, and Bonnie plopped Edmund just behind one of her protruding spines. A gust blasted Bonnie to the side, but the job was done. Now she could take her time gliding downward while keeping watch on the action up above.

Three Watchers and nine dragons flew all around *Merlin II*. The Watchers zipped from place to place, like shining dragonflies— speedy and miraculously agile. The dragons, slower and more methodical, created a ring around the plane. Two of the dragons now carried humans, Sir Edmund on one dragon's back, and Sir Newman dangling from another's teeth. The second dragon stretched her long neck and placed Newman securely between two spines on her back.

The two mounted dragons took places near each airplane wing. Two other dragons flew in front, two behind, and three seemed to be flying shotgun, aiming flaming missiles at any Watcher that dared draw near. Every few seconds a demon launched a black lightning bolt that streaked like a jagged stream of darkness toward a dragon. The dragons parried with fire, scorching any bolts that came near, evaporating them instantly.

Bonnie strained her eyes, trying to pierce the sheets of rain, but as much as she wanted to watch, she knew she had to keep her promise. She turned downward, looking for the airstrip or any open field to make a safe landing. Finding a small patch of grass, she glided toward it, her back and legs tingling as she neared the ground. She yanked down her hood and rubbed the back of her head. That bump against the plane must have given her a real jolt. Landing on the run, she splashed through a water-logged meadow, skidding a few feet before coming to a stop. She found a gentle slope with extra thick grass and lay on her back, spreading her wings behind her. As she watched the drama high above, she shielded her eyes to block the incessant downpour.

The airplane had flown away from the battle theatre, its propeller buzz barely audible as it descended toward the landing strip somewhere to Bonnie's right. Straight above, the dragons had created a line of defense, flying in a column of tight circles, coordinated so that two dragons would always be facing the Watchers and shooting an inferno blast. It seemed that the dragons always knew exactly where the demons were, guided undoubtedly by their sense of danger and the help of two experienced knights. Each volley of fire was a colorful laser shot that sent a winged villain diving to one side or the other.

63

Finally, Thigocia nailed a Watcher with a jet of blue sizzling flame. The demon was trapped in midair as slithering sapphire tongues wrapped around its body. Sir Newman's dragon joined in, shooting an orange flame so bright it looked like a geyser straight from the sun. The Watcher expanded to twice its size, as though absorbing the radiant energy until it seemed ready to burst with brilliance. Thigocia and the other dragon, virtually hovering, their wings beating madly in the driving rain, kept the rivers of fire trained on the demon. Now it had tripled in size. Beams of light shot from its eyes. Its whole body shuddered like a man being riddled with a million volts of electricity.

Seconds later, the Watcher exploded, shooting a halo of shimmering flames all around and splattering black liquid in a wide arc. The dragons curled their wings and dropped straight down, Sir Edmund clutching Thigocia's neck and Sir Newman gripping a spine on his dragon. The ring of fire passed over their heads and dissipated in the drenching rain, sending a circular plume of gray smoke into the clouds above.

One of the two remaining Watchers zoomed away toward the horizon, while the other descended out of sight. Bonnie jumped to her feet, trying to catch sight of where the second demon had fled, but he vanished into the forest. Eight dragons followed *Merlin II*, while Sir Newman's dragon skimmed the treetops, apparently in search of the missing Watcher.

Bonnie pulled the computer from her waistband and spoke into it. "Hi, Larry. Can you hear me?"

"Greetings. Your voiceprint reveals that you are Bonnie Silver. How may I help you?"

Bonnie rested a hand on her hip, slowly turning as she spoke. "I don't want to risk flying in this storm, especially with Watchers around, so I have to go on foot. Would you please guide me to the West Virginia airstrip coordinates?"

"With pleasure. Your security clearance grants you full access to my geo-guidance applications. A digital compass should appear on the screen. Proceed at a heading of ninety-four point five degrees, and I will correct your angle along the way."

Bonnie wiped the computer's display with her sleeve, but since her sweatshirt was sopping wet and the rain continued to pour, it didn't help much. She squinted at the digits and turned her body until the screen displayed ninety-four point five, then marched forward, heading for the forest edge. "How far is it, Larry?"

"Four point one kilometers. At your current rate, you will be there in forty-two minutes. Unfortunately, my maps indicate that you will be traversing more difficult topography soon, so I expect that you will slow down considerably."

"Well, try to keep me on high ground. The creeks are probably raging rivers by now."

"Will do." Larry began singing in a Scottish accent. "Oh! ye'll take the high road and I'll take the low road, and I'll be in Scotland afore ye; But me and my true love will never meet again on the bonnie, bonnie banks of Loch Lomond." Larry let out a robotic laugh. "Did you like that one? Bonnie, bonnie, banks for Bonnie Silver. Oh, I'm so funny, I think I'm going to pop a chip!"

Bonnie laughed, and Larry sang on, correcting her direction from time to time as she negotiated the hilly, forested terrain. Slick leaves and mud slowed her progress, but there were plenty of bare, skinny trees to grab as she sludged up and down slopes, both gentle and steep.

After she scaled a rise, the forest opened to a treeless expanse, flat and covered with water, more like a shallow, grassy swamp than a mountain field. It reminded Bonnie of the moat around Morgan's island back in one of the circles of seven, a marsh with dangerous serpents lurking in the dark waters. She took three steps into the field, then hesitated in ankle-deep water, letting the cool wetness seep in between her toes. It would be safe to fly now, wouldn't it? The higher ground on the other side couldn't be more than a hundred yards away, and there might be holes or ditches hiding under the rain-rippled surface.

Larry ended his song. "You stopped. Is there trouble?"

"No. I'm just getting ready to fly across this flooded field."

"Very well. If you wish to continue flying, bear eight degrees to the left. Walking in that direction would have been impossible because of a deep trench, so I had charted a safer land route. With flying, however, the improved angle and velocity will get you to the airstrip in less than five minutes."

65

"Only five minutes!" Bonnie shivered in the cold, wet wind. Her chilled body begged for something dry and warm to replace her saturated clothes. With a quick shake, her wings threw off thousands of droplets, then beat the air, lifting her off the ground. "I'm going for it, Larry!" She began zipping across the field as fast as she could, but the gale pummeled her body, beating her closer to the ground. With every desperate flap, she elevated four or five feet, only to be thrown down six by hammer-like gusts. Finally, she splashed back to the field, sliding for a moment on her chest before coming to a stop in about a foot of water.

Bonnie slapped her hand against the surface, splashing angrily as she rose to her knees, then to her feet. "Stupid decision!" she grumbled as she trudged forward. She raised the dripping computer to her lips. "Larry, I'm on the ground again. Give me a heading."

The computer remained silent. Only the swoosh of wind and rain passed into her ears.

"Larry?"

Still no answer.

Bonnie rolled her eyes. Brilliant move! Now she had to hoof it alone.

She pushed the computer behind her belt, then set her hands on her hips, scanning the forest ahead, quite a bit closer now. A new swoosh sounded from below. She tilted her head down. A black stream of buzzing particles streamed into the ground around her feet, instantly warming the water, thickening it into a sticky goo.

Bonnie tried to jump away, but like a serpent striking its prey, the black stuff caught her feet and began wrapping her up as though she were a mummy in need of bandages, first her ankles, then her legs, winding at a furious rate. She wrestled with the bands, trying to push them down her hips like overly tight pants, but they just wound around her waist, arms and all, binding her hands and wrists to her sides.

Seconds later, the black slime coiled around her chest, paralyzing her wings against her back. It then snaked its way up to her face, shrouding the world in darkness. The icky stuff oozed along her skin wherever it touched, as though the bands had been saturated with hot, runny axle grease. She kept her lips pressed tightly together, hoping the goo wouldn't seep into her mouth, nose, or ears.

A voice whispered, as if blended with the relentless wind, stretched out and wispy and lingering over the hissing words with a snakelike slither. "You are mine now, ssssweet princesssss. Alone and unprotected, yesssss. You were an eassssy catch, an eassssy catch. Do not sssscream or cry. We will fill the world with our offssssspring. The Nephilim will sssssoon live again." His slinking song continued, becoming peppered with suggestive, even obscene language.

As strong arms lifted Bonnie off the ground, she squirmed with all her might, but the gooey bands tightened with every move, crushing her lungs, squeezing her like a python would a doomed rabbit. She tried to stay calm, relax her muscles, shorten her breaths, but how could she? His disgusting words made her brain scream for escape.

Trying not to cry, she prayed for help, for God to send Billy or a dragon to blast this demon with fire and blow him to smithereens, but could any savior come in time? How could anyone possibly get her out of this mess? With the computer broken, Larry wouldn't be able to find her. *Merlin II* had probably landed long ago. Billy had no idea where she was or even that she was in trouble.

Bonnie gritted her teeth. She should never have tried to fly in the storm! That's probably what gave her position away. It was stupid!

As if he could read her mind, the Watcher continued whispering. "You are alone, ssssweet princesssss, yessss. No one can ssssave you now. I will teach you my artssss, and you will learn to enjoy my caressesssss."

Bonnie felt the demon's hand sliding along her leg. She shook her body violently and tried to flap her wings, wriggling with all her might. She would rather die than let that black-tongued monster touch her for another second, but the wrappings kept tightening, now clamping down on her throat. She could barely breathe at all.

68

THE HEALING DRAGON

Bonnie heaved her body upward. Suddenly, her stomach lurched toward her throat, and her backside slammed against the ground. Had he dropped her? Loud roars mixed in with the howling wind, then someone lifted her to her feet. A sense of new warmth coated her body. The goo sizzled in her ears. The tight band over her eyes popped, clearing her vision. A dragon stood next to her, shooting a precision stream of fire that melted the remainder of the black coat. Sir Newman sat at the base of the dragon's neck, his shoulders squared and his head erect.

Bonnie recognized the dragon immediately, the great Hartanna. She bounced on her toes in calf-deep water and cried out, "Mama!"

Hartanna's brow turned downward. She didn't answer.

Sir Newman waved his hand at Bonnie. "Keep still, Miss, and let her finish the job."

Bonnie froze in place. Vapor rose from the pool of water at her feet, making a cylindrical curtain of rising fog. The melting black stuff reeked of rotted flesh and body odor. As soon as her arms were free, she rubbed her hands and face with the falling rain to wash away the stinking residue.

Newman's voice penetrated the cloud. "The legends tell us the darkness spells are poisoned with doubt and despair. They drain your will and make you easy prey." The cloud thinned out. Newman slid off the dragon's side, dripping wet as he approached Bonnie. He grimaced at the gooey mess. "Hartanna has to destroy every drop, or it'll spread out again. Doubt is a cancer, and only fire can destroy it."

Bonnie squeezed water from her hair. "What happened to the Watcher?"

70

Newman laughed derisively. "When he saw us, he took to the skies in a hurry, I'll tell you. The darkness spell is a Watcher's only defense against dragons, and when dragons work together, they can easily melt away any direct hits."

Hartanna's stream of fire died away, and twin plumes of smoke curled up from her nostrils. "I think it is all gone now. Thank the Maker."

Bonnie leaped forward and hugged Hartanna's scaly neck. "It's so good to see you again!"

Hartanna's wing covered Bonnie's head, providing a welcome umbrella. "And you, too, dearest one. I am proud of you for risking your life to carry Sir Edmund to Thigocia's back."

Sir Newman bowed to Hartanna. "And I was pleased with your fine catch, High Dragoness. When I jumped from the airplane, I prayed for a miracle."

Hartanna dipped her head, apparently a return bow. "I just hope my teeth didn't scratch you, Sir Newman."

Newman rubbed the back of his neck. "Only a little. Much better than crushed bones on the ground, I assure you."

"Had I known you were an experienced dragon rider," Hartanna said, "I would have caught you according to custom, but few humans know how to use a dragon's tail to mount a flying steed."

"True. Although I am experienced, it has been well over a thousand years since I have attempted it." Newman pulled up his blood-stained collar. "All's well that ends well."

Bonnie ran her hands along her sleeves and shivered, a good shiver this time. Hartanna's fire spa had expelled more than demonic doubt; it had reminded Bonnie of her mother's love. Now much drier, her sweatshirt was a warm blanket instead of a cold burden. "So what now?" she asked. "To the airstrip?"

"Yes. It's very close." Hartanna lowered her neck. "You should ride with Sir Newman. The weather makes flying quite hazardous."

Bonnie laughed. "I found that out."

Sir Newman gave Bonnie a boost, then climbed aboard in front of her. "Hang on tightly to me, Miss. Hartanna is an expert flyer, but even she cannot make our ride a smooth one."

Bonnie grasped Sir Newman around the waist, her clothes getting soaked again. Seconds later, Hartanna launched into the air, fighting through needle-like rain and shifting blasts of cold. Sir Newman, upright and rigid, served as a steady anchor, seemingly unaffected by the storm.

From takeoff to descent, the flight lasted just a few minutes. Bonnie tried to peer through the rain, blinking constantly to see anything at all. *Merlin II* came into sight at the end of the

71

airstrip, a single dragon on each side. A human also stood next to the plane's tail, but he or she was too far away to recognize.

When Hartanna landed, Bonnie slid off, her wings parachuting her to the ground. Through sheets of rain, she saw Billy running toward her. He skidded to a stop, panting. "We have . . . a new meeting place . . . a secret place." He took her hand in his. "We need to hurry. These two dragons will guard the plane."

The knight marched behind Billy and Bonnie, while Hartanna flew just above the trees. As they splashed through the woods and down a muddy path, Bonnie peppered Billy with questions. "Did you find the book?"

Billy patted the front of his coat. "Got it right here."

"Did you hear that Professor Hamilton thinks the Watchers are causing all this rain?"

"He's right. One of them told me."

"You talked to a Watcher!?"

"Yeah. It's a long story. I'll tell it when we're all together. Walter's hurt, so we have to figure out a way to get him to a hospital."

Bonnie wanted to shout, "Walter's hurt?! How?" But the concern on Billy's face told her she was holding him back. She didn't want to be any more of an anchor than she already was.

The forest darkened, tree trunks conglomerating like wooden soldiers gathering for bivouac. With their nearly naked branches hovering in a tight network up above, the trees created a leaky umbrella of sorts, giving Billy and Bonnie a bit of a respite from the rain as the bark channeled streams of water earthward. Just when the undergrowth became so thick Bonnie thought they must have taken a wrong turn, they broke through into a small clearing. Six dragons sat in the grass, two with their wings spread to shelter the humans. Sir Patrick, Sir

Edmund, Ashley, Shiloh, and Karen knelt under one dragon's wings, while Walter lay in Marilyn's arms under another, his deathly still head resting on her shoulder. Hartanna glided downward to join them.

Bonnie dashed ahead and leaned over to join Marilyn under the leathery roof. She laid a hand on Walter's forehead. "How bad is it?"

Billy caught up and drew Excalibur from its scabbard. "Pretty bad. Just before he passed out, he said his arms and legs tingled and his heart was jumping." Still standing out in the rain, he summoned the sword's laser beam.

Bonnie pressed her hand on Walter's chest. She could feel a spasmodic thump and labored breathing.

"Arlo and I couldn't carry him to the road because of the flood," Billy went on, waving the sword back and forth. "So we got him as far as the airstrip, and Arlo said he could swim to a high outpost on another mountain to meet some rescue workers he contacted while I waited for Mom to land."

Excalibur's beam expanded into a huge photo-umbrella. The rain pelted the outer energy field and bounced off noiselessly. "Arlo might take hours to find help, so Mom and I carried Walter here. With the Watchers around, flying out again is too dangerous."

"What about Thigocia?" Bonnie asked. "Isn't she a healing dragon?"

Thigocia shook rainwater from her wings and folded them on her back. "I am a healer, but I have never had much success with humans, and I have failed with Walter so far." She touched one of Bonnie's wings with her own. "Since you are part dragon, I considered trying to heal you when you were dead, but there was no time. My methods might not have worked anyway."

73

Ashley stood, and with her hands behind her she walked slowly up to Thigocia. She tilted her head upward and reached a trembling hand toward the dragon's neck, then pulled it back. She seemed ready to cry.

Thigocia lowered her head. "You may touch me, young lady. I don't mind."

Ashley caressed the dragon's neck, petting her scales as she might a horse's withers.

"What are your methods?" Bonnie asked.

"One dragon breathes fire directly on me until my scales glow. Then I wrap my wings around the victim, and energy flows into his body. The energy enhances the ailing dragon's photoreceptors, enabling him to heal rapidly. Humans don't have photoreceptors, so, in theory, it can't work at all, though I have seen improvement in some cases."

74

"Really?" Bonnie said. "It worked in a human?"

She nodded toward Sir Edmund. "None other than this fine, brave soldier. During a storm much like this one, Sir Edmund and I were battling side by side with King Arthur to put down an attack from a group of barbarians. The king used Excalibur to great advantage, and the barbarians began to flee, but a spear pierced Edmund's armor and threw him off my back. I caught him before he struck the ground, but he was gravely wounded. I tried to break the shaft of the spear, but it came out, and he bled terribly. I thought to carry him home so he could die in peace, so I wrapped my wings around him to shelter his body until the battle subsided. I felt a sudden jolt, as if struck by lightning, and my rider began jerking around inside my wings. When I opened them, Sir Edmund burst out ready to charge the barbarian who speared him."

Ashley pulled back her hand, rubbing her thumb against her fingers. "A catalyst," she said.

"A what?" Bonnie asked.

Ashley waved her arms at the photo-umbrella over their heads. "Energy. It feeds our bodies. Every cell uses it to build and restore. All we need is a delivery system that transforms it into something the body can use. My guess is that the jolt of energy came from Excalibur while King Arthur was in battle. It passed through you and into Edmund, but to work on a human, it must have carried something more than dragon fire. Since you're a healer, your body must have transformed it from a destructive laser to a healing stream." She reached for Bonnie and lifted her multicolored bead necklace. "The regeneracy dome wasn't enough for you, but when Excalibur's beam ran along the ground, it shot through you and me while I was embracing you, and you revived."

Ashley stooped next to Walter and pulled him away from Marilyn. She wrapped her arms around him and nodded at Billy. "Point Excalibur toward me and strike the ground with it."

"What!" Billy cried. "Are you nuts? It'll fry both you and Walter."

Ashley pressed Walter's lolling head against her chest, her face contorting. "I analyzed that sword's beam and created my own translumination ray, so I know what it can do. I can't explain it all. Too much information can—" Walter's body began convulsing, his arms and torso twitching wildly. Ashley tightened her arms around him. "Trust me, Billy! Do it now!"

Billy brought Excalibur down, extinguishing the beam and evaporating the umbrella. As the rain poured, he pointed his body toward Walter and Ashley and angled the sword toward the ground. "Stand back everyone!" Both humans and dragons scattered, leaving Ashley and Walter alone.

Ashley positioned her body between Walter and the sword. "Go for it!" she yelled.

Tensing his face, Billy summoned the beam again. It shot into the waterlogged ground and ripped toward the huddled pair, boiling the water and sending up a line of steam. The laser streaked into Ashley. Her whole body stiffened. The beam forked and shot out her eyes, two spotlights illuminating the misty evening as she shook violently, her voice rattling. "Keep . . . it . . . going!"

Slowly turning her head, she guided her laser eyes toward Walter. They drilled into his pallid face. Light zoomed across his body, painting his skin and clothes, decolorizing him into a photo negative. Both bodies quaked. Ashley's head rocked, her voice shuddering as she screamed, "St-st-st-stop!"

Billy instantly doused the beam. A final streak sizzled across the ground and echoed through Ashley's eyes, popping through her sockets like blown out light bulbs. Her arms fell limp, and both she and Walter toppled over, splashing like used dishrags into the mud.

Billy rushed over. He grabbed Walter's arm and pulled him to a sitting position, bracing his shoulders to keep him upright. Bonnie lifted Ashley, joined seconds later by Marilyn, Karen, Shiloh, and Sir Newman. Ashley seemed conscious but groggy.

Walter's eyes flickered open, and he let out a moan. Sir Edmund helped Billy raise Walter to his feet. Walter shook his head, slinging water and mud from his hair. He wrapped his arms around himself and shivered, his teeth chattering like wild castanets.

"Hartanna!" Billy called. "Can you warm him up?"

"Dragons circle around!" Hartanna ordered. "Humans in the center!" Her glowing eyes locked onto Billy's. "Give us cover, son of Clefspeare."

As the company gathered, Billy lit up his sword, once again creating an umbrella. Six dragons surrounded the humans, their long necks reaching toward them. Hartanna bellowed, "It's time for the Sahara treatment. Hot air on, flames off." The dragons inhaled, then shot out jets of hot dry air, bathing the humans in luxurious warmth. In seconds, the arid blast slurped the moisture from their drenched skin, clothes, and hair.

Walter stopped shaking, a wry smile slowly spreading across his face. Billy punched him on the arm. "What's creeping through your mind, a new joke?"

"Sort of. I was just thinking about a new appliance combination. Instead of a washer and a dryer, you could have a Watcher and a dragon."

Karen grinned. "Walter's back!"

Walter brushed dried mud from the seat of his pants. "It's sure good to have dragons around." He turned toward Ashley and smiled. "But it's even better to have good friends."

Ashley took two tremulous steps and hugged Walter, her voice thin and rasping. "Glad I could help."

Walter cocked his head toward the pod of dragons. "Don't wear yourself out, girl. We still have to go dragon riding together."

Ashley smiled weakly. "I'm there."

Three of the dragons continued the drying treatment, slowing the jet streams to gentle, warm breezes. Thigocia stretched her neck until she came eye to eye with Ashley. "I sense a presence . . . a long lost love." The dragon took a long sniff, staring at her with flashing red pupils. "Is it really you?" she said softly. A great tear welled in the dragon's eye and splashed to the ground. "Are you my beloved Ashley?"

Ashley lifted hesitating arms and caressed the dragon's noble face. "Yes . . ." Her chin quivered. "Mother."

Thigocia lifted her head and let out a roar. "Praise the Maker! My daughter is alive!" She beat her wings, lifting her body as she seemed to dance in place. The other dragons sang a chortling song in a strange language, like short blasts from trumpets that played melody and harmony with a rumbling vibrato.

Walter let out a war whoop. Bonnie and Shiloh embraced. The two knights shook hands heartily. Karen flung her arms around Ashley and leaned her red head against her sister's chest. Ashley laughed, tears flowing down her cheeks.

Marilyn draped an arm around both Billy and Bonnie, then kissed Billy's forehead. "Did you find the book?"

Billy nodded and patted the front of his jacket. "Got it right here."

She placed a tender hand on his fist as it gripped Excalibur's hilt and leaned her head against his. "You do good work, son of Clefspeare."

LOSING PEBBLES

Nestled on the shoulder of one of the higher mountains, a company of dragons and humans gathered around a pile of wet debris—broken tree limbs, tufts of pine needles, and green, unopened pinecones. Hartanna shot a stream of flames, and within seconds, the collection dried, then ignited, erupting in a towering bonfire.

Sitting on the ground, Billy waved Excalibur back and forth to maintain the photo-umbrella and shield the campers from the curtain of rain. As daylight faded and mist began to rise in the chilled air, Professor Hamilton appeared in the distance, marching across the matted leaves. Shelly and the remaining knights followed close behind in single file, and a dragon flew just above the trees, circling like a gigantic vulture.

Billy stood and shouted, "Over here!" But he wasn't sure if Prof could hear him above the commotion of heavy rain and beating dragon wings.

The professor pointed toward the campfire, then halted and waved at the dragon. "Many thanks, Legossi," he shouted, his voice barely audible. "We would never have found them without you." He stretched his long legs over a rainwater ditch, and, once on the other side, he helped Shelly leap across. The knights tromped right through the channel, apparently oblivious to the mire of centuries-old leaf decay rushing down the slope. The new arrivals hopped over a narrow channel before finally coming to level ground at the campsite.

Billy extinguished the beam and let them in. "Hustle to the middle, and I'll fire up the shield again."

A new voice called from the woods. "Wait!" Seconds later, Carl Foley burst through a line of bushes and bounded over the channels, his agility belying his large frame. He jogged into the campsite, soaked to the skin and out of breath. "I got to the airstrip . . . a little too late. . . . Another dragon there told me to follow Legossi."

Billy recreated the umbrella, but the rain had already soaked the campers and extinguished the fire.

Hartanna beat her wings, tossing a fine spray all around. "Everyone gather at the center!" With newcomers swelling their ranks, the assembly of humans around the pile of wood had to stand elbow to elbow to fit into a single circle. The dragons provided another "Sahara" treatment, creating warm, swirling breezes within the sword's protective dome.

Hartanna then relit the wood, and after a few minutes, every camper rested on dry ground. Crackling flames leaped from the midst of the fire and coated their bodies with toasty heat.

With his companions warm and safe, Billy finally felt the freedom to rest his mind. His body, however, was another story. Having to constantly wave the sword kept his hands and wrists aching. Still, even in the peace of this gathering of friends, his danger sensor kept prodding him. Something wasn't quite right. He stared into the cloudy skies. Could the Watchers be prowling around, secretly spying on them? Did the other dragons feel the danger? Maybe since they were able to defend against the Watchers, they weren't very concerned. And what about oxygen? Could it pass through the shield? If not, would there be enough fresh air to sustain the group?

Walter tapped Billy's shoulder. "Take a break, and let me be the human umbrella for a while."

"You want to use Excalibur?"

"Sure." Walter shrugged. "Why not?"

"You've never summoned the beam before."

"I wouldn't have to," Walter said, pointing at Excalibur. "It's already blazing. Didn't you tell me it kept working when you put it in my hands back at the cave?"

Billy wanted to hand over the job, but if Walter failed, everyone would get drenched in seconds, and the dragons would have to turn on their drying jets again. Still, his arms really ached. "Yeah," he admitted. "I guess it did."

Walter reached for the sword. "Then don't hog the fun. Let me take over."

Billy passed the hilt to Walter. As he relaxed his grip, the beam dimmed for a moment, but when Walter fastened his fingers around the ornate handle, the shaft of energy flashed back to life. Walter raised the sword high, waving it with gusto. Deepening his voice, he mimicked a TV announcer. "And if you call right now, we'll throw in a ridiculously dangerous lightsaber. It slices, it dices, it even doubles as a demon-repelling umbrella."

Laughter echoed all around, but Sir Patrick sat stoically on a rotting log and studied Walter with steely eyes, his haggard

81

face resting in one hand. As Walter continued his antics, Billy stepped over to the log and pointed at the space next to Patrick. "Is this spot taken?"

Patrick slid over a few inches to make room. "Be my guest. It's damp, but serviceable."

Billy sat and rested his arms on his thighs. "It looked like you were in outer space. You trying to come up with a plan?"

"I have been formulating a concoction of ideas," Patrick said, picking at the log's loose bark, "but what captured my attention was Walter's ability with Excalibur. He is not a descendant of the king, nor of Merlin."

A centipede crawled out of a hole in the log. Billy brushed it to the ground. "I got the impression from Professor Hamilton that all you needed was to have holy hands, or something like that. I figured that since Walter has a lot of faith, he must qualify."

Sir Patrick let out a quiet, "Hmmmmm," stroking his chin with long, slender fingers. "I think you and I should have a private chat with your professor. There are some important facts that I have not yet revealed to you, because it would not have served any purpose. For now, it is best that we keep our intelligence and our plans among the three of us."

"You mean there's someone here you don't trust?" Billy held up his pendant. "This thing reveals if a Watcher is inside a person, and I secretly checked everyone. I feel like danger is somewhere close by, but with all the dragons around, the Watchers would be nuts to show their faces."

"I wouldn't be so sure," Patrick said, scanning the skies. "All the same, limiting the number of ears that listen to our discussion will also limit the number of lips that could tell of it." He rose from the log and brushed off the seat of his pants. "Bring *Fama Regis*. I will fetch Charles, and the three of us will reconvene at this log."

Billy shot to his feet, rolling the log back a quarter turn. "Sure thing." He hustled to the fireside and grabbed his wadded jacket, unwrapping it just enough to pull out the ancient book. Its texture and weight felt good in his hands, a feeling of importance and reverence bundled in tactile leather. It also felt good to trust Sir Patrick now. Pulling his jacket from the book reminded Billy of how Sir Patrick had stripped off his protective cloak in the final circle of seven, showing his willingness to die for the sake of others.

"Billy!"

It was Carl Foley. Now warm and dry in a gray Oxford-logo sweatshirt with rolled-up sleeves and dark blue denim jeans, he poked a long, thick branch at the embers on the edge of the fire. "I have a lot of news," he said, his beefy arms shaking as he stirred the fire. "I think we should have a powwow and exchange notes."

Billy glanced at Sir Patrick. Now standing next to the professor on the other side of the campfire, the elderly man half closed his eyes and nodded.

"Sure," Billy replied. While the others gathered around, Billy waited for his mother and Professor Hamilton to sit next to Carl and Shelly before he chose a space between Walter and Bonnie. Walter kept the hilt of Excalibur in his lap, waving it with one hand, just enough to keep the umbrella alive.

Sir Patrick sat cross-legged next to Shiloh, and the knights stayed erect, their eyes alternately watching the group and the surrounding forest. The seven dragons encircled the company, Hartanna and Thigocia stretching their necks into the crowd, Hartanna's head hovering near Bonnie, and Thigocia keeping close to Ashley and Karen.

Carl leaned forward. "First of all, are we in communication with Larry?"

Karen snapped the computer's casing back in place. "I was letting it dry out. We'll see in a few seconds." She turned it on and spoke into its built-in microphone. "Larry? Are you still high and dry?"

"My elevation has not changed, but my humidity meter indicates increased moisture. It is possible that the roof has been breached and water is leaking in. I am taking the programmed countermeasures."

Ashley bent over Karen's lap. "Larry, you'll find the mop and bucket in the hall closet."

"Very funny, Ashley. I rank that as the best mop and bucket joke I've heard all day."

Ashley giggled, seeming more happy and carefree than Billy had ever seen her. Walter winked at her, and she winked back.

"Okay," Carl said. "Let's get down to business."

Shelly tugged his sweatshirt. "But where's Mom?"

"She's watching Pebbles. I checked them into a suite at the Comfort Inn near Cumberland because of the media frenzy." He reached into his pocket and pulled out something, but he kept it cupped in his hand. "It was a good thing I did. My house and my office both got ransacked, I mean, really gutted. Someone was desperate to find something, and I think I know what."

Walter snapped his fingers and pointed at his dad. "The candlestone."

"Exactly." Carl spread out his palm, revealing a golf ball-sized crystal, then quickly hid it again. "But since the Watchers were bound to be looking for it, I plucked it out of my safe to, uh, keep it safe."

Walter beamed. "Cool bananas, Dad. Good thinking."

Carl patted Professor Hamilton's back. "It was Prof's idea to secure the stone, not mine."

Shelly reached out for her father's hand. "Ooooh! I heard Walter's stories about candlestones, but I've never seen one." She spread her hands under her father's. "Can I hold it?"

Carl pulled the gem back toward his chest. "Uh . . . Maybe I'd better hang onto it. We're not protecting it for Devin's sake, but he's in the only body Billy's father can use."

Shelly flashed an injured puppy look. "Don't you trust me with it?"

Carl's eyes darted around the group. "Should I? You go off in a car with a stranger at the airport without even checking with me. How hard would it have been to give me a call?"

Shelly's hands balled into fists, her teeth set on edge. "If you'd quit smothering me like an old blanket, maybe I'd think about it next time."

Carl stared at her in silence, his fingers still wrapped around the stone.

Billy's danger sensation grew. He tried to read the expressions around the campfire, but they all seemed uneasy about the family squabble rather than any imminent danger. One of the dragons let out a disapproving grunt. Shiloh took Sir Patrick's hand and held it against her cheek, gazing at him with sad eyes. Patrick patted Shiloh's knee, but his eyes were locked on Shelly, a deep scowl etched across his face.

Carl sighed and nodded. "Okay. For a minute." He slipped it into her hands. "But keep it covered. It's like Kryptonite to Billy and Bonnie and the dragons."

Shelly turned her back to the others and gazed into her cupped hands. The professor watched her for a moment, then stood, slid his hands into his pockets, and began walking around in the center of their huddle. "My idea," he began, his head tilted downward, "is that the Watchers need a dragon on their side to counter ours. It only makes sense that they want to get Devin out of that jewel." He stooped in front of Ashley. "I assume, Miss Stalworth, if they could duplicate your restoration dome, Devin would come out still in the form of a dragon?"

85

Ashley propped her arms on her knees. "I suppose so. But what good would one dragon be against nine?"

Thigocia flicked her tail and thumped the ground. "He would likely divide and conquer," she said. "He would try to isolate the females and pick us off one at a time."

Bonnie shifted her foot away from Thigocia's tail. "But he wouldn't be able to defeat you, would he, Thigocia? Didn't Sir Edmund say you're one of the greatest war dragons or something like that?"

Edmund, who had squeezed between two dragons to draw close, squatted near Bonnie. "I said she was the second greatest I had ever seen."

"Was Clefspeare the first?" Bonnie asked.

Sir Edmund let out a long sigh. "Indeed, he was."

Bonnie's wings fanned out slightly. "Who rode Clefspeare in your battles?"

86

Edmund stood and crossed his arms. "No one. He always refused to take a rider. He was the only dragon I have ever seen who could work well in a battle unit without a rider, and his heroism under fire is legendary."

Thigocia let out a throaty chirp. "He saved my life at least three times."

"And mine, twice," another dragon chimed in.

Hartanna snorted, sending a burst of flame into the campfire. The blaze erupted six feet high before settling down again, its cracks and pops echoing in the dome. "Self-sacrifice is the most honorable of attributes," she said in a low rumble. "Clefspeare's chivalry was unquestioned."

Billy glanced at his mother's reddening face. It was time to change the subject. He smacked his palm with his fist. "The solution is simple. We just don't let them get their hands on the candlestone." He watched while Shelly deposited the gem back in Carl's hands. "And, besides," Billy continued, "it's not just the body that goes into battle; it's also the mind. There's no way Devin could do what the real Clefspeare could do. He doesn't have the experience."

The professor began walking again. "Good point, William, and on that note, we'll move on in our discussion—how to locate your father's spirit."

Sir Patrick raised a finger. "May I interrupt, Charles?"

The professor paused, his eyes sparkling in the light of the fire. Patrick braced his hand on one knee and rose slowly to his feet. "I think the key to the mystery," he said, straightening his back, "lies in *Fama Regis* and its ancient runes, so we must use the Great Key to decipher its contents." He walked over to Billy and stared down at him, his protruding brow shadowing his eyes. "Have you discovered how to use the key, young Arthur?"

Billy caressed the ancient leather cover. "I think so, but it's not real fast at translating." He raised *Fama Regis* toward Sir Patrick. "I was thinking maybe you'd be able to read it since you lived back then."

Patrick waved his hand at the book. "After I became human, I began to learn the written language, but I had to flee what is now Europe before I mastered it, so it faded from my mind centuries ago. The same is true with Hartanna and the other dragons. I believe only Clefspeare remained in Europe, so he would be the only one who could read it now." He stepped over and joined Professor Hamilton. With both lanky men standing with their hands in their pockets, they seemed like mirror images, both strong and gentle, and both creased by time. "In any case," Sir Patrick continued, "there may be much more to the key's power than a simple reading of words. We shall see."

"What about the knights?" Billy flopped open the book and showed it to Edmund. "Think you can still read books from your time?"

87

"No, William." Edmund thumped his chest with his fist. "We were soldiers, not scholars. Although I have learned modern English quite well, back in our time, we were trained to fight, not to read."

Sir Patrick reached his hand down toward Billy. "I understand your desire to find an easier road, William, but I'm sure you've learned by now that scaling steep mountains leads to greater wisdom and strength."

Billy slipped his hand into Patrick's and enjoyed the surprisingly strong grip as the old man vaulted him to his feet. Raising his voice so that all could hear, Patrick gestured toward the old log. "Please excuse us. This may take awhile." He nodded at Walter. "I understand that the protective dome allows people to exit but not enter, so if anyone has to answer the call of nature, you will have to temporarily shut down the dome when he or she returns. Can you?"

Walter jiggled the hilt. "Just stop waving it, right?"

"Right," Billy said. "That'll kill the dome, but not the beam. Don't zap anyone with it."

Walter flashed an "Okay" sign. "Gotcha."

Sir Patrick, Professor Hamilton, and Billy walked side by side to the log. Since it had been moved from its original spot, hundreds of beetles and multi-legged arthropods skittered to and fro along the damp, bare ground. Billy gently rolled the log back in place, allowing the professor and Sir Patrick to sit.

Instead of crowding into the narrow space between the two men, Billy sat cross-legged in front of them and opened *Fama Regis* on his lap. Flipping to the poem the rubellite had translated for him, he held it up for his two mentors to see. "Look. The English words are still there. They used to be like those stick figure things on the next page."

The professor and Sir Patrick craned their necks forward, reading the strange words in the dim firelight. Patrick pointed at one of the lines. "This part is similar to a prophecy I heard Merlin speak in person. It's how I learned about the key." He read it out loud.

A dragon's key unlocks the truth
Of light's redeeming power to save.
Its eye transforms the red to white;
It finds the lost, makes wise the knave.

"But Merlin's poem was in the old language," Patrick continued, "and, frankly, I don't remember the words, just what it taught me."

Billy moved the pendant's light to the next page. "Let's see what this one says. It's not divided into lines like a poem this time." The blinking red glow settled on the top half of the page, focusing most of its energy on the title. Without the pressure of a flooded cave threatening to drown him, the characters seemed to morph more quickly than before. Within seconds, the strange runes wiggled out of place, squirming like thin black worms until they created new letters, spelling out "The History of Excalibur."

"Cool." Billy shifted the light down to the first line. "It's about Excalibur." As the "worms" continued to form new letters, Billy read out loud, the squiggling spellers keeping just ahead of him.

The story covered several pages, vividly describing how Arthur obtained the sword from a dark sorceress who claimed to be a water goddess, the Lady of the Lake. Once she bequeathed Excalibur to him, its powers could only be summoned by the king and his descendants, or by a trusted companion and his

89

descendants. Once chosen, that companion could not be changed. Naturally, Arthur chose Merlin. Whom could he possibly trust more?

Sir Patrick laid his hand on the book's page. "Stop!"

Billy jerked his head up. "What's the matter?"

"Bonnie is in Arthur's line," Patrick said, "and Charles is a descendant of Merlin, so it makes sense that they were able to use the sword." He slowly turned his head toward the campfire. "But why does it work for Walter?"

Professor Hamilton leaned forward and folded his hands between his knees. "Perhaps I can explain. Walter's father came to Oxford to research ancient documents. He had some evidence that he is a descendant of King Arthur, but he was never able to prove it. Since I am an expert in the field, he took several of my classes, and we became friends. Unfortunately, we never made the final genealogical connection." He nodded toward Walter. "Apparently we now have empirical evidence without the paperwork to back it up."

Billy dipped his head and whispered, "Walter's an heir to the king?"

"Yes," the professor replied, "and apparently a natural one, so he would supercede you in the line."

"That's weird," Billy said. "Why couldn't he pull Excalibur from the stone back when we first found it?"

"A good point, William. At that time, I considered his failure as final proof that he was not in the line."

"There are many heirs," Patrick said, "but only the one who could draw out the sword is destined to lead. God knows whom he has chosen and why he has chosen him. At least for now, William, you are the sword-bearer and the chosen one."

Billy picked up a stick and twirled it thoughtfully in his fingers. "That's too bad. I didn't want to be a king." He snapped the stick in two and tossed the pieces to the ground. "What about Shelly? She's older than Walter. Maybe she would come ahead of me. Maybe she could have pulled out the sword."

"Well, it doesn't really matter," Patrick replied. "The British royals would never recognize you anyway. But since Shelly's an heir . . ." His eyes grew dark. He thrust himself to his feet, his gaze searching the camp. "Where is she?"

Billy pushed off the ground. "I don't know. Call of nature, maybe?" He shouted over the pattering rain. "Walter! Where's your sister?"

Walter, seated between Ashley and Karen, pointed toward the forest. "She had to visit the trees."

"How long has she been gone?"

"Ever since you started your super secret meeting. About twenty minutes, I guess. She said she was cramping up, so it might be awhile."

Sir Patrick's face turned rubellite red, a taut vein pounding near his temple. "Dragons!" he shouted. "All but one of you search the forest from the sky! You must find Shelly immediately and bring her back by force if necessary! Knights, search from the ground. Split into pairs, and never leave your partner! She is a villain to be reckoned with!"

The dragons took to the air, plunging upward through the dome, leaving Hartanna behind. The knights charged into different sections of the woods, two by two.

Carl leaped to his feet, his face matching Patrick's crimson hue. "Villain?!" He stormed up to Patrick, meeting him almost nose to nose. "How dare you call my daughter a villain!" Sweat beaded on his balding head as curls of vapor rose from his scalp into the air.

"No time to explain!" Patrick backed away, continuing to shout commands. "Walter! Douse the dome, or it will block the

91

dragons and knights from returning." He quickstepped over to Hartanna, who dipped her head as he spoke into her ear. Walter loosened his grip on Excalibur, and the beam blinked out. Billy gave Walter a healthy slap on the back, and Walter returned the sword to Billy's scabbard. With rain cascading again in violent sheets, Marilyn huddled under Hartanna's wing with Bonnie, Ashley, Karen, and Shiloh.

Carl stood in the rain, his eyes darting all around and his mouth wide open. He seemed paralyzed by anger and fear. Billy and Walter joined him. Billy pulled up the collar on his jacket, feeling colder than ever. "I'm not sure how to explain all this, Mr. Foley, but . . ." A sudden brisk wind bit through his wet clothes. He wasn't sure what to say, and the chill made it hard to think.

"Carl." Professor Hamilton jogged over and placed a hand on his shoulder. "I think I can help."

92

Carl swept the professor's hand aside. "I have to find Shelly before the dragons do!" He took a long step toward the forest.

"Wait!" The professor grabbed Carl's bicep, nearly falling over as he strained to keep him in place. "There's something you have to know!"

Carl's nose flared, his voice sharpening. "What?"

Rivulets streamed into the professor's bushy eyebrows. He had to shout to be heard over the pounding storm. "Walter's ability to use Excalibur proves that you and he are descendants of King Arthur!"

"Yeah?" Carl replied, crossing his arms. "So? We suspected that for a long time."

"Exactly." The professor leaned closer to Carl's ear and lowered his voice. "But what you didn't know is that Morgan needed to possess a female in the royal line in order to survive. Since Shelly is also in the line, she is a prime target. She could be Morgan's hostiam."

"A hostiam?" Carl kept his voice low to match the professor's. "What are you talking about?"

The professor hugged his trench coat closer to himself. "There is no time to tell the entire story, but your daughter's behavior points to the probability that Morgan has taken control of her body. She left the airport with a stranger, only to reappear exactly where I was driving on a deserted mountain road. She shamed you into letting her hold the candlestone, and now she has disappeared."

"Ridiculous!" Carl fished in his pocket and withdrew the candlestone. It lay in his palm, a pool of water quickly gathering around it. "Isn't this what she was after?"

Billy laid his hand on his stomach. Nausea brewed inside, sending a burning swill into his esophagus.

Carl closed his fingers around it again. "Shelly could have stolen it, but she didn't."

Walter stepped in front of his father and held out his hand. "I need to look at it. It's important."

Billy couldn't see around Walter's body, but he guessed Carl was giving Walter a peek at the gem.

"When I dug it out of the wall of the abyss," Walter said, "I accidentally put a little notch in it with the sword. I guess these gems aren't as tough as diamonds." Although his hands were hidden, Billy saw his arms jiggling, like he was combing the candlestone for a flaw. "It's not the same one." Walter's voice sank with his drooping head. "Shelly . . . uh, Morgan, I guess . . . must have pulled a switcheroo."

Carl slid the gem into his pocket. He grabbed Walter's shoulders and looked into his eyes. "Did she hear me say where your mom and Pebbles are?"

Walter nodded vigorously. "She asked you, remember? You told her exactly where they are."

93

Carl jerked his cell phone from his belt and pressed a button. Snapping it up to his ear, he waited, bouncing on his toes. "Come on! Come on!" He rolled his eyes and let out an angry snort. "Voice mail." He nodded impatiently through the greeting. "Honey, listen! Get yourself and Pebbles out of the motel now! And don't go back. Just find another motel, any motel, and try to call me." He slapped the cell phone closed and spun toward Hartanna. "Karen? Can Larry get the number of the motel for me?"

Karen pressed the computer to her lips and marched out into the rain. "You listening in, Larry?"

"Yes. I have already found the motel and alerted the police in the community. I am now making the call to the motel itself. Please speak up if you want to add anything."

Karen gave the computer to Carl and slid her hands into her pockets. Ashley joined her and stood by her side in the downpour.

The sound of a ringing phone buzzed through the speaker. A young male answered. "Thank you for calling the gold-award-winning Comfort Inn and Suites in La Vale. This is Brian. How may I help you?"

Larry's voice morphed into an exact replica of Carl's, even copying his exasperated tone. "This is an emergency call from Carl Foley. I checked my wife, Catherine, and a little girl in there earlier, and someone is stalking them. Get me through to their room immediately!"

"Right away, Sir."

Another purring sound of a ringing phone repeated several times.

"I'm sorry, Sir. There's no answer."

"Then go to the room and leave this note on the door. 'Do not enter this room under any circumstances. Leave immediately and call Carl for further instructions.'" Larry paused. "Got that?"

"Got it, Sir. I'll put a note up there right away."

"I called 9-1-1," Larry continued in Carl's voice. "The police are on the way. Show them the room and give them this number." Larry recited Carl's cell phone number. "Have them report to me as soon as possible."

"Yes, sir. I'll watch the lobby door and catch your wife if she comes back."

"Good. Thank you very much."

"You're welcome, Sir. I'll take care of it." A click followed.

Carl's arms hung limp. "Larry, that was brilliant. I was so nervous, I don't think I could've done it."

"I knew your emotions had rendered your brain relatively incapacitated. My programming instructs me to help humans when they reach that point."

95

Carl shook his head slowly. "You're right." He gave the computer back to Karen and sloshed through the drenched leaves, raising his shaking hands. "I'd better go away and think for a few minutes."

Billy stood next to Walter. His friend's head drooped, rain dripping in front of his face. Billy wasn't sure if it would be manly to give him a hug, but he didn't care. He draped his arm over Walter's shoulders and pulled him to his side, then released him with a pat on the back. "Don't worry. We'll figure out how to save them all."

Walter kept his gaze low. His voice spiked with anger. "That witch has my sister, and now she's after my mom." He lifted his head toward Billy, his eyes red and his jaw tight. "I'm not going to let her keep them."

Billy patted his back again. Everything he thought to say sounded trite or sermonized, but he needed to say something to reassure his friend. "Have faith, Walter. God's never let us down before."

Walter nodded, drooping his head again. "Yeah. I know. Keep reminding me."

Sir Patrick returned, splashing through the puddles, apparently unaffected by the cold even though his light jacket clamped to his skin. "Hartanna and I are in agreement. Morgan is likely ready to execute the next step in her plan, so we must move ahead with plans of our own."

The professor nodded and crossed his arms. "But what is her next step?"

Patrick copied the professor's stance and raised a finger. "The flooding crisis brought Shelly to her in a way that would procure the candlestone, but I think she intended more than that." He tilted his head upward and sniffed the air. "Hartanna's senses are more acute than ours, and she says she has never smelled such a foul rain. There is something evil in the water."

Professor Hamilton took in a long breath. "I suspected as much when I heard the popping sound it made."

Billy kicked the leaves at his feet. "Could it be a chemical reacting with whatever it touches? An acid, maybe?"

Patrick shook his head. "No. I have heard it, too. The sound is too quick. Too sudden. More like the breaking of a tiny glass."

"Yes," the professor replied, pinching his chin. "That *is* the sound."

"Maybe it's like a delivery system," Walter offered. "Maybe every drop's like a vial of Morgan's witch's brew."

"Possibly." The professor spread out his hand, letting the drops pool in his palm. "But it seems to do no harm on contact."

Patrick pulled out a handkerchief, wrung it out, and mopped his soaked brow. "It seems harmless for now, but we should not underestimate Morgan's craftiness nor her arts." He squeezed a few more drops out of his handkerchief and returned it to his pocket. "After all, her teacher is Samyaza."

"At the very least," the professor added, "the rain is keeping everyone at home and out of her way. Perhaps it is nothing more than that, a tool to spread fear."

"And a fearful populace is an easily controlled one," Patrick added.

The professor pointed at Patrick. "Exactly."

"Excuse me, ladies and gentlemen."

Karen raised the computer so everyone could hear. "Go ahead, Larry, but speak up."

"I regularly scan Ashley's e-mail, and I have received an urgent message. Please authorize audio transmission."

Ashley pulled Karen's hands toward her and punched a series of keys into the computer. "Go ahead, Larry. Let's hear it."

"From Morgan Le Faye, queen of the ancient earth and mistress of the natural arts. To Ashley Stalworth, mongrel daughter of a dragon. Although our actions are truly undeserved, Samyaza and I have graciously decided to spare the world, and the rain will now cease."

Billy put out his hand. The downpour settled into a drizzle, then a sprinkle. How could they know exactly the moment they would hear the message? Could a Watcher be listening? He scanned the skies, but the clouds still hung low. There was nothing else in sight.

"Ashley, I'm sure you know what I want. You will receive further instructions very soon. If you cooperate, no harm will come to you. If you don't, you'll find that pebbles are easily crushed into sand."

97

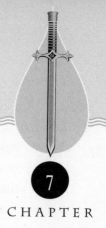

7

CHAPTER

Ashley's Choice

Carl held the cell phone to his ear with a flaccid grip, his face gray and sagging. His lips trembled, and his legs wavered as if he could barely stand. Bonnie crowded closer and leaned against his arm. Since her touch always seemed to help Billy calm down, she thought it might give Mr. Foley some comfort, too.

Thanks to another Sahara treatment from her mother, everyone was dry, but not exactly warm. Although the rain had stopped, the clouds kicked up cold breezes, delivering shivers and goose bumps as she hugged her sweatshirt to her body.

Sir Patrick stood several feet away from the group, tending the newly restored fire with a fallen branch, mindlessly watching the returning knights as they dried themselves in showers of hot breath provided by the dragons.

"Yes," Carl said into the mouthpiece. "I understand. I'm sure you'll do your best. Thank you." With a flick of his thumb, he closed the phone. "They're both missing. Pebbles and my wife." He shook his head sadly. "There was a note. It said . . . it said . . ." He kicked at the grass. "I don't remember. I had them fax it to Larry."

Bonnie took a sidestep away from Carl. "Does he have it yet?"

Larry piped up. "Received and ready to read."

Karen raised the computer. "Go ahead, Larry."

"Have the Bannister woman fly with Ashley in her airplane. We will pick them up in the air. After we have Ashley, as a sign of good faith, we will immediately release the Bannister woman unharmed. Do it by dawn, or we will begin delivering the Foley woman one piece at a time. No dragons. We will be watching."

Walter punched the air and let out a roar that echoed off a nearby cliff. "We have to save her!" His teeth clenched in rage. "Now!"

Carl grabbed his son by his arms, his grip so firm his knuckles began turning white. "But where do we look? We can't just go running out into the woods like madmen."

Walter locked forearms with his father, spitting out his words like an angry cobra. "I . . . will . . . find them!"

"Calm down, Walter," Ashley said. She began pacing, her wet shoes squishing on the saturated ground. "Finding your mother is simple, but saving her will be a lot harder."

Walter jerked away and spun toward Ashley. "You know where she is?"

She stopped and raised a finger. "Obviously they want me to get Devin out of the candlestone, and they know I'll do anything to save Pebbles. When I go with them, I'm sure they'll take me to wherever Pebbles is to prove they have her. Logically, they would use your mother as a caretaker and keep them in the same place." Lowering herself to a crouch, she plucked a long blade of grass and chewed on the end. "The problem will be letting you know where that is."

Karen leaned over and pressed the computer into Ashley's hand, her cheeks flaming. "Take this with you. Larry can track it. Just tell that gorgon queen you need his computing power to get the job done. She won't know any better."

Ashley twisted the grass stem between her lips, then threw it down. "Actually, I probably will need Larry. Who knows what kind of computing power they'll have?" She rose to her feet again and fastened the computer to her belt. "If they make me toss it, at least Larry can give you my last known location."

Karen's freckled face seemed to lose its fire. She hooked her arm with Ashley's. "Is it really worth you taking such a risk?" she asked. "Do you really think they would kill Pebbles?"

Sir Patrick rapped his branch against the ground. "Yes, they would kill her, but first they would torture her in unspeakable ways. Then, if you still didn't acquiesce, they would hunt down your other sisters one by one and savagely brutalize them as well. Their wickedness knows no bounds." He clutched an end of the branch with each hand and broke it in two. "But is acquiescing really the right thing to do?" He pointed one part of the branch at her, his arm shaking. "You are Morgan's only hope for restoring one of the most wicked creatures in the universe, and in so doing you would provide the Watchers with a weapon that would neutralize our only hope for defeating them." He threw both branches to the ground, and one stuck in the mud. "You might save a life or two, but you would put the entire world in jeopardy."

Professor Hamilton spread out his arms. "But if it is in our power to save lives, shouldn't we do it? Shouldn't we try to save Pebbles and trust God to save the world? Shouldn't we try to free a wife and daughter and trust God to liberate the rest of mankind?" He lifted one hand toward the sky. "God has long been in the business of providing the savior the world needs.

Our part has always been to reach out to one soul at a time." He pulled the branch out of the mud and threw it into the woods, a hint of anger in his voice. "Wouldn't you have saved Shiloh from the circles if you could, even if it meant releasing the Watchers?"

Sir Patrick's lips parted as if to reply, but for a moment, no sound came out. His bottom lip trembled. "Charles, you are sounding more like Merlin all the time." He lowered his head. "I bow to your superior insight."

The professor laid his hand on Patrick's shoulder, his tone now gracious and calm. "Nonsense, my friend. You have a heart for the world. You have lived for centuries and have seen a bigger picture than I, so you have taught me a great deal." He gave Patrick three hearty pats. "We sharpen each other."

Billy stepped in between Sir Patrick and the professor, waving his hand. "Now, wait a minute. If I understand this plan right, Ashley and my mom are just going to take off and fly around until some Watchers come and get them. Then, we're supposed to wait for a computer to tell us where they went and figure out a way to get there with a bunch of dragons, even though they've probably made their hideout dragon-proof. And even though they really won't have any use for my mother after they've picked up Ashley, we're supposed to trust that they'll take good care of her." Billy shook his head. "I'm sorry, but this plan really stinks."

Marilyn bounced on her toes, shivering. "As long as they need Ashley, I think they'll keep their word. Besides, what choice do we have?"

"We have until dawn." The professor pulled out his pocket watch and read it in the light of the fire. "That gives us about nine hours to consider the matter, but I would counsel for a much earlier decision. In our emotional states, I think it best to have a time of prayer and meditation now. We will reconvene in one hour to decide our plan. That would be ten fifteen. All agreed?"

Carl nodded, his fists tight. "Agreed." He reached for Walter, but Walter just spun around and headed for the woods, his hands deep in his pockets. "Walter! Wait!"

He didn't wait. With trees dripping all around, he disappeared into the shadows.

Carl sat down heavily near the fire, grabbed a stick, and poked the coals at the edge. The knights slowly separated, each one finding a spot to either sit or stand with skyward gazes. Professor Hamilton reached into his coat and withdrew a pocket Bible and his spectacles. Sir Patrick returned to the log and picked at the wet bark while Billy sat nearby, thumbing through *Fama Regis.*

Bonnie glanced around at all the quiet activity. "Isn't anyone going with Walter?" she asked. "He looked really upset."

Marilyn spread one arm around Ashley and one around Bonnie. "There's something I've learned about men. They're indispensable. Well, not all men, I suppose, but at least the good ones. In one way, they're fiercely independent, holding their own beliefs and passionately following visions that no one else can see. They need time alone to gather their thoughts, seek God's counsel, and get reenergized. But, when they get back together, they lay aside their differences and forge an unbreakable unit, like a single sword that rips through their enemies with furious rage."

Ashley pulled away from Marilyn's embrace. "I think I understand what they're feeling. I'd like to be alone for a while, too." She strolled toward the trees, waving behind her. "I'll be back."

Marilyn kept her arm around Bonnie. "Looks like it's you and me, kid."

"That's okay." Bonnie shoved her hands into her pockets and rocked on her feet. "There's something I wanted to talk to you about anyway."

Marilyn sat on the ground and patted the space next to her. "Let's talk."

Bonnie sat, not really wanting to look her in the eye. She gazed at the clouds breaking apart, catching a glimpse of a star as the gray masses breezed by. "You know a lot about how men think, don't you?"

Marilyn pulled her knees close to her chest and shrugged. "I suppose so, but since my man is . . . was . . . a dragon, my perceptions may be a bit skewed."

"Actually," Bonnie said, watching the moon peek around a cloud, "that's perfect, because I want to ask you about Billy, and he's both—man and dragon, I mean."

"Okay . . . go ahead."

104

Bonnie lowered her gaze, catching Marilyn's. Her matronly eyes seemed so full of love and understanding, it wasn't hard for Bonnie to spill what was in her heart. "Well, I guess you know the prophecy. It looks like Billy and I are supposed to get married someday."

"Yes, I know." Marilyn took Bonnie's hand and clasped it tightly. "And I can't imagine a more wonderful girl for him."

A surge of warmth flooded Bonnie's cheeks. "Um. Thank you." With her wings fully exposed, she never felt wonderful, more like a freak than a girl. "Anyway, do you think I'm a distraction for him? I mean, am I getting in the way of him doing what he's supposed to be doing?"

"A distraction? If you mean, does he notice how pretty you are?" Marilyn's cool fingers caressed Bonnie's hot cheek. "He'd be blind not to notice."

A tingle spread across Bonnie's arms. The compliment was sweet, pleasant, but she didn't want to focus on her looks. "What I mean is, if Billy has a job to do, and I'm with him, he might be thinking about taking care of me, you know, protecting me when he's in battle or something. That kind of distraction."

Marilyn folded her hands over her knees and nodded slowly. "I see what you mean. Let me think about that awhile." For a moment, she was silent, her eyes focused on her lap as she hummed a quiet tune. Finally, when her song finished, she turned back to Bonnie. "I think the best thing you can do is to let him decide if you're a distraction. I think you can trust him to keep his thoughts straight. He's gone through so much. It's like each victory in the circles added a piece of armor that protects him from temptations that might come his way." She wrapped her arms around her legs and pulled them closer. "Trials change a man, you know. They make a godly man stronger, wiser, a better leader, and, believe it or not, more humble."

Marilyn nodded toward Billy. He was shining the pendant's light on a page of *Fama Regis*, carefully studying the glowing letters. The light flashed back into his face, trimming his skin in scarlet and brushing his hair with reddish highlights. Bonnie smiled. Billy looked more like his father than ever before.

"Whatever you do, Bonnie, give him room to be a leader. Give him time to fill out his masculine frame, always supporting him with love and encouragement. If he drags himself home from a defeat on the battlefield, impatient nagging will just cut his legs from under him, but an encouraging word will puff his chest out and make him charge back into battle. He needs a woman to inject him with power and purpose, because a good man draws his sword for only one reason, to protect his wife and children."

105

Another tingle raced across Bonnie's skin, and her heart thumped. Her soul drank in the words as Marilyn continued.

"The mind-numbing complaints of a shrieking shrew will pour acid in his cuts and squeeze dry his masculine energy. But the tender hands of a loving wife will salve his wounds and open the floodgates to power from above."

Marilyn's smile wavered. "I still have faith that my husband will return. He will find a way back to me. And I'm . . ." She cleared her throat. With her voice failing, she hurried through her words. "I'm sure he'll never be the same again."

Bonnie threw her arms around Marilyn and pulled her close. "I'm sure, too. He'll find a way." She felt Marilyn's heart drum, beating faster by the second, then gentle shaking as Marilyn wept.

The growling whispers of two dragons caught Bonnie's attention. Beautiful in form and sparkling in the firelight, they exemplified the glory of the dragon race. Beautiful, yes. But not human. Could that be what Marilyn was thinking? If her husband did return, would he be a dragon? If he had a choice, would he become human again? Did she suspect that during those long centuries in human form, Jared really wanted to go back to being a dragon, even if it meant leaving his wife?

Bonnie pulled her closer. She cried, too, each tear a salty pearl falling silently to the ground. Shiloh's story came back to her, the fifteen-hundred-year-old story of Valcor speaking to Irene. He had said, "How rare were the tears of a dragon. We once lived in Paradise, and because of the corruption of an angel disguised as a dragon, all the world was cast into darkness. Now, as humans, we shed many tears—for what was lost, for what might have been, and for the end of friendships." But Valcor seemed satisfied to be Sir Patrick, a wise old man who held the secret of remaining human when all the other dragons regained their scales. Did he have a choice? Was the dragon paradise lost, making him decide to keep his place in the world of corruption in order to help redeem it somehow?

These questions were too deep. Too difficult. Bonnie decided to wait and wonder, and just let this godly, broken-hearted woman weep in her arms.

Shelly sat on a lumpy sofa, curling her legs underneath her body. With the fireplace still radiating stifling heat, she fanned herself with a newspaper. Only a hint of incense remained in the air, and her mind felt much clearer than the last time she had come to this cabin. She dug her nails into her arm, cursing herself. How could she do that to Dad and Walter? Sure, Morgan said they were keeping a friend of hers inside the stone as a prisoner, so she had the right to take it, but she still felt like a conniving thief. And it was getting worse and worse. Now Morgan was threatening Mom and that little girl. World peace was worth a lot, but not that much.

A low, marble-topped table covered most of the wood floor between her and the roaring fire. A chessboard in a mid-game arrangement lay on the table next to a hard-shell ring box and a narrow, rectangular case. Shelly knew the candlestone lay inside the ring box, but the other container was a mystery. If she had been by herself, she would have snapped it open by now, probably finding a set of ancient pens or maybe even a magic wand. Yes, that was it. Morgan was a witch of some kind, so that was likely her wand. But since the witch was lurking somewhere in her mind and body, snooping in strange boxes was out of the question. Morgan probably already knew what she was thinking anyway.

She grabbed a throw pillow and slung it toward the fire-place, missing the fire but knocking over a set of tongs that had been leaning against the wall. She jerked her hand back,

107

pain ripping through her arm. "Okay, okay," she said. "You don't have to be mean about it. I did exactly what you wanted, didn't I?"

A voice entered Shelly's mind. *You did very well, but your anger demonstrates lack of faith in my plans. Patience. You will soon learn how the angels will defeat the dragons. Remember, your family and their friends have been deceived by Merlin, and the only way to rescue them is through the power of another dragon. And once the dragons are swept aside, the angels can establish their peaceful rule.*

Shelly picked up the other throw pillow and hugged it to her stomach. "Can we eat soon? I'm getting hungry."

Not yet. Call my sister. I have decided how to counteract Merlin's plan.

Shelly grabbed the newspaper, wadded it up, and threw it into the fire. "Yo! Elaine!" she shouted. "Morgan wants to talk to you."

Now prepare for me to take over your voice. I will be gentle.

A petite woman glided into the room, her long, silky gown giving her the appearance of a floating ghost. "Yes, Sister?"

Shelly felt her eyes rolling upward, her mind drawing back into her head, burning like fire, as though someone had grabbed her soul with a pair of tongs, impaled it with a spit, and roasted it in a broiler. Her vision turned cloudy, sort of like looking through glasses with the wrong prescription, or maybe more like watching a play through a fuzzy camera lens. She could still hear her surroundings, echoing as if from a distant valley. A voice erupted from her throat, deeper than her usual tone, but still recognizable as her own.

"Still no ill effect from living on the earth?" Morgan asked, using Shelly's voice.

"None at all, Sister. As I explained—"

"Yes, yes, yes. I've heard it too many times. You never married a Watcher, so you don't have to cocoon yourself to survive another century."

Elaine folded her hands and bowed her head. "How many lives do you have left?"

Morgan frowned and raised a single finger. "I can regenerate only one more time. That's why I can't afford to leave this hostiam. I must save my last life for an emergency." She leaned over the chessboard and slid a black pawn forward. "I finally understand Merlin's strategy," she continued, "and I need you to visit Dragons' Rest to block his next move. Do you know how to enter?"

Elaine nodded, her head still down. "With a dragon's eye?"

"Yes, but since you are not a dragon, you must not take it off until you are ready to leave that place. Do you understand?"

"I understand." Elaine tilted her head up, regaining eye contact. "What am I to do there?"

109

Morgan slid the chessboard's white king behind its knight. "Young Arthur will try to rescue his father and the other dragons. You must stop him." She opened the rectangular case on the table and withdrew a dagger. Its gnarled wooden handle and primitive stone blade made it seem old, even prehistoric. She held it up, caressing the rough edge with her finger. "This is perhaps my most valuable treasure, a sublime weapon of stealth and betrayal that leaves its victims no hope. It can kill anything forever, even wraiths like you and me. Cain used it to murder his brother Abel, and Brutus plunged it into the heart of Julius Caesar. Only a direct touch from the word of God himself can reverse its power, and Dragons' Rest is void of any such influence."

"But isn't Merlin orchestrating a sacrifice and resurrection? Wouldn't we be playing right into his hands?"

Morgan picked up the black queen and raised it in her fingertips. "Sister, you are wise to see this as playing. Merlin and I are at war in a supernatural game of chess, and the stakes are high. He foiled my queen's gambit in the circles. I did not get the hostiam I desired, and Devin lies trapped in the candlestone. But I have recovered my position on the board. The Watchers are free, and I have advanced my pawn to gain a new hostiam."

She set the queen down two spaces from the white king. "Now Merlin will launch his final attack, expecting the boy king to follow the trail of the human messiah. But he makes a dangerous move." She pulled the white bishop next to her queen. "Merlin wishes to play the bard and retell the crucifixion tale. It is a tired, old story that many have rehashed in doggerel verse, but Merlin's living play is the worst abomination of all." A painful cackle erupted from Shelly's throat. "And to top it off," Morgan added, "Merlin would use the Great Key as the stone of the tomb, rolling it away to present the risen king as he leads forth captives from the other world. What a hopeless romantic!"

"But would it work?" Elaine asked. "Would it set the dragons free?"

"Oh, yes. It would work. . . . If not for this." Shelly saw the dagger turn in her hands, the hilt now extending toward Elaine. "If Judas had stabbed the Nazarene in the heart with this staurolite blade, perhaps there would have been no resurrection."

Elaine grasped the hilt, admiring the simple, yet deadly weapon.

"Use it on the boy," Morgan said. "We'll give the old bard a funeral dirge he'll never forget."

Elaine dipped into a curtsy, a thin smile spreading across her lips. "With pleasure, Sister."

Shelly felt a laugh erupt from her belly. "You're still scornful that he spurned Naamah's advances, aren't you?"

110

"And why not?" Elaine asked, spreading her arms to display her perfect figure. "No man ever resisted me before, whether I chose to wear the face of Naamah or not." She rubbed a wide scar on her wrist. "An eye for an eye, a cut for a cut. I will pay him back for his insult."

"What form will you take this time?"

"I haven't decided. Whatever will be the most likely to deceive him." Elaine spun in a slow circle, and her body transformed into the shape of a young man. "Perhaps a male body this time? I could be a comrade. I could be his Judas Iscariot."

"That would be an interesting approach, but remember, males are not as easily deceived by other males. Their hearts are made proud and deflated by the fairer of the genders."

"True." Elaine turned again, reverting to her original form. "I will seek Lucifer's counsel and decide the best shape to conjure."

"Excellent, but before you go, tell Samyaza it's time to gather our troops."

"He has already gathered them, six hundred of our father's angels at our disposal. Samyaza has instructed them where to hide, and they await your command to mobilize."

"Six hundred warriors and only nine dragons to conquer. Excellent. We will overwhelm them with sheer numbers."

Light footsteps tapped the floor and faded away. The fire crackled and hissed. A low voice seemed to meld with the dry heat, hanging in the air like a bitter smell, half spoken, half thought. Morgan picked up the black queen and knocked the white bishop over. "Checkmate, Merlin. The end of the dragon race is at hand."

Shelly felt her brain floating back toward her eyes, as though she were being pulled from the depths of a mineshaft, passing through both icy wind and oppressive heat until her vision cleared and she was back on the sofa. Elaine was gone, and the fire was slowly dying.

Nausea churned Shelly's stomach. Dizziness spun the world as her head pounded a savage drumbeat. She grabbed the pillow again and hugged it close, too sick and scared to move.

Ashley stole through the woods, using a penlight to guide her way in the darkest parts of the forest. Panting as she scaled a steep rise, she paused at the top to survey her surroundings. The clouds had parted, letting the moon's glow bleed through the bony treetops. She jerked her head back and forth. Her gaze latched onto a familiar rock formation. That way!

She hustled down the slope, surfing on wet leaves to the bottom. With breathless whispers, she urged her legs up the next rise. "Have to hurry. They'll notice I'm gone soon." Finally breaking into a clearing, she found what she was looking for, the airstrip and *Merlin II*, still guarded by a pair of dragons.

Ashley folded her hands behind her and nonchalantly approached the plane as she caught her breath. "Good evening, dragons. Remember me? Ashley Stalworth?"

Both dragons perked their ears and swung their heads toward her. "I didn't feel you coming, Miss Stalworth," one of them said. She let out a rumbling chuckle. "Obviously, you pose no danger to us."

"Not at all. What are your names?"

"Mine is Legossi," the dragon replied. She then stretched her neck toward the other dragon. "This is Firedda."

Ashley laid her hand on the fuselage. "Well, thank you for guarding the plane so well, but I have to take it now. I'm sure you'll be able to find Thigocia and the others, right?"

"Yes. I led your professor to the campsite."

Ashley shifted on her feet. "Oh, yeah. I forgot about that."

"Be careful in that flying machine," Legossi said, stretching out her wings. "The wind is still unpredictable."

"Don't worry. I will." Ashley climbed the rear airstair and pulled it closed. Leaning over to avoid bumping her head, she walked up the narrow aisle to the airplane's cockpit. After seating herself in the pilot's chair, she paused. Was she stealing? Was saving a life more important than asking permission? She didn't believe for a minute that the Watchers would spare Marilyn, or Mrs. Foley. The Watchers were liars. As long as they held Pebbles, they had all they needed to get Ashley to do whatever they wanted. Morgan and her monsters drank murder for breakfast. They wouldn't hesitate to spill as much blood as they could as long as it didn't interfere with their plans.

Ashley flashed her penlight on a tri-fold startup checklist, hurrying through each step and mumbling their completion. "Okay, cabin doors secure. Check. . . . Brake set. Good. . . . Fuel tank selectors, on. . . . I think I can skip some of these. . . . Fuel quantity. Hmmm. Not great. No idea how long it'll last." By the time she finished the list and started the engine, the dragons had taken wing and were nearly out of sight.

"My turn to fly," she whispered. She taxied the plane to the end of the runway, pressing the steering pedals to maneuver into position. "Okay. Flaps, twenty degrees. Temperature within limits. Brakes released." She pressed the throttle, her heart thumping like a thousand bongo drums. "Here we go!"

Merlin II raced down the runway, bumping along the uneven surface. Ashley watched the speedometer, waiting for the right moment to adjust the flaps. Then, with a breath-taking lift, the plane launched into the sky.

Ashley leveled the plane, feeling much more confident in her ability to cruise, but anticipation kept her teeth on edge. When would the Watchers come? What would they do? And

113

when Legossi and Firedda showed up at the campsite, would a platoon of dragons rocket into the sky to try to stop her?

Ashley turned *Merlin II* away from the campsite and accelerated, flying as fast as she dared. She knew the Watchers could catch her, but the dragons probably couldn't. They might mess up everything. She had to go alone.

Billy angled his watch toward the moonlight. The hour was almost up. He closed *Fama Regis* and tucked it under his arm. He had read enough. He knew what to do.

After balancing the book on the log, he withdrew Excalibur from its scabbard. The beam exploded from its tip, blasting light throughout the campsite. Humans and dragons alike gazed at him, their eyes wide and shining.

"Everyone gather around," Billy said.

While the humans made a circle around him and the dragons arced in a second circle behind them, Billy pivoted in place to survey the group. Heat blazed from his toes to his tongue, words spilling out almost unbidden. "Too many obstacles have been set in my path. Too many delays have stolen precious time. I have a mission set before me, and I intend to fulfill it." He paused, a nagging voice whispering tremors of doubt, but he brushed them aside. "I can't let Watchers, or witches, or floods, or even Pebbles stand in my way." He paused again, his throat catching, narrowing, threatening to pitch his voice to soprano. "I . . ." He cleared his throat and swallowed, deepening his tone. "I have to find my father, and I'm only allowed to take one person with me. I will have to leave everyone else under the protection of the dragons, but the book taught me how to give some of you a valuable gift that will help."

Billy removed the pendant from around his neck, the chain catching for a moment in his tousled hair. "*Fama Regis* offered

114

this protection for women and girls." He approached his mother and laid the chain around her neck, allowing the gem's octagonal frame to rest on her bosom. Her eyes glowed with heavenly pride. He waved Excalibur over her head in a circular motion, completing seven orbits before he pulled it back. An almost imperceptible aura remained, white and sparkling, like a blurry angelic halo. He did the same for Shiloh and Karen, then for Bonnie, waving the sword a few seconds longer over her than over the others.

He backed away and searched the faces in the circle. "Where's Ashley?"

His mother fingered the pendant lovingly. "She hasn't come back yet. Neither has Walter."

Billy checked his watch. Two minutes until their scheduled meeting time. "I'll cover her before I leave." He doused the beam and rested the sword on his shoulder. "Anyway, the halo protects females from the Watchers. It's called the king's cap; it's sort of like a spiritual cloak. The book says demons won't even be able to see a girl who wears one."

Billy swung around to Professor Hamilton. His old friend and teacher crossed his arms and nodded, his face solemn. Billy walked toward him, a lump growing in his throat again, but this time he couldn't swallow it away. The professor's brow wrinkled. His chin quivered.

Billy extended his right hand. "Take my hand, please, Professor Hamilton."

The professor grasped Billy's hand, his cold fingers wrapping it up, shaking ever so slightly.

"Do you remember how our friendship started, Professor?"

A wrinkled smile grew wide on his face. "You had to visit the water closet, and I joked about you having too much tea."

Billy laughed. "Right. A lot has changed since then, hasn't it?"

"Indeed. You were a boy then." His grip tightened. "Now you are a man."

Billy pulled in his lips and bit them hard. He could barely whisper. "Only because of you." Then he drew back, releasing the professor's hand and laying Excalibur's hilt in the old man's palm. "I can't use it where I'm going, and I don't know how long I'll be gone." He stretched his arms back and slid out of the scabbard belt. "I know I can count on you to use it well," he said, handing the belt over.

He helped the professor strap the scabbard on, then checked his watch again. "They're late." He glanced around the woods. "Where could they have gone?"

Hartanna unfurled her wings. "Dragons approaching! Friendly visitors, but unexpected."

Thigocia swished her tail. "I sense two. Firedda and Legossi. Why would they leave the airplane?"

The two dragons circled low, then landed gracefully in the clearing, each one glowing in the moonlight.

"Why have you returned?" Thigocia growled. "Legossi! Who told you to leave your post?"

"There is no post," Legossi replied. "The young lady, Ashley, has flown away in the airplane. There was nothing left to guard."

"What?" Marilyn screamed. "She couldn't! She wouldn't!"

"She would!" Karen countered. "In a heartbeat. You told her she could probably fly the plane."

"But I was just . . . I meant she . . ." Marilyn clenched her fists. "Oooooh! She probably really could fly it, the little twerp!" She kicked a branch, sending it spinning. "But why would she?"

"The Watchers wanted her," Karen replied, "not you, so why risk your life?"

Professor Hamilton scanned the skies. "An excellent point, Marilyn. It was a brave and noble act."

"But where's Walter?" Carl asked. "I know he was upset, but it's not like him to stay out of the action."

Barlow drew a knife from a sheath on his hip. "I volunteer my knights. We will search the woods once again, and—"

"Wait!" Billy shook his head, his eyes closed, trying to make himself heard without yelling. "I can't have any more delays!" He opened his eyes again. They felt wet and raw. "Walter's proven he can take care of himself. And I can't worry about him right now. It's just another distraction that might keep me from my mission." He choked up again, his voice barely squeaking. "I have to find my father."

Sir Patrick clapped Billy on the shoulder. "Exactly. There is nothing more important. Leave Walter and Ashley to us." He leaned close to Billy and whispered. "Am I correct in assuming that you will not choose one of the knights as your companion for this quest?"

"You are correct." Billy whispered back.

Patrick cupped one hand at the side of his mouth and shouted, "Knights and dragons! To the forest! Two dragons stay here for protection."

The knights dashed away by twos again, and the dragons took to the skies, knocking *Fama Regis* off the log and scattering leaves as their wings fanned the ground. Billy hustled over and tucked the book under his arm.

"I'm going with the knights!" Carl shouted. He sprinted after Barlow and Fiske.

Sir Patrick massaged Billy's shoulder. "Whom will you be taking with you?"

Billy, unable to speak, extended his hand toward Bonnie.

Bonnie pointed at herself and mouthed, "Me?"

Billy could only whisper, "Who else?"

"But won't I be a distraction?"

Billy swallowed again. This time, his voice returned. "Remember when I didn't want you to fly me over the moat to Avalon because I said I should be carrying you?"

Bonnie nodded, tears glistening in her eyes, her response like a hymn's refrain. "I told you to be careful what you wish for."

He extended his hand farther. "I'm being careful, and I'm wishing that you'll come with me. I learned that day that I can't do this without you." The lump started growing again. "Help me find my dad."

Bonnie dashed to his side, her wings shuddering. "Billy, you lead, and I'll follow. And if I ever become a distraction, just send me away. I'll understand." As her wings settled down, she stopped bouncing. "Where are we going?"

"To the darkest place of all." He opened *Fama Regis* and laid the spine over his hands. Standing with his back to his mother, he nodded at the professor. "Prof, I'm going to read a prayer, then I would like you to transluminate us with Excalibur."

"What?" Marilyn gasped. "No!"

The professor lit up Excalibur's beam. "This is no time for doubt, Marilyn. We must proceed."

"Don't worry, Mom. We've done this before." Billy winked at Bonnie. "Ready?"

With wings spread out behind her and a radiant halo over her head, Bonnie truly looked like an angel. "Ready!"

Billy placed a finger on the page and read the words as reverently as he could.

The blade that bears the light of truth,
The word of God made sharp and bright,
O send us now our God we pray
To chasms filled with holy light.

The dragon's gem, the walls of red
Must now become a house of white.
Rejecting pride reserved for knaves,
The dragon bows to take a knight.

Billy gave the book to his mother, then took Bonnie's hand.
Inhaling deeply, he nodded again at the professor. Bonnie's hand
squeezed his fingers, and their rubellite rings clicked together.
The professor, his face steeling like the bronzed image of a warrior, swung the beam straight toward them. A flash filled Billy's
vision. Sparks flew everywhere. He lost all feeling—no weight,
no touch, no sense of shape or proportion. It was like being
back in the candlestone, except there was no roller coaster ride
down a waterfall of light, no sense of floating in a black void
with an anchor pulling back. It was more like liquid consciousness, real, yet unreal. Still, he sensed a presence, and he
"thought" out loud, much like he did in the candlestone.

"Bonnie? You there?"

"Right next to you. . . . I think. . . . Where are we?"

"According to *Fama Regis*, it's called Dragons' Rest. It's sort
of like limbo, where the souls of dragons go."

"Don't dragons go to heaven?"

"I don't know. The poem in the book was really confusing,
but I think I caught the gist of what I'm supposed to do."

"Okay. I'll just stick close and try to help."

"Let's figure out how to move around. I have no idea how
much searching we have to do, but my dad's in here somewhere,
and we're going to find him."

Ashley tried to read every gauge at once. Altitude was fine.
Speed was high, but it would work. The fuel gauge said
. . . Uh-oh. Those Watchers had better show up soon.

119

A new voice broke her concentration. "So what's the next step?"

Ashley spun her head and yelped. "Walter!" She slapped her hand against her chest. "You scared me half to death!"

Walter slid into the copilot's seat. "Well, I had to wait till we were airborne. Otherwise you wouldn't have let me come along. Besides, I thought you'd just read my mind like you always do and figure out I was here."

"I don't read minds!" She shook her finger at him. "This is dangerous! Why did you stow away?"

"'Cause I knew you'd do this," he said, waving at the dashboard. "Besides, dangerous is my middle name. Or is it Dangerfield? Anyway, I'm not getting any respect here."

She shoved him against the window, a little harder than she intended, but she kept her voice firm. "Cut the clowning. This is serious. Either we're going to get picked up by Watchers, or we're going to run out of fuel and crash. Pick your poison."

Walter eyed the dashboard. "No door number three, huh? You can't land this thing?"

"I didn't consider that an option when I took off." She tapped the fuel gauge. It budged a little, but the wrong way.

Walter leaned over the dash, his eyes filled with wonder.

"You don't look scared at all," Ashley said.

He waved his hand. "Nah. After you've faced a dark sorceress and a bunch of demons in Hades, you kind of run out of the heebie-jeebies."

A loud bump sounded from underneath the plane.

"Hide!" Ashley ordered. "You're not supposed to be here!"

Walter crawled down the aisle and climbed into a crate in the back.

The engine died away. The plane kept flying with no change in altitude, but it began accelerating so fast that Walter's crate slid to the back of the cabin.

"Remember what I said about heebie-jeebies?" Walter called, his voice muffled. "I think I found a few."

"Shhh!" Ashley withdrew her hands from the yoke and pulled the computer from her belt. "Larry, you got my position?"

"Tracking you at a speed of 352 knots at an altitude of—" The computer suddenly exploded in Ashley's hand. Sparks flew through the cockpit. She dropped the fried remains, leaving her palm a raw, sizzling mess. Grabbing her wrist, she moaned, her fiery fingers splayed.

A low, sinister voice penetrated the cabin from somewhere outside. "Bad form, my dear." It breathed a mocking tsk, tsk, tsk. "I know, I know. I didn't tell you not to bring a tracking device, so technically you haven't violated our demands, but surely you knew Morgan would not be pleased if anyone followed you."

Ashley found a half-empty water bottle and poured it over her stinging hand. "Cut the blather, will you? I'm not here to please Morgan, and you know it."

"Very well, I will forgo diplomacy." The plane suddenly shook, rattling everything inside. Ashley clutched her seat, hanging on like she was riding a raging bull. Walter's crate bounced. Books and papers flew all around the cabin. The voice returned, now growling. "Since you prefer to speak to Samyaza unmasked, you will get your wish."

121

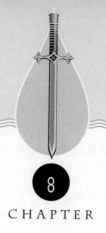

THE KING'S CAP

Excalibur's beam wrapped around Billy and Bonnie, instantly transluminating them and leaving a pair of sparkling silhouettes. Their remains streamed toward the pendant on Marilyn's chest. She heaved in a breath and held it, fixing her gaze on the silvery ribbon as it flowed into the rubellite. Seconds later, the stream vanished in a splash of sparks.

The professor extinguished the beam and lowered the sword, his shoulders sagging. "May God bless your journey, my friends."

Marilyn slowly exhaled, then caressed the pulsing gem. "So, Sir Patrick, they're actually inside this thing?"

"Yes, it would appear so." Patrick extended his hand toward her. "May I see the book?"

Marilyn handed *Fama Regis* to him. Patrick flipped the book open, turning to the most recently translated page. Professor Hamilton joined him, looking over his shoulder. Both men murmured in base tones, their eyebrows scrunching as they turned page after page.

Marilyn tried to peer over their arms. "What does it say?"

"It's quite remarkable, Marilyn." The professor slid his hands under *Fama Regis*. "May I read it out loud, Patrick?"

"By all means." Sir Patrick pulled away, leaving the book with the professor. "While we are awaiting word from the search team, there is nothing else to be done. We can't leave without Walter."

"Very well." The professor, his spectacles still on, stood erect. "I will begin here with the explanation of the 'king's cap.' Apparently Merlin is speaking to King Arthur about protecting Guinevere from Morgan. It seems that Morgan had demon cohorts back in the sixth century, not Watchers, but some other rank of fallen angels. This is important, because it leads to the decision William made about his journey to find his father." He placed his finger on the page and cleared his throat:

124

The king paced about the room, his head hanging low. "So, you are saying, Master Merlin, that while a battalion of my finest men cannot protect Guinevere from those devils, a mere wave of my sword can?"

"Actually, seven waves, Your Majesty, in a circular pattern. It creates a covering called the king's cap. Although its most extraordinary power is unleashed when a father applies it to his daughter, it makes any female wearer invisible to demons."

"Invisible!" The king stopped in his tracks. "And by what authority do you know this? A magic spell?"

Merlin's jaw tightened as he sat in the chair beside the throne, but his voice remained calm. "You know I do no magic, Sire. I am a prophet, and God has told me what to tell you. Is this any different than Moses being told to strike a stone to draw water?"

"No. I see your point." He resumed his pacing, now circling Merlin. The prophet remained motionless, not bothering to follow the king with his eyes.

At length, the king asked, "Then why did your own wife fall prey to Morgan? Could you not conjure up a protective device for her?"

Merlin's cheeks burned. "A day will come when Morgan—" He cast a sideways glance at the scribe. "My king, at this point I beg for privacy. Must our words be recorded?"

"Yes, they must, Merlin. This discussion may help my sons for generations to come. But, if you lack trust in my royal scribe . . ." The king waved his hand. "Palin. Leave us now."

Palin laid the book in the king's hands and bowed before leaving the hall.

King Arthur closed the book and laid it on a table at his side. "I will record the remainder of this meeting with my own hand this evening, and I hope my memory serves me well enough to be a faithful scribe. I will add my pages to the book after Palin has left my service, so he will never see them." He nodded at Merlin. "Go on."

Merlin's cheeks faded to pink. "A day will come when Morgan will pay for all her sins. I told her about the hostiam, because I had hope that she could be redeemed. And how did she repay my kindness? She poisoned my wife." Merlin's chin trembled, and his voice lowered to a growl. "Her hellish food robs both life and soul. The meat and meal of devils chokes out life, then empties the soul of its vitality. And now she wanders in the so-called Dragons' Rest, like one of the dragon spirits without a heaven for a true resting place . . . or a hell to reap the bad seed they have sown."

"Dragons' Rest?"

"Ah, yes. Of course you don't know. There is much I have to teach you, and there is so little time." Merlin stood slowly, looking older than usual, and braced his back as he straightened. He strode toward the corner of the chamber, gesturing for the king to follow. "Come with me on a short journey. It would be best if I show you so that you will never forget."

Merlin pushed on a panel at the back of the room, opening a door that had blended perfectly with the surrounding wall. The two ducked under the low exit, then stepped cautiously on a craggy stone floor. Only a tapered shaft of light from the chamber illuminated the room, revealing a narrow passage under a low ceiling. A scruffy rat sat up on its hind legs, its eyes twinkling. With a skittering of its claws, it scurried into the shadows. A musty odor filled the passage, a reminder of abandonment—melancholy, but not unpleasant.

Merlin took an unlit torch from a metal wall bracket. As he closed the door, darkness swallowed the remaining light. His voice echoed as if several Merlins occupied the long corridor. "Your Majesty. If you please."

A bright sword suddenly appeared, Excalibur shedding its royal glow, its hilt firmly grasped in the king's hands. Merlin set the end of the torch against the blade and whispered, "*Eshsha.*" First as a tiny spark, then spreading across the torch's fiber and fuel, a flame came to life.

"A magic word, Merlin?" the king asked.

Merlin led the way through the carved-out tunnel. "No, but you probably grow tired of my denials. I simply commanded fire from Excalibur in Hebrew. Since its light represents truth and knowledge, it responds to quite a number of commands."

The king followed close behind. "Do you know any other languages?"

"Yes. Latin, of course. And if I am dealing with evil forces of pagan origin, I often use Greek commands to counter them."

The two tramped down a slippery stone slope for several hundred yards before leveling off and beginning a climb back to the surface. The ceiling and floor drew closer together until both king and prophet had to stoop to continue, ending on their haunches when they finally reached a dead end. Merlin handed the torch to the king, then pushed up on a wooden panel above his head and straightened his body. Pressing his hands on each side of the opening, he lifted himself out of the tunnel and stretched. The king followed, his sword still in hand, and slowly turned to gaze into the surrounding woods while Merlin put the hatch back in place and covered it with dirt and leaves. "I tamped out the torch," the king said. "We can use it again on our return."

The moon's glow framed a dark forest, shedding light on phantasmic oaks that stretched out their branches to snatch up unwelcome wanderers. Merlin nodded toward a thin line of dirt that weaved the narrowest of paths through the darkest part of the forest. He took a deep breath, his chest rattling slightly. "This way."

As the two stole through the woods, Excalibur's light leading the way, Merlin whispered, "Remember this path. It is the way to Blood Hollow, a place Devin likely does not know. It is also the hiding place of one of the former dragons, one with whom I have gained a close bond."

They waded across a knee-deep stream, then followed a path so obscure that it must have been made by deer or perhaps rabbits. Descending once again, they pushed through thick brush and came out into a clearing, an elliptical, rocky space that resembled a miniature, sunken amphitheatre.

Merlin stood at the center point, lifted his head, and whistled a nightingale's call. He then stooped, signaling for Arthur to join him. "Devin will soon launch his rebellion," Merlin said, "and I will conduct my greatest, and my last, experiment." He bent close to the king, as if fearing that someone might be hiding in a bush to eavesdrop. "Valcor will be here soon. When he

127

comes, you will learn a secret about dragons even the dragons themselves do not know."

Bushes rustled. King Arthur rose to his feet, Excalibur at the ready. A man emerged from the darkness, his hands raised, palms out. "I am Valcor, unarmed and at His Majesty's service." He bowed low.

The king returned the sword to its sheath, then touched the man's head. "Arise, Valcor. I recognize you from the day of transformation. You seem more fit than ever."

"Enabling me to serve you with more vigor, my king."

Merlin laid his hand on Valcor's shoulder. "You have learned diplomacy well, my friend." He waved his hand across the depressed clearing. "I have chosen this place because the dividing wall between this world and the world to come is as thin as papyrus. Here, creating a portal to that world requires only the paltriest skill."

Merlin knelt and placed a gem at the lowest point of the depression. Its crimson glow pulsed, like a dragon opening and closing its eye. "This rubellite," he explained, "belonged to your father, Makaidos. As dragon king, he was aware that Devin would target him first when the war against dragons began, so he told me where it would be hidden should anything happen to him.

"As you know, the gem itself represents the essence of a dragon's soul, beautiful in form, as is the dragon, yet scarlet, the color of the unredeemed. What you may not know is that when a dragon takes the stone as his own, his soul becomes tied to it, and it becomes his gateway into the dragon afterlife, a place where humans are not meant to go. I expect, however, that any rubellite will absorb a dragon's spirit, for not all dragons have their own gem.

"But, if a dragon has one, as long as there is the slightest glimmer of a dragon's soul remaining, his chosen rubellite will be red, and when he passes through the gateway into Dragons' Rest, the gem becomes a pulsing beacon, indicating his presence there for the benefit of those he or she left behind in this world."

Merlin laid his hand on the rubellite, capping its glow for a moment. Then, raising his hand slowly, the glow seemed to follow his hand, growing into a vertical column, a rising scarlet pedestal that finally stopped when it reached the prophet's height. Merlin drew an oval around it with his finger, and the pedestal seemed to bleed in all directions, filling up the frame Merlin had drawn until it formed a scarlet ellipse.

Merlin backed away, joining the king and Valcor as they gaped in silence. He waved his hand, his palm pointing toward the flaming halo, and spoke in a resonant tone.

O make the passage clear to men
Who wish to see the gate,
The path no dragon deigns to cross,
For death is not their fate.

From top to bottom, the halo's red hue faded to pink, then to white. A horse-trodden path appeared, straw lying here and there, and as people crossed from one side of the road to the other, they trampled the straw under their feet. The scene appeared to be a marketplace—two young women standing in front of a hut, their handmade wares displayed on the tops of wooden tables; a burly man carrying a pole with a deer carcass hanging from its hooves; and a matronly woman bearing a fruit basket in each of her meaty arms.

Merlin took two quick steps forward. "There!" He pointed near the top of the ellipse. His voice grew excited, even agitated. "See the woman standing next to the nobleman? The one carrying the scrolls?"

The king leaned closer, squinting. "The gray-haired lady handing him a scroll right now?"

"Yes! Yes! She's the one!"

The king stroked his chin. "She is familiar to me, Merlin. Very familiar."

"She should be." Merlin's face reddened again. "She is my wife."

"Your wife? So we are looking upon Dragons' Rest?"

Merlin's expression turned vacant, as though his mind had flown into the scene before them. His fingers hovered over the image of his wife, caressing her face from afar.

"Merlin?" The king shook the prophet's arm. "Is that Dragons' Rest?"

Merlin tore himself out of his trance and stepped back from the oval. "Yes." He took a deep breath, now keeping his gaze on the king. "As I told you, Morgan's food not only kills the body, it drains vitality from the human soul, and this dungeon is reserved for the dead who enter into eternity without a living, human soul. Now my wife languishes there, not knowing who she really is or why she is there."

The ellipse suddenly grew dark, shifting to gray, then black, the darkness seeping out of the oval like a night fog. Billowing smoke crawled along the ground, then rose into a column, slowly solidifying into a human form, slender and feminine, the shape of Morgan Le Faye.

King Arthur drew his sword, but Merlin raised his hand. "Not here. Not now. She has yet to fulfill her purpose."

Morgan, dressed in a silky black gown, waltzed up to Merlin, laughing. "I saw you mooning over the gateway. Do you miss your sweet wife, my old friend?"

Merlin clenched his fists, and his lips turned white, yet he neither advanced to attack nor raised his hand. Serrated words slipped through his grinding teeth. "Leave it to you to attack a man by killing his defenseless wife."

"Oh, but Merlin," she crooned, "there is no more effective tool. Taking a man's woman is the same as ripping out his heart and pouring his life's blood on the ground." She patted his cheek, pursing her lips as though speaking to a child. "And watching you wither over the past three years has been such a joy." She turned and gave the king a mock curtsy. "Your Majesty. It is an honor."

King Arthur drew back his sword. A brilliant ray erupted from its tip and shot into the sky. "Merlin, step aside, and I will slay this foul witch where she stands."

Merlin stayed put. "She is a wraith, more dead than alive. In your hands, the sword would do nothing more than reveal her nature. Killing her requires much more."

The king pushed forward and shoved Merlin aside. With a wild swipe, he sliced through Morgan's waist. Her body absorbed the sword's light, like sunlight coursing through her veins. Her face transformed. A sultry, painted mask melted away, replaced by a bloody raven's head, its mouth agape in a raging scream and its red eyes aflame.

Arthur fell to his seat, and the sword's light died away. Valcor rushed to his side, sliding his hand behind the king's shoulder. Morgan, returning to her female form, glowered at the king. "You are all such fools. Knowing about my strategy will not protect your wives now or in the future. All who oppose me will feel my wrath, and no loved one is safe, man, woman, or child."

Morgan sublimated to black fog and disappeared into the ellipse. Seconds later, the portal cleared to a pulsing red glow.

King Arthur jumped to his feet. "That sorceress from hell will not kill my queen." He waved the sword in the air. "I will apply the king's cap and ward off her evil minions."

"That will shield her from the demons," Merlin said, "but I don't know how it will affect Morgan's ability to see her. She is not one of them."

The king relit Excalibur. "In any case, I must do what I can." With the sword lighting the way, he sprinted down the narrow path.

Professor Hamilton's shoulders slumped, his face ashen, his eyes joyless. His voice carried the death rattle of a moribund man. "There are two poems at the end, but I have no more strength to read."

Sir Patrick took *Fama Regis*, keeping it open to the same page. "One of the poems is the prayer Billy read as he departed, the other is one for him to recite once he gets to the dragon resting place." He put his finger on the page. "A final note tells him to take along one companion, a worthy one who, as it says, 'would never leave or forsake you, no matter what.'"

Patrick hugged the professor, patting him on the back. "Do you believe your own wife is in the dungeon?"

The professor's arms hung limp, his voice still barely audible. "Yes. . . . Yes, I do."

Patrick released him, keeping one hand on his arm as he helped him sit. "Then let me tell the rest of the story, for, as you know, I was there with Merlin. What happened that night has replayed in my dreams countless times, especially the prophetic song I will relate. I have long known what a flashing rubellite means, and when you hear the story, you will understand why I could not tell Billy what I knew."

Patrick closed the book and laid it in the professor's lap, then stepped back and addressed the group as if ready to deliver a lecture. But unlike any stoic or monotonous university teacher, his eyes came alive with adventure, as though he were still viewing the events he was about to relate. Reaching out his arms to hug empty space, he spoke in a vivid storyteller's voice:

When the king departed, I embraced Merlin. "My dear friend, what can I do to help? I will go to that place myself and rescue your wife if you will only tell me how."

Merlin pulled away from my arms. "At this time there is no way for a living person to enter that place. If you were to die, however, you would go there, for it is the haunt of dead dragons."

"Dead dragons?" I peered into the aura, but red mist clouded my view. "Then why did they appear to be humans?"

"They walk there as the humans they would have been had they been born to Adam's offspring or else transformed into humans as you were. But since they were designed never to die, they wander in futility—without a human soul, without hope, and without a redeemer."

133

I lifted a thin, leather cord that hung around Merlin's neck. A crude, wooden cross dangled at the bottom. "Humans have a redeemer. Why not dragons?"

Merlin wrapped his palm around the cross and drew his fist to his breast. "The human messiah, fully God and fully man, was sent to rescue the offspring of Adam, a creature made in the image of God. A messiah for dragons, who were made in the image of man, would have to be fully man and fully dragon."

"Fully man and fully dragon?" I pointed at myself. "Isn't that what I am?"

"Almost." Merlin released the cross and placed his hand on my chest. "Although you have a human body, you still lack an eternal human soul. If a dragon redeemer were to come, you would then have the choice to step fully into the human condition. You would lose all dragon genetics and receive a human soul."

I placed my hand over Merlin's. "And then the human redeemer would lead me to everlasting life."

"Indeed." Merlin's face beamed like a proud grandfather's. "In any case, the gateway has not yet been made ready. While I am away on my journey, it will be my mission to open a passage to Dragons' Rest, using a device that I will call the Great Key. It will unlock the door that divides the two worlds. I believe there will come a time when that passage will be the salvation of both mankind and dragonkind."

"Of both races?"

"Yes. The Watchers, the powerful demons of old who were banished to the abyss, are seeking a way out. Unfortunately, it seems that such an escape is possible, and all of mankind would be threatened by their reappearance." Merlin lifted his head and gazed into the sky, a slight puff of white visible in his breath. "Hear the word of the Lord, my friend."

While dragons seek the Holy Grail,
A star is plucked from seas of light.
He journeys through a tempest wind
And plunges into darkest night.

And finding dragons lost in ruin,
He sounds a trumpet to restore,
But as he sweeps the scattered bones,
The vermin follow to make war.

The foulest snakes of Satan's brood
Will fly from pits on demon wings.
With loins on fire they lust for flesh
And seize the thrones of sleeping kings.

Merlin lowered his head, moving his gaze to the red aura. "I do not know the full meaning of this prophecy, but the Watchers are surely the foulest snakes." He let out a long sigh and turned to me, his voice as thin as the vapor escaping with his words. "Is it a sin, Valcor, that my motivations sometimes veer toward self-interest? Although my first desire is to help the dragons find their way out of their prison, I also hope, in so doing, to provide a way of escape for my wife."

I clasped Merlin's shoulder. "It is no sin to seek what is best for your wife."

"True enough, but I also have this yearning within. We were together for so many years, my soul longs for hers as though I am half a man without her by my side, perhaps even less than half."

"God put that yearning in your heart when he joined you together. How can it be a sin?"

Merlin firmed his jaw and nodded, his voice strengthening. "I will oversee the salvation of the dragons. I will travel across the boundaries of spiritual realms and guide the paths of those God has chosen to fulfill his plan." He gripped my wrist, excitement spiking his voice. "As Elijah returned in power and spirit in the form of John the Baptist, so I will return in one of my descendants. That son of mine will also play the part of the magi, going to the place of the messiah's birth, bearing three gifts—faith, truth, and wisdom—though each one of these gifts is a treasure the dragon messiah must also gain on his own, for it is impossible to lend someone your faith."

Seeming stronger than ever, Merlin strode to the portal and set his hand on top. He pushed it down, squeezing the aura into the rubellite sitting on the ground below. As it compressed, a stream of energy popped out, like a frazzled lightning bolt. The stream spun around Merlin and me three times, then shot into the sky.

With my arms stiff at my side, I watched the sparkling current fade in the distance. "What was that?"

"I have no idea!" Merlin replied, his hand still on top of the portal.

"Is it a sign? Part of the prophecy?"

"I will seek wisdom on this mystery, but for now—" Merlin pressed the portal into the gem and picked it up—"I want you to take this rubellite. It was the gateway to the underworld for the last dragon king, and I intend to use it as the Great Key. Keep it safe. When I have set the plan of redemption in order, I will make sure the way to use this key is added to the king's chronicles."

He laid the stone in the palm of my hand. "Master Merlin! The rubellite is no longer pulsing."

Merlin rocked the gem with his finger. "Makaidos! He has either died, or . . ." He gazed into the sky. "He has escaped."

"My father? Escaped?" I tried to find a trace of the energy trail, but it had vanished. "What will happen to him? Where will he go?"

"I am not sure. He died before the transformation, and he has no body in which to reside. Unless he finds a way to reanimate his dragon carcass, he will be a wandering spirit."

I held the gem in my fingertips. "Shall I tell Irene about this? After all, Makaidos was Irene's father too, and you know what happened to my other sister."

"Yes," Merlin said, covering the stone with his hand, "but guard what you say. Tell her that the rubellite once belonged to her father and reflects the vitality of his mortal essence, but keep the rest to yourself. Since we don't know what really happened to Makaidos, speculation about his fate would be foolhardy. The secret of the rubellite's property as a gateway to Dragons' Rest must remain a secret until after the new dragon king enters the prison. When he comes, he must find his own way."

Patrick folded his hands over his waist. "When I showed the rubellite to Irene, she kept it for a time, then passed it back to me after Merlin's departure from this world. For my part, I built my home where Merlin and I met the king. The oldest section of the house still stands, and its outer window is framed directly over the spot where the rubellite unveiled Dragons' Rest. That very window became a portal to the human underworld, through which Billy and Bonnie entered the circles of seven."

Patrick reached for the sword on the professor's back and rested his hand on top of the hilt. "So you see, Charles, when I dubbed you Merlin, I was hoping, as his descendant, that you were the one about whom the original Merlin spoke. You have been God's instrument, his voice crying in the wilderness to make straight the way of the dragon messiah. You were the magus who sojourned to the place of his birth and brought him gifts of truth and wisdom, then led him to faith in his own messiah. In so doing, you raised up the one who is called to lead the dragons out of their prison so that they, too, will have the opportunity to find the ultimate savior."

A gentle smile grew on the professor's face. "You and Merlin composed an ingenious plan, my old friend. When you sent me to West Virginia in search of the king's heir, I had no idea that you already knew he was there. How could you be sure I would find him and give him the gifts?"

Patrick moved his hand from the sword to the professor's shoulder. "Because you are the magus, and you followed the star, the guiding light that led you westward. And I also knew your character, that you possessed the royal gifts of faith, truth, and wisdom, and you would undoubtedly give whatever you could to the coming king." He straightened his body and crossed his arms over his chest. "I had nothing else to do with it. God and Merlin did the rest. I merely waited for you to bring Billy to England for his own wilderness journey."

The professor rose to his feet, a hint of anxiety in his expression. "And does he now take the road to Jerusalem? Will this be his Via Dolorosa?"

"I am not sure how closely Billy's journey must parallel that of the human messiah." Patrick tapped the cover of *Fama Regis*. "All I know is that he has read the king's portion of the story, and he has gone into the prison to rescue the dragons in whatever manner God chooses. He also read that Merlin's wife is there somewhere, and, knowing him, he will try to rescue her as well."

138

Professor Hamilton's head dipped slightly. "But he doesn't know my wife is there."

"No," Patrick replied, shaking his head. "I don't see how he could."

Marilyn, who had listened intently to the stories, collected herself enough to speak. "Professor, I have a question." Closing her eyes, she laid a hand on her forehead as if suffering from a bad headache. "When you said Via Dolorosa, were you talking about the road to Calvary?"

"Yes, Marilyn. It means the way of sorrows, the way of the cross."

"That's what I thought." She wiggled her fingers over her tightly shut eyes. "So are you saying to be this dragon messiah, Billy has to die?"

After a few seconds of silence, the professor finally replied, his voice soft and caring. "Not necessarily, Marilyn. I think he will have a choice. But knowing William—"

"Stop!" Marilyn shouted, raising her hand. "I know what you're going to say!" She slowly opened her eyes and wrapped her fingers around the flashing pendant. "I . . . I'm sorry Professor," she said, patting him on the back. "This isn't your doing." She gave him the brightest smile she could. "I know that."

Marilyn walked several steps away from the two gentlemen. Taking in a few shallow breaths, she looked up into the dark sky. "Dear God . . ." Her voice pitched higher, trembling. "Please bring my son back to me. I—" She grimaced and shook her head. "No. . . . No, that's not it." Taking a deep breath, she swallowed, a single tear tracking down her cheek. "You know what I need, Lord." She lifted the pendant toward the sky. "But let your will be done."

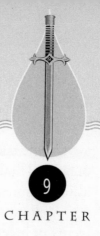

9

CHAPTER

DRAGONS' REST

Ashley tapped her jaw and caressed one of her molars with her tongue. A slight vibration tickled her gums. She lowered her hand and released a long breath. Whew! The tooth transmitter was working.

Leaning forward to get a better view of the ground, she raised her voice a notch. "So, Mr. Samyaza. Where are you taking me?"

His gruff voice answered from the underbelly of the plane. "To a facility we equipped just for this purpose."

"Equipped?" Ashley pressed her nose against the side window, trying to get a glimpse of the demon, maybe a wing or a foot, but she could see only darkness.

"You'll recognize pieces of your Montana laboratory."

Samyaza's voice seemed agitated, as though Ashley's questions irritated him, but she didn't really care about staying on his good side, so she continued her probing. "You salvaged my lab? I thought it was in a shambles."

"The parts we collected are in need of repair."

"I'll bet." Ashley slid out of the pilot's seat and tiptoed toward the back of the plane, ducking her head under the low ceiling. "Thousands of pounds of rocks don't mix well with delicate equipment."

"Well put, but we are confident in your abilities. You'll have plenty of incentive."

She lifted the lid on the crate, her hand still stinging from the burn. Walter's eyes peeked out, as big and white as ping-pong balls. She pressed a finger to her lips and whispered, "Remember, you're not on board. I'm putting on an act."

"What did you say?" Samyaza growled.

Ashley raised her voice again. "Is the inner core intact?"

"If you mean the lead box, it was bent but not broken."

"Good." She replaced the crate lid, noting a two-inch gap on one side, enough to provide air. She whispered into the gap, "After I'm out of sight, count to ten and try to find me."

"What is out of sight?" Samyaza asked. "I can't hear very well through the fuselage. It sounded like you're trying to find something."

"Is the engine out of light?" Ashley shouted. "Is the lens fried, or is it fine?"

"The engine is producing light, but the lens is shattered."

Holding onto the seats on each side, she walked back up the aisle. "I'll need a special kind of glass and a grinder for a new lens. Do you know where I can get those?"

"We anticipated that. There is a nearby town with several glassmakers. I'm sure we can procure whatever you need. Is there anything else, Your Majesty?"

"Look, Mr. Demon, I'm just thinking ahead." She settled back into her seat and buckled her belt. "If you think you know how to do this, then be my guest."

142

The plane shuddered. Ashley bounced in her seat, her belt keeping her from slamming against the ceiling. Walter's crate banged against the cargo door.

"I am no fool," Samyaza roared. "Don't play me for one."

After a few seconds, the ride smoothed out again. "Okay." She held her hand against her chest, gasping. "I get . . . the picture. How long till we land?"

The plane began descending. "Soon enough."

Ashley leaned toward the window. "Wow! The moon's really bright. I see a long, skinny lake down there. What's it called?"

"What do you think I am? Your tour guide? Don't say another word until we land, or I'll shake this plane so hard, you'll hear your own bones rattle."

Resisting the urge to snap back with a stinging remark, Ashley chewed on her tongue. That was too close. She needed to be careful. After all, she was dealing with one of the head honcho demons, not some backwoods wannabe bad guy. No telling what he was capable of doing. If he didn't need her to rescue Devin, he probably already would've . . .

She bit the edge of her finger. Time to change the subject. It looked like she would have to go ahead and get Devin out of the candlestone, but how could she make sure everyone was safe before she did it? She released her finger and wiped it on her shirt. After she did the job, they wouldn't need Pebbles, Mrs. Foley, or her anymore, so they were bound to go ahead and kill them. Why risk letting them go? And they sure wouldn't let Pebbles go before she finished. Otherwise she wouldn't have any reason to do what they wanted.

She pulled in her bottom lip. Then again, maybe they would kill the others. Maybe they didn't know that she'd rather die than let that maniac out. But what options did she have to keep the others safe? She had Walter on board, and Larry was

143

just a breath away, but was that enough to mount a rescue attempt?

Ashley scanned the dashboard, trying to decipher all the instruments. Altimeter, air speed . . . Aha! The GPS! She flipped on the switch and waited for the system to lock in on her location. Within seconds, the screen showed a tiny airplane in the middle of a map. Using the control buttons to zoom in tight, she calculated their location—Deep Creek Lake State Park in Western Maryland. At their rate of descent, they would land in minutes. But how could she tell Larry without letting Samyaza know what she was doing? He had already warned her to be quiet.

As the plane flew low over the massive lake, Ashley mumbled in the back of her throat, "Morse code," then coughed to cover it up.

The plane shook, angling heavily to the right. "No more warnings! I know you're up to something."

Ashley pinched her nose. "I said dis is the worse code I've had in a long time. I think I'm getting chills." She began chattering her teeth, making long and short clicks to match the dashes and dots of Morse code.

"You asked for it!"

Merlin II rattled like a bag of marbles in a toddler's hand, pitching, then barrel rolling. Instruments all over the dashboard exploded, pouring out sparks and smoke. The cargo door flew open. Walter's crate skidded sideways. It teetered on the edge of the doorway, then plunged into the void. A rush of wind sent papers flying out in his wake.

Ashley tried to scream, but her tongue cleaved to the roof of her mouth. When the plane finally settled down, she bent over the side of her seat and clutched her abdomen, swallowing an eruption of bile as she desperately tried not to vomit. Tears filled her eyes, hot, stinging tears. She sobbed, quietly mouthing, "Walter! Oh, Walter!"

As Billy tried to propel himself forward, his mind felt like it was breaking apart and the pieces were scattering in a hurricane. Just seconds ago, he was able to think clearly, but now the simplest thoughts proved to be a struggle. Even as he tried to formulate an idea for his next step, he forgot his previous thought, forcing him to start over. All he could remember was his mission and that Bonnie was somewhere nearby. Could he still contact her? Was this brain-splitting stuff happening to her, too?

He steeled his consciousness, calling on all his energy to keep his sanity. He spoke out in his mind. "Bonnie? You still there?"

"Yes!" Her thought seemed agitated, frightened.

"Okay," Billy "said," trying to calm his thoughts for Bonnie's sake. "Get ready . . . for a change."

"What . . . kind . . . of change?"

"I don't know." Every word Billy expressed was like spitting out a cannonball. "A big one . . . I think."

"Okay. . . . I'll do my best."

Billy drew up every last atom of strength and spoke firmly in his mind.

I have no sword or shield in hand,
No weapons of a knight.
I come to save a wandering soul
From shadows of the night.

My eye has seen, my ear has heard,
'Tis love that sets men free.
To make scales flesh, to make red white
O give us eyes to see.

As his words died away, Billy's awareness of himself increased—first a sense of feeling in his fingers, toes, and skin, then a flood of scarlet filled his vision. The substance slowly thinned, like strawberry gelatin melting into liquid.

Flexing his fingers and arms, he could tell that his body was again intact, though he was unable to see anything through the red stuff. A voice reached his ear, echoing across an expanse like a call from a man on a distant shore. "Take this. You will need it later."

Billy suddenly felt a lump in his hand, as if someone had pressed a small object into his palm and rolled his fingers closed. The voice continued. "Give it to the first person who mentions your father's royal name. A ring is the only ticket to the theatre. As soon as you find the theatre, you must enter. Only then will you learn how to rescue the deathless."

146

The liquid slowly dissolved into gas—red mist, then pink, and finally white vapor that melted away, like fog evaporating in the heat of mid-morning. Billy's eyes focused on a quaint village setting—a cobblestone street with a horse carriage tied up on the side and a planked sidewalk filled with streams of people window-shopping as they passed by a feed store, a dry goods shop, and a butcher.

He opened his palm revealing a rubellite ring. "Will you look at that!" he said, turning to Bonnie. "I already have one. I wonder why—"

She breathed in a loud gasp. "Billy! My wings! They're gone!"

The sound of galloping ripped through Billy's ears. He jerked Bonnie back, just in time for a team of stagecoach horses to tear by. "Whew!" Billy shoved the ring into his pocket and mopped his forehead. "We were in the middle of the street."

With one hand still on Bonnie's shoulder, he turned her gently to get a look at her back. "No wings. Cool!"

Bonnie spun around, a hurt expression on her face. "Cool? You like it better this way?"

"No! It's not that! I was just thinking the weird stuff that's happening here is kind of exciting. *That* kind of cool." He shrugged his shoulders. "I don't necessarily like it better."

Now near the edge of the street, Bonnie set one foot on the raised planks and one in the sand that had collected at the berm. She eyed Billy carefully, her lips tight.

He shrugged again. "It's just different. That's all."

Bonnie turned away and dipped her head. "I know. I'm just kind of upset at myself. I was excited too, like I was glad they were gone, like I'll be sorry if they come back when we get out of this place." She crossed her arms over her chest and sighed. "I should know better."

"Don't worry about it." Billy drew a line in the sand with his shoe. He wanted to cheer her up, but what could he say? Everything that came to mind seemed inadequate, either too contrived or too romantic. He decided to go for it. Better to tell the truth than to worry about how his words sounded. "Bonnie, I would like you, wings or no wings. It doesn't change how important you are to me."

Bonnie lifted her head, a tender smile gracing her lips. "Thank you," she whispered. "You know, it feels really weird, almost like I'm off balance. I have to be careful not to fall forward, because I'm so used to carrying a load on my back."

"I've changed too." Billy laid a hand on his stomach. "I don't feel anything brewing down below. I think my fire breathing's gone."

"So we don't have dragon traits anymore?"

147

"Seems like it. I had no idea those horses were coming, so I guess my sense of danger bit the dust, too."

Billy surveyed the stores and the signs hanging overhead. Sunlight filtered across them from a pink horizon. Although it had been late evening at their campsite, it seemed to be earlier here, the time when afternoon began giving way to dusk. Candles glowed in windows, and people meandered into various buildings, locks clicking as they shut the doors behind them. Closing time.

A man strolled by, tipping a black bowler. "Evening, Miss," he said to Bonnie.

"Bat?" she said softly. But the man didn't turn. He repositioned his hat and ambled down the walkway.

"Bat?" Billy repeated. "Who's Bat?"

"Bat Masterson." She spread her arms, her eyes wide. Her face was so pale, she seemed as dead as when Billy carried her to the bridge in the seventh circle. Her fingernails dug into his hand. "I'm back!"

"Back? Back where?"

"The sixth circle. But it's . . . it's different somehow." She pointed at Bat. "Shiloh and I were here in this village, and we saw that very man." She strode across the sidewalk, teetering forward, then plopped down on a bench that abutted the outer wall of a shop. "This is where we sat when he walked by." Bonnie searched the back rail with her fingers. "But Shiloh's marks aren't here."

Billy sat next to her. "What marks?"

"The ones Shiloh used to count the years." Bonnie caressed the dark, weathered wood on the seat. "This is the bench. I'm sure of it."

Billy intertwined his fingers behind his head and leaned back. "I guess quite a few things are different. You told me the people acted like you weren't there"—he nodded toward the man in the bowler hat as he turned into an alley—"but that guy talked to you."

"Right. When I was here before, Shiloh pulled on Bat's arm and begged him for food, but he didn't even glance at her."

Billy tilted forward and propped his chin in his hand. "Hmmmm."

"What are you humming about?"

He kicked a pebble out to the street. "This town. The story in *Fama Regis* made it sound like it was older, sort of medieval. Maybe it got modernized somehow."

"To make it look more like home for new arrivals?"

"I guess. Whatever 'home' is." Billy paused for a moment. A lady in a floral-print dress sashayed by, staring at them for a moment before quickly looking away. Billy pulled at his shirt through his unzipped jacket—dirty, wrinkled, still damp. Bonnie's clothes didn't look much better. A dark, vertical smear soiled the back of her sweatshirt, shading most of the opening where her wings once came through. Mud speckled both of her denim pant legs.

When the lady rounded a corner, Billy continued. "All I know is that this place is full of dragons in human form, and Merlin's wife is here, too."

"Merlin's wife?" Tight lines furrowed Bonnie's brow. "I guess I should've known he had one, since the professor is his descendant." She stretched her arms and yawned. "But I never thought about it before."

Billy stood, took off his jacket, and propped it behind Bonnie's head. "You look really tired."

"I am." She slid down on the bench and lay on her back, folding the jacket on the armrest behind her head. Her eyelids fell to half-mast as she pulled her knees up to make room for Billy. "I haven't had much sleep lately."

149

"A lot less than I have, that's for sure."

She let out a quiet chuckle.

"What's so funny?" Billy asked.

She squirmed on the bench, scratching her back on the seat. "I can't do this at home. My wings would get in the way."

Billy sat down again and laid an arm over the back of the bench. "Well, enjoy yourself, and I'll tell you the whole story."

While Billy told Bonnie what he read in *Fama Regis*, her eyes kept blinking. It was obviously pure torture for her to stay awake. With darkness deepening over the village, he came to the part about Merlin seeing his wife with the scrolls.

Bonnie interrupted with a yawn. "So you're supposed to find her and your dad and get them out?"

"I think so." He returned a yawn and slid down on the bench. "I thought she would be easy to find, someone handling scrolls for the town big shot, but now that the town's so different, I'm not sure what to look for."

"What about everyone else?" Bonnie asked. "Can you get them out of here?"

"I think I'm supposed to try. After the two prayers, *Fama Regis* just said, 'Though you lead, not all will follow, for many are called, and few are chosen.' I'm trying to figure it all out as we go, but I do know one thing to do. I heard a voice when we got here, the same voice I heard in the candlestone when Merlin carried me. He said I have to go into a theatre."

Bonnie yawned again, her voice dying away as she spoke. "I remember a theatre. . . . It's where . . . I found Palin . . ." Her breathing settled into a heavy, buzzing rhythm.

"Okay, then," he said, unlacing one of Bonnie's shoes. "We'll find it first thing in the morning." He pulled off each of her shoes, exposing her damp, muddy socks. The evening air was parched and warm, perfect weather for drying out a bit. He kicked off his own shoes and settled back on the bench, closing his eyes. The streets were quiet. The pleasant aroma of wood smoke hung in the air. A soft breeze began to blow, carrying a faint violin song, sad and lonely.

He let his head droop onto his chest, sleep drawing his mind into its comforting arms. A distant bell gonged eight times, each one snapping Billy's head back up for a second, but when the last gong faded, his mind drifted into a dream. He stood at a wedding altar, Bonnie at his side. As the pastor quoted the vows, Billy kept glancing at Bonnie out of the corner of his eye. Although he could see her face, for some reason he wanted to check her back to see if she had wings. In his mind, he kept trying to stretch his vision. He had to know if they were there. What could be wrong with that? He was marrying her, wasn't he? Shouldn't he have the right to know if she had wings or not? But he couldn't quite see her back.

The pastor continued. "In sickness and in health, for richer, for poorer, for better, for worse . . ." Billy's thoughts drifted. His mind interrupted. "With or without wings?"

The pastor, who suddenly looked exactly like Professor Hamilton, said, "William!"

Billy shook away the distraction. It was time to say, "I do." He tried to stretch his vision one more time, but Bonnie's back was still barely out of sight. He cleared his throat and opened his mouth.

The clock sounded again, jolting Billy from his dream. Still half asleep, he counted the gongs as they plodded their way to twelve. When the last toll died in the breeze, the wind shifted. The bells sounded again, but this time as if played backwards, the echo building up to the initial gong. Then, after only a few seconds, they chimed eleven times. A few more seconds, and ten backwards gongs sounded, then nine. As the clock passed

151

the eight o'clock signal, darkness faded away, and the whole town brightened a hundred times faster than a dawning day.

Billy couldn't tell if he was asleep or awake. This was too real to be a dream, but too weird to be real. After a minute or so, the light dimmed again, rapidly giving way to darkness. The clock continued to signal the time—four o'clock . . . three . . . two . . . one, then, after a longer pause, the breeze changed directions again and an echo of a single gong drifted by, pulling all consciousness from his mind.

Female voices drifted into Billy's ears.

"Homeless waifs?"

"Yes, probably a brother and sister. Looks like they've been on the road a long time."

"Poor things. No home. No bed. I wonder why they're here."

"Well, I don't trust strangers. They're probably up to no good, right Constable?"

"They might be running from the law."

That was a male voice. Billy tried to wake up.

"I'd better get them off the street," the man continued, "or folks'll think this town is a haunt for hoboes."

Billy held up his hand and forced his eyes open. "No. Please wait, Constable." He yawned, trying to focus his bleary vision. Three women stood before him, each wearing vintage, nineteenth century dresses—long sleeves, floor-length hems, and simple patterns in muted colors. All three had their hair tied back, tightening the skin on their faces. One of them stood only shoulder tall to the other two. Her dress accentuated her figure, slender and curvaceous. Her youthful face seemed familiar, and her smile kindled a warm sensation.

A man walked around the women and stared at Billy. Brass buttons fastened his blue, long-sleeved shirt all the way up to the collar, a shoestring tie wrapped around his neck, and a gray, snap-brim hat adorned his head.

"We're travelers," Billy said. "We just had to rest somewhere." He nudged Bonnie's leg. "Don't worry. We won't be here long."

Bonnie sat up, her eyes blinking rapidly. Pushing her hands through her hair, she smiled. "Good morning."

"Well," the constable said, "you two had better get washed up and into some proper clothes, or I'll run you out of town myself."

"Sorry. We just got here." Billy stood and brushed some of the mud off his jeans. "We'll get cleaned up." He grabbed his shoes and began putting them on.

The man and two of the women walked away, but the shorter woman lingered. "My name is Constance," she said. "Please come to my hostel for a hot meal. I also have clean beds for tonight." Her long black hair shone in the morning sunlight. "My beds are not the finest, but they are much better than a hard bench. And I have heard that strange things happen on the streets during the night. It is not safe to be out." She backed away, smiling with each step. "Camelot Inn. Middle of the town square. You can't miss it." She turned and hurried along the walk.

Billy's gaze followed Constance for a moment. There was definitely something familiar about her, something enchanting. She was certainly a friendly one. He leaned down and finished tying his laces. "Know where there's a clothing shop?" He straightened and pulled out his wallet.

"Maybe," Bonnie said, rubbing her eyes. "I remember seeing a sign for a seamstress when I was here, so it could still be around somewhere."

He rifled through the bills in his wallet. "I hope they take modern American money."

153

Swinging her feet to the planks, Bonnie stood and stretched her arms. "I guess we'll find out." She pulled the hem of her sweatshirt down and wiggled her socked toes. "What happened to my shoes?"

Billy slid them toward her with his foot. "My mom never let me sleep with my shoes on."

Bonnie bent over and slipped her feet into her shoes, tying them quickly. After collecting Billy's jacket, she gestured with her head toward the street to their right. "Come on."

They marched quickly, weaving through a line of morning pedestrians. Bonnie made a right turn around a corner, then immediately ducked under the awning of a store. Billy shadowed her, keeping a lookout for the people who had awakened them. He wanted to avoid the constable if he could help it.

Bonnie pushed open the door, jingling a bell, and Billy followed her inside. The seamstress shop boasted a bright array of mannequins draped with colorful dresses—silky evening gowns, gingham riding frocks, and long, flowing prairie dresses.

Bonnie picked up a hem of a sky blue prairie dress and rubbed it between her thumb and finger. "Isn't this nice? Simple and pretty, and I love the color."

A lady at the counter peered over her spectacles, her gray hair pinned in a bun. A bewildered smile spread slowly across her face. "May I . . . help you?"

Billy marched to the counter. "Yes. My name is Bi—uh, William, and this is Bonnie."

The lady stepped around the counter and extended her hand. "My name is Dorcas."

Bonnie covered her mouth, a slight gasp sneaking through her fingers. Billy glanced at her, then shook the lady's hand. "We're travelers, and people are looking at us kind of funny, so we thought we should do something about it."

"I should say so," Dorcas replied, her smile now more friendly. "Your garments are quite odd." Her gaze shifted lower on their bodies. "But I thought you were locals, seeing that you're wearing rings."

Billy raised his hand up to eye level, rolling his fingers into a fist. The gem in his ring had turned white. "Our rings?"

"Yes, of course." Dorcas pushed her hand into a pouch in her smock. "Everyone in town wears one. But I see now that yours are different."

He held out his fist for the lady to see. "Because they're white?"

"Yes. The others are red and blink like a fiery eye, but no one knows the reason."

Billy wanted to ask more questions, but he felt the need to hurry. "Well, I guess once we get some new clothes, we'll fit right in."

Dorcas tapped Billy's hand. "Just twist the ring so the gem faces your palm, and no one will notice its color." She picked up a slate and a piece of chalk from a cutting table, bent low, and felt the crease in Bonnie's jeans. "Blue jean material with rivets? I read about this in a fashion catalog." She looked up at her, a motherly scold crossing her face. "Why are you wearing trousers, young lady?"

Bonnie bit her bottom lip. "It's, uh, our style back home."

Dorcas straightened up and laid a hand on Bonnie's head, then floated her hand back toward herself, touching the bridge of her nose. She chalked a note on her slate. "Do women dress like men where you come from?"

Bonnie half closed one eye. "I guess you could say that some of them do, but usually not so much that you can't tell the difference."

Dorcas tucked the slate under her arm, cupped her hands around Bonnie's waist, and nodded. "The dress you admired will likely fit you well." She turned to Billy and laid her practiced hands on his shoulders. "Hmmm. Square and strong. I like that." Copying her method of checking Bonnie's height, she measured Billy's, the edge of her hand striking her brow. She made another note on her slate. "You and Remus are the same height. The suit I made for him will do fine."

Billy leaned forward, trying to read the notes on the slate. "What about Remus? Won't he be coming in for his suit?"

"No." Dorcas fished for something in her pouch. "His wife came by and paid me for it, saying to give the suit to the poor. She said ever since he started going to the theatre, he changed from a miser to a philanthropist." She withdrew a thimble and slipped it on. "He's given away nearly everything he had."

"To the theatre?" Billy asked. "What movie is playing there?"

Dorcas squinted. "Movie?"

"Uh . . . the show? You know, the play that's showing at the theatre?"

"Oh," Dorcas said, waving her hand, "it's not that kind of theatre. I hear it used to be a playhouse at one time, but now it's been converted to the waiting room."

"The waiting room?" Billy repeated. "What do people wait for?"

Dorcas flushed. She glanced at the window, then back at Billy. "Well, supposedly," she said, lowering her voice, "back when it was a real theatre, an old man appeared out of nowhere at the end of the play, like a ghost floating in a sea of red mist. He told the audience that a king would come to the theatre someday and take them to a better life." She picked up a spool of black thread from her sales counter and reeled off a couple of feet, her gaze still flashing back toward the window every few seconds. "But, the only people who could go to that life would have to come to the theatre. So, I guess folks who aren't satisfied with their lives decided to believe the old man and wait for this king to arrive."

Billy peeked at the window out of the corner of his eye. Nothing there. "How many come, and how long do they stay?"

"I'd say about twenty on a regular basis, sometimes more, and they come for the posted showtime and stay about three hours." She picked up a needle and expertly threaded the eye. "They wait in the dark theatre, usually without saying a word, then come back and try to make up for lost time in whatever jobs they normally do, though they feel quite weary when they come out."

"So, do you go to the theatre?" Billy asked.

"Oh, no." Dorcas laughed, a hint of nervousness blending in. "I'm only telling you what I've heard. I tried a few times, but it seems that when I get to the door, I just can't go another step, as if there's an invisible wall in my way. The others in line try to help me, but no matter what we do, the wall remains." She flapped her arms against her sides. "I seem to have been singled out, like a black sheep, I suppose."

157

"That's weird," Billy said, glancing at Bonnie. She shook her head sadly.

Billy nodded toward the door. "Can you tell me where the theatre is?"

Dorcas pointed toward the street and began drawing directions in the air. "Turn left out of my shop, two blocks, left again, then look for the first side street on the right. You'll see it."

"Thank you." Billy pulled out his wallet and tried to separate the damp bills. "Um. What kind of money do you take?"

"Your suit is free. Like I told you, Remus wanted it given to the poor." Her head tilted up and down as she examined his clothes again. "And I think you qualify."

"Okay," Billy said, laughing. "I won't argue with that." He spread out a twenty, two tens, and two ones, each one bent and wrinkled. "How much for Bonnie's dress?"

"We usually barter," Dorcas said, eyeing the money curiously. "Some people use precious metal coins, but I'm not familiar with this kind of currency."

Billy laid his palms on the counter. "I don't have anything to barter with." He noticed her eyes focusing on his ring, his father's ring. He covered it with his other hand. "I can't trade this. It belongs to my father."

Dorcas smiled and shook her head. "Oh, no, dear boy. I wasn't coveting your ring. I was admiring it. As I told you, we don't see white gems here." She picked up a ten and the two ones, pinching the ends and letting them hang from her fingers. "This money will do fine." After putting the bills away, she pulled a suit of clothes from a cubbyhole in the counter and handed it to Billy, nodding toward a corridor in the back. "Dressing rooms. The lady to the left. You to the right. You'll also find washbasins back there. When you're finished, come out, and I'll see how they fit. Bring your old clothes too, and I'll have them laundered."

After several trials, with tedious pinnings and alterations in between, Billy and Bonnie sported sharp new clothes. Billy stretched his arms to test the fit of his pressed long sleeves and button-down vest. Bonnie wore a simple prairie dress and pinafore that swept just above the floor. With her matching blue eyes, her shining blond-streaked hair, and her barely visible halo, she radiated heavenly beauty.

"Now you look like a fine young gentleman," Dorcas said, straightening Billy's cuff. "This Oxford shirt is perfect for . . ." Her voice drifted away.

"Something wrong?" Billy asked.

Dorcas shook her head, blinking her eyes as if warding off a mist. "Oh, nothing." She paused for a moment, then sighed and pulled the hem of Billy's vest down to his waistline. "I don't know why I'm telling you this, but have you ever heard a word that struck you as though it is very important somehow, yet you cannot quite grasp why?"

"I think so." Billy tapped a finger against his temple. "Sort of like a tune in your head, and you can't remember the words."

Dorcas pulled a loose thread from the vest. "Maybe like a tune, but I think it might be more like an echo. When I hear the word *Oxford,* it echoes in my mind over and over. It seems that it has become my favorite shirt just so I can say its name. I have no idea why." A tear came to her eye, and she wiped it away. "Aren't I a silly old biddy? Look at me, crying over a shirt!"

Bonnie reached out and held the lady's hands. "You're not silly at all. You just miss your husband."

"Husband? I have no husband. I'm just a foolish old spinster who has already talked far too much."

Bonnie kept holding her hands, caressing her bare ring fingers with her thumbs. "You don't belong in this town, do you?"

Dorcas squinted at Bonnie. "What makes you say that, child?"

"You said everyone in town wears a ring, but you don't."

Dorcas pulled her hands back and thrust them into her smock's pouch. "I must have lost it." Her eyes darted to the window and then back to Billy, her smile now fragile. "I don't remember ever having a gem."

A change in the light prompted Billy to turn around. The constable opened the door, making the bell jingle, and poked his head inside. "Are these two vagrants bothering you, Dorcas?"

Dorcas waved her hand. "Not at all, Marlon. They're buy-ing clothes."

A tall woman peeked in the window next to the door. With high cheekbones and a puckered face, she was the epitome of the tight-haired schoolmarm. Dorcas glanced at her, then back at Marlon, but her gaze kept darting to the window.

The constable pulled his pants up an inch. "So they're trad-ing goods? Well, that's a surprise."

"Yes, they are." She waved her hand again, this time as a good-bye. "Thank you for checking on me, Marlon. I'll be fine."

The constable tipped his hat. "You're welcome"—he forked his fingers at Billy and Bonnie—"but I'm keeping my eye on these two." He closed the door. The bell sang once again. On the walk outside, the woman shook her finger at the constable, her jaw moving as fast as a nibbling rodent's.

As they hustled away, Dorcas swallowed and nodded sharply toward the door. "I think you should leave now."

"Is that woman trouble?" Billy asked.

"That's Jasmine," Dorcas said. "She's the mayor and fancies herself a prophetess. She's been warning the town against strangers for as long as I've been here, spouting her silly songs and poems. Doom and destruction. Poverty and pestilence. That's all she knows." She wrung her hands together. "But it would be best if you stayed away from her."

Billy gestured with his head. "C'mon, Bonnie."

Bonnie leaned forward, urgency reddening her face. "But, Dorcas, you have to remember your husband. You—"

Dorcas raised her voice, her hands trembling. "I don't have a husband!"

Billy pulled Bonnie back and led her toward the door, mak-ing the bell jingle again as he heaved it open. "We'd better get to the theatre."

Once outside, Bonnie shook his hand away. "I know who she is!"

Billy peered down the street. The constable was nowhere in sight. "Yeah, but she was getting really upset." He reached up and straightened a sign hanging over the door, "Stitches in Time." "You think she's Merlin's wife? Did she change from scroll-bearer to seamstress?"

"No." She pulled Billy close and whispered, "She's Professor Hamilton's wife!"

THE DRAGON'S EYE

Karen pointed toward the line of trees. "Someone's coming. I heard a phone ringing."

Carl Foley emerged from the forest, his cell phone at his ear. "Got an update, Larry?" He rejoined the other campers near the fire, his skin ashen. Karen edged close and laid a hand on his arm.

"So where do you think they're going?" Carl patted his pockets as if looking for something. "I don't have a pen. Can you text message me? . . . Good. Send the info when you have it. . . . Fine. We'll pick it up." He kept the phone flap open and watched the screen, sweat beading on his forehead. "Okay, here's the scoop. Ashley and Walter are in the airplane, and it's being carried by one of the Watchers. The handheld computer isn't functioning, but Larry can hear Ashley through her tooth transmitter, so she's giving clues to where she is."

Karen tried to peek at the phone's screen. "Did Larry come up with where she might be?"

Carl angled the phone toward her. "He's calculating the possibilities based on the speed and direction they were traveling when the computer died. And the Watcher told her there are glassmakers nearby, so Larry's going to send a list of manufacturers. That should help narrow it down." He glanced around the camp. "I never caught up with the knights. Are they still out in the woods?"

Hartanna rose to her haunches and beat her wings. "I will call off the search party." With three mighty flaps, she launched into the air, then made a low circle as she climbed into the misty sky, trumpeting a shrill note as she ascended.

Carl drew the phone closer to his face. "Here it comes." His eyes darted from left to right several times. "Okay. Cumberland, Maryland, has glassmakers, and Ashley's giving more clues. She saw a long, skinny lake from the airplane. Larry's sending a list of nearby bodies of water that fit the profile. He says the most likely is Deep Creek Lake."

164

Professor Hamilton pulled a driving cap from his coat pocket and slipped it over his scattered white hair. "I have seen pictures of that lake while studying the region. I believe it is easily accessible, but I am not sure of which roads to take."

"So we need to get a map." Carl fished his keys from his pocket. "I'll drive my car. Larry wants me to pick up Ashley's laptop so we can communicate better."

"Her laptop has a mapping program," Karen said, hooking her arm with Carl's. "Let me come with you. I know old silicon brain better than anyone here, and I'll bet Ashley's already given him more information by now."

Carl covered Karen's hand with his own. "Fine with me."

The professor tipped his cap toward Mrs. Bannister. "Marilyn, will you accompany me? I think we make a good team."

Marilyn copied Karen's move, sliding her hand around the professor's elbow. "With pleasure." She pressed the pendant against her heart. "And Billy and Bonnie are coming, too."

The professor straightened his cap and nodded toward Sir Patrick. "Do you have any counsel, my friend?"

Carl closed his phone and slid it into his pocket. "Sorry. I got so worked up, I forgot to ask the most informed guy here."

Sir Patrick retuned the professor's nod. "I do have counsel. I think—"

The thunder of running footsteps broke through the mist. Sirs Edmund and Newman sprinted back into the clearing, followed by the other four knights. A sweating Sir Barlow trailed the others, clutching a hefty branch. "We heard the news," Barlow puffed as he strode toward Patrick. "Is the word given to embark on a new quest?"

Sir Patrick slapped him on the back. "The word is given, good knight. We are organizing a new search strategy now."

The moon cast a moving blanket of shadows over the circle, and eight dragons settled to the grass, gusts of wing-whipped winds buffeting the humans. Shimmering in the cold light, the dragons formed a line in front of Thigocia.

Sir Patrick paced before the reptilian squad. "Since you dragons are the only enemy the Watchers fear, you will be the attack force. Thigocia, will you be able to sense Ashley's presence?"

"Yes. Now that I have met her, I am sure of it. But from how far away, I cannot tell."

"We'll leave it to Ashley to guide us." Patrick gripped Sir Barlow's forearm. "Will the dragons and knights join together in battle as in the days of old?"

Sir Barlow laughed. "I have ridden a dragon only once and that by accident. But I accept the challenge and relish the opportunity to fight for the life of a fair maiden."

Thigocia flipped her tail toward the end of the line of dragons. "Two of my group have neither fought nor flown with riders, but we have enough experienced fighters to carry these valiant knights."

"Excellent." Sir Patrick folded his hands behind him. "The world already knows that there are dragons in their midst, but you had better fly low and try to stay out of sight as best you can. We will all rendezvous at a remote point near the lake and rest for the remainder of the night. I can only pray that Morgan will allow Ashley to rest until morning as well."

He stopped in front of Thigocia. "Your main objective, once we find the captives, is to draw Morgan and the Watchers away from Ashley. Engage them in battle if you must, but keep them occupied. Professor Hamilton and Carl will escort Marilyn, Shiloh, and Karen as close as possible to the hideout. From there, the ladies can infiltrate the facility under the protection of the king's cap."

Karen linked arms with Shiloh. "Yeah! Girl power!"

Marilyn tapped Karen's shoulder. "Don't get cocky, Red." She grinned. "Sneaky, yes. Cocky, no. Remember, Morgan might still be able to see us."

Sir Patrick leaned down and placed both hands on Shiloh's shoulders. "I will ride with the dragons, dearest one. They need someone who is familiar with Morgan's tactics. I promise not to ride in the battle itself. Do you mind?"

Shiloh's nose wrinkled. "A little. But we both have to do what we have to do. I'll just hang with Karen and sneak past a few dangerous demons."

He pushed a wisp of hair out of her eyes. "Are you up to the challenge?"

Shiloh raised four fingers. "After four decades in the circles, I think I should pay Morgan a visit and thank her for her hospitality, don't you?"

Carl wagged his finger, half smiling, but concern radiated through his reddening face. "Don't forget. That's my daughter she's possessing. We have to take her alive somehow and figure out how to get Morgan to leave."

Sir Patrick straightened, his face solemn. "That will be Excalibur's job. Only it can divide soul and spirit, but what it might do to Shelly's body, I cannot tell."

Marilyn picked up *Fama Regis* and folded her arms across it, pressing it against her chest. She let the pendant dangle over the leather cover. "I'll see if the rubellite will translate more of the book, but I can probably do that on the way to the lake."

The professor buttoned his trench coat. "Let us hope the flood hasn't washed out the roads." With a long stride, he headed down a narrow trail, Excalibur's hilt protruding from his back scabbard. "Step lively, men and ladies. The new quest has begun!"

Billy watched the seamstress through her shop's window. "Prof's wife! What makes you think that?"

Bonnie pinched the cuff of Billy's sleeve. "You heard what she said about Oxford. Couldn't she be remembering that her husband was a professor there?"

Billy furrowed his brow. "That's kind of a stretch, isn't it?"

"By itself, maybe, but the professor told me his wife was a seamstress, and he said something about Peter not being around to raise Dorcas from the dead."

"And the seamstress is also named Dorcas." Billy pressed his lips together, nodding. "Okay, that's too many coincidences to ignore, and Morgan said something about going after her enemies by killing their wives."

Bonnie set her hands on her hips. "The professor would be one of her enemies; that's for sure."

Bat strolled by, tipping his bowler hat once again. This time Billy took note of his pulsing ring as he lowered his hand from the brim.

"So we add Dorcas to the list." Billy stepped off the raised planks and onto the street. "Now we have to find Dad and Merlin's wife and rescue all three." The crowd had thinned.

Horses stood idle, harnessed to carriages or tied to posts. Apparently, the morning "rush hour" was almost over.

Billy scanned the stores lining both sides of the street. "But would my father even be at the theatre? Maybe if we find him, he can sort it all out."

Bonnie folded her hands over her waist, copying the pose of many of the women in town, and walked slowly on the planks before hopping down to the cobblestones. "Let's see. He liked to fly, but I don't think they have airplanes here. What else did he like to do?"

"He loved to read and study. Any bookstores around? Or maybe a library?"

"I think I saw a bookstore when I was here." Bonnie stroked her chin. "Let me think a minute."

Billy shoved his hands into his pockets. "Well, if we see it on the way to the theatre, we can stop in and check it out."

Bonnie's eyebrows lifted. "Frankie!"

"Frankie?" Billy repeated.

Bonnie pointed across the street. "The guy with the flowers, over by the fertilizer store."

"You know him?"

"Sort of." Bonnie waved for Billy to follow. "Come on."

The teenager, dressed in a newsboy cap, baggy white shirt, knickers, and black suspenders, paused in front of the store, digging in his pocket for something.

Bonnie ran up to him, Billy following close behind. "Young man!" Bonnie yelled. "Wait!"

He swung toward Bonnie and flashed a big smile. Cradling fresh flowers in his other arm, he pulled his hand out of his pocket and tipped his cap, a sweet Irish accent spilling from his lips. "Do I know you, Miss?" He tipped his cap at Billy, his smile fading. Billy returned a tight-lipped nod.

Bonnie dipped into a quick curtsy. "Bonnie Silver, and, no, you don't know me. We're from . . . out of town."

"Brogan's the name." He straightened his cap and repositioned the flowers. "Why did you call me?"

Bonnie propped up a drooping carnation that protruded from his bundle, but it flopped back down. "I just wanted to ask you a question."

Brogan pulled out a long-stemmed daisy and handed it to her. "By all means."

Bonnie twirled the stem. "Is there a library or a bookstore in this town?"

"Indeed we have both." Brogan pointed down the road, his palm closed around something. "Go to the city square. You'll find them between the constabulary and Town Hall. The library is inside the bookstore. You can't miss it. Just follow the bell tower on top of Town Hall."

Bonnie followed the line of his arm, then turned back to Brogan. "I have another question, a personal one, if you don't mind."

Brogan shifted his head back a bit, a quizzical look on his face. "If it's not too personal, I'll have a go."

"That silver dollar in your hand," Bonnie said, pointing at Brogan's tight fist. "What are you going to buy with it?"

Brogan's smile returned. "These flowers are for my mum, and I'm going to buy some marbles for my sister for the Founder's Day picnic. Marvin stocks them in his fertilizer shop for decorating gardens."

Bonnie fingered the beads on her necklace. "Marbles?"

"Yes. I don't know why I decided on marbles. I guess an angel must have whispered in my ear." He gazed at his hand, slowly unwrapping his fingers from around the coin. "By the by, how did you know I was holding a silver dollar?"

169

"I think the same angel whispered in my ear." Bonnie stared at Brogan's soiled palm. "I never noticed your ring."

Brogan closed his fist again and turned his knuckles toward her. "Haven't you seen a dragon's eye?"

"A dragon's eye? Why is it called that?"

"Folks say it can see into other worlds." Brogan blew on the gem and polished it on his shirt. "It's superstition, of course, but we all wear them, just the same. Sort of a village trademark, you might say."

"Everyone in town?"

Brogan nodded toward the seamstress shop. "Well, I noticed Miss Dorcas doesn't wear one, but seeing that she works with her hands all the time, it might get in the way. Oh, and I think the new librarian also, but he's a bit of a crackpot, if you know what I mean. Proper folks always wear their rings." He tipped his cap. "Nice talking with you. I work at the florist's. If you want more daisies or some nice carnations, come and see me." He smiled again and vaulted up the steps to the fertilizer store.

Billy took Bonnie's hand. "C'mon. If we try to find the bookstore first, maybe we can—"

"Wait." She pulled her hand away. "Wasn't that a rubellite in his ring?"

"Pretty sure it was." He glanced down at his own ring. "It looked just like mine used to."

"The dragon's eye," Bonnie said, twisting the ring on her finger. "What do you think it means?"

"I'm not sure." Billy took her hand again. "But we'd better get going before Brogan comes out again."

Bonnie pulled him back. "Why? Is your sense of danger working after all?"

170

Prickles crawled along Billy's neck. He wasn't sure he should say what he was thinking. "No, it's just that . . ." He gave a sigh of resignation. "Well, he was kind of flirting with you."

"Flirting?" A slight blush tinged Bonnie's cheeks. "He was just being friendly."

Billy mocked Brogan's accent. "I work at the florist's. If you want more daisies or some nice carnations, come and see me."

Bonnie bent the daisy's stem. "Okay, I get the point."

Billy waved it off. "You're a pretty girl. Who can blame him?"

Bonnie's cheeks turned pomegranate red. "Okay, Mr. Smooth Talker, now who's flirting?"

Billy's new suit suddenly felt hot and tight. "Uh . . . I . . . uh . . ."

Bonnie dropped the daisy and took his hand. "Never mind. Let's find the bookstore."

They hustled to the center of town, always peeking up at the cone-shaped top of a belfry that towered above the other buildings. A familiar gong chimed loud and clear, ten base tones that echoed through the streets. Each one reminded Billy of the gong in his dreams and the weird sensation of time slipping backwards. Was the sound a warning? Could it be tolling for a reason beyond the telling of time? He shuddered. The eerie vibrations seemed to portend something dark and sinister.

Arriving at the town square, they crossed the street to a traffic island that acted as the focal point of the road network. Scattering pigeons as they jumped up to the island, they stopped in the middle of a patch of green grass where a statue of a man on a rearing horse rested atop a brick pedestal. "Here's the plaque," Bonnie said, pointing at the cornerstone of the foundation. "Captain Timothy Autarkeia . . ." Her lips turned downward. "It's different. When I was here there was a poem underneath. Now it just

171

says, 'Founder of Dragons' Rest.' And there's no pitcher pump that watered Shiloh's plant."

A little pug dog sniffed at Billy's shoe. Billy jerked his foot away, and the dog barked at him, obviously indignant. He laughed and knelt, petting its wrinkled, round head. "Was this dog here with you and Shiloh?"

"Yes." Bonnie rested her hands on her hips, her head swiveling as she searched through the dozen or so people milling about. "Look for a woman with a parasol. She's its owner." The pug darted away, chasing the pigeons and scolding them with a blitz of scornful yips.

A few people, including Jasmine, had gathered at a building with iron bars in one window. The constable stood next to her, fiddling with a pocket watch dangling from his vest pocket. He nodded over and over while listening to Jasmine and glancing periodically at Billy and Bonnie.

Billy dipped his head, not wanting to provoke Jasmine. He hoped his new clothes would smooth over any suspicions, but he didn't want to take any chances. His gaze moved to the building next door. "There it is," he whispered.

He nodded at the constable and walked straight to the bookstore. A garland of fresh greenery in the front window surrounded a handmade sign that read, "Pages of the Ages." Billy pulled on the door, but it wouldn't budge. He peered through the window, but with the morning sun reflecting on the glass, he couldn't see anything inside except a light coming from a room far in the back. He searched the front for another sign. "See anything that tells when it opens?"

"No," Bonnie replied. "I guess everyone in town just knows."

"Eleven o'clock," another voice said.

They turned to see Constance walking toward them from the direction of Town Hall, her hair now tied up under a kerchief.

With her navy blue dress sweeping the planks and her lacy sleeves covering her wrists, she seemed the picture of a more innocent age. She stood no more than five feet tall, making her look like an early-blossoming twelve-year-old, yet her eyes revealed the maturity of a woman.

Wiping her hands on a long white apron, she stepped between Billy and Bonnie. "She'll be here in less than an hour." With her head tipped upward, she gazed into Billy's eyes. "Have you had breakfast? There's plenty left at the inn. I saw you over here while I was washing the dishes, and I thought you might like a bite to eat."

Billy rubbed his stomach. "Sounds good to me."

Bonnie reached around Constance and touched Billy's elbow. "What about the theatre?"

Constance widened her eyes and stepped out of the way. "Oh, don't let me keep you from anything. I wouldn't dream of it." She waved her finger between them. "So are you two . . . related?"

Bonnie closed the distance between them and took Billy's hand. "I guess you could say we're covenanted," she said, smiling sweetly.

Billy felt Bonnie's fingers tightening. "Yeah," he said. "It's sort of like a prearranged deal."

Constance pressed a finger to her chin and nodded. "I see. It's a shame your parents won't let you decide on your own."

Bonnie's lips thinned out, and the corners turned downward.

Billy cocked his head. Obviously, Bonnie didn't trust Constance. But why? Did the remark about her parents upset her? Maybe it would be a good idea to change the subject. "Well, we don't want to starve," he said, "but we have to make it quick."

Constance took Billy's hand and began leading him away. Billy glanced back at Bonnie. Her frown deepened as she followed.

After passing Town Hall, a post office, and a linen store, they entered the double doors of an old inn. When they had crossed the threshold, Constance peered down the sidewalk and closed the doors quietly.

"Something wrong?" Billy asked.

Constance kept her voice low. "I thought I heard Jasmine. She's been gossiping about you two from one end of town to the other." She curled her finger. "Let's go to the dining room, and we can talk. All my guests have already eaten."

Constance seated them at a small, round table. A gray tablecloth draped the top, blue napkins enfolded silverware at four place settings, and a white pillar candle decorated the center, a tall flame biting its wick. "Eggs and toast okay?" she asked.

"Sure," Billy replied. Bonnie just nodded, a slight crease just barely noticeable in her brow. Constance disappeared through a swinging door.

Bonnie lowered her head and whispered. "There's something strange about that woman."

Billy unrolled his silverware. "Well, she's kind of short, but—"

"That's not it. She's . . ."—Bonnie wiggled her fingers—"creepy."

Billy laid his napkin on his lap. "I wouldn't call her creepy. Maybe friendlier than most." He balanced his knife on his finger. "No one else offered to feed us."

"Friendly is right. She's hunting for a man, and she's got a bulls-eye painted right on you."

"What makes you think that?"

"Don't you remember? She said she saw us while she was washing dishes." Bonnie rolled her eyes. "Billy, the kitchen is at the back of the building. She had to be looking for you."

Constance pushed the door open with her foot, carrying three plates in her arms, each one heaped with scrambled eggs and wedges of toast. "I have not had time to eat, so I'll join you." After setting the plates on the table, she scooted away again, her voice ringing gaily. "I'll be right back with coffee and tea."

As soon as she left, Bonnie switched her plate with Constance's.

"Wow!" Billy said, dropping his knife. "You don't think she'd poison you to get me, do you?"

Bonnie set the plates in the exact positions Constance had left them. "I'm not taking any chances. Besides, there's something else weird going on. Do you think they ate eggs back at whatever time period this is supposed to be?"

"Probably." Billy poked the eggs with his fork. "They had hens, didn't they?"

Constance reappeared with two steaming pots and a stack of three china cups. As she set them on the table, she kept her eyes trained on Billy. "Coffee or tea?"

"Tea, please."

She turned to Bonnie. "And you?"

Bonnie turned her cup over. "None for me, thank you."

Constance squinted at her for a second, then poured tea in her cup and Billy's. When she sat down she began talking immediately, keeping her voice low. "Jasmine is the minister of the church and the mayor of Dragons' Rest. She watches over the spiritual lives of the citizens and their public behavior. She also supervises the constable and acts as judge in all criminal cases."

Billy scooped his fork under the eggs but waited to see if Constance would eat hers. "Isn't that a lot of power for one person?"

"Too much, if you ask me." Constance flapped her napkin and laid it on her lap. "She speaks from a fiery pulpit, though, and her prophecies have always come true, so the people trust her . . . or fear her." Constance took a bite of toast, then sipped some tea.

"I take it you don't trust her." Billy took a bite from his own toast. He noticed Bonnie hadn't touched her food at all.

"No, but I do fear her"—Constance pointed at Billy—"and so should you. She's telling people your white rings prove you're the fulfillment of a calamitous prophecy. She would have your head in a noose if she could do it discreetly. That's the penalty her prophecy proscribed, but she would want to first prove your guilt in order to save face with the people."

"How could she prove guilt?" Billy asked. "We haven't done anything wrong."

"She'll watch you, or have others try to catch you doing something that proves what she is already calling you." She paused, apparently waiting for the obvious question.

Billy obliged. "What's she calling us?"

Constance reached for the base of the candle and turned it slowly. "Oracles of fire. She's been prophesying against them for as long as I can remember. She says the oracles will tell about the destruction of our world and of new life in other worlds." The flame reflected in her eyes, and an aroma of wildflowers tinged the air. "Actually, it sounds pretty good to me," she continued, "I get an odd sensation when I walk through town, when I serve customers, when I sweep the floor. Haven't I done all this before? Isn't today just like yesterday, and the day before?" Her eyes misted, and she sighed. "It's a feeling . . . like I don't belong here. I feel a coldness, even on warm days . . . loneliness, even when I'm surrounded by people. It's almost as if I'm . . ." She glanced upward as if searching for a word.

"Far away from home?" Bonnie asked, a sympathetic curve in her brow.

Constance smiled as she continued rotating the candle, her eyes still fixed on the flame. "Yes. . . . Yes, I think that might be it."

Billy was glad to see Bonnie soften toward Constance. He knew Bonnie well enough to listen to her advice about anything she doubted, and he really wanted to trust Constance. With Jasmine whispering murder in the streets, they could use all the help they could get.

"Do you ever go to the theatre?" Bonnie asked.

"I did for a while." She sighed again, this time staring right at Billy, her fingertips inching onto his. "But a promise left unfulfilled for years is like a flower without water. It eventually withers and dies."

An odd warmth flowed into Billy's ears, sending a hot flash across his cheeks and into his eyes, as if her voice carried more than sound waves through the air. The candle's scented smoke stung his eyes, making him blink sleepily. He cleared his throat, hoping his face hadn't turned red. "I . . . uh . . . I think I understand."

Bonnie slipped her hand into Billy's and pulled it away from Constance, her tone sharp and urgent. "We'd better go." She slid her chair out and stood, holding Billy's hand at her side. "I apologize, but we have a lot to do and no idea how much time we have to do it all."

Constance dabbed her lips with her napkin. "But you have hardly touched your breakfast. I thought you were hungry."

Billy knew better than to doubt Bonnie's discernment . . . or her resolve. He rose quickly and stood next to her. "I really appreciate the food, but she's right. We don't have time to hang around."

Constance lowered her head and closed her eyes. "If that is your wish." She stood, glancing first through the passage to the

177

front room, then back at Billy, a flush of pink rising in her cheeks. "I will visit the theatre today, but I do not know if I will stay long. We are having our Founder's Day picnic at the town square at one o'clock. Everyone is expected to participate, but whatever you do, stay far away. Jasmine will surely look for an opportunity to condemn you there."

Billy flashed a thumbs-up sign. "Stay away from the picnic at one. Got it."

He headed for the door, stopping to open it for Bonnie. Constance lingered at the dining room entrance, a teacup cradled in her hand, her sad eyes watching them as they crossed the threshold.

Bonnie halted on the planks outside and waited for him to close the door. "I'm sorry, Billy, but I had to get out of there." She hugged herself and shivered. "Her voice was like icicles under my skin."

Billy pulled the front of his vest and flapped it against his chest. "That's too weird. I felt the opposite, like I was in a sauna." He looked back through the window. Constance was nowhere in sight. "I got the impression that you were starting to feel better about her, like maybe you trusted her."

"Well, I guess I do feel sorry for her, but . . ." An elderly woman hobbled by, leaning on a cane each time her right foot touched the planks. Bonnie waited for her to pass, then shook her head. "I'd better not say any more."

Keeping his eyes open for Jasmine and the constable, Billy stepped out onto the street and checked the clock. "That's strange. It's ten-thirty. I didn't think we were in there that long, did you?"

Bonnie shivered again. "Sitting across from Miss Antarctica made it feel like an hour to me."

"Maybe hours and minutes aren't the same here. Or maybe . . ." Billy raised his arm and sniffed his sleeve. The candle scent lingered in the material. "Maybe something in the air messes up our perceptions of time somehow."

Bonnie took in a whiff of her dress. "A drug of some kind? Was the candle like a scentser?"

Billy pulled on his cuffs, straightening his sleeves. "It could be, but I had a dream last night that time went in reverse, and the day started over again. So maybe it's just something about this town, like time bends funny here."

"Could be. But I'm not ready to trust Constance, no matter how pitiful her story is."

"Fair enough." Billy scanned the walkway, watching two women and a man window-shopping. Still no constable in sight. "We won't trust anyone until they prove themselves."

"Look!" Bonnie said, pointing. "There's a light in the bookstore."

179

"Let's check it out. My father always told me to find the answers in books, and we're already hip deep in questions."

11

MERLIN APPEARS

Bonnie peeked through the bookstore window. "There's a lantern on the counter. Someone must be inside."

Billy tried the handle. "Unlocked. I guess it's okay to go in."

Bonnie backed away. "I remember this place now. When I was here with Shiloh, an old lady disappeared when she went in the door." Bonnie flared her hands. "Poof! She was gone. Scared me half to death. But then Shiloh told me they did that all the time."

Billy eyed the doorframe. "Looks safe to me." He entered first, grimacing. When no energy field zapped him, he breathed a sigh of relief, took another step into the store, and motioned for Bonnie to follow.

Stained glass in a side picture window cast a dazzling hodge-podge of flickering colors all around the little shop. Books filled shelves that lined three walls, each book spine wearing a different shade of the spectral splash. An aroma of pine rose from the spotless wooden floor.

Billy tiptoed toward one of the shelves. Most of the books seemed to be novels—some romance, some action and adventure, and a few mysteries. He found a book on Italian art and flipped open the cover. A handwritten note said, "On consignment from Mr. Collins."

Bonnie pulled a cookbook from a low shelf and thumbed through it. "What are we looking for?"

"I just thought we'd do a bit of detective work while we're waiting for the owner. I'm looking for a history book or maybe a biography, something to explain what this town is all about."

While Bonnie searched one side of the room, Billy searched the other, moving from shelf to shelf and sliding out book after book. The process seemed to take forever, but with the mystery of Dragons' Rest deepening, he was determined to get some kind of clue that might help them find Merlin's wife.

From a high shelf along the far wall, he removed a small, leather bound book. He traced the imprint on the cover with his fingers. Aha! Here's something. He carried it to Bonnie. "Take a look at this."

The shadow of her head dimmed the cover as she whispered the title. *"The Prophecies of Jasmine, the Seer."*

Billy opened it to the first page, and they read together silently.

What is past, is past, and only ghosts lurk in its shadows. Memories are but dreams, and they fade with the rising sun. Only a fool worries about the troubles of days gone by, and no wise man puts his faith in yesterday's triumphs. For both troubles and triumphs are wilted roses, and neither thorns nor fragrance will remain at the season's end.

So let the shadows of the past fly away, for they are hopeless thoughts, dreams of addled minds, invisible playmates of street urchins. We are no longer children, nor are we foolish enough to entertain the oracles of fire.

A loud clap sounded from the rear of the store. Billy closed the book and stooped low, pulling Bonnie down with him. The squeak of door hinges ushered in an angry, female voice.

"If you know what's good for you, you'll do just what I say. Report every word they speak to you, or I'll run you out of town with the rest of the underborns."

"Jasmine," another female voice answered, "you should know by now that your fiery rhetoric is neither intimidating to my senses nor welcome in my establishment."

"Mark my words," Jasmine snapped back, "your rebellious tongue will someday dig your grave."

The bell in the tower gonged, interrupting the quarrel. Billy laid the prophecy book on the shelf and tapped Bonnie's shoulder. "Let's get out of here." Staying stooped, they sneaked to the entrance. Billy threw the door open and ran outside, checking to make sure Bonnie was following. With her long dress clutched in one hand, she bolted through the doorway and sprinted behind him.

They flew down the street, first backtracking toward Dorcas's shop. Slowing to a furtive march as the eleventh and final gong sounded, they followed the directions to the theatre. After turning onto the side street, they came upon about ten people waiting in line for something, each one dressed in black. As Billy hesitated, a matronly lady with a gray bonnet joined the line, then a short, swarthy man wearing chaps and a shirt ripped on one shoulder.

"Think this is it?" Billy asked.

"It has to be."

They walked past the waiting line and stepped up to the box office window. A sign on an adjacent wall read, "The Waiting

Room. Doors open at noon; close at three." Billy cupped his hands on either side of his eyes and peeked in through the cashier's cage. Not a soul lurked inside the theatre lobby. Several empty chairs lined the walls near a set of double doors, probably the inner entrance to the seating area. On the wall, posters with yellowed paper and marred lettering advertised a play called "Witnesses" and another entitled "Of Things Unseen." Next to a long table that looked like a food service counter, a pendulum clock on the wall read eleven thirteen.

Billy backed away from the window, then turned to Bonnie and muttered to himself. "Obviously there must be a caretaker. Someone has to wind the clock." He studied the growing line of people, trying to read their expressions. Their somber faces revealed only grim resignation, neither sad nor mournful—faraway gazes, flat-lined lips, and pale complexions. No one said a word.

Billy walked to the front of the line where the old lady they had seen at the inn leaned on a knobby cane, her shoulders bent. A wrinkled face and scant wisps of gray hair told of many years of strife, and her gleaming eyes begged for someone to ask her to share from her library of ready stories.

Billy took a few steps closer and nodded politely. "I hear you're waiting for a king."

She pushed on her cane, straightening her body slightly, her voice quavering with her unsteady legs. "Oh, no, young man. Not *a* king . . . *the* king. I was there myself when the prophet announced his coming, and I intend to be there again when the king arrives to take us to a new country." With a flick of her head, she gestured behind her. "We all feel the same way, even though most of the town thinks we're crazy, especially the mayor."

"What's your name?" Bonnie asked.

"Martha Stone." She looked at Bonnie long and hard. "Who's asking?"

"Bonnie Silver." She extended her hand, but Martha just stared at it. Bonnie pulled her hand back and cleared her throat. "I'm pleased to meet you."

Billy leaned toward the door. "Is anyone allowed to go in there now?"

Martha steadied herself and pointed at the door with her cane. "According to the prophecy, none but the king can open it before the hour. I tried it a few times years ago, but it won't budge until noon."

Billy took two steps, grasped the handle, and pulled. The door swung open easily. Trying to ignore the sound of gasps behind him, he strode inside, snagged a chair in each arm, then hustled back. "Here," he said, setting one of the chairs next to Martha. "Have a seat." With Bonnie's help, he retrieved enough chairs from the lobby for every woman in line. Each lady, whether young or old, patted his hand or gazed at him with adoring eyes. He bounded to the front of the line again and spread his arms to quiet the murmuring crowd. "Everyone listen! I'm going inside, but I think all of you should wait until noon to come in."

Billy backed toward the open door, gesturing for Bonnie to follow. A man stepped out of line and rushed forward, but Martha whacked him on the knees with her cane. "You heard him, Remus! Not until noon!"

Billy ducked inside with Bonnie and closed the door behind him, his heart racing. "They think I'm the king."

"Why shouldn't they?" Bonnie said, laughing. "You opened the door, didn't you?"

"Yeah, but I don't know how to take them to a new country. I don't even know where I am now."

"There's not much time till noon. Let's get going." Bonnie jogged to the inner doors and pushed one open. "Hmmm. Pretty dark in there."

185

Billy joined her, trying to adjust his eyes to a dim red glow that barely illuminated the theatre. They shuffled down a carpeted slope, passing between long rows of empty theatre seats. Finding a short flight of stairs, they climbed up to the stage and faced the closed curtain. Pulses of scarlet light bled through its threadbare material.

Bonnie found where the curtain parted, bundled part of one panel in her arms, and drew it to the side. Billy did the same with the other panel while pulleys squeaked somewhere in the rafters. When he and Bonnie had opened a twenty-foot gap, he hurried back to center stage and surveyed the newly exposed scene.

A floor-to-ceiling glass partition walled off a forest landscape, three-dimensional, alive, and active, though saturated with a red hue, as if a cameraman were recording it through a color-coated lens. Trees and sky bounced up and down in time with the cameraman's gait as he seemed to be trying to keep up with a man who marched away into the background. The man in front wore a black trench coat and scabbard. White hair protruded from his cap. "Professor?" Billy whispered. Everything was so real, it seemed to be an extension of the stage, as though they could walk right into that scarlet world.

Billy inched toward the screen, putting out his hand to find where reality ended and the image began. His fingertips finally touched smooth glass. He sighed. He wasn't sure why, but finding the boundary filled him with sadness, as if he had run out to play in the fields but found instead a set of iron bars that blocked his way.

Bonnie tiptoed to his side, and they watched the scene, mesmerized, almost hypnotized by the undulating trees and sky. Suddenly, a shadow loomed over the entire screen, a human form slowly shrinking as if stalking them from behind. Billy instinctively reached for his sword, but it wasn't there. Before

186

he could think of another way to fight, a quiet, soothing voice drifted toward them from the screen. "Do not be frightened."

The stalking shadow shrank to human size, and a man stepped onto the stage, yet remained behind the glass partition somehow, as if he were part of the screen image and in the theatre at the same time. When he reached the center, he stopped, steady and calm, while the scene behind him continued to oscillate.

He spread out his hands. "Welcome, my friends. I have been waiting for you for a very long time."

Although he seemed to wear a red mask, the man's face was clear. Billy set both palms on the glass. "Professor?" He pointed at the man in the trench coat still walking in the living view port. "I thought that was you over there."

The man held out the fringes of a robe and laughed. "I don't think your professor ever wore anything like this, but looking through the gemstone's wall you probably can't tell that I'm wearing scarlet." He made a half turn and waved his arm at the forest scene. "Your first guess was correct. There is your professor, fulfilling his duty to guide your mother to an appointed task and protect her to the best of his ability. It is still night there, for time in two different dimensions rarely coincides. I have noticed that there are periods when the two are in sync, then one might streak ahead, fast forward, if you will, while the other seems to plod along in slow motion. In all my centuries of traveling across the dimensional boundaries, this phenomenon has been among the most interesting."

187

Billy's legs wobbled again, his voice barely finding any breath. "Merlin?"

Merlin nodded. "Yes, Billy. It is I." He bowed toward Bonnie. "Welcome, my tender blossom. You look lovely in that dress."

Bonnie curtsied, a smile bursting forth. "Thank you, kind sir."

Rising up again, Merlin's eyes sparkled. "You are most welcome, fair maiden." He clapped his hands together, his voice lively. "Now, we have much to do—"

Billy held up his hand. "Wait a minute! Aren't you going to explain why and how you're here and what this place is all about?"

A gentle smile spread across Merlin's face. "Ah, the young king still has so many questions. After all you have seen, do doubts still plague your mind?"

"Not doubts, really. I just want to get a handle on what's going on. I'm so confused, I feel like I'm walking in a nightmare."

"Fair enough, but since time is of the essence, I must be brief." Merlin raised a finger. "To answer your first question, when Excalibur transluminated me, I transformed into an existence that allowed me to travel across almost all spiritual dimensions—into the candlestone, through the circles of seven, and even to the outer courtyard of Paradise. If you'll remember, I even inhabited your professor for a time." He tapped on the inner wall of the glass screen. "This partition between us is the gem of the pendant, the Great Key that opens the passage between your world and Dragons' Rest, and it now rides on a chain around your mother's neck. Although I am able to stand inside the rubellite, the vestibule of the world you are in, I cannot penetrate the final barrier."

"Why not?" Billy asked.

"I am not a dragon," Merlin said, spreading out his arms. "Those in the village are the spirits of the dragons who never allowed the Nephilim to control their minds. I suppose you could call them the uncorrupted dragons."

"Uncorrupted?" Billy smirked. "There's at least one in here who seems plenty corrupted. She's been a pain ever since we got here."

188

"Is that so?" Merlin asked, a hint of concern in his voice. "What does she do?"

"Her name is Jasmine. She calls herself a prophetess and tells the townspeople not to think about the past. A couple of them have told us she'd like to kill us if she could. She's been saying we're something called 'Oracles of Fire' and deserve to die."

Merlin stroked his chin. "I see. Very interesting. I suppose she could be a self-corrupted dragon. Although the Nephilim never took residence in her body, perhaps she sought power from dark sources and uses it to control the others." He folded his hands at his waist. "I did not expect someone like her to exist in Dragons' Rest. I advise you to avoid her."

"Yeah," Billy said, adding a chuckle. "We guessed that. But why are the dragons here?"

"They are in there," Merlin replied, "because their souls have nowhere else to go. Dragons were designed to rule with mankind in the original paradise of earth, but when man fell, paradise collapsed. As you know, the dragons who were killed after they became humans were sent to the seventh circle of Hades. They were dry bones in need of a spiritual awakening that you provided as a representative of the human messiah. The dragons you see in this village were killed as dragons, so they went to this holding place not meant for humans. They had no messiah to rescue them . . . until now.

Billy pressed his thumb against his chest. "You mean me? How?"

Merlin pointed at the floor. "Convince them to come here, and you will all see together. They know that deliverance has long been prophesied. I'm sure many are already awaiting your coming."

Billy nodded toward the doorway. "Well, not that many, maybe a couple dozen at the most."

189

Merlin's lips turned downward, but they slowly recovered as he lowered his brow, a wave of determination steeling his face. "Then you must convince more to come. Earth depends on their numbers, and their deliverance depends on their faith in you, the chosen one." He raised a fist and rapped on the screen. "They cannot be saved unless they follow you to this stone, and even when they come, their faith will be tested. All who have enough faith to line up will believe when they see you pass through the stone, and only a chosen anthrozil, fully human and fully dragon, can lead them through the passage."

Bonnie laid her palm on the glass. "What will happen to the dragons when they go through?"

Merlin lowered his fist and flapped his arm against his robe. "Actually, I am not quite sure. These dragons have died, so they will likely not return to physical life, but"—he pointed at the glass barrier—"there are not only dragons in there. You must also find two souls who do not belong."

"Your wife?" Bonnie asked. "Billy read about her in *Fama Regis*."

"Yes. My wife still has her mind, but her human soul has died within her, making her like one of the deceased dragons. I searched through the circles to find her, especially the sixth circle, but I never saw her among the spirits there. Perhaps her image is unable to appear in the human realm because of the unusual nature of her captivity in Dragons' Rest." A glimmer of a smile brightened Merlin's face. "But if you can get her out, I can take her to a place where she will be restored."

"Don't worry," Bonnie said. "We'll do everything we can to find her."

Billy breathed a sad sigh. "Then I guess the second one must be Professor Hamilton's wife."

Merlin half closed one eye. "Is Dorcas in there?"

"Yes," Bonnie said, nodding. "She's a seamstress, just like she was in our world."

"Well, then, Morgan murdered another enemy's wife. I should have guessed. She is predictable, if nothing else."

Billy drew a smudge line on the glass with his finger. "Then who's the other one who doesn't belong here?"

Merlin leaned close to the barrier. "Your eyes give you away, Billy. Yes, your father is likely in the village, though I cannot tell you where to look. He doesn't belong there, and he, above all, must be convinced to come. The fate of the world may rest on his shoulders."

Billy lifted his eyebrows. He didn't want to get too excited. Not yet. "So, if he doesn't belong here, then he's not dead?"

"No. Not at all. He is merely without a body. When you sent Excalibur's beam into the abyss, his spirit passed through the pendant's rubellite and entered Dragons' Rest. Since an evil spirit now controls his dragon body, I cannot say what will happen should you bring him out, but you must persuade him, for your coming marks the end of the dragon's redemption story. They will all make their choice, and there will no longer be any need for this place. It will be utterly destroyed." He paced to the edge of the barrier and back, then leaned close again. "For some reason, God doesn't tell me exactly how he will carry out his plans, but I do know that your decisions, Billy, will make all the difference. Mark these words well, for they are words of prophecy.

> The path to grace, a path of blood,
> Will cost the king his greatest gifts.
> Of life, of love, he must resign
> And give his all for souls adrift.

191

"Give his all?" Billy repeated. "What does that mean?"

Merlin paced again, faster this time, his head down and his arms lifted. "I don't know!" he said, his voice strained. "It could mean a lot of things." He stopped at the center and took a deep breath, closing his eyes as though fearing to gaze into Billy's. Finally, he looked up again, tears flowing and his voice barely a whisper. "Just be ready for anything, even if it means following in your savior's footsteps. No matter what happens, even if you should die, you will never be forsaken."

The sound of shuffling feet filled the theatre. Martha hobbled to the very front row, her eyes sparkling in the glow of the red screen. "Look!" she cried. "The king has parted the curtains!" Cheers erupted as the people hurried to their seats.

Merlin ducked low and whispered. "These people have awaited your coming for many years, so they won't mind when you tell them you will return with as many of their fellow villagers as you can. But mark this well. A portal to and from this realm requires an extraordinary amount of spiritual energy to maintain, even for just three hours. Although the power to open the portal originates in heaven, it comes in response to the prayers of the faithful ones who wait here every day as they adhere to the schedule God has ordained. So, at three o'clock the screen's passageway will close, and you must return by then and lead them to salvation. May God give you the right words to say, both here and in the village." Merlin turned to the side and marched away, his shadow growing again, then fading.

Billy turned and faced the onlookers, slowly walking to the front of the stage with Bonnie at his side. Their bright and eager faces gazed up at him as if begging for a single word, like puppies hoping for table scraps. Bonnie slipped her hand into Billy's, squeezed it three times, then let go. The warmth of her touch sent a stream of courage through his body.

Billy cleared his throat. "You have come because of the prophecy a man made here many years ago, and you were wise to believe him. I assume you have told many others, right?"

Martha waved her cane. "Everyone I knew and some I didn't. I even made my own tracts and handed them out, but people just laughed at me."

"Same here," a man in the second row shouted. "My own wife thinks I'm crazy."

Constance stood near the back. "I tell all my customers at the inn about the coming king, but most of them call me a fool." A rumble of agreement passed through the audience.

Billy waved both hands, his palms down. "But you still want them to come, right?"

Silence fell upon the theatre. Billy glanced around at each person, a glow of red pulsing on every emotion-torn face. After a few seconds, a middle-aged woman stood up in the third row, her hands wringing. "I want them to come." Her head turned from side to side. "We all have loved ones who just won't listen." Reaching into a dress pocket, she withdrew a handkerchief and wiped her eyes. "My own son is kind and thoughtful, but he refuses to believe the prophet." She returned her hand to the pocket, this time retrieving a carnation. "He brings me flowers, but he won't give me what I long for more than anything else, hope that he'll escape this place with me."

Bonnie clutched Billy's wrist. He knew what her signal meant.

"Is his name Brogan?" Billy asked.

The lady's eyes lit up like two crimson sparklers. "Yes! How did you know?"

"I've met him. I can't promise anything, but I'll try to find him again and tell him to come."

Shouts from the audience peppered Billy with names, obviously loved ones the desperate people wanted him to find. He

193

waved his hands again to settle them down. "I'll bring everyone I can, but I'd better get going. There isn't much time." He turned and looked at the screen. The walking motion in the other world had stopped, and the professor had turned around. Mr. Foley and Sir Patrick stood next to him. The three seemed to be discussing something important, each one carrying stern expressions. "Just watch the screen until I get back," Billy continued, "and tell me if anything really interesting happens."

Billy jumped down the stairs, Bonnie following close behind. They ran up the slope toward the theatre exit and dashed out the door and onto the street. Billy stopped and surveyed the area, waiting for his eyes to adjust to the sunlight. "Okay. First back to the bookstore. Maybe Jasmine will be gone and we can talk to the clerk."

"True," Bonnie said, "but with time passing the way it is, it won't be long till one o'clock. She'll probably be close by."

With a slight nod of his head, he gestured at the people streaming toward the center of town. "Think we can play follow the leader and blend in?"

Bonnie checked her ring to make sure the gem was on the palm side. "You lead," she said, curling her fingers into a fist. "I'll follow."

The airplane hovered over a field next to the lake's shore, its propeller quiet. Samyaza barked, "We're low enough. Jump out."

Ashley unbuckled her seatbelt, hustled down the aisle, still clutching her stomach, and stopped at the cargo door. She looked down at a field of wet grass sparkling in the moonlight. A cool breeze wafted in and chilled her body, making her shiver.

With the lake on one side and tall trees on the other, the long, narrow meadow acted as a border to the forested state park, probably a fun playground under normal circumstances. Tonight, however, it would be a field of nightmares where she would have to meet an enraged demon face-to-face. She swallowed, tasting again the caustic bile that so recently passed through her throat, then leaped from the plane.

Trained as a long jumper in school, she knew how to land, bending her knees when she struck the ground and thrusting forward again to ride out her momentum. She rolled to her back, the airplane and demon now in full view. As big as an elephant, yet as striking as a sculpture of a Greek god, Samyaza gripped *Merlin II* under its wing structure, then, with his bare feet set like a boy throwing a toy glider, he slung the plane into a stand of trees and sent a stream of dark red flames behind it. The Cessna ripped apart, and the trailing flames ignited the remaining fuel, creating a fireball that engulfed nose, wings, and tail almost instantly.

Ashley sat up and gulped. Walter had barely escaped that explosion, but was his watery plunge any better? She jumped to her feet, turned a half circle, and gazed at the lake's waves lapping at the shoreline. Could he have survived the impact after falling from such a height? Even if he had, could he survive the frigid water?

Samyaza stomped toward her, his pointed teeth bared. "Enough playing nice." Ashley grabbed a thin branch, but how could such a feeble weapon ward off a monster? With a sweep of his arm, he scooped Ashley up and carried her toward the forest as if she were a teddy bear, his grip squeezing her breath away. She chattered her teeth, still encoding their location, and broke off a piece of the branch.

"It's not that cold," Samyaza growled.

Ashley dropped the piece and gasped through his crushing hold. "It *is* cold, . . . and you're scaring me . . . half to death!" She broke off another thumb-length fragment and dropped it.

He tightened his grip even more, compressing her stomach and making her feel like her liver was about to explode and spew into her esophagus. She heaved for each breath, her lungs catching teaspoonfuls of oxygen. Forget chattering Morse code! She just had to survive!

Cold rushed through Walter's crate. "Gahhh! I'm falling!" His limbs stiffened. His lungs grabbed for air and held it tight. Then—

Splash!

The impact whipped his head against an inner wall. Jets of ice-cold water sprayed his face and soaked his clothes, keeping him from blacking out. Thrusting upward with both arms, he threw the lid off and found himself bobbing on the surface of an enormous lake, bright moonlight shimmering on choppy waves as far as he could see. A brisk wind raced across the wide expanse and pummeled him unhindered, biting through his wet jacket and shirt like a thousand dagger-sharp icicles.

His joints locked in the frigid water. The wooden crate, although not even close to sea-worthy, kept him afloat, but would he be able to swim if it started to sink? Maybe he could paddle to shore with his hands before it got waterlogged. He could see lights, probably houses at the edge of the water, but he had no way to judge how far away they were. Could he possibly get there before he turned into a human popsicle?

He picked a single light on the shore and surged toward it, paddling in the direction the wind was blowing. He felt like a mouse in a flooded coracle as he bobbed in an endless expanse of white-capped water. Every stroke brought a stab of pain. Every wave splashed ice water into his hair. Every gust of wind snatched breath out of his lungs, breath he sorely needed as he slogged across the lake.

A huge fireball erupted to his right. He gasped. "Ashley!" The towering column of flames marked his new course, a two o'clock heading. He had to fight the wind somewhat, but the explosion sent a shot of adrenaline into his heart and limbs. He thrust his arms through the water, new energy giving him new hope. But how long would it last?

197

JARED BANNISTER

With more people filling the town square, Billy felt safe weaving through them as he and Bonnie headed for the bookstore. Still, he eased the door open, entering slowly and scanning the room for Jasmine. When he stepped to the side to give Bonnie room to enter, a plank groaned under his weight.

An elderly woman glanced up from the sales counter, smiling as she peered over her spectacles. "May I help you?" she asked.

Billy ambled to the counter, trying not to appear too anxious. "Yes. I'm looking for someone—a man, over six feet tall, slender and kind of muscular. Reddish-brown hair."

"You've described my librarian to a tee. Are you a friend?"

"Uh . . . a relative."

"I see. Reginald didn't tell me about relatives coming to visit, but you are certainly welcome." She gestured toward a set of swinging double doors. Billy took note of the fingers on the one hand he could see, her right hand. No ring.

"He is working on a research project," she continued, "but you may interrupt him."

At the sound of "Reginald," Billy's heart sank. He was hoping for "Jared," but somehow the name seemed familiar, as if Reginald might be a relative from long ago, maybe a great uncle he had never met but had seen listed in a family tree.

"Bonnie," Billy whispered as they approached the door. "She doesn't have a ring. Are you thinking what I'm thinking?"

"Merlin's wife?" Bonnie asked.

"Books are like scrolls. Why not?"

"Let's see what we can find out."

With Billy following several feet behind, Bonnie strode to the counter and extended her hand. "My name is Bonnie. May I ask yours?"

The clerk tilted her head and stared. "Yes, young lady," she said, slowly putting her hand in Bonnie's. "My name is Sarah."

Bonnie shook her hand firmly, her smile growing from ear to ear. "I'm pleased to meet you." She picked up a book from a stack on the counter—Jasmine's prophecies. Apparently it was required reading among the townspeople, and an ample supply lay within easy reach. "How long have you been selling books here?"

"Oh, as long as I can remember, but I rarely think about such things." She held her hand out for the book. A hint of sarcasm spiced her tone. "As Jasmine says, dwelling on the past is an unprofitable venture."

"I see." Bonnie passed the book to her. "Are you married?"

Sarah took off her spectacles and laid them on the counter. "Young lady, I adore your smile." She touched the tip of Bonnie's nose. "But I think your nose is getting rather long, if you understand my meaning."

Bonnie rubbed her nose, then blushed. "I'm so sorry. I hope I didn't offend you."

200

"Apology accepted. Since you are obviously not accustomed to our practices here, I have three pieces of advice for you. One, gentlemen shake hands. Ladies curtsy. Two"—she pointed at Bonnie's finger—"keep the gem in that ring hidden. Turning it is not enough. Three, refrain from asking anyone about the past. Four, stay away from Jasmine, the mayor."

Bonnie held up three fingers. "Uh, you said three pieces of advice. That was four."

"Here is a fifth," Sarah replied, holding up her hand, her fingers spread. "Be careful about correcting an old woman. We rarely enjoy being reminded of approaching senility."

"I see." Bonnie curtsied. "And I apologize again."

Sarah's smile lit up her face, making her look like a delighted grandmother. "No need, dear girl. I apologize for being abrupt with you about my marital status."

Bonnie folded her hands over her waist. "I was only asking because we're trying to find the wife of a man named Merlin."

Sarah's eyebrows lifted. "Merlin, you say?"

Bonnie nodded rapidly. "Have you ever heard of him?"

"The name is familiar . . . very familiar." Sarah rolled her eyes upward and tapped her finger on her chin. "Perhaps I knew him at one time, but I cannot remember him now."

Bonnie twisted her ring nervously. "Uh . . . may I ask why you don't wear a ring?"

"You may ask"—Sarah rubbed her naked finger, her hands trembling slightly—"but I have no answer to mysteries I cannot understand. To hear Jasmine's interpretation, I am an underborn, that is, a member of a lower class, so I am not privileged enough to receive a ring."

Billy took two steps closer. He didn't want to interrupt Bonnie—she was doing a great job—but the conversation was becoming so interesting, he didn't want to lose a single word.

"How many others are there like you?" Bonnie asked.

"I know only of Dorcas, the seamstress, but Jasmine tells of dangerous foreigners who have no dragon's eye, and they are driven out whenever they set foot in our town. She allows Dorcas and me to stay, because we are harmless old women."

Bonnie touched the book on top of the stack. "How does Jasmine keep everyone from asking about the past? Don't you wonder where you came from or how long you've been here?"

Sarah rifled through the pages of the book in her hand. "Not everyone here is spellbound by her prophecies." She slapped it closed and set it down. "We are simply accustomed to thinking only in the present, so the past does not occur to us."

"What about the people who go to the theatre? Are they influenced by Jasmine?"

"By her prophecies? No. By her power to punish? Yes. But she allows them to go. She sees it as simple foolishness that amounts to nothing. The people still seem to get their work done."

Bonnie picked up a piece of paper from another stack and scanned it. "Do you ever go?"

"I tried twice." Sarah shook her head sadly. "But it seems that underborns are not allowed."

Bonnie glanced up from reading the page. "Did a strange wall keep you from going through the door?"

"Yes," Sarah replied, her eyes narrowing. "How did you know?"

Billy stepped up to the counter. "The same thing happened to Dorcas." He pushed his hand into his pocket, wishing he could give her the ring, but he knew he had to wait for the sign he'd been given. "We'll go back and see Reginald now, if it's all right."

"Of course," Sarah replied. "But be warned. Although Reginald is harmless, he is a bit eccentric."

Billy and Bonnie returned to the area near the back of the store. "What do you think now?" Bonnie asked. "Is she Merlin's wife?"

"Makes sense to me. When you mentioned his name, it seemed to ring a bell." Billy pushed one of the doors and peeked into a much larger room. Row after row of standalone bookshelves, rising from the floor and reaching to the ceiling, blocked much of his view. Old dusty books sagged the rows, as if threatening to collapse the shelves at any second.

Swinging the door farther, he walked in, feeling like he should tiptoe in the hallowed sanctuary of ancient codicils, as though the books themselves might shush him if he even swallowed too loudly. Bonnie followed, her anxious breathing sounding like the wheezing of an old woman. They padded through a corridor between the rows, Bonnie whispering the labels on each shelf as they passed. "Alchemy. Allegories. Art. Astrology. Biographies. We could get a lot of information here."

The room opened up into a bleak studio, the only light coming from a series of transoms near the ceiling. Two long wooden tables covered much of the dusty floor, dozens and dozens of books spread across them, some open, some piled high in precarious stacks. A musty odor pinched Billy's nose as he drew closer.

A man stood at the side of one table, his head down and his hands flipping page after page of a book. He jotted notes on a piece of paper, grabbed another book off the top of the nearest stack, then slapped it open on the table, starting the process over again.

The man looked familiar—reddish hair, strong hands, confident motions, but his face remained hidden, buried in his work.

Billy cleared his throat. "Reginald?"

203

The man looked up, his tawny face haggard, his eyes bright and inquisitive. "Yes?"

Billy squinted, not daring to believe what he saw. That face! Those eyes! His stomach flipped. He could barely breathe. "Dad?"

The man's lips parted, mouthing Billy's greeting, but his brow lowered as if he was unable to grasp the meaning. Picking up a book and clutching it in both hands, his eyes darted back and forth. He appeared to be wrestling with a memory, something that begged to break through to the surface, but he just muttered quietly with a British accent. "Parenting books are in the 'Self-help' section behind me, four rows in, turn right." He lowered his head again, returning to his frenetic study.

Billy gulped, trying to push down a familiar lump in his throat. This man looked so much like his father he wanted to sprint forward, vault the table, and give him the hug to end all hugs, all the embraces he had missed over these many months of torture. But he couldn't. This was Reginald, a man who seemed not to recognize him, or at least pretended not to, and although his voice carried the same low tones, Dad's accent had never sounded British at all.

Billy grabbed Bonnie's hand, glad to hold onto someone who knew who he was. He whispered, "Let's get closer and ask some questions." He strolled to the table and picked up a book, pretending to be interested in the title. "What are you studying?"

Reginald pointed at the book, then at the table, barely looking up at all. "Put that down, please. I will need it in a moment."

Billy dropped it back in place. "Sorry."

Reginald placed both palms on the table and sighed. "I apologize. It is my job to help the library's patrons. Please forgive me . . . what did you say your name was?"

"I didn't. It's Billy." He cocked his head toward Bonnie. "This is my friend, Bonnie."

"Billy. . . . Billy. I know that name from somewhere. Have you been in here before?" He tilted his head upward, tapping his finger on his jaw. "Oh, I am sure you have. You checked out books on . . . Oh, what was it?" He snapped his fingers. "Oh, yes! Art. Pencil sketches, to be precise, of various beasts. Didn't you specifically search for examples of dragon art?"

Adrenalin surged through Billy's body. Reginald had to be his father! Who else could know about his interest in art and dragons? At the same time, however, he felt as though a vacuum cleaner had sucked out his insides, heart, breath, and soul. What good was it if his dad didn't know who he was? This was the worst torture of all. This man was like a visible picture of Billy's memories, a father he loved but who could give no love in return. Watching him was like hugging a portrait, the joy of a familiar face, but aching hollowness when no arms hugged him back. Still, "Reginald's" latent memories had to mean a spark of hope existed somewhere in his mind. All Billy had to do was figure out how to fan it into a flame.

"I see from your reticence that you have forgotten," Reginald continued, "but I distinctly remember you from somewhere, definitely something to do with art and dragons."

"Oh, sorry. I got lost in thought. But you were right. I'm an artist, and I'm interested in dragons." Billy pointed at Reginald's pencil lying atop his notes page. "May I show you?"

"Yes. Please do."

Billy drew a quick sketch of a dragon and slid it in front of Reginald, desperately hoping to prod his memory. "What do you know about them?"

"Mythical creatures," Reginald replied, glancing at the drawing. He nodded toward the shelves on his left. "Mythology is between Music and Names. But if you want my opinion, they're not worth the time or effort to study."

Billy laid his hand on a book, remembering not to pick it up this time. "Whatever you're studying sure seems important."

"It seems that it's only important to me." Reginald opened a binder filled with newspaper pages. "But I'll tell you about it. I am already considered the village idiot, so what difference does it make if you think me mad as well?"

Billy grabbed Reginald's forearm, hoping his touch might have some effect. Reginald tried to pull away at first, but when Billy wouldn't let go, Reginald's arm relaxed. "Please trust me," Billy said softly. "I won't think you're mad."

Bonnie sidled up to Reginald and peered at the newspaper pasted to the facing page of the book. "Is this your town's news-paper? *The Daily Herald?*"

"It is a simple, one-page newspaper for the locals." He tapped on the page with his finger. "Notice the date?"

Billy scanned the paper, drumming the pencil on the table. "Uh, no. I don't see a date anywhere."

"Exactly." He turned the page. "Now, do you see any simi-larities between the two issues?"

Billy took the page and flipped back and forth between the two. "Yes. They're identical as far as I can tell."

"Exactly, again." He pointed at the headline. "For example, read this story on the Founder's Day picnic."

"I saw this on Sarah's counter," Bonnie said. She put her fin-ger on the article and moved it slowly down the page. "Looks like everyone's getting ready for the big event at one o'clock this afternoon, so they're supposed to get their shopping done early today." She ran her finger along the last line. "There will be food, fun, and friendship, so come on out and celebrate with your neighbors."

Reginald fanned through the pages in the binder. "I collect them and put them in this book, and every single issue is the same. Every day the entire village attends a community picnic, and they never seem to realize that they did it the day before. And as I watch the people in this community, and myself, for that matter, I get the distinct impression that the picnic isn't the only repetitive event. Everyone goes through the same routine every day. And it seems that I am the only person who is aware of the repetition."

"Have you shown anyone your collection of papers?" Billy asked.

"I have shown the mayor and the constable."

"What did they say?"

Reginald let out a "humph," then closed the book with a thud. "They accused me of collecting a stack of copies of today's paper and concocting an insane story in order to get attention."

The door between the library and the bookstore squeaked. Billy lowered his voice. "But they can't be serious. Why would they accuse you of lying?"

Reginald didn't bother to lower his own voice. "They are serious, and as sincere as a mother's love. They have no idea they are racing on a hamster's wheel. And as each day goes by, I feel as though I am beginning to repeat my own actions. I seem to forget what I did the day before, so I often do it again, remembering that I did something yesterday only after I have repeated it today. Therefore, I am convinced that I am slowly becoming one of them, and I will fall into a repetitive pattern day after day, blindly stupid to the fact that I am treading the same ground I trod the day before."

Reginald waved his hand across his books. "Even as I do my research on the origins of this town, I get vague notions that I have read the same books, analyzed the same thoughts, and come to the same conclusions, only to forget them by the time I awake in the morning." He drew back his arm and slung the binder across the room, scattering the newspaper clippings through the air. "Ha! I won't be reading you again anytime soon!"

Breathing heavily, he ran his fingers through his hair. "I . . . I apologize. As you can see, this could easily drive a man mad. I think I would be better off as one of the robots, unaware of my condition, happily repeating my daily routine." He suddenly gave Billy a strange look, his brow lowering. "But if you are one of them, you must have come in here yesterday, which means that I have forgotten your visit." He picked up another book and slammed it on the table. "There is no hope! I am doomed to a fate worse than hell!"

Billy couldn't help himself any longer. He wrapped both arms around Reginald and hugged him with all his might. "No!" he cried. "You're not doomed! There's a way out of here."

208

Bonnie joined in the embrace from Reginald's other side. "God will clear your mind. I know he will."

Billy felt Reginald's heart race, thumping against his ear like a ravenous woodpecker. A deep voice oozed from Reginald's lips, barely a whisper. "God? . . . Did you say . . . 'God'?"

"Yes," Bonnie replied softly.

He pushed Billy gently away and pulled free from Bonnie as he turned to face her. He placed his hands on her shoulders, his eyes filling with tears. "That word haunts my nightmares, but I can't remember what it means. I try to remember, and it seems for a moment that I understand, but then the memory is lost and I am left with a vague impression. It is a fish in a stream that I try to catch with my hands, but it swims away just before I close my grip, and I can only feel its tail as it slips through my fingers."

Reginald picked up a thin pamphlet with the words "The Waiting Room" on the front. "There have been others like me.

I see it in their eyes. When I ask them about God, I catch a glimpse of a tiny spark, but it is quickly snuffed like a paper match in a gale." He opened the pamphlet to the first page. "Look. Here is a tract an old woman handed me this morning." He motioned toward a stack of pamphlets on a nearby chair. "I have dozens of them, so I suppose she brings me one every day. In any case, it seems that a prophet has predicted the coming of a king, and all who believe the prophecy are supposed to go to the theatre and wait for him."

He closed the pamphlet and tossed it to the table. "When I read these pages, I feel that spark, the same one I felt when I heard you mention God, and I hear a siren song to join those mad folks who wait in line." He ran his hand through his hair again. "Everyone already thinks I am crazy, so I often ask myself why not go to the theatre? After all, who is the madman, the fool who sits in a dark theatre waiting for a show that never begins, or the fool who is quite happy living day after day in endless monotony, not even noticing that he has carried a bucket of bolts from a shelf to a workbench and back again ten thousand times over his tedious years?" He bent down and rested his elbows on the table, intertwining his fingers behind his head. "Either way I choose, I play the fool."

Billy leaned over to look into Reginald's eyes. "But you would be the biggest fool of all if the king showed up and you were still here studying old books and newspapers."

Reginald spread out his arms. "But the whole story lacks credibility!" He picked up the pamphlet again and turned to the last page. "You see, according to the prophet at the theatre— whom only a very few people heard, mind you—this deliverer king is supposed to open a doorway to a new world, and those who pass through will meet a greater king who will determine whether or not they go to everlasting peace." He pointed at a

209

line on the page. "But here is the crux of the problem. The prophet said, 'Every person who chooses to follow the king must give up his will and become the king's servant.'" He threw the booklet down again, spinning it on the table. "Servitude is not exactly the kind of salvation I had in mind, so why should I believe a story that promises a deliverance of chains? It just makes no sense."

Bonnie picked up the pamphlet and opened the cover. "Servitude's not so bad if your master is fair and noble."

"True enough, but . . ." Reginald pressed his fist into his palm and twisted it like a pestle in a mortar. "I must be more than wheat in a mill. I cannot believe that I have only these two choices—to suffer this daily gristmill or else submit myself to a king who will also grind me as he pleases. Is servitude really better than toiling in this village? At least here I have a shred of hope that I can . . ." He stroked his chin. "How should I put it?"

"That you can run the grinder," Billy said. "That you can be in control."

"Exactly!" His face reddened under a furrowing brow. "What did you say?"

"I said, 'That you can be in control.' You don't want someone else deciding your fate."

Reginald's eyes narrowed, the red in his cheeks deepening. "But do I deserve the same fate as all the mindless robots in this town? Since I am able to see through this veil of despair, is it right that I must stand in the same line as those who cannot see past their noses, only to learn that at the end of the line we will be fitted with rings for those same noses?" He slammed his hand on the table. "I am not a lemming who leaps into a void simply because my fellow lemmings have done the same. What do they find at the bottom? Nothing but dead lemmings."

He crossed the aisle to a parallel table and threw open another book, an old tome filled with heavy parchment, yellowed and empty. "Look here. This is the work that helps keep me sane and proves that I do not belong here." He turned the parchment leaves back to the first page. "As you can see, there are quite a number of old runes."

Billy leaned over, bracing himself with his palm on the table. "I've seen writing like that. It's ancient English, right?"

"Of a sort. While I was trying to figure out where to shelve this book, I opened to the first page. Since it was blank, I assumed it was a logbook that no one had bothered to use, but suddenly these letters appeared as if by magic. I knew deep in my soul that this was new, that I had not done this the day before." He turned the page. "I immediately translated the words to modern English, believing that writing on a blank page was a sure sign that I was doing something new."

Billy read the words silently, his gaze riveted to the parchment.

A warrior craves the power of light.
Yet strength alone will not avail.
For keys to mysteries hide from men
Who think their eyes can pierce the veil.

A dragon's key unlocks the truth
Of light's redeeming power to save.
Its eye transforms the red to white;
It finds the lost, makes wise the knave.

For light explores the darkened heart,
Igniting souls with probing flames.
It cuts and burns away the chaff—
The flesh of dragons, knights, and dames.

The way of darkness traps and keeps
Its captives naked, cold, and blind,
But light revealing words of truth
Will open doors that snare and bind.

Billy's heart pounded. This was the same poem that appeared in the cave when he was trying to escape drowning in the flood! How could the words appear in both places along with their translations at the same time? Did his father somehow provide the translation for him? It was just too weird, too coincidental to happen at all. But what else could possibly explain it?

He mopped his brow with his shirtsleeve and drank in the verses once again. When he had first read them, they meant little more than a way to escape, but now they rang with new truth. They meant so much more.

He read the second quatrain again. He knew the rubellite in the pendant was a key, because it had acted as a gateway into Dragons' Rest. But he had taken it off—otherwise he couldn't have gone through it. Still, the poem said "*A* dragon's key," and not "*The* dragon's key." Could any rubellite work the same way? He balled his hand and gazed at his ring. How should he use it?

He read from the last section out loud. "But light revealing words of truth will open doors that snare and bind." He thumped his pencil eraser on the page. "It sounds like we have to find this light if we don't want to stay trapped in this place."

Reginald blew out a long breath, nodding. "Agreed. But how do we find it? I've searched everywhere."

Bonnie closed the pamphlet and laid it back on the table. "Did you search the theatre?"

"No," Reginald said. "I am told that the theatre is dark. Why would I search for light there?"

"Light shines in a lot of strange places," Billy replied. He laid his palm on the table and splayed his fingers. "I heard that almost everyone in town has a ring like this one. Why don't you?"

Reginald waved at the ring, a look of disdain on his face. "The dragon's eye is for the superstitious, not for scholars. Besides, yours is white, so it must not be a dragon's eye."

Billy jerked off his ring and slapped it down, then moved his hand away slowly. "What color is it now?"

"Well, now, that's a clever trick. It's red."

Billy clenched his teeth. Dad had always been tenacious, but now he was fighting like a thousand-pound marlin. What else could he do to reel him in? His father had always been as sharp as a saber, but maybe in his confused condition he would fall for a bluff. It was worth a try.

Billy banged his fist on the table, making the ring jump. "You're hopeless!" He spun on his toes and stormed toward the entrance. "C'mon, Bonnie. Maybe someone else will listen."

Bonnie reached for him, grabbing empty air. "But Billy—"

Reginald lunged and grasped Billy's arm, pulling him back. "No! I need you. If you leave, I'll—" He suddenly let go, straightened his body, and smoothed out his clothes. "I'm terribly sorry. That was out of line." He lowered his head, flipping through a book's pages once again. "Go on," he said, gesturing toward the door with his hand. "Your destiny is your own."

Billy sighed. The bluff didn't work, yet feeling his dad's powerful grip, even for that brief moment, brought back a rush of memories from a fateful morning that seemed ages ago—a dream about gazing into a rubellite and seeing the face of a dragon, a Pop-tart for breakfast, his mother's hummed song about remembering the past, a wrestling match in the middle of the kitchen, and a scalding kiss on his mother's cheek. Why

213

could he remember so much, yet his father's mind seemed vacant? Those images had to be in there somewhere, didn't they?

Billy regripped the pencil and turned to a blank page of parchment in the old book. With lightning fast jots and swirls, he sketched a woman's head, adding short, dark hair and sad, longing eyes. Bonnie pulled up a stool and sat down to watch, nodding at Billy as though she knew exactly what he was doing.

Reginald glanced up, his face aflame. "What are you doing to my book?" He scooted over and jerked it away. "How dare you? That was my only link to sanity!"

Billy wrestled it back, smacked it down on the table, and pressed his finger on the drawing. Heat flashing through his cheeks, he yelled, "What do you see, Jared Bannister?"

Reginald stared at him, his mouth dropping open. "What did you call me?"

"Jared Bannister!" Billy grabbed Reginald's shoulder and turned him toward the page. "Just look at the picture and tell me. Without thinking, what comes to your mind? Tell me now!"

"Ma . . . Ma . . ."

"Say it!" Billy screamed.

Reginald's eyes slowly widened. "Marilyn?"

THE FELLOWSHIP OF SUFFERING

Yes!" Billy shouted. "Marilyn is your wife's name!" He threw down his pencil, wrapped his arms around Reginald's torso, and wrestled him to the ground. Reginald instinctively fought back, pushing Billy to the side and wriggling his hands in between his chest and Billy's arms to free himself.

Billy had seen his father try this move a hundred times, and it had always worked. But now he was stronger than the boy his father had wrestled in the past, much stronger. Struggling for position with their heads close together, he grunted a pained whisper. "What . . . are you . . . thinking . . . now?"

Reginald gave no reply. He strained to push Billy away, but Billy pushed back even harder, turning the bigger man's body and pressing his shoulders toward the ground, nearly pinning him. Billy grunted. Only . . . another . . . inch. Sweat now streaming down his cheeks, he strained with all his might, as if pinning his father would mean so much more than a simple wrestling victory. "I told you I'd pin you one of these days, remember?"

Reginald's eyes glimmered as though something prodded a new thought. "So . . . you want . . . to know . . . what I'm thinking?"

"Yeah. Tell me."

With a double-fisted thrust, Reginald threw him to the side and jumped to his feet. He leaned over the table that held the parchment book, panting. Mopping sweat from his brow, he looked down at the book as if searching for lost thoughts. "The words, 'not a chance' came to my mind. Does that mean anything to you?"

Billy scrambled up to meet him. "Yes! That's it! That's what my father always used to say when I said I would pin him."

Reginald looked again at the picture of Marilyn, then turned to a fresh page. "Your father used to say?"

"Yes, you—"

Reginald pressed his forearm against Billy's chest. "Look! New runes!" He frantically searched the tabletop. "Where is my pencil?"

Billy found the pencil on the table and presented it to him, sighing. "Here."

Reginald grabbed it and began scratching down an English translation on the next page, flipping back and forth between the pages. After a few minutes, he dropped the pencil on the table. "I think it's done."

"What's it say?" Billy asked. Bonnie got up from her stool and moved closer.

Reginald picked up the book and laid it open over his palms.

"Clefspeare, I dub you Jared, son of Arthur. By this decree, I name you my son, though truly you are closer than any of my natural offspring." He turned and tapped the lady's shoulder. "And you, dear Hartanna, I dub Irene, for your very presence brings peace to my soul. You are now my daughter, a treasured princess, who I hope will always find peace within the walls of my palace. For your protection, I have entered your names as Reginald Bannister and Tabitha Silver in the official records as my adopted son and daughter. Hide your identities well, for if your enemies discover them, you will be chased by bloodthirsty hounds for centuries to come. I suggest choosing different surnames for yourselves for the time being, though you may return to Bannister and Silver to protect your inheritance when the time comes."

Reginald's color seemed to drain from his forehead to his chin. He murmured, "Jared Bannister. That's the name you called me."

Billy felt like his brain was swimming in a boiling sea. "Reginald. . . . That's your royal name." He pulled the ring from his pocket. "Bonnie, remember I told you someone gave me this ring when we first got here?"

Bonnie drew close and eyed the ring. "Yes."

"The voice said to give it to the first person that calls my father's royal name."

"Well," Bonnie said, "Sarah was the first one to say, 'Reginald.'"

He laid the ring on the table next to his own, and all three stared at the gold circles and red stones. Billy drew his eyes closer, peering into the light. "A dragon's key," he continued softly, "finds the lost."

Reginald straightened and rapped the table with his knuckles. "I have made up my mind. I still have no conscious memory of your claim to be my son, but you have convinced me that I must make a new search for the light. I will go to the theatre."

217

Bonnie threw her arms around Reginald. "You won't be sorry!"

"There's one problem," Billy said. "We found out that you need a dragon's eye ring to get in."

"And I don't have one." Reginald's shoulders sagged. "Do you have a solution?"

Billy snatched up his own ring, grabbed Reginald's hand, and thrust it over his finger.

"No!" Reginald twisted the ring, pulling it toward his knuckle. "How will you get in if I—"

Billy strangled Reginald's fingers. "This was your ring before it was mine. There's another way for me to get out."

Reginald tried to pull away, but Billy wouldn't let him. "But how?" Reginald asked.

"If you're such a scholar, then ask yourself how I knew so much about you. I knew your name. I pulled thoughts out of your head you didn't even know were there. I even drew a picture of your wife, and you didn't even know you were married." He released Reginald's hand and picked up the other ring. "If I know you better than you know yourself, then who am I?"

Reginald stared at him, caressing the dragon's eye, his voice barely audible. "The deliverer king?"

"Come to the theatre and find out." Billy jumped away from Reginald, wrapped an arm around Bonnie, and marched from the library, retracing their steps and squeezing through the gap between the shelves. As they approached the partition to the bookstore, a shrill voice broke the silence. He eased the door open a crack and peeked through. Bonnie stood on tiptoes, her chin on his shoulder.

A knot of people had gathered around Sarah, most looking angry or scared, a familiar woman in the front shaking a ringed finger—Jasmine. "I'll bet your crazy friend is hiding them in the library. I've been watching those strangers, and I'm sure they came in here. And I saw their dragon's eyes. They were white, I tell you. They must be the ones I've been warning everyone about." She altered her tone from a rant to a chant. "Two eyes of white will change our ways. They'll purge our world and end our days."

"Yes," Sarah replied, "I heard your soapbox sermon this morning, but I tell you, they're not here."

Jasmine huffed. "Spoken like a true underborn. You have no dragon's eye. What would you know?"

Sarah raised her voice. "I know enough to realize that you would have those two killed if you had your way."

Billy let the door swing shut. Sarah was clearly trying to make sure he heard that warning. He whispered, "Let's see if there's a back way out." He and Bonnie turned, but they ran right into Reginald.

Reginald gestured with a sharp wave, keeping his voice low. "This way."

Billy and Bonnie followed him through a maze of bookshelves, noiselessly winding their way toward the very back of the library.

Jasmine's voice pierced the silence again. "Reginald! If you don't give those two demons to us, you'll suffer their fate!"

Reginald led them to a door in a dim corner, too far from the transoms to take advantage of their light. He lifted a wooden beam from two brackets, propped it against the wall, and pushed on the door. It didn't budge.

"Reginald!" Jasmine's voice grew closer, accompanied by the sound of a dozen tromping shoes. "I know you're in here somewhere!"

Reginald put his shoulder to the door and launched his body against it. It flew open, squealing on its hinges, and he tumbled to the ground outside, grunting. Jumping to his feet, he waved his arms. "Go! I'll keep them at bay and meet you later at the theatre."

Billy and Bonnie sprinted down the cobblestones, more of a back alley than a road. When they reached the corner of the main street, Bonnie grabbed Billy's arm. "What about Dorcas? We have to get her to come! She needs a ring!"

"But the extra ring is for Merlin's wife. We have to get it to her somehow."

Bonnie yanked off her own ring and held it in her fingers. "I've got one." She dashed away, her long dress flapping in her wake.

Billy sprinted behind her, catching up just before they reached the seamstress shop. They stopped at the door, puffing. "How will you get into the theatre without one?" Billy asked.

"Whatever way you do. I'm not leaving your side."

Bonnie pushed through the door. The familiar bell jangled. Dorcas was sitting on a stool at her cutting table, several pins squeezed between her lips. "Did you come for your old clothes?" she asked, mumbling through the pins. She nodded toward a pile on the counter. "Right there. All clean and pressed."

Bonnie marched straight up to Dorcas, grabbed her right hand, and pushed the rubellite ring onto her index finger, but she couldn't get it past the second knuckle. She held the ring in place and looked up at the elderly lady, her face pleading. "You have to come with us to the theatre right away. We'll take you to a man who'll tell you why Oxford means so much to you."

Dorcas dropped the pins into her hand and laid them on the table. "Didn't I tell you that I tried? I just couldn't seem to go in."

Bonnie moved the ring to Dorcas's smallest finger and slid it all the way on. "You can go in if you wear this ring."

"But why the rush? I have a dress to finish. The Oxford mystery can wait."

Billy stepped over to Dorcas's cutting table. "No, it can't. Jasmine's on our trail." He picked up a stub of chalk and began drawing on her slate. In less than two minutes, he had sketched a striking portrait of the professor. He handed the slate to her, dramatically tapping on it with the chalk. "Charles Hamilton, Professor at Oxford University."

Dorcas stared at the portrait, her eyes growing wide as she brought it closer to her face. "I . . . I know him." She gently rubbed her finger across the man's hair, smudging the lines. "I can't say how, but I know him."

Bonnie leaned her head against the trembling woman's shoulder. "He's your husband."

Dorcas reached into the pocket of her smock and pulled out a dainty ring. Tiny gold blossoms lined both edges. "I've often wondered why I have this." She slipped it over her finger, caressing the blossoms as if encouraging them to grow. A tear rolled down her cheek. "Did . . . did he like flowers?"

"Yes," Bonnie replied, laying her own fingertip on the ring. "He said you loved carnations."

Another tear followed the track of the first. "I adore carnations." Dorcas sniffed, still caressing the ring. "But where is he now, and why don't I remember?"

Bonnie took her gently by the arm. "Everything will become clear very soon," she said, lifting Dorcas to her feet. "Just go to the theatre and sit down. Billy and I will meet you there."

The town clock gonged a single time. Billy gathered their clothes, opened the door, jangling the bell once again, and allowed Dorcas and Bonnie to exit. Dorcas pulled up a shawl and shuffled along the planks next to the deserted street.

221

Bonnie wrapped her arm around a pole, watching the old lady head for the theatre. She swung around and faced Billy. "Two hours to go. Is that enough time to tell the whole town?"

"Yep, because the whole town will be gathered in one place."

"The Founder's Day Picnic?" Bonnie asked.

"Yep." Billy leaned his shoulder against another pole. "Trouble is, our prophetess friend will be there, too. She might want to turn the picnickers into a lynch mob."

Lugging Ashley's laptop case, Karen labored from the Bannister house, trailing Shiloh. They halted at the station wagon, and Karen set the case on the pavement in the glow of the streetlights. "I think Ashley must've packed the kitchen sink and the bathtub with it."

Carl, who had parked in front of the professor's wagon, leaned against the back of his SUV. "Did you get a report from Larry?"

"Yeah. He wants to talk to you." She unzipped the case and pulled out the computer. "Something weird's going on."

While Karen began the boot-up process, the professor and Marilyn exited the house. With *Fama Regis* tucked under her arm, Marilyn locked the door, then strode toward the cars with the professor. Her voice filtered through the night sounds, growing clearer as she drew near. "The gem quit working. It showed the adoption story, when King Arthur took Jared and Irene into his family, but I couldn't get it to translate anything past that."

The professor nodded. "So the rubellite's powers are intermittent. How strange."

Karen laid the laptop on the hood of the professor's car, making sure it could be seen under the streetlamp. "Larry. Repeat to Mr. Foley what you just told me."

"Ashley is sending a set of clues that I cannot decipher. I will play some of it for you."

The speaker emitted a strange noise, like marbles clicking together in a random sequence.

Carl tapped the computer case. "Prof, have you heard this yet?"

The professor stepped close. "No. I did not speak to Larry. I was making sure the house was secure. It has been ransacked, but it seems that whoever did it is no longer inside."

Everyone leaned toward the computer, listening to the odd clicks.

"Is she cracking her knuckles?" Karen asked.

"Not quite," the professor replied. "Although the clicks are intermittent, they are too sharp and defined for knuckles."

"A pencil striking a table?" Shiloh suggested.

Karen snapped her fingers. "It's her teeth. If it's coming through the transmitter, it's got to be her teeth. But it's not really chattering, so I'll bet she's sending us a code."

The professor began nodding at each click, his eyebrows rising every few seconds. "Could it be Morse code?" He turned the keyboard and pulled up the word processor. "R," he said, typing in the letter. With every new series of speaker clicks, his index finger fell on a key. "E . . . E . . . K . . . L . . . A . . . K . . . E."

"That's it!" Karen shouted. "Ashley's at Deep Creek Lake!"

Marilyn clamped her hand over Karen's mouth. "Shhh!"

The professor continued announcing the letters. "S . . . T . . . A . . . T . . . E . . . P . . . A . . . R . . . K . . . W . . . A . . . L . . . T . . . E . . . R . . . M . . . I . . . S . . . S . . . I . . . N . . . G . . . D . . . E . . . E . . . P . . . C . . . R . . . E . . . E." He stopped typing. "It seems to be repeating now."

Shiloh clapped her hands together, her British accent more pronounced than usual. "That girl is brilliant!"

223

Karen smiled in spite of the fingers over her mouth. She crowed in a muffled voice, "That's my sister!"

Marilyn released Karen and laid a hand on Carl's shoulder. Every line in his face had turned south. "Missing means just that, Carl. Maybe Walter's hiding somewhere. You know how resourceful he is."

Carl sighed, shifting his weight from foot to foot. "At least we know where to go now, and Ashley's sure to help us close in."

Still leaning over the computer, the professor found the mapping program and brought up Western Maryland on the screen. "This may suit us quite well." He zoomed in, magnifying the lake, and pointed at its central section. "Here is Ashley's probable location." He slid his finger down the screen. "Hartanna told me the dragons would land as soon as they find the lake, so I assume they will congregate at this southwestern cove." Turning the keyboard toward Karen, he straightened his body. "It would be better if we can draw the Watchers out over the water and use the lake as our battle theatre."

"Why is that?" Carl asked.

"Two reasons. The dragons are as adept in the water as they are in the air, and staying away from land will minimize the risk of danger to humans. The Watchers will not take care to keep their flaming arrows away from the innocent."

"We already know that," Carl said, jangling his keys. "And standing around while they're holding my family is driving me nuts."

"Then let's make haste," the professor replied. "But we still must be careful. We can't afford to do anything to call attention to ourselves. Even the authorities may be in the pocket of the enemy."

Samyaza flew low over the ground. Ashley dangled from his arm, the tips of her shoes scraping the gravelly path below and the demon's torturous grip crushing her breath away. As her feet brushed the gravel, she stretched her toes, hoping for enough contact with the ground to boost her body just an inch higher and free her lungs. She pushed hard. It didn't work. She pushed again. Nothing. With her vision turning dark and her head ready to burst, she gave one last lunge. Samyaza's hands slipped lower.

Ah! Air! It wasn't much, but every shallow breath tasted like heaven.

In the distance, moonlight bathed a wooden deck that skirted the upper floor of a two-story structure. A pair of incandescent lamps illuminated a sign on the wall, but with lack of oxygen blurring her vision, Ashley couldn't make out the words until she was close enough to touch the sign. "Deep Creek Lake Discovery Center." At the lower level, another Watcher, with a grotesque smile on shiny silver lips, held open a glass door.

After landing at the threshold, Samyaza hustled Ashley through the entry and slung her to the floor. Sprawling across the tiles, she gasped for breath, her chest heaving. Tremors shot through her arms. She pushed herself to her knees to take the pressure off her lungs. As precious oxygen filtered through her body, her mind and vision cleared.

The door slammed. She brushed her hair away from her eyes only to see Samyaza marching toward her. He kicked her in the lower abdomen so hard she nearly lifted off the floor. "Get up!" he roared. "You have work to do!"

Ashley clutched her pelvis and fell back to the floor, pain ripping through her body. At that instant, she knew for sure Samyaza would kill her when this was all over. She stretched out one arm, trying to push up to a sitting position. The other demon laughed, flapping a set of dark red wings and muttering in a strange, guttural language. The tone sounded insulting.

Suddenly, Ashley's whole body lifted into the air, the pain zipping from her pelvis up to her head. She blinked open her eyes. Samyaza held her over the floor by her hair.

"Stand!" he ordered.

With her scalp burning and her face feeling like it was about to rip off her skull, Ashley extended her legs, groping for the tiles with her shoes. When they touched, he lowered her to the floor.

"Amazing what a little persuasion will do." He glided along the short hallway. "Now come with me."

Ashley bent over double and shuffled forward. Nearly toppling at every step, she tried to focus on the winged monster in front of her, tears blurring her vision. Every thought stabbed at the horrible beast. If he so much as bruised a finger on Pebbles . . .

She didn't know how to finish her threat. She felt powerless and alone. As she slowly took in her surroundings, a fresh dose of sanity seeped into her mind. The signal! She wrapped her arms around herself and shivered, adding her coded chattering seconds later.

Samyaza turned left and banged open an inner door. Ashley followed him in, the pain finally subsiding enough to walk more upright. "Sleep here until dawn," Samyaza growled, "but the dragon must be freed by midday tomorrow." He left the room and slammed the door.

Ashley spun and grabbed the knob, but the lock had already been set. She leaned against the door and ran her fingers through her hair. She had to collect herself, get her bearings, and check out the room. First, she scanned the walls for possible escape routes. Two glass doors and two windows lined the wall to her left, but Venetian blinds made it impossible to see through them. She hobbled over to one of the doors and tugged the drawstring, rotating the horizontal slats to their open position. Peering through, she could see the rear of the visitor center and the path over which Samyaza had carried her.

Ashley grasped the door handle, but it wouldn't turn. Of course her captors weren't that stupid, but it was worth a try. She set a hand on her hip, eyeing the other sets of blinds. Why not open all of them? If anyone happened to be looking for her, it made sense for her to give a potential rescuer as much help as she could.

After snapping open each set, she turned her attention to the rest of the room. A collection of broken or mangled equipment, some of which she recognized, filled three tables in this makeshift laboratory.

Her eyes locked on the middle table. The lamp from the restoration dome lay at its center, jagged pieces of glass lining its inner rim. Immediately to the right of the lamp, a leaden box sat on a pedestal. She reached for it and slowly opened the hinged lid, her scorched hand still pulsing with heat. Streams of light swirled toward the inside, dimming the room but lighting up a glowing gem that sat on a tiny bed of purple velvet. She picked up the candlestone and laid it in her palm, wishing she could smash it and get this all over with.

She clenched her fist around it. Maybe she should. How many lives might she save if she just threw the stone on the floor and ground it into dust? Sure, they'd kill her, but she didn't care. She would just—

The inner door banged open. Carrying Pebbles in his massive arms, Samyaza stepped inside. "As soon as the job is done," he said, hoisting the little girl higher, "you'll get your reward."

Ashley shuffled toward them. "Pebbles!" she cried. "Are you all right?"

227

Samyaza raised his hand. "Stop!"

The force of the command seemed to stiffen Ashley's joints. She halted, stretching her arms, but she couldn't quite reach Pebbles.

Samyaza crooned in the little girl's ear. "Ashley has some work to do, so I'll take you back to Mrs. Foley now. As soon as Ashley's done, you can be with her." Pebbles cried, her tiny face puckering. As the demon turned, he glanced back at Ashley, flashing a set of claws at the ends of his fingers, more like eagle talons than human fingernails. The door closed behind him with a dull thud.

Ashley clenched her fist so tightly, the edges of the candlestone inside bit into her skin. She walked back to the worktable, slowly opening her palm. As light swept toward the gem, she imagined the creature inside, a dragon with the mind of the devil. Should she bring it out? Could it really do much harm to nine other dragons?

As she returned the gem to its velvet bed, the image of Pebbles's tear-streaked face flashed across her mind. She snapped the lid shut. She had to let the dragons take care of themselves. For now, her job was to save an innocent little girl.

She surveyed the equipment on the three tables. The one on the left held a tangled pile of metallic debris, the pieces of equipment the demons had salvaged from the earthquake in Montana. The middle table held the restoration lamp with the broken lens and a rectangular piece of lead that looked like a gray brick with two thick wires coming out of one end.

On the table to the right, piles of circular pieces of glass covered the surface, some of them finished lenses, some coarse hunks of thick glass representing a variety of colors. Against the back wall, a huge machine of some sort stood on the floor, a confusing array of meters and dials surrounding a central monitor.

It resembled a lens grinder she had used back at her own laboratory, but with all the extra controls, it seemed more advanced.

Glancing around the room, Ashley spotted three video cameras attached to the wall near the ceiling. Could the room also be bugged for sound? With Pebbles in the clutches of that maniac demon, she didn't want to risk speaking to Larry directly. She wrapped her arms around herself, pretending to shiver. Time to get clicking again. Remembering a sign she saw outside the building, she began tapping out "Deep Creek Lake Discovery Center" with her teeth. After three repetitions, she quit, knowing it would be nearly impossible to concentrate on her coding and the monumental task of fixing the restoration engine.

She stepped up to the table on the left and picked through bent metal boxes and broken plastic casings. She found most of the pieces of her engine, at least all the parts she needed to make it work. Though warped and dented, everything fit together. The wires were also sound, and the hard drive and CPU in the main box seemed intact.

Ashley pieced together the first unit, sort of a huge metallic shoebox. A glass cylinder, about the diameter of a toilet paper tube, projected from one side. In her mind, she drew the diagram of the restoration process. This tube was the energy collection channel. The light energy would gather in one end of the tube, pass through data collectors, and emerge at the other end after the computer decoded it. Of course, without a dome to cover the emerging light, she would have to assemble a separate unit for the restoration ray, maybe a gun-like device to aim at the energy as soon as it came out. Otherwise, it might just disperse.

The main unit's lid had obviously been ripped away from the hinges, so she just left the box open and moved it to the center table. It didn't really matter how pretty it looked. It only needed to work one more time. Finding an outlet, she plugged

229

in the power source. Tiny bulbs on the circuit board flashed to life, blinking at her as if waking to a new day.

Ashley straightened and rubbed at the sore spot from Samyaza's kick. At least the computer still functioned. As long as she had the brains behind the decoding engine she could probably make this work.

Finding another metal casing, a small one that fit well in her hands, she laid it on the table and placed the leaden brick, the nuclear core of the restoration ray, inside. She found the cap that had originally been on top of the glass cylinder of the restoration dome and pulled out its laser gun and tubular extension. Both gun and extension fit nicely next to the nuclear core. She then fastened the wires from the core to the gun's energy input. With a quick twist and click, she attached the broken lens to the end of the laser's protruding tube.

After closing her eyes for a moment and breathing a quick prayer, she flipped a rocker switch on the laser. The engine hummed. A white energy beam shot out of the tube, brighter and brighter as the hum grew louder. The beam struck a wall, slowly burning a hole through the beige plasterboard.

Ashley flipped the switch off. Okay, it worked, but it wouldn't restore a dragonfly, much less a dragon, unless she made the lens filters just right.

Moving to the last table, she picked up a blue lens. Too dark. Too thick. And who could guess what the refraction would be?

She carried the glass to the lens machine and flipped through the pages of a spiral-bound operator's manual, comparing the illustrations to the dials on the control board. After reading the last page and closing the book, she rested a hand on her hip and gazed at the panel. This would do just fine. She set the glass inside the machine. It wouldn't hurt to mess up a few lenses to see what the contraption could do.

As Ashley worked, moonlight reflected off the lake and shone through the glass doors. She glanced at the cove nearest the building. Walter was out there somewhere. Was he alive? And if he survived, was he hurt, lost?

She wagged her head, trying to shake the morbid thoughts away. She had to get this lens exactly right. When it was finally time to use it, she wouldn't have the luxury of trial and error. This candlestone probably didn't have an inner crack that would allow Devin to escape to the exit channel, so she would have to break the stone and catch his light energy.

She took out the blue lens and laid it near the corner of the table, mentally calling it her rejection pile. Setting her hands on her hips again, she gazed at the dozens of glass disks that lay in regimented order. Her shoulders slumped. There were so many, and she had such a short time to find just the right one.

Pain stabbed her abdomen as though Samyaza were still there, savagely kicking her again and again. With tears welling in her eyes and a hand massaging her stomach, she picked up another lens, this one clearer than the first and wearing a tinge of orange instead of blue. Carrying it shakily back to the machine, she set it in place and flipped open the manual again. Using a corner of her shirt, she dried her eyes. Keep working. No time to stop now.

Dizzy and disoriented, she stumbled back to the worktable again. She stretched into a wide yawn, then rocked back and forth from heel to toe. Forcing her eyes open, she picked up the broken lens and stared at it. There was so much to do! It might take all night to get it all working again. How could she possibly risk going to sleep?

With her lips trembling, she set the lens back down. She folded her arms on the table and rested her head on them, whispering, "I'm not going to cry . . . I'm not going to cry." She sniffed again. A tear moistened her arm. Then, like a river ripping through a dam, Ashley sobbed, her body heaving in great convulsions. As her whole world turned dark, she gritted her teeth, chiding herself for ever dreaming her silly Morse code idea could work. She was stupid to think she could do this alone. Nobody would come to rescue her. Nobody.

Walter climbed out of his waterlogged crate and dragged his feet through shallow water. A wide swath of grass grew along the lake's higher-than-normal edges, making for a slippery climb up the incline to dry land. He found a stand of trees and flopped down in their midst, shivering and chattering so hard he thought his teeth might crack. As he warmed his hands in his armpits, he gave himself a pep talk. "Ju-just try t-t-to rest f-f-for a m-m-minute. Then you-you'll be f-f-fine."

Remnants of the smoke plume rose between his shelter and a thicker forest. He shook his head hard. "C-can't r-r-rest. Gotta f-f-find Ashley." He forced himself to his feet and lumbered along a grass-covered field, his right foot dragging, still half-frozen. When he reached the forest edge, his knees locked in place. He surveyed the scene—twisted metal wrapped around charred trees, strings of smoke rising from smoldering piles of blackened upholstery, and a bent propeller wobbling in the breeze.

He shuffled toward the wreckage, his legs aching. Was Ashley somewhere in that heap of junk, maybe lying scorched and broken under a blackened piece of fuselage? How could anyone have survived a crash like that, much less the fireball that erupted after impact? As he drew nearer, the stench of burnt fuel and rubber assaulted his senses, but the broken fuselage radiated a welcome warmth over his chilled skin.

Frantically kicking sheets of metal aside, it didn't take long for him to realize the truth. He breathed a long sigh. "She's not here! She survived!" He spread his arms, now fully enjoying the heat from the pile of smoking debris. After a few minutes, his ears began to sting, then his fingers and toes. A new rush of blood surged into all his extremities until they burned like fire. Dizziness overwhelmed him. He backed away from the debris and dropped to his knees, feeling like a toppling oak as his body crashed to the ground. The warmth of the plane wreckage wafted over his body, and a sense of darkness flooded his mind, peaceful and soothing.

A bird chirp pricked Walter's ear. Pushing to a sitting position, he twisted his neck and scratched his head. Where was he? Why did his body ache so badly?

The first rays of dawn filtered through the tree branches and cast a soft glow on the lake's rippled surface. Walter slammed his hand on the ground. "How long did I sleep?" He jumped to his feet, groaning at the pain in his stiff legs. Quickly scanning the area, he trudged toward the wreckage. It was cooler now, but smoke still curled from the half-buried engine.

He searched the ground for footprints, finding nothing until he moved to a grassy area where two impressions dug deeply into the soft turf. Not far away, he spotted two more divots and a single handprint. He crouched to pick up a broken stick and mentally traced a line from the divots to the stick, then extended the line and continued searching in that direction. After several steps, he found another stick, then a third.

The trail of clues ended at a gravel path, certainly easy enough to follow, but he couldn't just traipse right up to wherever the bad guys were holding Ashley. They'd see him from a mile away. He ducked into the woods that lined the trail and scampered from tree to tree, pausing at each to peer ahead and listen.

The gravel path widened into a blacktopped road that led to a building in the distance. Walter continued his stealthy approach, and when he sneaked to within a hundred feet of the wood-framed structure, he crouched behind a broad evergreen tree. A sign on the wall read, "Deep Creek Lake Discovery Center."

He spotted a parking lot on a hill on the opposite side. Was he approaching the back of the building? Would anyone be watching this path from the lake? He sprinted to the building and flattened his body against a wall, then peeked around the corner. An ugly creature with red wings opened a set of glass double doors. He jerked his head back. "That ain't Bonnie," he whispered.

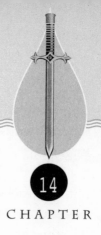

SEEKING THE LOST

Walter edged along the wall toward the demon-guarded door, staying as flat against the siding as possible. He had spotted a closer, unguarded glass door during his sprint toward the building. What he wouldn't give to get a peek in there, but a stone column stood in his way.

Dropping to his belly, he crawled on the wooden deck inch by inch. One of those Watcher creeps might walk or fly by at any second, but, even though the slightest movement could give him away, he had to risk it. He could have pretended to be a visitor to the center and acted as if he didn't know it had been closed down for the flood, but the Watchers had seen him in the seventh circle. They weren't likely to be dumb enough to forget him.

Just as he rounded the column, the sound of flapping wings filtered through the breeze. He jerked his head up, then froze in place, his palms flat on the deck. A Watcher glided down to the entry door, and a second one joined him. They seemed to be conversing with the red-winged demon he had seen earlier, but the few words he could hear sounded more like Klingon than English.

With the Watchers occupied, Walter continued his crawl until he reached an alcove created by two columns framing the nearer door. Still sore and stiff, he sat up with his back against the stone and waited for his heart to stop pounding.

After glancing at the demons, he rose to his haunches and peered through the glass. Venetian blinds hung over the inside, so he tipped his head and peeked between the slats. Something moved on the near side of a table. A female shuffled sideways to another table, her back toward him and her shoulders sagging.

Walter jerked back and squatted low. Ashley! He searched the skies, then the ground between him and the conversing demons. The coast seemed clear enough. He tapped the glass three times and peered in again. Ashley held a metal cylinder up to her eye, but she didn't look his way.

As he poised his knuckles over the window, a stream of blackness splashed across his eyes. "Arrrg!" Walter clawed at his face, but the stuff adhered to his skin as if it had octopus suckers. Like hot tar, it oozed down his cheeks and neck, feeling more like a hundred crawling legs than dripping liquid. He felt trapped. Lost. Back out on the water without his crate to keep him afloat.

Something grabbed him by each arm and yanked him to his feet. "What are you doing here?"

Walter spat through the spreading goop. "I was—" He grimaced at the bitter taste. "I wanted to buy a souvenir at the visitor center, but some scary creatures were guarding the door, so I was trying to signal that girl inside."

"There are signs on every road. Didn't you know the place was closed?"

The icky stuff spread to Walter's lower torso and squeezed like a tight vest. Every second seemed to drain away his usual courage. "No. I came in on a boat." He had to gasp to catch his breath. "I didn't see any signs."

The voice spoke a strange word that sounded like a command. The goo released him, running down his body and slithering to the ground like an army of black worms. The mass of black streamed toward a pair of bare feet, crawled up a leg, and disappeared under a white robe.

Walter's gaze followed it upward until he was face-to-face with one of the Watchers. The demon's huge hand shot forward, grabbed the front of Walter's jacket, and lifted him into the air. "I know you!" it growled. "You were in the circles."

Walter swallowed, trying to keep calm, but his dangling legs trembled. Shivers spread throughout his body, but he felt his moxie slowly returning. "Yeah. I helped set you free, remember?"

237

The Watcher threw Walter back to the deck, rapping his head against the stone column. The crack on his skull sent a shock wave down his spine. As a black aura swept across his vision, he took in long, slow breaths, trying not to faint. Desperate thoughts swirled through his brain. "Have . . . to . . . save Mom . . . and Ashley," but he didn't know for sure if the words really escaped from his lips. His body crumpled to the cold, wooden planks.

Carl pulled his SUV into a lot next to the park's headquarters and turned off the engine. He twisted around in the driver's chair, his eyes wide and glistening. "It's time for courage, ladies." He nodded toward the professor sitting on the passenger's side. "Prof and I would charge in, but we would only succeed in getting ourselves killed. So, here's the plan. Ashley sent a message about a discovery center, and the only one we could find on the map is less than half a mile away. I saw a lot of trees between here and there, so sneaking up to it shouldn't be a problem. Marilyn, you'll take Shiloh and Karen into the building and look for Ashley, just like we planned earlier."

Karen turned down the volume on the laptop, silencing a recording of Ashley's chattering teeth. "When will the dragons show up? They don't know about the visitor center."

The professor opened his door and gazed toward the sky. "They left from the south side of the lake shortly after we did, so they should be closing in on this section. I think we can count on Thigocia to locate Ashley."

"And when the dragons arrive," Carl said, "the Watchers will probably fly out to battle them. Of course, they will expect us to try to rescue their prisoners, so Professor and I will pretend to be the rescuers. That will be the ladies' cue to sneak into the center and look for Catherine and the girls."

"And Walter," Karen added.

"Right. He might be a prisoner, too."

The professor pointed toward the lake. "I see something."

"Yep," Shiloh said. "The dragons are coming."

Carl opened his door, but hesitated. "Professor, would you please pray for us all?"

"My pleasure." After everyone bowed their heads, the professor lifted his voice, his British accent sounding more refined than sterling silver. "Our gracious and powerful heavenly father, we call on you now in our desperate time of need. We are faced with the most terrifying danger we can possibly imagine, demonic forces who influenced mankind to commit myriad abominations, leading you to destroy this world with a flood so long ago. Yet, even that flood reminds us that you are the one who holds sway over the waters, who commands mountains and trees to uproot and be moved, and who keeps us safe in the palm of your mighty hand. Go before us now, we pray. Prepare the battlefield for us. Confound our enemies. Make straight the path of a conquering deliverer, whether he be armed with scales, human flesh, or the power of the Spirit. And we will give you all the glory for the great victory, whether we live or die, in the name of Jesus our Lord. Amen."

Carl squared his shoulders. "Marilyn, are you ready?"

Marilyn displayed a cylindrical bottle and a roll of clear tape. "Ready. I have a few surprises for Uncle Screwtape and company."

A lynch mob?" Bonnie said. "Do you think they'd go that far?"

"You heard her in the bookstore." Billy laid their old clothes on the walk. "And I've been wondering about this whole dragon savior deal." He turned away from Bonnie and kicked at a pile of sand. "I'm starting to think—" he swallowed, trying to keep his voice in check—"that I'm really supposed to . . ."

"Die?"

Billy watched a dark cloud as it passed in front of the sun. It seemed warmer today, and the cloud covered the town with a welcome shadow. He unfastened the bottom button on his vest. "I'm trying not to think about it. I'm doing all this by the seat of my pants. I guess I'll just face up to whatever happens."

She picked at a collection of lint on his sleeve. "Are you afraid to die?"

"I . . . I'm really not sure." He watched her fingers, soft and loving as they pecked away at the white dots. "Are you going to try to talk me out of it?"

Bonnie pinched the last dot. "No, Billy." She sat down on the edge of the raised sidewalk and patted the spot next to her. "I know time's running short, but we have to talk."

Billy sat by her side, trembling a bit. She propped her feet on the walk and pulled her knees up to her chest, spreading the hem of her dress over her ankles. A breeze played with her hair, blowing wisps around her glowing face and delicate neck. She pursed her lips and swallowed, the dress's high neckline moving in and out with her throat. White lace trimmed a line of dainty buttons all the way down to her veiled feet. Lace also adorned her wrists like bracelets of baby's breath. Billy's heart thrummed. Her startling beauty nearly took his breath away.

"Billy," Bonnie began, her eyes imploring. "Don't be afraid to die. I know after all the awful places you've had to go, it's hard to imagine how good heaven can be, but I've seen it, and no words can describe it." She waved her hand toward the cobblestone road in front of them. "Saying that the streets are made of gold would insult the streets of heaven and give gold too much credit. An angel led me down one of the streets . . ." Her eyes grew wider. "Such a beautiful creature! We've seen the Watchers, and they can make themselves lovely of form and face, but when you see a true angel of God, you'll know that the demons are sick, grotesque forgeries of the real thing. They are to the real angels what a toddler's dough molds are to a Michelangelo masterpiece.

"And remember that twisted tree in the first circle, the tree of the knowledge of good and evil? Well, I saw the tree of life. Oh, Billy! The fruit was so big, a family took one piece and carved it like a turkey! When everyone had eaten their fill, there seemed to be just as much left over as when they started! I wanted to try a bite, but the angel who led me down the streets told me to wait. He said once I tasted of heaven, I could never go back to earth, because food on earth would forever taste like dust, and I would wither away pining for the fruit of paradise. It

240

was then I knew that God planned for me to come back to this place of misery. It felt like someone pricked a hole in my skin and vacuumed out all the joy. How could I leave such a glorious life, a paradise of faithful saints?"

She clutched Billy's sleeve, her eyes widening even more as though she could still see the glory. "Look! There's Moses gazing upon the stone tablets with awestruck wonder, even after all these centuries. And there's Paul, welcoming a believer into heaven, overjoyed that his ancient epistles filled a longing in another lost soul's heart and led her to the savior." Bonnie's voice quaked. "And then . . . I saw *him*. . . . And he saw me. . . . He took me . . ." She swallowed and wrapped her arms around herself. "He took me in his arms and hugged me so tight, I felt . . . I felt . . ." She drooped her head and sighed. When she finally looked up again, tears streamed down her face. "It's worth it all, Billy. We've both lost a parent, we've been beaten and bruised, and we've gone through hell together. I even died. And I can tell you . . . giving up everything to serve God is worth it all."

Moisture filled Billy's eyes. Bonnie, his angel from above, had given him a glimpse of heaven.

"Like I said," Bonnie continued, "I'm not trying to talk you out of it." She wiped away the stream of tears. "I'm trying to give you strength to do whatever you need to do, whether you live or die. If you have to die—" She bit her lip, and her voice rose an octave—"I'll miss you . . . but I will never . . . *never* . . . doubt God's will." She grasped his shoulder, her strength seeming to radiate into his skin. "You're just the man to do his will, Billy. I know you can do whatever God calls you to do."

Billy's heart swelled with strength. He sat up straighter and inched forward in his seat, ready to jump into action. He gazed

241

at Bonnie, soaking in her faith and zeal, watching her tears of sincerity track down her lovely cheeks. He caught one of the tears on his finger, and the drop of warmth seemed to strengthen him even further. Words spilled into his mind. Eloquence borrowed from Bonnie? Maybe. But no matter what it was, the words were just too beautiful to keep to himself. "Remember when we were running away from the slayer and you covered me with your wings to keep me warm?"

"I remember. It seems like ages ago."

"Do you remember what I said to you?"

She nodded, her voice trembling. "Forever and ever, Bonnie, I will always be your friend."

"I was trying to encourage you." He reached for the pile of clothes and pulled a folded sheet of paper from his cargo pants pocket. "But you're the one who made me strong." He opened it slowly, displaying a portrait of Bonnie, her wings spread behind her and Excalibur in her extended hands, a miniature of a larger portrait he had drawn months ago. "Wherever I go, I carry this symbol of how you delivered the sword to me—I mean, the real sword, the truth."

Bonnie's hand flew to her mouth. A new tear trickled down her cheek.

Billy folded the paper and returned it to his cargo pants. "And now you covered me again, but with words instead of wings. I couldn't feel more protected if I was wearing a suit of armor."

Bonnie placed a hand on Billy's cheek. When she withdrew it, Billy continued. "Without you, I would be lost forever. My father never taught me about faith. The professor couldn't give me his. But you showed faith to me. You lived it." He laid his palm against his chest. "Because of your friendship, this squire has become a knight."

242

Bonnie's eyes sparkled. "A knight in shining armor." She hugged him briefly, then pulled away.

"Speaking of armor—" Billy picked up the pile of clothes and rose to his feet—"I'd feel better if I had my old clothes on." He extended his hand. "How about you?"

Bonnie grasped Billy's hand and pulled herself up. "Probably more practical, that's for sure."

They hustled into the seamstress shop and changed back into their clothes, then hurried toward the center of town. "First stop," Bonnie said, holding out her palm, "the bookstore."

"Right." Billy handed her the ring. "Let's hope Jasmine's not there."

The tall statue of Captain Autarkeia guided them as they waded through the thickening crowd—men carrying picnic baskets, ladies scurrying around looking for a place to spread a blanket, and various peddlers pushing wheeled carts that boasted steaming hot dogs, buttery-smelling popcorn, dark bottles of bubbling brew, and billowing plumes of cotton candy on long paper tubes. The townspeople congregated in the square, many of them already sitting on blankets and nibbling on treats, excitement spilling out in buzzing chatter.

243

Billy halted, waiting for a caravan of street peddlers to pass. "Think there'll be a speaker who'll start the festivities?" he asked Bonnie.

"The article said the mayor would speak at two, after everyone's had a chance to eat."

Billy glanced up at the clock. "Twenty minutes." As his gaze returned to the street, he spotted the constable circling around the statue, scanning the crowd from the elevated center island. Billy turned Bonnie around. "Don't let him see you."

"Who? The constable?"

"Yeah. I think he's looking for us. Let's get to the bookstore while we have the chance." He hesitated. "But we can't afford to both get waylaid. Let's go one at a time."

Billy strolled through the square with Bonnie trailing several yards behind. When he reached the door, he opened it quickly and ducked inside. Two people stood in front of the sales counter. Billy froze.

Sarah and Jasmine both turned his way. "Aha!" Jasmine said, smiling. "Here you are. Where's your—"

Bonnie opened the door and stepped inside next to Billy.

"How convenient," Jasmine continued. "Right on cue."

Sarah waved a finger at Jasmine. "Don't you dare touch them. They know nothing about oracles of fire or any of your prophecies. They're just children."

"But they wear the white gems," Jasmine said as she approached Bonnie. "They must be the two oracles."

Billy stepped in front of Jasmine and showed her his hand. "We got rid of them. Are you happy now?" Bonnie also lifted her hand, showing her empty fingers.

"Oh," Jasmine said slowly, "I see." Putting a finger to her lips, she walked around Billy and Bonnie. "Getting rid of your rings, of course, doesn't alter your identity. I'll just have to find another way to convince the crowd that you deserve to die. The white gems would have made it easier, but I do have other options."

"Like what?" Billy fired back. "Claiming we're underborns or one of those shadows in the past you're so afraid of?"

Jasmine laughed and continued her orbit around the teens. "If only you knew how close you are to the truth. The people of Dragons' Rest eagerly accept my advice to forget the past, because they fear it. If they searched deep within, they would learn the secrets of their origins, and they would realize that they live here without hope." She stopped in front of Billy and shook a finger at him, anger rising in her voice. "Are you willing to dredge up those sad memories? Do you want them to know how futile their lives are here?" She spread out her arms. "This is a place of eternal forgetfulness, and knowledge for these people means torture."

Jasmine glanced at Sarah but seemed unconcerned that so many secrets were coming out into the open. "I take care of the people," she continued. "And most of them trust me to drive out or alienate anyone who might shine the light on the deep recesses of their minds."

Billy spread his hands. "But we want to take them to a better place, and the only way to get them to go is for them to realize what they were. They have to remember the past to understand why they need a new life. If you really cared about your townspeople, you'd let us tell them."

Jasmine shook her head. "There is no better place for them. With their memories locked away, they are perfectly happy in this town. That's why I named it Dragons' Rest."

"*You* named it?" Billy said, glancing at the statue in the middle of the town square. "I thought Captain Autarkeia was the founder."

Jasmine gestured toward the statue with her hand, a proud smile on her face. "Captain Autarkeia was my father, and we founded this place together. He taught me how it came to be, how we must learn to be content with who we are and what we have here, but he disappeared long ago, so I have taken his place."

Bonnie peered out the window. "But being content without knowing the truth is just being gullible. It's like . . . it's like . . ."

"Being a lemming," Billy prompted.

"Right!" Bonnie spun back to Jasmine. "What good is that? They're all just jumping off a cliff."

245

"I prefer to think of this as a psychiatric ward," Jasmine countered. "The past is a haunting ghost that keeps them from being happy here, so I medicate them with forgetfulness. Would you take away their eternal happiness by telling them they will toil in meaningless labor forever? I don't believe my father would have."

Billy kept his gaze on the statue. The image of a heroic figure riding high in the air reminded him of something, something he had read in *Fama Regis*. The connection finally registered. Yes! Captain Autarkeia had to be him! The first murdered dragon, and a king at that. Of course he was the founder! Billy focused on Jasmine again, half closing one eye. "Does Makaidos mean anything to you?"

The color in Jasmine's face drained away. "Makaidos? Where did you hear that name?"

Billy smiled, trying not to sound too triumphant. "I'm glad you recognized it as a name. It was your father's dragon name."

Jasmine's cheeks turned from white to red. She shook her finger at Billy again, screaming, "Memories are poison! You will pay for spreading it in my town! I'll see to that!" She stormed out of the building and slammed the door.

Bonnie jumped up and down, clapping her hands. "Way to go, Billy!"

Sarah kissed Billy on the forehead. "I have never seen anyone fluster her before."

Billy felt a blush in his cheeks. "Maybe. But she's definitely out to get me now."

Bonnie pulled Sarah's ring from her pocket and laid it in her palm. "You've got to believe us now. Merlin gave Billy this ring to give to you." She dropped it into Sarah's hand. "Will you wear it to the theatre? Your husband is waiting for you."

Sarah slipped the ring onto her finger. "I'll go out the back way." As she shuffled to the door, she smiled back at them.

"This is so exciting! I feel like I'm on a blind date to my own wedding!"

As the rear doors swung shut, Billy laughed. He put an arm around Bonnie's shoulders and turned her toward the window. His smile faded. Out in the streets of Dragons' Rest were a thousand thirsty souls. And besides them, a small audience patiently waited in a dark room in a theatre just a few blocks away. They were counting on him.

Billy opened the front door. "I'm going straight to the statue. Everyone's sure to see me up there."

Bonnie placed both hands on Billy's cheeks and looked him in the eye. "You'll be great. Everyone will listen to you." Her skin felt as cool as ice water, but her words seemed to travel through her hands and set fire to his heart.

They exited the bookstore together and marched toward the center island, maneuvering through the stream of people. A high-pitched peal of laughter cut through the chatter, and a chill prickled Billy's neck. At the base of the statue, Jasmine stood with the constable. She glanced away from him, and her eyes locked on Billy's. Her wide smile melted.

"Trouble," Billy murmured. "Do you want to come with me or head back to the theatre?"

"Is that a serious question?" Bonnie smiled. "Lead the way. I'm right behind you."

Billy edged between a peddler and a man on stilts, then headed for an open space, checking over his shoulder every few seconds to make sure Bonnie was keeping up. After stepping around a blanket, he halted and looked back. No Bonnie. He retraced his steps, pushing past a juggler and spilling his collection of flying fruit. He finally caught sight of Bonnie, her arm clutched by a young man wearing knickers and black suspenders. Brogan!

247

"Let me go!" Bonnie hissed.

"I just want to talk to you for a minute. My sister said—"

"Let her go!" Billy ordered, loud enough to make several heads turn. He strode forward and jerked Brogan's arm down. "Don't touch her again."

Brogan took two steps back and jerked the cap off his head, his voice trembling. "I meant no harm, Sir. I assure you my intent is honorable. I just wanted to deliver a message."

Billy stepped in front of Bonnie. "Then deliver it to me."

Brogan backed away another step. He lowered his gaze, shifting his weight nervously as he threaded the edge of his cap through his fingers. "I told my sister that you suggested the marbles, and she was so happy, she wanted me to find you and thank you."

Bonnie stepped around Billy and stood at his side. "But the marbles were your idea, not mine."

248

"Oh, no, Miss." He dug into his pocket, then withdrew his hand, his fist still closed. "I said that an angel whispered the idea in my ear, and I wasn't lying. You see, I used to have this dream every night that someone who looks just like you comes up to me and asks me to play marbles. But I was too busy for such nonsense. The dream always ended the same way. I'm holding a bunch of flowers and a ruddy silver dollar, and I just go about my business and leave her crying."

Bonnie's lips parted, but she didn't make a sound.

"Today," Brogan continued, "you told me that I had a silver dollar in my hand. How could anyone know that but the angel in my dream?" He nodded at Bonnie's necklace. "The angel wore the same beads, to be sure." His gaze wandered to just above her head. "And now that I know who you really are, I can see your halo."

Murmurs rippled through the crowd. Dozens had gathered around and were now listening to the conversation.

Brogan extended his trembling fist, his eyes welling with tears. "Heavenly angel," he said, his voice shaking with passion. "What am I holding now?"

Bonnie lifted her necklace, fingering each bead as she passed it through her hand. Finally, she slipped her palm under his fist. "A blue bead."

Brogan slowly straightened his fingers and dropped a shining blue bead into her hand. "Yes, dear angel," he said, dimples hollowing his cheeks. "I will play marbles with you."

A gasp erupted from the crowd, then a shout. "I see it! I see the halo!" The people began pushing in, the mass of bodies pressing heavily. As Billy and Brogan formed a shield around Bonnie, more shouts confirmed sightings of her halo.

"Stop!" Billy shouted. "Get back!"

Brogan lifted his hands and waved at the crowd. "You'll hurt the angel. Back away!"

The pressure eased a bit, but the throng of people still roared—buzzing, shouting, some even crying.

Bonnie leaned over and whispered into Billy's ear. "No time like the present."

Cupping his hands around his mouth, Billy shouted, "Listen to me everyone!" But he couldn't seem to make a dent in the noise.

Brogan squatted and pointed at his back. "Up you go now!"

Billy straddled Brogan's shoulders and balanced himself while the young man straightened his body. When Billy looked over the sea of faces, he immediately caught sight of Jasmine arguing with five or six townspeople. That was exactly what he needed. Bonnie's miracle just might be the distraction to keep Jasmine at bay.

As Billy shifted his body to get more comfortable, he prayed for the right words. The din slowly ebbed, every eye focusing

249

on him. "You have all heard of The Waiting Room," he began, his voice much stronger than he expected. "And most of you have probably heard about the deliverer some have been waiting for. After all these years, that deliverer has finally come to the theatre, and he will lead the way to the new world for all who wish to go." Billy glanced at the clock. "The door to the new world will close in less than an hour, so I urge you to come. When the deliverer leaves, this world will be no more."

"He speaks the truth!" a woman called out. It was Constance, her lovely face beaming. "I saw him enter the theatre before noon, and he drew the curtains aside. The screen shows another world, and it's filled with beauty and wonder." She extended her folded hands. "I came here to beg you to join us in the theatre. There isn't much time left."

"Liar!" Jasmine pushed her way through the crowd and pointed a finger at Billy. "You have come to destroy us. We are safe here, but you would lead us into a world of dragons and demons, of wars and floods, of rape and theft and murder." She shook her finger at him. "Do you deny it?"

Billy glanced around at the expectant faces in the crowd. How could he deny it? His own world was full of evil, exactly as she described it. But how could he explain that it was better than a life of worthless repetition?

As Jasmine's anger settled into satisfaction, a devious smile bent her lips. She had nailed Billy, and she knew it. She crossed her arms over her chest, a cold stare matching her icy voice. "As you can see, my friends, he doesn't deny it. He is not a deliverer. He is a destroyer who has come with his demonic soothsayer, to beguile you all."

New murmurs scattered through the crowd, arguments lobbing back and forth. "She's right. . . . No, there has to be a deliverer . . . Maybe she is a demon. . . . She can't be; she has a halo."

Billy shouted over the noise. "If I were a destroyer, I would have denied her claims right away, but I am not a liar like she is. There is evil in the new world, but I need you to go there to battle against the evil forces that threaten to destroy us."

Jasmine paced in front of Billy and Brogan, waving her arms. "Why should we go to your world and battle your evil? We're safe right where we are! We live in peace and contentment."

"But what good is it to live in peace if you're living a lie? You just repeat everything over and over, because you're scared to see what you really are. If you would just . . ."

Billy paused and repeated his words to himself. *See what you really are.* He slowly curled his ringless fingers and held up his fist. "Listen! Have you ever wondered why you wear the dragon's eye? Look into the gem right now, and tell me what you see." He waited while every head dipped down to look. Jasmine maintained a defiant glare at Billy.

Billy shouted again. "What do you see?"

Brogan yelled from underneath Billy. "I see a dragon!"

An old lady in a shawl echoed him. A young woman holding a box of popcorn cried out, "So do I! What does it mean?"

The crowd fell silent. Billy shifted again, wondering if Brogan could hold him up much longer. Jasmine held her tongue, allowing him to speak. "Search your memories. You were all once dragons in my world, but when it became cursed, evil forces killed most of your race, and your spirits now rest here waiting for the deliverer. The reason you've been taught to ignore the past is so you won't remember what you are. Yes, it helps you live here in peace, but the truth will show you the way to a better life."

Jasmine pointed a long finger at Billy. "And if we were really dragons, who killed us, pray tell? Humans, like yourself?"

251

"Yes, humans did the killing, but they were corrupted humans, not—"

"Did you hear that?" she yelled, raising her hands above her head. "He claims that his kind killed you and banished your souls here." She spat on the ground at Brogan's feet. "You know our law against false prophets, but some gullible fools have already forgotten it and the prophecy I announced when the clock struck one today.

They call you dragons, dead and lost.
In circles now you toil and swirl.
The very ones who slew your race
Have come to lead you to their world.

They cast your bodies to the void,
And now your souls they wish to claim.
Reject these fiends and send them back
To hell's abode from whence they came.

"And now here they are, just as I predicted, and the little she-devil is performing false signs and wonders to get you to fall into their trap!"

"The mayor's right!" A tall lady shook a collapsed umbrella. "I heard her prophesy those very words."

Loud rumbles arose from the crowd, punctuated by angry shouts, rising in volume like the barking of watchdogs.

"No!" Billy shouted, waving his hands. "I'm telling the truth. She's the one who's lying." The noise of the mob grew louder. Billy motioned for Brogan to let him down. When his feet settled, he yelled as loud as he could. "Anyone who wants to come to the new world, follow me!"

Billy took Bonnie's hand and marched away double-time, enduring insults that seemed to pierce their backs like poison-tipped arrows.

"Devils! False prophets! Kill them!"

"It's getting too rough," Billy said to Bonnie. "I'll come back when I know you're safe."

Brogan kept pace alongside, glancing to the rear. "I don't think anyone is following us yet. In fact, I think they are planning a rough going-away party, but that was one rousing speech you gave."

Billy really wanted to look back, but he knew better. Jasmine's poisonous words gave him a sick feeling. He imagined a Joan-of-Arc-type pyre, complete with a burning stake and mounds of kindling all around, he and Bonnie tied back to back with tongues of fire licking their feet.

Billy shook the picture from his mind and kept his pace strong and consistent. It wouldn't help for him to show anything but complete confidence.

"I'm glad you're coming," Bonnie said to Brogan. "Your mother's already there."

"Yes, I know. She goes to the theatre every day. I always thought it silly, but I never told her so, out of respect, you understand."

When they reached the theatre, Billy stepped up to the doorway and stopped, balling his hand into a fist. "We don't have our rings. Think we can get in?"

Bonnie reached her hand toward the doorway, but Billy grabbed her wrist. "No! Let me!" With a slow extension of his lower leg, he pushed his shoe toward the opening. Just as the toe met the plane, it stopped. He then pressed his palm on the doorway, and it flattened as though he were pushing against a wall. "It's not an energy field or anything. It's like a solid barrier."

253

Brogan stepped in front of the door. "I have a ring. I'll try it." With a confident stride, he marched right through the door, then turned and looked back. "Now that's a brilliant device. The very people who are supposed to go through are left out in the cold." He twisted his ring. "Here, I'll toss mine back, and we'll go through one at a time." He pulled, stretching his finger until his face turned bright red. "It won't . . . budge."

Still pulling, he walked back outside. "There," he said, sliding his ring off. "It's easy on this side of the door." Pinching the ring, he extended it to Bonnie. "Shall we let the lady enter?"

Bonnie raised both hands. "No. I'm staying with Billy. We'll figure out a way together."

Brogan tried to push the ring into her palm, but Bonnie jerked her hand away. "I said no. That's your ring, and—"

"Excuse me," a strong voice called out.

Billy swung around. It was Bonnie's Bat Masterson.

He tipped his bowler, adding a polite bow. "I have come to the theatre, as you suggested. I have long pondered the meaning of life in this village, and everything you said makes perfect sense to me." He nodded at Bonnie. "But it was this lass who melted my heart."

"How? I didn't say a word to you."

"Nevertheless, I felt as though you were pulling on my arm, begging me to come with you. A tiny voice cried out in my mind, 'Please listen to me.'" He bowed his head. "So I listened, and here I am."

Billy swept an arm toward the door. "Then go inside and wait. I'll be in there as soon as I can."

He took off his hat and held it at his waist. "There are others who wish to join us, but the crowd has been stirred by Jasmine's evil tongue, and they are holding captive all who wish to go to the theatre. I was able to come, because I did not verbalize my intent."

Brogan nudged Bat with an elbow. "Mr. Collins, these two need rings to get in. If they don't enter the theatre, then all is lost."

"Said is as good as done." Mr. Collins pulled off his ring, and he and Brogan presented theirs to Billy and Bonnie.

Billy waved his hands at the rings. "No. Without your rings, you're stuck here. I can't let you make that sacrifice."

"It is no sacrifice," Mr. Collins said. "Without these rings, you cannot enter, and if you cannot enter, we are all lost."

Billy kept his hands raised. "Look, it's really great that you'd do that, but there's got to be another way. We didn't come this far to be beaten just because we're missing a ring or two." He ran his fingers through his hair, clutching it as he gazed at their willing faces. "Okay, I need one of you to go inside and make sure everyone knows what's going on so they don't worry about us, and I need the other one to go with me in case I need help to rescue the people who want to come to the theatre."

"I'm going with you." Brogan straightened his cap. "I'm younger and faster."

"I don't suppose I can argue with that." Mr. Collins pulled a chain and withdrew his pocket watch. "Only thirty minutes to go. Arguing would waste precious time." He nodded and slipped his ring back on. "Godspeed to you all."

255

THE SACRIFICE

K aren broke through the edge of the forest and crossed the deserted street, walking cautiously between Marilyn and Shiloh as they followed the professor and Carl toward the front entrance of the visitor center. Up above, nine dragons flew in tight circles over the lake, six with riders, who, for the most part, seemed comfortable on their spiny mounts, their commands echoing on the lake as they piloted the magnificent, shimmering creatures.

A black stream shot through the sky, then another. Karen paused and searched for the source of the stream. There, near the edge of the forest! A Watcher. Two of them! Three! The winged demons soared through the early morning haze, firing rivers of darkness at the dragons. With pinpoint turns and sudden dives, two dragons flying in tandem dodged the missiles, one launching an inferno at the lead Watcher just before plummeting toward the lake.

The demon darted out of the way, and the dragon's blast knifed into the water, sending up a plume of steam. Streams of fire and darkness zipped across the sky, dragons and Watchers fighting in chaotic turmoil.

Barlow's voice resonated over the water. "Edmund! Tell the dragons to fall back and regroup!"

A shrill whistle pierced the furious commotion, first a warbling, flute-like sound, then a blitz of screeches punching the air in short bursts. Like show planes flying in a precision drill, the dragons swept upward and formed a line, each one firing back at the Watchers to create a wall of flames.

Karen felt a hand on her back. "Now, Karen," Marilyn whispered as she swept past. "Mr. Foley is waving for us."

Karen jerked her head around and dashed forward, running as fast as she could to keep pace with Marilyn and Shiloh. As they closed in on the visitor center, she saw the professor and Carl on the wooden deck that skirted the center, hiding with their backs against a wall to the right of the entry.

258

The professor raised a finger to his lips, and Carl signaled for everyone to stay low. The girls slowed to a jog, hunching and padding as quietly as they could on the planked walkway that stretched from the parking lot to the deck.

As they approached, the professor whispered, "There's a guard at the door, an especially ugly beast with black wings." He withdrew Excalibur from its scabbard. "I will entice him into battle. When the door opens, you three sneak inside. Be as quiet as you can. Though they won't be able to see you, they likely can still hear you."

With the sounds of combat raging overhead, Professor Hamilton lit up Excalibur. Holding the sword vertically, he stepped in front of the door.

Shiloh stayed close to Marilyn as she inched around the corner next to the door. Karen tiptoed behind them, trying to ignore the awful screeches in the sky. The glass door flew open, and the black-winged demon glided out, a wrinkled smirk cracking his face. "Do you think that little toy can hurt me?"

Karen froze at the sound of his nails-on-chalkboard voice. Marilyn sneaked past the Watcher, spun around, and gestured for the girls to follow. Shiloh grabbed Karen's hand, pulling her so hard she almost toppled over.

The professor kept his gaze locked on the demon. "Feel free to stand there and mock me, you foul devil. I await your move."

Staring at the demon's hideous face, Karen tiptoed beside Shiloh, holding her breath as they passed. Marilyn pressed a finger against her lips and shepherded them into the center's foyer. As the door clacked shut, Karen spun around. The Watcher stalked directly toward Professor Hamilton.

259

Tightening his grip on the sword, he swept the beam across the demon's waist, slicing through it like a knife through Jell-O. Karen leaped backwards to dodge the beam as it blazed through the glass door and into the visitor center. The Watcher let out an ear-shattering screech and lumbered closer to the professor, still intact. Suddenly, Carl lunged at the Watcher and tackled him to the ground.

Marilyn grabbed Karen's hand. "Let's go," she whispered urgently. "We have work to do."

Karen began to follow but caught a glimpse of the professor and Mr. Foley running away from the entry, a dazed Watcher stumbling after them. When they disappeared from sight, she turned her attention to Marilyn. The older woman crept along the hall with furtive steps, pausing at intervals to spray something onto the floor from a tiny aerosol bottle. As Karen followed, she noticed a flowery scent, pungent and sweet. She wrinkled her nose. Was it perfume?

A huge display room dominated the upper floor of the center, providing no place to house prisoners. Marilyn tiptoed through the room and down a flight of stairs at the back, spraying the perfume every few steps. In spite of the dread crawling across her skin, Karen kept urging herself forward. "Girl power," she kept repeating to herself. But with Mr. Foley and the professor fighting a powerful demon right outside the door, and male knights and female dragons in heated battle up above, her rally cry seemed kind of silly. They were all in this together. Karen firmed her chin. Now it was time for her to do her part.

W alter rocked his head back and forth, trying to open his eyes, but his lids kept fluttering closed. A cool sensation bathed his forehead, like water trickling from a spring. Finally, he forced his lids up and held them open. His blurred vision slowly sharpened, the shape of a woman's face becoming clearer and clearer.

"Mom?"

"Yes, I'm here." She dipped a cloth into a basin of water and squeezed a few drops on his forehead, then gently wiped his face. "He's coming around, Pebbles. Can you get another ice cube?"

Walter heard the patter of shoes, then a halt, then the patter returning. "No more ice," a little girl's voice announced.

"That's okay, honey. This will be enough. Just go sit with your book. I'll read to you in a minute."

The sweet massage continued, the scent of his mother's subtle cologne making him feel like a little kid again. "The Watchers don't give us much," she explained. "Just whatever they can steal from the vending machines, crackers and ice chips mostly."

Walter's memory snapped back to life. "The Watchers!" He pushed the cloth away and bolted to a sitting position. His head ached and the whole world spun, but he managed to clamber to his feet, shifting his weight back and forth and spreading his arms to keep his balance. "Where are we?"

"The Deep Creek Lake Discovery Center." She laid a hand on a four-foot-wide metallic box. "Locked in the furnace room, apparently."

Walter grabbed a ladder leaning against the wall and braced his body. He opened a gray fuse box, then slapped it shut again. "Anything around to pry open the door?"

"No. I tried a broomstick and a paint scraper, but they both snapped." She pointed to a broom handle on the floor next to a mop, a bucket, and a jug of Mr. Clean.

With the room still spinning, Walter sat down on the floor and buried his face in his hands. His legs and arms tingled as if every limb had fallen asleep and needed a good massage to wake up.

He felt his mother's touch on his shoulder. "Just rest, sweetheart. You probably have a concussion."

Bare fluorescent tubes flickered from the ceiling, casting a dancing white light that filtered between Walter's fingers. "I can't rest." He watched a tiny roach skitter through the dust near the furnace. "I mean, who's going to find us here? Nobody even knows where we are."

His mother's voice stayed calm and reassuring. "God knows where we are."

"Okay, you got me there." He lowered his hands and looked his mom in the eye. "I have faith and all that, but you know me. I'm the kind of guy who prays with his sword drawn."

She gently stroked the back of his head. "You and your father both." She sighed and took his hands in hers, gripping them firmly. "These hands will do great things, Walter. I can't believe God would craft such powerful tools, inflame a heart with godly passion, and then leave his handiwork locked and unused in a roach-infested closet."

"That's a cool speech, Mom. Thanks."

"I practiced it while you were out cold."

The doorknob rattled. As the hinges squeaked and light poured into the room, Walter squinted through the dimness. A Watcher filled the doorway, clutching a leash that led to a huge, menacing dog.

The demon—Walter recognized Samyaza immediately—stomped inside and pointed a clawed finger at him. "Morgan wants to see you. Follow me."

Still dizzy from the blow to his head, Walter stumbled through the hallway, following Samyaza and the dog. In his muddled vision, the demon seemed to bounce, like it was riding a hobbyhorse or playing hopscotch. As they passed by a staircase, Walter caught a glimpse of a shadow on the landing above. He slowed and strained his eyes. Was someone coming, or had he imagined the shadow? Samyaza flung open a door and barked, "Get in there. Morgan will be here soon."

Marilyn and the girls reached a landing and paused. The stairs reversed direction and descended to the lower floor. At the bottom, a Watcher with a leashed, multicolored dog at his side slammed a door to the left of the stairway.

Marilyn pushed herself and the girls against the wall and flattened her body. Karen held her breath and pressed herself back as hard as she could. As the Watcher strolled past the stairwell, the dog's head perked up, its blue and red ears twitching. It looked directly at the women and stalled, a low growl rumbling from its throat. The Watcher jerked the leash. "Keep moving. There's nothing here."

The dog resisted, whining. It hung out its rainbow tongue, then barked, but the demon kept pulling it forward. "Yes, I smell it, too. Morgan's hostiam is wearing perfume." When it passed out of sight, Marilyn led the girls to the bottom of the stairs and peeked around the corner. Karen, standing on tiptoes one step above, stretched herself over Marilyn's head and peeked with her. The Watcher and the dog passed by another demon standing next to a windowless door on the left. After the two demons exchanged a string of odd words, the dog and its handler entered an office just beyond the guarded room and closed the door.

Marilyn crouched on the bottom stair, and the two girls leaned into a close huddle. She laid a hand on the back of each girl and whispered so softly, Karen could barely hear her. "Good job. Stay strong. Keep praying." She stood again and gestured with her head for them to follow.

263

Marilyn edged forward. The guard demon's red eyes scanned the corridor. His head nearly touched the ceiling, and white armor covered his muscular physique. Karen gulped. What a monster! It definitely needed one more piece of armor, a helmet to cover its vampire teeth and ugly scowl.

Marilyn walked right past the guard. She knocked on the outside of the door, then backed away.

The Watcher put a hand on the knob. "What do you want in there?"

Marilyn reached into her pocket and drew out her roll of tape. She sneaked up and knocked again.

"Be quiet!" the demon barked.

Marilyn peeled off three strips of tape and stuck them to her arm. She knocked a third time.

The demon jammed a key into the lock and threw the door open. "Be quiet, or you'll get no food or water tonight!"

Reaching underneath the Watcher's arm, Marilyn pressed the strips of tape over the latch. Then, pulling the little bottle out of her pocket, she sprayed a mist into the air and backed away. The Watcher sniffed, swiveling his head from side to side.

Nausea rumbled in Karen's stomach, worse than the air-sickness on *Merlin II*. What was Mrs. Bannister up to? Wouldn't the smell give them all away? Karen covered her mouth, knowing that spilling her guts would mean their deaths.

The Watcher, still sniffing like a curious beagle, closed the door and walked right past Marilyn, Shiloh, and Karen. He stopped at the bottom of the stairs. After looking both ways in the hall, he took a long sniff and climbed the steps, disappearing from sight.

264

"Come on," Marilyn whispered. "Mrs. Foley and Pebbles are in there." She pushed the door open, and the three slipped inside.

Brogan led the way, running along a deserted street, then darting into an alley strewn with vegetable crates and various wilted greenery, mostly lettuce and carrot greens. Breathless, he leaned against a dirty wall, his gaze uplifted.

Billy followed his line of sight. "The roof?"

Brogan nodded. "We wouldn't want to march right into their clutches now, would we?" He grabbed a crate and threw it on top of a larger one, then stepped up. Billy handed him another, and together they fashioned a staircase to the roof.

Brogan tested it, marching quickly to the top, then back down again. It shook a bit, but it seemed stable enough. "Ladies first," he said to Bonnie. "We'll catch you if you fall."

Bonnie took the first two steps, but the staircase wobbled. Billy placed both hands on the precarious crate to secure it. "If I had my wings," she said, "I'd fly us all up there."

Brogan laughed. "Oh, the angel has wings now, does she?"

"You'd be surprised." Bonnie made her way to the top, then looked back down, bracing her hands on her knees. "Next?"

Billy, then Brogan, hurried to the roof. "You see"—Brogan pointed toward the town square—"we can make it all the way to the constabulary without going down again."

A throng still knotted the village hub, and unintelligible shouts rose to their ears. "I don't like the looks of it," Billy said, "but we'd better get going. Time's running out."

Zigzagging from roof to roof, sometimes sidestepping along narrow ledges, they snaked their way to the roof of the constabulary. From there, the scene below was quite clear. Jasmine stood before the raging crowd, spitting venomous rhetoric. Ten people, five of them ladies, sat in the midst of a tight circle of men, their knees pulled up to their chests. Billy recognized Constance in the group of prisoners.

A woman near the front of the crowd pointed at the roof. "There they are!"

Jasmine spun around and looked up, smiling. "I knew you'd come back! Couldn't bear to miss the excitement, could you?"

Billy glanced at the clock. Twenty minutes left. "What are you going to do with these people?"

Jasmine spread her arm toward the captives. "When the clock strikes three, we'll let them go, but for now we want to shield these fools from you and your march to destruction."

Billy instinctively reached for his missing sword, but his hand swiped at air. The lack of a weapon sparked a memory, several lines of Merlin's poem.

A warrior comes with sword and shield,
With truth and faith in hand,
Exposing lies and cutting through
The darkness in the land.

Has eye not seen, has ear not heard,
The love that sets men free?
From scales to flesh he softens hearts;
From red to white he bleeds.

Like a symphony of trumpeted words, all of Merlin's prophecies came roaring back into his mind, so fast it sounded like an auctioneer's voice played at double speed. Still, Billy comprehended every word, and now, for the first time, he understood what the poems had been trying to tell him for so long. Ever since his father had returned to his dragon form, he felt like he lost his dad, and the abyss in the seventh circle led him even farther away, ripping his father's body from his soul. Billy's search had consumed him ever since, but now he had to let it go. Jared Bannister had to decide his fate on his own.

Ten sad faces in the circle of captives stared up at Billy, quiet and expectant. Each face represented an eternity of meaningless existence. Besides him, they had no other hope of salvation.

Billy clenched a fist. There was simply no choice. It was time for him to give up everything for the sake of these lost souls who had nothing. He took a deep breath and let it out slowly. "I'll make a trade with you."

"A trade?" Jasmine whispered something to a man who then promptly dashed into the constabulary. She looked at Billy again, wincing at the sunshine. "I'm listening."

266

"For your part," he said, pointing at the corralled people, "let them go to the theatre, and give me a dragon's eye ring from one of your followers."

The man returned from the constabulary carrying a rope with a hangman's noose fastened on the end. Jasmine took the rope and slid the knot up and down. "And for your part?"

Billy gulped. A strange tingling sensation tickled his neck. He took a deep breath and pointed his thumb at his chest. "You can have me."

Jasmine waved her arm at the circle of captives. "You will trade places with these?"

He gazed at their faces. A few of them shook their heads, obviously disapproving of the deal. Constance stood and gazed at him, her eyes wide and adoring.

Billy firmed his chin. "I will trade."

"Agreed." Jasmine took a ring from the man who had brought the noose and tossed it toward the roof. Billy snatched it out of the air and reached for Bonnie's hand, but she jerked away. "Billy, what do you think you're doing?"

"Saving souls." He grabbed her wrist and forced the ring over her knuckle. With shaking hands he pushed his fingers through her hair and intertwined them behind her head. "Do you know how many times you've told me to trust you?"

Bonnie's lips trembled, her halo glistening in the sun. She nodded slowly.

"Well, I'm asking you to trust me now." He turned and clutched Brogan's arm. "You two will lead these captives to the theatre. As soon as you can, get everyone on stage as close to the red screen as possible. If I understand all this prophecy stuff, if I can get the people to believe who this prophetess really is and how she's been keeping the truth from them, maybe they'll come with me. Maybe I won't have to die after all."

"And then what?" Bonnie asked.

He hugged Bonnie and whispered in her ear. "I think the Great Key screen will turn white, but if I'm not there to lead everyone through it, you'll have to. And if I do have to die . . ." He pulled back, his arms aching to hold her forever. "I'll see you in heaven."

Bonnie's voice cracked. "I . . . understand."

Billy glanced around the surface of the roof. "Can you two get down?"

"Yes." Brogan bounded to the next building and pulled up a trap door. "My florist shop is right underneath."

Billy noted the time again. Fifteen minutes to go. "Hurry! Go now! I'll get down another way."

268

Bonnie and Brogan hustled down a ladder. The door dropped closed behind them with a thud. Seconds later, they ran out the florist shop, Brogan waving his arm at the prisoners. "Follow us! Hurry!"

The ring of men split apart, allowing the prisoners to leave, one strapping man carrying an old lady as they hustled down the street. Constance sidestepped the crowd and lingered, looking up at Billy.

Jasmine spread out her arms. "As you see, I have completed my part of the bargain." Two men draped the hangman's rope over the statue of Captain Autarkeia. The noose swung freely about six feet off the ground.

Billy walked to the edge of the roof. "Why did you trust me? I could still run away."

"Because I . . ." She looked back at the crowd.

Billy jumped to an awning and slid down to the end of its canvas, launching outward like a ski jumper. Bending his knees, he landed deftly on both feet directly in front of Jasmine, then glared at her, speaking softly. "Because you knew I'd keep my word." He raised his voice to a shout. "She knew I'd keep my word. And why? Because I tell the truth. I'm not a liar like she is."

New murmurs rushed through the crowd. Jasmine's henchmen grabbed Billy and hustled him to the center island. The stoutest of her gang pulled the noose lower and draped it around Billy's neck, giving it a tug to make it tight. Another man, smelling of tobacco and cheap wine, tied his wrists together behind him.

From his higher vantage point, Billy could see a lone man in front of the bookstore, bending his tall frame to lock the door. Billy drew in a breath to shout to his dad, but the rope cut his air supply, squeezing off his yelp. His shoes lifted into the air. He stretched his feet, trying to get his toes to touch the ground, but it was just out of reach. The rope knifed into his skin. Pressure flooded his head, pounding his skull. His lungs demanded air. His chest heaved. His whole body felt like it was on fire.

Jasmine shouted over the crowd's growing buzz. "You heard him agree to give himself over to me. As your mayor, because of our law condemning the oracles of fire, I have sentenced him to death by hanging."

"No!" Constance jumped up to the island and grabbed Billy's legs, propping him up. "You can't do this! He's had no trial!"

Billy gasped for breath. The rope relaxed, and precious gulps of air filled his lungs. Constance pushed him higher, her strength more than he guessed it could be. The smelly hangman lunged at her, but a taller man came out of nowhere and threw him to the side. The tall man then grabbed the stout hangman by the nape of the neck and tossed him to the street, sending

269

him tumbling across the cobblestones. Billy's rescuer shoved Jasmine with his fingertips. She fell backwards and landed heavily on her seat. Several in the crowd applauded, some making catcalls.

While Constance kept her stranglehold on Billy's legs, another pair of hands lifted the noose, freeing Billy from its painful grip. His body slipped downward, and he found himself face-to-face with Constance, her fairy-like eyes blazing with passion. For a brief second, a flash of familiarity brushed his mind, but when a masculine voice spoke from behind he swept the memory aside. "You may have won a few more converts, Billy. You'd better lead them to the theatre."

Billy spun around and looked up into the eyes of his father. "Dad?"

Reginald patted him on the back. "I am not convinced of that yet, young man, but, madman or not, I knew I had to stop a murder." His deep brown eyes glistened. "And now I'm ready to see what is playing at the theatre."

Billy wanted to embrace him, to wrap his arms around his muscular frame and welcome his dad back into his heart, but he couldn't. Not yet. Not until Dad's memory returned. Not until he knew for sure that he was Jared Bannister.

Billy jumped down from the island, rubbing his neck. Jasmine scooted back, her eyes wide with terror, but Billy passed her by and waved to the crowd. "We have to hurry. If you want to go to the new world, follow me." Dozens of new converts gathered around, whistling and shouting, and they all turned toward the theatre.

"Wait!" Constance hooked her arm through Billy's and nodded at Reginald. "You lead everyone to the theatre. Billy needs a ring to enter, and I know where to get one that no one else needs."

270

Reginald turned slowly, glancing back at her before calling out, "Follow me!" The mass of believers hustled down the narrow road, while the rest, muttering curses and insults, filtered toward the other buildings, leaving soiled blankets and spilled food strewn across the square.

Billy pulled his arm away from Constance. "We have to hurry. Where's the ring?"

"I have it right here." Constance reached into her dress pocket and gazed into Billy's eyes. For a brief moment, that flash of familiarity returned, a glimpse of feigned innocence in her nymphean eyes. "Don't you remember me?" she asked.

Billy took a step back. "Naamah?"

Her appearance changed again, this time altering to the slender wraith Billy saw with Morgan in the third circle, the black-hearted sister who obeyed Morgan's every command.

"Elaine?" Billy lurched to the side, but Elaine's vise-grip fingers wrenched his shirt. Her eyes flashed with malevolence, red and shining like bloody lasers.

A sharp pain jolted Billy's senses, a horrible pain. His head drooped. The hilt of a dagger protruded from his chest, her delicate fingers wrapped around it. Elaine, an unearthly smile on her face, drove it farther in, piercing his heart, her sleeve sliding up to reveal a scar around her wrist. Her words spat out, each one punctuated with venom as she twisted her grip. "Nobody . . . turns . . . me . . . down."

Billy fell backwards, his hands groping for the dagger, gasping and gurgling. As a curtain of red fog filtered into his eyes, he grasped the hilt and pulled it out. Warm liquid spilled over his hands. His mind seemed to drain away, sinking between the cobblestones under his back, then a sense of floating took over, as though strong arms had lifted him from the street. The red mist changed slowly to white. Then, darkness.

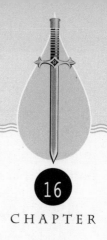

16

CHAPTER

RETURN OF
THE DRAGON

The door slammed behind Walter. As the room swirled
around his dizzy brain, he braced himself on the doorframe. A strange mix of tables and machines seemed to orbit a
. . . a person?

A pair of strong arms latched around his chest. "C'mon,
Walter," a female voice said. "There's a chair over here."

Giving up some of his weight to the support, he let his feet
drag.

"Oof! You're heavy."

The voice finally registered in Walter's mind. He tried to
hold his head erect. "Ashley?"

"Glad to hear you still know me." Tender fingers searched
through his hair. "I've been praying like crazy that you survived
the fall. What did you do? Knock yourself out?"

"Just the usual stuff." His voice sounded as dizzy as his head. "Falling out of airplanes, paddling in a broken crate through miles of ice water, duking it out with a demon. You know. A normal day at the office. . . . And you?"

Ashley laughed, her fingers moving to the back of Walter's head. "Oh, here it is. You have a class A-one knot back there, boy."

"And it was my first day as a sailor. Not bad, huh?"

As Ashley caressed the lump, his vision seemed to improve, each second bringing her worried face more clearly into focus. The room stopped spinning, and even the stabbing headache changed to a tolerable throb.

"Well," she replied, "I guess you can say I've been working for the devil. Not that I'm enjoying it."

"Oh, yeah. The candlestone. Did you get Devin out yet?"

"No, but everything's ready to go." Ashley pulled her hands away and set them on her hips. "Morgan's coming to attend the grand restoration."

"In Shelly's body?"

"Yeah. It'll be weird for you seeing your sister like that. I hope you can take it."

Walter rubbed his head. "I think at this point, I can take almost anything."

The door opened again, and Shelly shuffled in, her head down. Now in a black dress, she looked like a widow at a graveside. With her hands folded in front of her, she lifted her head, a look of complete shame covering her face. "Walter, I'm so sorry! She's making me do these things. I wish I had never—"

Shelly's head snapped back. Her eyes rolled upward, leaving only the whites showing. Clutching her chest and gasping, her eyes slowly rolled back in place, her pupils now dark red. She croaked, "Welcome, Walter." Her voice was sort of like Shelly's,

274

only deeper and rough. "Since you put Devin in the candle-stone, I thought it appropriate to invite you to his welcome home party."

Walter seethed. A hundred snappy comebacks rolled through his mind, but each one died on his lips. Heat burned in his chest and rose up into his throat, his head ready to explode. He looked past that familiar face and saw the evil sorceress behind the curtain, a demon who held captive the mind of his sister. He saw Morgan Le Faye for the hideous creature she really was.

The anger that had built ever since he first received word of Shelly's capture seethed inside him. The volcano finally erupted. "Get out of my sister!" Walter screamed. He rushed for Morgan, grabbed her shoulders, and pressed his nose against hers. "I see you in there, you cowardly witch! You pick on little girls, but when you have to face a man you hide behind the skirts of a college coed!" He raised a fist and shook it. "Come out and fight me. I'm not afraid of you!"

"You think I'm stupid enough to fall for your little taunt?" Morgan smiled and patted him on the cheek. "Come now, Walter, give your new and improved sister a little more credit than that." She pulled free from his grasp. With a sweep of her long, silky dress, she glided to a glass door at the outer wall of the room and raised the blinds. "I will give you the fight you want soon enough, but first I must make a larger door for Devin's escape." Placing her hands on each jamb, she pushed against the wall. Two streams of black smoke poured through her nostrils and adhered to the glass like dark textured paint. Morgan backed away several tottering steps, then fell on her seat. With a resounding crash, the wall, the door, and a window exploded. Glass, plaster, and cinder blocks crumbled to dust and shards. The black smoke retreated and coalesced into a cloud before streaming back into Shelly's nostrils.

On the other side of the hole, a gravel path wound toward the lake. In the distance, dragons and Watchers darted in and out across the sky. A handful of humans scurried about, but they were too far away to recognize.

"That should be large enough for a dragon." Shelly's body rose from the floor and dusted herself off. "Now, Ashley, let's get on with it."

Ashley crossed her arms and set her feet. "Release Mrs. Foley and Pebbles first."

Morgan glided toward Ashley, a smile belying her blazing eyes. "Removing your incentive to get Devin out would be rather foolhardy of me, don't you think?" She stopped, the fire in her pupils dying down. "But I see your point. You believe I would kill all my captives once you've done my bidding, so what would it profit you to continue?" She picked up a glass lens from the table and flipped it in the air like a coin. "We seem to be at an unfortunate impasse." She caught the lens in her palm. "How about, 'Heads, I kill Mrs. Foley right now. Tails, I kill Walter instead.' Would that put a dent in your stubbornness? Either way, Pebbles would still be alive to make sure you finish your assignment."

Walter stepped between Morgan and Ashley. "If you let them go, you'll still have me." He flicked his thumb over his shoulder at Ashley. "She'll still have incentive to do the job. When it's done, I'll take the candlestone so I'll have a fighting chance to survive even if you go back on the deal."

Morgan extended her hand—Shelly's hand—and caressed Walter's cheek. He steeled his face. If he flinched at all, she'd know he was really scared spitless. He imagined himself as a granite cliff. That helped . . . a little.

"I admire chivalry, even in my enemies," Morgan said. "I accept your offer." Her red eyes focused on Ashley. "Agreed?"

Walter could almost feel Ashley fuming behind him. He had come up with the idea without thinking much about it, hoping she would calculate all the options, but his rash decision might have taken her by surprise.

"We both know you're a liar," Ashley replied. "Why should we trust you to keep any kind of deal?"

Morgan's eyes flashed, like a fire fed a splash of gasoline, but she recovered quickly. "Then you have misunderstood my curse," she said, sweeping past Ashley with a graceful stride. "I can keep nothing that is not given to me, so the Watchers capture and hold all prisoners." She spun back toward them, her black dress twirling. "But if someone gives me something, I am bound to do whatever I can to keep it from perishing. That is why I never killed King Arthur when he gave himself into my care." She rubbed her hands along her hips. "Shelly is also safe within this body, and now that Walter has offered to be my prisoner, I will keep him whole."

Silence blanketed the room. Morgan stared at Ashley through Shelly's corrupted eyes. A loud roar erupted from somewhere outside, a dragon's cry of pain. An answering screech reverberated. Was it a Watcher's cry of celebration?

Walter rubbed the knot on his head. The injuries were mounting, and the battle outside sounded pretty bleak. It was no wonder Ashley didn't want to give the enemy another weapon, but she really didn't have any choice. "You have to get Devin out," he said. "I'll be her prisoner. I've been through worse."

Ashley sighed and nodded. "Okay. But I want to see Mrs. Foley take Pebbles out of this place first."

"Consider it done." Morgan clapped her hands. A Watcher entered, his red eyes flaming. "Release the other prisoners." She waved her hand as if dismissing a servant.

277

"Don't treat me like a slave," the Watcher growled. "If your plan fails, Samyaza will not protect you from us."

Morgan's face burned. "Be gone!" she yelled, thrusting her finger toward the door. "My word *is* Samyaza's."

The Watcher scowled at her and left the room, leaving the door partway open.

Marilyn stood at the furnace room door and pressed her ear against it. "It's quiet now."

Karen leaned close, bending over Marilyn to listen. "Any idea what that noise was?"

"An explosion of some kind. No clue." Marilyn pulled back, her jaw tense. "We'd better make our move now."

Catherine closed Pebbles's book and tucked it under her arm. "Are you ready to go?"

Pebbles wrinkled her eyebrows. "How are we going to get past the monsters?"

Marilyn lifted Pebbles into her arms and kissed her cheek. "So far the Watchers haven't seen anything I've been carrying, so they won't be able to see you either." Her confident smile probably fooled Pebbles, but Karen knew better. Marilyn wasn't really sure at all.

Catherine laughed nervously. "Can you carry me too?"

Marilyn shifted Pebbles higher in her arms. "I think this big, brave girl is all I can handle, but we'll get you out of here. Shiloh and Karen will create a diversion in the stairwell, and we'll head for the exit door."

Karen's throat suddenly dried up. "Uh, what kind of diversion?"

"Just scream and yell and stomp your feet, then scoot far away from where you made the noise."

"Okay." Karen swallowed through her parched throat. "Then what?"

Marilyn laid her hand on the doorknob. "Then try to find Ashley."

Shiloh put her arm around Karen's shoulders. "We can do it. Girl power, remember?"

"Yeah," Karen said, shuddering. "But I think this girl's batteries need a recharge."

Marilyn opened the door a crack and peeked out, then shut it quietly. "A Watcher's coming!" She set Pebbles down and raised a finger to her lips. "I have a new plan."

The door opened again, and the shining head ducked under the top of the doorframe. Staring quizzically at the latch, he began peeling away Marilyn's tape. "What happened here?"

Marilyn slipped around the demon and signaled for Shiloh and Karen to follow. As Shiloh tried to squeeze past him, the Watcher's terrible eyes glowed. "Who put tape on the latch?" he bellowed.

Shiloh managed to get through and joined Marilyn on the other side of the hall. Karen's turn. She stood and tiptoed toward the door, her legs trembling as she looked up at the demon's sneering face.

Catherine picked up the roll of tape Marilyn had left behind and showed it to the Watcher. "I was waiting for a good time to escape."

With the Watcher blocking most of the doorway, Karen had to flatten herself against the frame. Even so, her belt buckle grazed the demon's thigh. He twisted his head toward her. "Is someone else here?" He jabbed his clawed hand at Karen, but she dove into the hall just in time, hitting the floor with a grunt.

"Someone *is* here!" Bending over and waving his arms, the demon searched for invisible intruders. Karen scooted away on her backside, but she didn't have time to scramble to her feet. The Watcher pursed his lips and whistled a long, piercing signal. "Iridian!" he called. "Come!"

Catherine grabbed up Pebbles. "Hold on tight!" She dashed out of the room toward an exit door at the end of the hall.

In a flash of white armor, the Watcher flew after them, catching up in seconds. He grabbed Catherine by the scruff of her jacket and lifted her off the floor, making her feet dangle inches from the tile. Pebbles let out a terrified wail. Catherine wrapped her arms around the girl even more tightly as the Watcher stood near the door, stroking his chin. "Trying to escape was a foolish move. Maybe I should send you back to your people with a few broken bones to show our displeasure."

280

Karen jumped to her feet and joined Marilyn and Shiloh in a huddle, so close to the demon its shadow covered their bodies. Marilyn placed a hand on each girl's head. "We have to separate," she whispered, her words nearly drowned by Pebbles's crying. "I'll try to save Catherine and Pebbles. You two look for Ashley."

Iridian bounded into the hallway, the red colors in his coat glowing.

Marilyn sneaked past the Watcher and slammed the door to the furnace room, then ran toward the stairwell, clacking her shoes loudly.

The Watcher pointed in the direction of the noise. "Iridian! Fetch!"

The dog lunged ahead, galloping like a racehorse. Marilyn made a sharp turn toward the stairs but slipped and crashed into the wall.

Karen was about to cry out, but Shiloh clamped a hand over her mouth. Pebbles screamed. The Watcher set Catherine down near the wall. "Stay there and keep her quiet!" he ordered. Catherine hugged Pebbles to her chest.

The dog leaped on Marilyn and wrapped his massive jaws around her throat, thrashing her twice before dragging her back to the Watcher, a trail of blood marking their path. Marilyn hung limply from his mouth, her eyes closed. The rubellite pendant dangled from her neck, the bottom tip scraping the floor.

Shiloh hustled Karen past Iridian, her mouth close to Karen's ear. "He can't bark or chase us," she whispered, pointing at the stairwell. "Let's get out of sight."

The Watcher groped around the dog's jaws. "What did you catch? Ah! Feels like a human." His fingers ran through Marilyn's hair. "A woman, I think." As his hand drew near her throat, the demon smiled. "I think you might have played too rough, little puppy. What a shame. But I suppose this one's death will be enough punishment. We'll just deliver her body when we release our two prisoners."

Karen's heart felt like it slid up into her throat, beating so hard she could barely breathe. When they arrived at the stairs, Shiloh placed her hands on Karen's cheeks and looked her in the eye. "We can't help Mrs. Bannister now," she whispered. Shiloh's hands were cool and calm, and only a trickle of sweat on her brow revealed any hint of worry. "It's up to us to find Ashley. Do you understand?"

Karen gulped and nodded, but her voice was still buried in her throat. Her whole body trembled as the demon carried Catherine and Pebbles through the exit door, the dog dragging Marilyn in his wake.

Shiloh took her hand. "Try not to worry. Forty years in the circles taught me one thing; never doubt God, no matter how bad things look."

Karen's heart slowed enough to let her squeak out a reply. "They . . . They can't look much worse."

Shiloh nodded toward a set of wooden doors, one of the few passageways they had not yet explored. "It's ajar," she whispered, then peeked inside. Her hand tightened around Karen's. "I saw a shadow . . . and a black dress."

Karen backed away from the door, her voice still feeble. "Is it Morgan?"

"They're coming out!" Shiloh jerked Karen's hand. "Quick! Up the stairs!"

Ashley plugged two wires together in her restoration box. "There's only one problem. My computers were destroyed in Montana, so I don't have the processing power to decode Devin's body." She lifted a circuit board from the box. "This unit has a microprocessor that I used when the device was in prototype phase, back when I was restoring mice. It's programmed to do the job, but it'll take hours to work on a dragon. I really need Larry, my supercomputer, to do it quicker."

Shelly's red pupils pulsed, a wicked smile spreading across her face. Morgan was still in full control. "Can you send data to Larry through your tooth transmitter?"

"Tooth transmitter?" Ashley cocked her head to one side. "What are you talking about?"

Morgan scowled. "Oh, don't play dumb, my little brainiac. Do you think Samyaza is incapable of intercepting your transmissions? We have been listening to your coded messages. Quite ingenious, but not unexpected from someone like you."

Ashley set her fingers on her cheek. "So you let the messages go through? Why?"

"Because it suited my purposes perfectly. Your handheld computer would have brought them too quickly, but your clever clues drew all the dragons here at exactly the time I wanted them to arrive. The Watchers are merely waiting for Devin and my other reinforcements to attack en masse."

Ashley tapped her jaw. "Larry!" she shouted. "It's a trap. Tell the dragons to pull back!"

"Too late, my dear." Morgan swept her arm toward the hole in the wall. "As you can see, the battle is already engaged. The dragons cannot retreat now."

Outside, streams of fire and darkness clashed in midair. On the ground, a Watcher glided by carrying a woman and a child, followed by a dog dragging another woman's body.

Ashley laid her hands on the table. "He has Pebbles!"

Walter shielded his eyes from the sun's glare. "He's got my mom, too. But what's that dog carrying?" He laid a hand on his stomach. "It . . . It looks like Billy's mom."

"They are taking the prisoners to your friends." Morgan grabbed one of the rejected lenses and broke it on the table, leaving a sharp fragment in her hand that she wielded like a weapon. Her face stayed perfectly calm. "I kept my part of the bargain. Now it's your turn."

Walter flared his nose. "Don't be afraid of this chicken-hearted witch, Ashley! Break the candlestone and run for it! I'll make sure she doesn't follow you."

Snatching a handful of Walter's hair, Morgan pulled his head back, stretching his neck. She pressed the glass fragment against his throat, drawing a trickle of blood. She glared at Ashley. "Finish . . . the . . . job."

283

"All right, all right. Don't hurt him." Ashley searched the table for a sharp instrument, anything with a point. Her glance landed on a screwdriver. She picked up one of the more polished lenses and checked her reflection, angling the glass to show the inside of her mouth. She inserted the screwdriver and popped out her tooth transmitter, then laid it in her palm and talked to it. "Larry. Listen. The receiver's not in my mouth anymore, so I won't be able to hear your answer. I'm going to modulate the data to you through this transmitter. Run it through the alpha/omega algorithms and send me back the stream in binary."

Ashley used the screwdriver to pry a microchip out of the open restoration box, then set the transmitter chip in the gap. Grabbing a couple of discarded wires and a soldering iron, she talked while she worked. "The new chip doesn't have the same prongs, so I have to hardwire the I/O."

284

As smoke rose from the soldering iron, Ashley's shirt dampened. "It's crude technology," she said, "but it should work." Finally, she laid her tools down. "I have to break the candlestone to let him out, so there'll be no going back. I also don't know how much ionic energy is left in the nuclear core. I haven't recharged it with photoreceptors. Even if it didn't leak during the earthquake, it might not have enough juice to complete the restoration."

Morgan pulled Walter's head back farther. "If it doesn't work, then you will have broken our deal, and I will no longer be bound to it. Walter will die, and you'll be next."

Walter bared his teeth. The jagged glass dug deeper, and a faster flow of blood painted a red ribbon down his neck.

Ashley placed the candlestone in one end of the box next to the glass collection tube and aimed the restoration light at the tube's exit point. She poised her screwdriver on top of the gem and struck the top with a hammer, driving it through the crystal and slicing it into jagged halves. A dazzling eruption of sparkling light flowed into the tube, and seconds later began spilling out the other side into the glow of the restoration ray. The sparkles seemed to pile up into a tall column, each one zipping into an assigned position, like an animated jigsaw puzzle putting itself together. Once a sparkle found its place, it flickered out, leaving a solid piece behind, a reddish-brown fragment of dragon flesh. As the pieces collected, the shape grew slowly, expanding to fill half the room.

Slowed by the altered data transmission, the restoration process took longer than it ever had in the Montana laboratory. And, after all, this was the biggest thing Ashley had ever restored.

As the shape solidified, the dragon began to move, awkwardly testing its weight and lowering its head and long neck to avoid the ceiling. He seemed covered with reflecting sequins, glittering from the tip of his snout to the abrupt end of his tail, which Walter had severed in their last battle. A crack appeared in the pattern on one of his forelegs, a gash also provided by Walter. Finally, when the last sparkle of light winked off, the dragon let out a terrible roar. "Where is that little brat who trapped me in there?"

Walter gulped. The long neck swung the dragon's head around. His red eyes flamed with vengeance. Morgan released Walter's hair, and he fell to the floor, clutching the wound on his neck. "Devin," Morgan said in a singsong voice, "I'm glad to see your anger in full bloom. You'll need it for the battle ahead."

"I want to make a torch out of that boy first." Devin sent a sizzling blast of fire toward Walter, but he rolled out of the way just in time. The volley splashed against the wall, leaving a smoldering hole. Some of the fiery drops spattered on strewn paperwork, igniting several small blazes.

Morgan held up her hands. "Patience, Devin. He has agreed to remain my prisoner, so I will deal with him in due time."

285

Walter scrambled to his feet and scooted over to Ashley. He gave her a healthy shove toward the gaping hole in the wall. "You did your part, now get going. I'll handle this overgrown lizard."

Ashley set her feet. "But I can't leave you with—"

"That was the deal!" Walter pushed her again. "Go! With the battle raging out there, they'll need you to heal the wounded."

Ashley ran to the hole in the wall, pausing at the crumbling frame to look back. With smoke from the fires filling the room, a mist of gray veiled Walter's face. She tried to smile, but her lips could only tremble. "Dragon riding tonight," she said, pointing at him. "Don't stand me up." She ducked behind the exterior wall and peeked back in, biting her finger as the dragon's head floated around the smoky room.

Walter picked up the two halves of the candlestone and fitted them back together. He held the restored gem, pinching it to keep it in place. "How do you feel now, snake?"

Devin flicked out his tongue. "Except for the wounds you gave me, fine."

"Enough chitchat!" Morgan pushed a long black sleeve up to her elbow, exposing Shelly's delicate forearm. "The candlestone has lost its power, so Walter is defenseless." She pointed toward the hole in the wall. "Now get out there and aid the Watchers. My army is awaiting your arrival to attack, and you will soon activate my secret weapon."

Devin lumbered from the room, keeping his wings folded in to fit through the hole in the wall. Ashley lurched to the side, pressing her hand against her chest to quiet her heart. Devin came within inches, but he didn't see her. The near miss made her feel sick. Steeling her courage again, she peeked back into the room.

Walter coughed, waving at the thickening smoke. "Army? What army?"

"The Lord Satan has sent reinforcements, but since they are not as powerful as the Watchers, he would not allow them to come until I had a dragon on my side. You will soon see why." Morgan grabbed the nape of his neck and led him toward the door to the hallway. "This way. I want Samyaza to join us."

When they left the room, Ashley stepped back in. She batted at the smoke and coughed, tasting a chemical coating on her tongue. She wanted to follow, but Walter was right; they needed her help with the wounded. Holding her breath, she dashed past the growing fire and yanked the tooth transmitter from the restoration machine. When she broke back through the wall of smoke, she stopped outside and pushed the transmitter between two bottom molars and lodged it in place with her tongue and upper teeth.

Gasping for breath, she tapped her jaw. "Larry?" She coughed deeply, dropping to her hands and knees. "I need your help."

The computer's voice buzzed in the back of her mouth. "Ashley, I detect extreme distress. Initiating security measures."

"No! Don't lock me out!" She coughed again, barely able to speak. "Pass code . . . beta . . . omicron . . . gamma."

"Security lockdown terminated. How may I help you?"

With a final cough, Ashley cleared the tickle from her throat and rose to her feet. "Just keep listening." A loud shriek pierced the sky, and a ball of fire shot over Ashley's head. She sprinted toward the source of the sound, her voice shaking as she ran. "We're all pretty frazzled, so we may need your logical brain to keep us cool."

A hideous, serpent-like monster dove at her, black-eyed with dual fangs in its gaping mouth. She dropped to the ground and rolled out of the way just in time. Fire spewed over her body, engulfing the beast in flames. A familiar voice shouted from a circling dragon. "Are you all right, Miss?"

Ashley stood and brushed off her clothes. She recognized Legossi's flying style, smooth and graceful. She banked, taking the knight in a wide circle, obviously staying in the air in case of another attack. "I'm okay, Sir Barlow," Ashley shouted. "What was that thing? It wasn't a Watcher."

With a flurry of wings, Legossi finished the circuit, bringing the knight back into view. "No, Miss," he said, speaking rapidly. "A new kind of demon has begun to rise from the lake. Foul creatures, to be sure. They have strange powers we are just learning to understand. I don't know how long we can last."

Legossi took him high into the air again. Ashley yelled at the top of her lungs, jumping into the air. "Any losses on our side?"

Swerving at a sharp angle, Legossi swooped down. "Two dragons missing," Barlow said as he approached. His face came clearly into view, his eyes wide with distress. "And Marilyn is dead." Legossi flapped her wings and shot back into the air. "Thigocia is in the heat of battle," he called back as they rose higher. "She cannot heal her, so you're Marilyn's only hope."

Barlow guided Legossi away, her scales flashing as they surged toward a cluster of dragons in the distance. Underneath the battle, a small group of humans darted around in a grassy field near the edge of a forest. Ashley broke into a dead run, wincing as she passed the hideous, burning demon, wondering how an evil spirit could catch on fire.

She shook the image out of her mind and locked her gaze on the humans as she sprinted down the path to the lake. Would she have enough strength to endure another healing procedure? Might Marilyn be too far gone to save? Who would use the sword to generate the healing energy? The professor?

She kicked into her highest gear. There was only one way to find out.

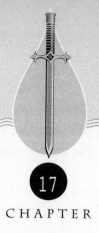

THE DEADLIEST POISON

W alter stood on the gravel path between Shelly, still possessed by Morgan's evil spirit, and a Watcher. He stared at the battlefield on the border between war and peace. Behind him was the door to the visitor center, a symbol of peace and security. Before him, brave dragons and humans fought for the safety of millions who were still under orders to remain in their homes, cruelly unaware that their lives hung in the balance in this battle between good and evil.

While the Watchers engaged several dragons in battle high in the sky, Devin isolated another in a one-on-one shootout. His dexterity in flight was far better than Walter expected. What would it be like for Clefspeare himself to possess that magnificent body and combine such raw, brutal force with experience and wisdom?

Devin collided with the smaller female, then whipped around and slapped her wings with his shortened tail. She tumbled in flight, spun downward, and plunged into the lake, her body sending up a geyser-like splash. Walter cringed. If this kept up, the battle wouldn't last much longer.

Suddenly, the lake seemed to boil, huge bubbles popping on the surface. Then, from each bubble, a black snake-like creature arose, slithering through the air as if swimming upstream. It was hard to tell how big they were from so far away, maybe six to eight feet long, each one with a set of sharp-tipped black wings.

"My endgame strategy is at hand," Shelly crooned in her Morgan-possessed voice. "The queen will now send her knights across the board. Since Devin has arrived, the dark angels can join in battle."

Devin spewed a short burst of fire all over the body of one of the snakes.

Walter raised his eyebrows. With Devin firing on his allies, maybe there was hope after all. He snorted. "Your dragon is killing your secret weapon for the good guys."

"Fool," Morgan scoffed. "Dragon's fire increases the dark angel's strength."

"To a point," the Watcher said. "If the angel catches on fire . . ."

"Silence!" Morgan's face darkened. "This battle will end soon. When the dark angels bite the humans, their death is certain."

The snake demon flew away, its scales steaming like hot tar. Five sleek, shining dragons swooped down, blitzing the boiling lake with waves of fire. Walter silently clenched his fist. Yes! That was Thigocia leading the charge!

Morgan breathed a low tsk, tsk. "Your dragons won't even make a dent in our forces."

A snake demon rose into the flames. Three dragons locked their fiery jets onto its body. As fire encompassed it, its body hardened, then burst into flames. The snake writhed as if in pain, and when Thigocia's flame intensified, it finally exploded. Thousands of glowing pieces rocketed over the lake.

The dragons circled as one and zeroed in on another rising serpent. Walter grimaced. Morgan was right. They couldn't possibly get them all, not even one percent of them!

Morgan stepped forward a few paces and clapped her hands. "Excellent! Most of my troops are eluding the fire. The dragons will busy themselves with our horde while the Watchers free themselves to assemble the new recruits for battle and make ready for the next step. I will have a supercharged army of warriors, and your dragons will be no match."

Walter shifted from foot to foot, itching to charge out and join the fray. With Morgan standing several feet in front, she'd never be able to catch him if he bolted to the side. He glanced up at the hulking, winged monster to his right. No way. Mr. Ugly would probably make it the shortest combat mission in history. If only he could—

291

Walter felt a tug on the back of his shirt and heard a low "Shhh." He peeked over his shoulder. Shiloh and Karen crouched near his heels, glowing auras hovering above their heads. Shiloh rose and sidled up to him, a broken broomstick tightly wedged in her grip. She whispered, "The Watcher can't see us. We'll keep him and Morgan occupied while you make a run for it."

Walter shuddered at the thought of leaving the two girls to deal with a pair of ghouls, but if the Watcher really couldn't see them, maybe they had a chance. He nodded, hoping Shiloh and Karen wouldn't hurt his sister too badly.

Shiloh drew back the broomstick and tiptoed up to Morgan, Karen padding a few steps behind. With a home run swing, she smacked Morgan's head, and the two girls leaped on her back, knocking her flat on her face.

The Watcher pushed Walter away and stormed to Morgan's side. Shiloh swung the stick upward between his legs, then she and Karen jumped off Morgan's body and ran. Walter launched into a sprint, heading for the battlefield like a freight train out of control, passing so quickly over the gravel path he could barely feel his feet hitting the ground. The field drew closer. A couple of humans turned his way, one woman with her arms outstretched. His mother!

He slowed just enough to run into her embrace without knocking her down. "Mom! You're okay! You got out!"

She squeezed him tightly, running her fingers through his hair. "And you, too! Praise God!"

Walter felt a strong hand on his shoulder. "Good job, son. Ashley's here, and she told us what you did to save her and your mother and Pebbles." His father patted him on the back. "I'm proud of you."

Walter breathed a long, cleansing sigh. For a brief second, he let himself feel proud, too—proud to be a valiant knight who saved a fair maiden, and proud to be the son of Carl and Catherine Foley.

He pulled away and surveyed the scene. The professor, resting Excalibur on his shoulder, stood by a tree where Ashley crouched over a woman reclining against the trunk. Pebbles poured water from a thermos bottle into a cup and handed it to the professor. Sir Patrick was dragging a carcass away, a colorful animal that looked like the dog he had seen earlier, now decapitated. A dragon swooped low, tracking one of the snake demons as it zipped by. The wind from the dragon's wings sent a fresh breeze across Walter's face.

Pebbles ran up to him and lifted a cup of water. "Want some?" she asked, a concerned look on her lovely Oriental face. Walter smiled and took it gladly. Finally, a few seconds to rest.

As he sipped, the water rippled at the top of the cup. He couldn't stop the trembling in his hands.

He gazed across the field hoping to spot—Yes! There they were! Shiloh sprinted down the path, Karen close behind. Reaching the group, they stopped, huffing and wheezing, each with a hand on her chest. Shiloh dropped the broken broomstick on the ground. "This might come in handy again."

As Walter helped Pebbles pour water for the new arrivals, he glanced around, then turned back to his father. "So, where are Billy and Bonnie?"

Carl's shoulders sank. "They entered the rubellite in the pendant's gem. Apparently, Billy's supposed to look for his father in there, but we don't know yet when or how they'll get out." He pointed toward the woman leaning against the tree, but, with Ashley blocking their view, he couldn't see her face. "The pendant's over there. Brace yourself, son."

Walter edged closer to the tree, his legs feeling weaker with every step. Ashley eased to the side and faced him, her cheeks stained with tears. When he recognized the woman, her eyes tightly closed and her skin pale, he leaped forward and fell to his knees at her side. "It *was* Mrs. B!" He grabbed her limp hand. "Is she . . . Is she . . ."

Ashley nodded, her lips thin and trembling, her face nearly as pale as Marilyn's.

"Well, can't you . . ." Walter gestured wildly with his hands, gripping an invisible sword and swinging it at the professor. "Can't you do the healing thing with Excalibur? Didn't you just hit the ground with it and buzz Ashley or something?"

"That's correct," the professor said. "The energy travels through the ground, somehow picking up trace elements that aid healing. The process—"

293

"I don't care how it works!" Walter spread out his hands. "Let's just do it!"

"We tried it already." Ashley ran her fingers through her hair, but the stringy locks fell back in her face. "I don't know what's wrong. I think I'm just completely drained."

Walter swiveled his head. "Where's Thigocia? Can't she do it?"

Ashley nodded toward the sky. Walter tilted his head upward, scanning the blue backdrop. He saw five or six dragons firing streams at dozens of snake demons, but the Watchers were nowhere in sight. As the black angels swarmed, the dragons slowed, their tired wings barely able to keep them in flight. Finally, he spotted two dragons battling head to head, shimmering in the sun's glow—Thigocia and Devin.

Thigocia dipped below Devin's swiping tail, folding her wings just in time to avoid getting slapped. She spun back and shot a thin stream of flame at his eyes, blinding him while she lunged forward and latched her jaws onto his tail.

Devin roared and slung her away, her teeth dragging his scales and sending a spray of sparkling blood into the air. Thigocia dove, then glided, circling around for another attack.

Walter shook his head. "That could last for hours. How can we get her to come down?"

Carl opened his palm, displaying the candlestone Shelly had planted as a decoy. "We still have this," he said, "but I'm not sure what to do with it. I guess it would weaken Thigocia, too."

"Maybe not. She's a healer like Ashley." Walter scooped up a handful of dirt and let it run slowly through his fingers. He gazed again at Ashley and Marilyn, both limp and ragged. Ashley's sad, weary eyes gave him an idea. Thinking about actually carrying out his idea knotted his stomach, but he couldn't come up with anything better. "Dad, keep that rock handy. I have a plan that just might work."

Carl closed his fingers around the candlestone. "What do you have in mind?"

Walter winked at him. "Just trust me." He stood, grabbed Ashley's sleeve, and jerked her to her feet. He screamed into her face. "What's wrong with you? Can't you do your job? You're supposed to be a healer!"

Ashley's mouth dropped open, her eyes wide, bewilderment mixing with exhaustion.

"Walter!" Catherine shouted. "No!" She ran toward him, but Carl held her back.

Sir Patrick grabbed Karen's arm and whispered into her ear while the professor stepped toward the field, Excalibur poised in his grip.

Ashley stared at Walter, her chin trembling. He peeked up to the sky. Thigocia swerved around and stared in their direction.

Walter grimaced. One more ought to do it. He gripped Ashley's biceps and shook her. "This is no time to wimp out on us! Get some backbone, girl, or I'll . . ." He raised his hand as if to slap her.

Thigocia dove toward the trees. Ashley's knees buckled. Walter pulled her into a full embrace, holding her head in his hand. "I'm so sorry, Ashley. I'm so sorry." He set her down near Marilyn's body and knelt. "I had to make you think you were really in danger." He nodded toward the sky. "Look. Here comes your mom."

Thigocia glided to the edge of the forest and pawed the ground like a mad bull, snorting jets of fire. "Where's my daughter?" she roared.

Walter jumped up and waved his arms. "It's okay! Ashley's fine."

Devin swooped toward them, twin flaming torrents erupting from his nostrils. The professor swung Excalibur and caught the flames in its laser beam. The stream curled around the beam, adhering to it like a snake around a pole. With a flick of his wrists, he slung the fire back toward the dragon, but it just glanced off his scaly hide.

Carl held up the candlestone. Devin banked into a hairpin turn, beat his wings twice, and headed back toward the skies. Carl cupped his other hand over the gem and exhaled loudly. "At least he won't be back for a while."

Thigocia thumped her tail on the ground and roared again. "What is the meaning of this?"

Walter took an awkward step back, stumbling at the impact of her rage. "We need your help." He took three more backward steps and knelt again next to Ashley. She had taken Marilyn's lifeless hand in hers. "It's Billy's mom," he explained. "She's dead. We need you to try to heal her."

Thigocia's ears twitched. "I have never raised someone from the dead. Only Ashley has done that."

"Can't you at least try?" Walter pleaded. "Ashley's healing engine is fried."

The other dragons glided to the ground, five in all. Sir Barlow dismounted the lead dragon and collapsed to the ground, panting. Standish, Fiske, and Woodrow joined him, each one tugging at sweat-drenched shirts as they dropped to the forest floor. Pebbles ran to Barlow with the thermos, and each knight took a quick gulp and tossed it to the next man.

Legossi's eyes flashed. "I sense grave danger in every direction. The demons retreated, but not because we were winning."

"You have fought well." Thigocia dipped her head toward each dragon. "Three are missing. Where is Hartanna?"

Legossi flopped to the ground, her voice weak. "She and Newman chased a Watcher until I could no longer see her. Neither she nor the Watcher returned."

Thigocia swung around to address the knights. "Did anyone see Sir Edmund? He fell into the lake during my fight with Devin."

Barlow wiped his wet mustache with his sleeve. "Not I. He is a fine swimmer, but that lake is cold and rough."

"Then we must find him, he's—"

"Hey!" Walter stepped in front of Thigocia. "I hate to break up this troop inspection, but you have a dead woman to heal!"

Thigocia stretched out her neck and drilled her pulsing scarlet stare at Walter. "You have a lot to learn about war, young man. Many march into battle and never return. It is my job to minimize that number."

297

Walter squared his shoulders and stepped forward, meeting her stare. "And you have a lot to learn about compassion. Billy risked his life to save dragons he didn't even know. If not for him, you'd still be a bucket of bones collecting dust." He gestured toward Marilyn, keeping his stare fixed on the dragon. "This is his mother we're talking about."

Thigocia gazed at Walter, the fire in her eyes fading. "You have both the wisdom and the courage that my own son had." Her ears twitched again. "Very well. I will try."

The professor stood about thirty feet from Marilyn's body and waved Excalibur. "Everyone kindly stand back. I'll need a clear path."

As the dragons and humans backed away, Thigocia lumbered forward and settled near Marilyn. The professor energized

Excalibur's beam, sending it rocketing into the sky. "Are you ready?" he asked.

Legossi blared a trumpet-like blast. "Danger!"

Sir Barlow thrust his finger toward the sky. "A Watcher is flying this way! And it's carrying Shelly . . . uh, Morgan, that is."

The professor spun around, now wielding the sword in a defensive stance. The dragons stood, and the knights leaped aboard. Barlow caressed Legossi on the side of her neck. "We are all tired, so we will not fight unless we must. But show them the fire in your eyes and make them believe we will attack at any moment."

The Watcher landed gracefully and set Morgan on her feet. She looked less like Shelly than ever, her face contorting like a twisted rag, the red in her eyes as bright as ruby lasers. Her calm voice, however, belied her wrathful expression. "I think it is time that we end our conflict," she said, rubbing the back of her head. She clapped her hands, and a wave of snake demons flew down from the sky and settled behind her in a mass of wiggling blackness. Eight Watchers landed at the front of the dark army, one dragging a wet human body in his hand.

298

Walter gulped. It was Sir Edmund. His head hung limply, and his chest neither rose nor fell.

The Watcher threw Edmund into their midst. His body slid to a stop between Karen and Shiloh, his dripping hair and clothes forming a puddle at their feet. Walter rushed to his side and laid a hand on his neck. Warm and pulsing. Still alive!

Finally, Devin glided to the ground and landed at Morgan's side. "You have fought valiantly," she called, "but you are obviously outnumbered. If you continue to fight, I will be forced to kill you all where you stand. I offer you, however, the opportunity to surrender. If you do, we will only kill the dragons. The humans will go free."

"In a pig's eye," Barlow muttered.

Walter glanced at his allies. "We're not afraid of her!" he yelled. "She's just a category five hurri-pain who's nothing but hot air."

Each knight's chin drew taut, and they puffed out their chests a bit more. Walter massaged his fist. His words seemed to help, if he could judge by how the troops carried themselves. They'd all need resolve in the face of those insurmountable odds lined up behind Morgan.

His gaze trailed to his dad whispering with Sir Patrick and Professor Hamilton. What were the three of them up to now?

Morgan held up Shelly's fingers. "You have ten seconds to decide." She began closing her hands one finger at a time. "Eight seconds . . . seven . . . six."

Carl grabbed Excalibur from the professor, stepped to the front of the group, and stood shoulder to shoulder with Walter. "You have to release my daughter," Carl said.

299

Walter grabbed his dad's arm. "No! We can't surrender!"

He shook loose from Walter's grip. "Did you hear me, Morgan?"

Morgan lowered Shelly's hands. An evil grin crawled across her face. "I see. You want to add another condition."

"It's not a condition!" Carl marched ahead, closing the gap between him and the evil army, Excalibur's beam shooting upward. "I'm telling you to let my daughter go. You can't have her."

A Watcher sent a jagged bolt of darkness at him, but he set his feet and batted it away with the blade.

Morgan raised her hand. "Stop! He can't hurt us with that sword. Only Merlin knows how to do that." Her confidence, however, seemed to fade as Carl marched closer, brandishing Excalibur like a seasoned warrior.

Carl lowered the beam, angling it so the bright shaft of light hovered over Morgan. He waved it in a tight circle, as if painting a halo over her head—two rotations . . . three . . . four.

The red in Morgan's eyes faded to pink. She seemed to teeter for a second, but she locked her knees and stood firm, speaking through clenched teeth, her voice only half as strong as before. "She gave herself to me. She's mine."

Five rotations . . . six. Carl spoke in a low, calm tone. "I am her father. I renounce her vow and apply this shroud of protection." He completed a seventh rotation and lifted the beam. "Now she's mine."

Shelly dropped to her knees, her eyes rolling back. Smoke drained from her nostrils, collecting in a column next to the closest Watcher. As the smoke solidified, Shelly toppled forward. Before any of the demons could react, Carl scooped her up and retreated, running as fast as he could, Excalibur still in his grip.

The smoke coalesced into a female shape, a floating black hag of a woman. She lifted her ghostly hands to her withered face and screamed. With her eyes bloody red again, she thrust her arm forward. "Devin! Activate the poison!"

The dragon heaved a long, hot stream of air, blowing across the field like a Sahara storm. As the scalding breeze passed over the ground, thousands of "pops" sounded from the dirt. Strings of black arose, engulfing Walter and his allies with spewing fountains of noxious gas.

Walter stared at Morgan through the gathering haze. A vague form floated beyond the field of black fog as she cackled. "The rain worked perfectly. Now, if the doubt doesn't destroy their hearts, the cyanide will snuff out their lives."

Both dragons and humans fell to the ground like rubbery bowling pins, coughing and retching. Walter keeled over, dropping to his knees and clutching his stomach. He wheezed, trying to suck oxygen out of the poisoned air, but the pungent scent of almonds and choking gas clamped his throat shut.

Walter clawed helplessly at the ground. Was this it? Was it all over? Their struggles had been meaningless, futile attempts to do good in this world of sorrows. Why had he even tried? Mankind had been doomed ever since Adam ate the fruit, so why try to save people who didn't want to be saved? They weren't worth the effort. Every second he had suffered was a futile waste of sweat and blood.

Writhing in the dirt, he desperately tried to gasp a good-bye to his parents. Most of the bodies lay motionless under a blanket of gloom. Yet, one person stood upright, sleek and lovely, her blond-streaked hair shining in the rays of sunlight that filtered through the fog. Shiloh!

She leaned over and plucked something from the wet spot near Edmund's face. It looked like a flower of some kind, a tall stalk that ended in a round bulb. It hadn't been there earlier, so it must have sprouted and budded in a matter of seconds. She peeled back the bulb's covering, then broke off a piece of white stuff inside. After putting a piece in Karen's and Edmund's mouths, she hurried to Walter and pressed a fragment through his lips.

With his senses failing, he could barely hear her gentle British tones. "Chew it quickly." She jumped up and disappeared into the mist.

Walter made a feeble effort to grind the fragment in his teeth, then swallowed hard and forced it down his throat. It was sweet, sort of like honey, but as soon as it reached his stomach, it turned bitter. Gas erupted in a painful belch. Cramps wrenched his muscles. He curled into a fetal position and moaned. Heat blazed from his gut and radiated to his skin. Sweat spilled from every pore, drenching his body.

301

When the pain eased, he opened his eyes. His vision had cleared. His stomach muscles relaxed, allowing him to stand. With the smoke breaking up, he could see Shiloh giving some of the plant to one of the knights. Other people rose from the ground and straightened their frames. Barlow. Newman. Even Edmund began climbing to his feet. The other two hoisted him the rest of the way and patted him on the back.

Walter dashed to his parents and offered his mother his hand. His dad brushed himself off and lifted Shelly to her feet. She seemed woozy, but even her bleary eyes were an improvement over Morgan's scarlet spotlights. When she saw Walter, she gave him a weary smile. "Forgive me?" she asked.

Walter gave her a warm hug. "You bet."

She pulled at the sides of her black dress. "I think I need to change . . . a lot of things."

Walter clasped her shoulder. "I know what you mean. . . . We'll talk."

His dad retrieved Excalibur and waved it over his wife's head.

She coughed. "Carl?"

"I'm applying . . . a protective halo . . . so the demons won't see you." When he finished, he handed the sword to Walter. "Take it," he gasped. "I'm too weak to fight with it."

Walter encircled his fingers around the hilt, and the blade brightened in his grip. As if drawn by Excalibur's beacon, Karen ran to Walter's side and clutched his arm. "Do you think they'll attack when the smoke clears?" she asked.

Walter tried to peer through the smoke, but he could only get a vague sense that something was still moving out there. "Don't worry," he said. Karen leaned against his shoulder. Her touch sent a surge of strength into his flexing muscles. "I'll do whatever it takes to protect you."

Bonnie and Brogan raced to the front of the rubellite screen. About twenty people had gathered on the stage, each one anxiously watching the image.

"For a while it was blank," Martha said, "like something covered it up, but all of a sudden I could see an angel and two girls. Then the screen started bouncing. For a few seconds, I saw a horrible dog with green and orange teeth, then just a floor of some kind. It changed so quickly, it was hard to keep up with, but there was a lot of grass and people's feet. After a few minutes, I could see faces, worried faces. There was a big man. I could tell right away he was a friendly sort, and strong too. He was carrying a little girl in one arm, and a pretty woman hung on to his other arm. She was crying . . . sobbing, really. The big man hugged and kissed the woman, quite a passionate kiss, if you ask me, and then he walked out of view. Then an old man struck the ground with a flashing sword, and a girl with rays of sunshine coming through her eyes looked at us. The light actually came right into the theatre and lit up the whole room. After a few seconds, her eyes returned to normal, and she started crying. Since that time, we've been watching blue sky with flying dragons passing across the screen every once in a while."

Bonnie had a hard time taking her eyes off the red glass. Whoever was wearing the pendant now was keeping it perfectly still, giving them a good view of what was going on. A battle raged in the air, mounted dragons shooting jets of fire at the Watchers as they dodged and darted about, battling back with bolts of darkness emanating from their eyes. Bonnie counted only six dragons. Hartanna wasn't among them.

Bonnie paced in front of the screen and glanced more and more often at the door to the lobby. Billy had to come at any second now. He would bang the door open and march in with a hundred new believers. But the door, like an unanswered

303

prayer, remained shut. She clasped her hands in front of her and breathed another silent petition for Billy's safety. This was no time for doubt. God's timing and wisdom were perfect.

A gaunt old man stepped forward, his voice shy and apologetic. "Excuse me, Miss. We have less than ten minutes. When do we leave?"

Bonnie wanted to give him a confident answer, but how could she? Her own confidence was as fragile as burnt thread, and she had no answers. "Well, I think this screen is supposed to turn white, and then . . . we'll go through, I guess."

Sarah, as if reading Bonnie's mind, laid her arm around her shoulders. "I can already feel my memory coming back, and I know what my husband would say. We cannot predict how God will work, only that he will always succeed."

"Where is Billy?" a voice interrupted.

Bonnie spun around. Merlin was again standing inside the screen, his brow low. She glanced at Sarah, who smiled and eased back into the crowd, seeming almost bashful as she stood next to Dorcas.

Bonnie stepped closer to the screen. "We separated," she explained. "He told me to come here while he tried to rescue some people." She flashed a broad smile. "Your wife's here!"

Merlin beamed. "Excellent!" But he quickly doused his delight, looking like a man who knew he had to get down to business. He beckoned for Bonnie to come closer. She peeked at the whispering crowd, each face darkened by worry, then took the last step between her and the crystal wall. Merlin spoke in a low, serious tone. "Did it seem that the villagers wanted to kill him?"

"Some did," Bonnie whispered. "Jasmine for sure."

Merlin's brow dipped even farther. "If they succeeded in killing him, who will bring his body here so he can be raised?"

Bonnie gulped and peeked back at the onlookers again. Brogan had drawn closer, obviously listening while pretending not to. "I . . . I don't know," she said. "Billy thought I could take the people through, so I—"

Merlin raised his voice and gestured toward the people on the stage. "Only the king can pierce the veil! If he doesn't come in time, none of these faithful ones will be able to pass."

Bonnie's stomach knotted. The whole world seemed to be crumbling, and she could do nothing about it. She laid her palm on the crystalline screen. "Merlin, I'm so sorry! It was all so confusing. We just had to guess what to do."

Merlin pressed his palm up against Bonnie's. "Yes, it seems that God often works that way. He lets his children step out in faith, even though they don't always know exactly what they're doing, and he makes their choices work." He slid his hand into the deep pocket of his robe and withdrew a large hourglass. "But still, God's prophecies cannot fail. The king must open the door." He set the hourglass by his feet. The sands in the top half were almost gone. "Time is running out. There are fewer than seven minutes remaining."

305

"I'll go and drag him back here if I have to," Brogan offered. "Those others aren't worth dying for, are they? They never believed before."

Bonnie pointed her finger directly at Brogan's nose. "Did you ever come to the theatre before today? Why should you get to go and not them?"

Brogan backed away and bowed his head. "Touché, fair lass. A well-placed blow." He hurried to the edge of the stage and began descending the stairs. "But still, the practical truth is—"

The door banged open. A tall figure walked in carrying a body, but the darkness in the back of the seating area concealed his identity. Dozens of others filed in after him, each face veiled in the dimness, each pair of feet shuffling. Only their wide white eyes were visible, darting this way and that.

The lead figure strode down the aisle, his form becoming clearer by the second. As he marched up the stage steps, Martha cried out, "It's Reginald! And he's carrying the king!"

Reginald stopped in front of Bonnie. Billy's arms dangled, blood dripping from his fingertips. Tear tracks striped Reginald's blood-stained cheeks. "I brought him here as quickly as I could, though I cannot see how any hope remains."

Bonnie grabbed Billy's hand and pressed it to her cheek. He had no ring. How could he come into the theatre without one unless he was . . . "Oh no!" Her whole body shook. She felt for a pulse. "Is he . . ." She swallowed hard, unable to squeak out another word. With her gaze fixed on Billy's blood-soaked chest, she begged it to take in a single breath. It didn't move.

Reginald kept his head angled away from Bonnie, his face streaming with new tears. "Yes, my precious girl. A betrayer killed him." He dropped a dagger at his feet, and it clanked on the floor. "But she will not kill again."

Bonnie ran her trembling hands up and down Billy's dark sleeve. "But he can be raised . . ." She looked back at the rubellite screen. "Right Merlin?"

"Bring the dagger to me!" Merlin ordered.

Brogan snatched up the stone blade and rushed it to the glass wall. Merlin eyed it for a moment, then clenched his fist. "It's the staurolite dagger! Morgan's work. It will take more than the power of the rubellite to raise the king now."

Several people on the stage murmured. More than one began to weep. Martha fell to her aged knees wailing a vague lament.

Reginald set Billy's body on the stage floor and knelt beside him, covering his face with his hands. "I was close by. I should have stayed with him. Now all is lost!"

"No!" Merlin shouted. "Even in death, he can still pierce the veil, but he must be carried."

Reginald slid his hands under Billy's body again. "Shall I carry him?" he asked.

Merlin shook his head. "Did Billy tell you your physical body is inhabited by someone else?"

"If he did," Reginald said, laying Billy's hands on his chest, "I was too dense to listen."

Merlin pointed at the stage floor. "Then you must stay here until a body is secured for you. Otherwise you would disperse in the air as a cloud of energy if you tried to cross over."

"Then who will carry him?"

"There is only one who is able," Merlin replied, "the only other one here who is fully dragon and fully human, the only one who can split the barrier between the two worlds."

Merlin turned his gaze to Bonnie. "You have carried Billy before, both physically and spiritually. Although he has been a valiant warrior, he could never have taken the first step, much less the next ten thousand, without your support. You are the virgin who gave him spiritual birth. It is only right that you should be his shroud and carry him on his last great journey."

Bonnie could only nod in reply. She crouched next to Billy, her legs trembling so badly, she wondered if she'd be able to get up again. She slid her hands under his back and legs, and Reginald helped her lift Billy's body until she could stand up and set her feet.

When Reginald pulled his hands away, Bonnie let out an "oomph." Billy's full weight bent her back and anchored her feet to the stage floor. Rippling pain shot through her arms as she strained to keep them curled. With no wings to help her lift and with her legs wobbling, she could barely stand, much less walk.

A young woman stepped forward from the crowd, now swollen to a hundred or more souls. "You can do it, dear angel! If not for you, I would be lost with the rest of them. You are a messenger from the Maker!"

Brogan whispered in Bonnie's ear. "That's my sister, Darby. I told her all about you and my dreams."

Mr. Collins joined Darby, clutching the brim of his bowler hat. "And I, Miss, would never have believed had I not seen you."

Bonnie shuffled her feet toward the screen. Billy's arm fell from his chest and dangled again. She choked back a sob. "So, I just walk right through?"

Merlin picked up the hourglass and stepped to the side of the crystal veil. "Yes. As the king enters, the red in this gemstone screen will fade to white. The rest of the faithful will follow the passage to freedom."

"Except for me," Reginald said, backing away. "Finding a body for me is a hope beyond hope. Who would be willing to die and allow me to take his place?"

Bonnie felt as if her face was about to explode. "You can't stay! You're the main reason Billy came!" With her arms aching and time fleeing, she couldn't argue. "Merlin! What can we do?"

"Nothing that I know of, fair maiden. When the prophecies run dry, all I can do is watch in wonder as God completes his master plan." He held up the hourglass. Only a few grains remained at the top. "As for you, you have to trust and obey. There are only seconds left."

Bonnie gulped. It became so quiet, she could hear Billy's blood dripping onto the stage. She leaned back, slid her arm up higher on his shoulders, and blew a strand of hair out of her eyes. With her weight creaking the planks, she slid one shoe forward, then the other. The gemstone screen pulsed its red beacon signal as though warning her to stop, go back, never return.

"One more step, Bonnie!" Brogan shouted. "You can do it!" A chorus of cheers erupted.

Merlin faded away at the side of the screen. In the center, she could see Walter holding Excalibur, its beam blazing. As she took the final step, the crystalline barrier flashed with white light.

When the smoke cleared, the army of demons had dispersed. Morgan half stood, half floated next to the biggest Watcher. Two other Watchers remained behind them along with twenty or more of the snake demons.

Excalibur vibrated in Walter's grip as if it wanted to fly into battle. He gazed at his hand on the hilt, then slowly followed the blade up to the point, staring at it with wonder.

Morgan screamed, "They're still alive! Samyaza! Gather the forces and strike them down at once!"

Samyaza blasted a single bass note that vibrated the ground at Walter's feet. The snake demons assembled into formation again, flying down from the sky, their black bodies shimmering like polished obsidian. While they congregated, Samyaza barked orders. Walter glanced at his friends. Most were now on their feet, but it seemed that the dragons were still groggy, their bodies swaying as they tried to keep their balance. There was no way they could survive another assault. The knights seemed dazed as well, but at least they were up, encouraging the dragons to dig deep for one last battle.

Ashley knelt with Professor Hamilton next to Marilyn. With her body propped up against a tree, Mrs. B's arms hung limp, her head tipping to one side. Blood painted a wide circle under her neckline, staining her gray sweater.

Walter's heart ached. That was Billy's mom, and somehow Billy was inside the pendant that lay on her chest, having no idea that his mother was dead. He was probably in there spilling his guts to do anything God commanded him, and if he ever made it out alive, he would find a new tragedy. Walter wrung Excalibur's hilt with both hands. It was up to him to prevent it.

Ashley waved at Walter. "Bring Excalibur! I'm feeling stronger, so the professor wants to try again before it's too late!"

Ashley's cry echoed in Walter's brain. Excalibur vibrated, sending a tremor into his heart that echoed with a surge of power from deep in his soul. His muscles flexed on their own, extending the sword into the air. Power erupted from his chest and into his arms, ripping upward toward the blade. When the energy hit his hands, the blade ignited into an explosion of brilliant light, much brighter than he had ever seen it.

"Stand back, Prof!" Walter yelled. "I'll do it."

310

As the professor crawled away, the knights and dragons perked up their heads. Shelly, Shiloh, and Karen stood like statues, their eyes bulging. Walter's dad hugged Shelly, and his mom stooped between the younger girls and drew them close. Ashley pulled Marilyn's body into her embrace, then nodded.

Walter slashed the beam downward, sending a streak of light shooting across the ground. A series of sharp pops erupted in its path, and tiny puffs of smoke dotted the line like black toadstools. The bolt slammed into Ashley. Her arms locked around Marilyn. Her hair turned bright white. Laser beams shot through her eyes, and her whole body shook.

Ashley pointed the beams at Marilyn's heart. They struck the pendant, sending a huge splash of bright sparkling crimson all around, a constantly exploding fireworks display that nearly shrouded Ashley in red flares.

Walter kept the energy going, not knowing when to shut it off, and not really sure how. The sparks turned from red to pink, then to white, like a constant storm of shooting stars.

Ashley cried out, her voice shattered by the streaming flood of high-voltage light. "S-s-s-stop, Walter. S-s-stop!"

Walter swung the beam clear, letting it rocket into the sky. He glanced back at the army of fiends as they formed rank again. Devin flew in and landed gracefully next to Morgan, completing their front line.

Ashley's laser eyes flashed off. The gem pulsed white, still sending streams of sparks into the air. Suddenly a huge burst of light popped through the rubellite, a million flashing molecules that formed a walking statue in the air. The collection of energy floated to the ground and materialized into a winged female holding a large mass.

Within seconds, the figure transformed into Bonnie Silver carrying Billy in her arms. She set him on his feet, and he walked in place as if testing his legs. She lunged at him and threw her arms around his neck, her wings fluttering. "You're alive! Praise the Lord, you're alive!" The shower of sparks from the gem continued, throwing sequins of celebration on their heads.

Walter choked out a gasp. His chest heaved. The beam died away, and he ran to Billy and Bonnie, dropping Excalibur and wrapping both his friends in his arms. They wept together, laughing and crying at the same time.

Walter socked Billy on the arm. "What a bum, letting Bonnie carry you like that! She ain't your personal flotation device!"

Billy punched him back, then gazed at Bonnie's sparkling eyes. "No, but she's a life saver!"

Walter roared, "I love it!" He slapped Billy's back. "I'll have to steal that joke from you."

"I got a pulse!" All three spun around. Ashley was pressing her fingers on Marilyn's wrist. She drew the limp arm up and kissed the back of her hand. "She's alive."

THE VEIL IS TORN

B illy ran to his mother and gripped her hand. "What happened?"

Amidst a continuing shower of energy, Ashley touched a nasty wound on Marilyn's throat. "A dog attacked her—Morgan's devil dog." She patted Billy's shoulder. "I think she'll be okay now."

The sparks from the pendant died away for a moment but quickly returned, erupting in a series of punctuated bursts. Each burst expanded into an enormous mass that floated above the ground like a glittering ghost. The first mass sprouted limbs, then what looked like a pair of wings on its back. A half dozen others followed, each one slowly morphing into a dragon shape. The eyes of the first "pendant dragon" glowed a brilliant blue. It dipped its head as if bowing politely. In its sparkling, disembodied form, it seemed unable to speak, but somehow Billy knew who it was. He smiled and bowed in return. "Welcome, Brogan!"

As the features of the other pendant dragons clarified, Billy thought he recognized Martha and Mr. Collins, but he couldn't be sure. Only the color and shape of their eyes differed from one shining dragon to the next. An army of pendant dragons slowly took shape, but with non-physical bodies of pure light, would they be able to help in the battle?

A tuba blast sounded. Billy jumped up and joined Walter and Bonnie. "What was that?"

Walter kicked dirt toward their enemies. "Samyaza's calling the troops. He's so full of hot air, he has to get rid of it somehow."

The demon army, hundreds of viciously ugly vermin, coiled on the ground like vipers ready to strike. Ten Watchers lined up in front, looking taller and stronger than ever.

Morgan lifted her thin arm into the air. "Attack!"

Each Watcher shot a stream of darkness from his eyes. The professor snapped up Excalibur and sculpted a photo-umbrella over his human and dragon allies. The energy field deflected the black jets into the air.

The Watchers halted at the edge of the professor's strobing dome. The vipers surrounded the sphere and stopped, their tongues flicking madly. Morgan floated to a spot in front of the professor. Only a few feet of earth and a shield of light separated them. "That was a quick move for an old man, Charles Hamilton, but you'll see that I have more up my sleeve than a dram of poison for your sweet wife."

The professor's face turned red, but he stood erect, unflinching.

Morgan picked up one of the winged serpents. As she looked into its eyes, it curled its six-foot-long body around her waist. "Time for your feast, Zimsko. Strike the one with the sword first and devour him slowly." She set the serpent down, and it immediately dug its snout into the soil, burrowing furiously.

Hundreds of other demons joined in, each one picking a spot around the dome and digging underneath the shield.

The professor's arms trembled. "Any ideas, William?"

When the snakes' bodies disappeared underground, Billy turned to the dragons. "They're coming across! Get ready to blast them!"

Seconds later, Zimsko's ugly head popped up inside the barrier, his tongue flicking over the professor's shoes. The professor stomped its head, splattering black goo under his soles, but dozens more popped up, hissing loudly. The humans in the group stomped on the openings, but there were far too many heads to squish. The dragons shot blasts of fire, engulfing several demons until they burst into flames, but the heads kept appearing. The dark thick bodies squeezed through their burrows until the ground was blackened by writhing serpents with fluttering wings.

Ashley stood in front of Marilyn, her feet set for fighting. More bursts flew from the pendant, joining with the others—twenty dragons . . . fifty . . . too many to count—but they still had no substance, just pure energy in dragon form. The first few now had red eyes, pulsing like the rings they once wore in Dragons' Rest, and they began testing their wings with great fervor, like old soldiers reliving days of glory.

Two demons struck at the professor's legs. He deftly leaped over them and lowered the beam, swiping it across the ground and frying at least six snakes. The photo-umbrella collapsed, leaving nothing to protect them from the Watchers.

Morgan's shrill voice pierced the commotion. "Kill them all!"

Streams of darkness flew toward them. Four of the pendant dragons blew blasts of energy that cut off the black streams, vaporizing them into clouds of smoke. Several more pendant dragons launched a salvo of electricity balls, each ball grabbing

315

a serpent with a pair of sizzling, claw-like arcs of energy and devouring its flesh. When the snake disappeared, the ball crumbled into gray ashes.

The physical dragons spewed fireballs, like bursts from a cannon, into one of the Watchers, pounding his chest until he exploded in a titanic blaze. The Watchers levitated as if on a high-speed elevator until they were nearly out of sight. Devin flew to join them while the serpent demons continued their assault.

The knights mounted their dragons. Edmund whistled a shrill note. "We'll take on the Watchers. Whoever these other dragons are, they can handle the snakes! Fly!" The physical dragons vaulted into the air and zoomed upward, following the path of the Watchers.

Half of the serpents took to the air and struck at the remaining men from above, ignoring the women and girls. The pendant dragons fired their electric snake-eaters, but they weren't always quick enough. One viper bit Sir Patrick on the ankle. He grasped the serpent by the tail and slung it away.

Bonnie squished the crawling demon with her foot and yelled at Shiloh. "Keep stomping! I don't think they can see us!" Shiloh smashed her foot down on one of the biggest serpents. Catherine, Shelly, and Karen hopped from snake to snake, raising splashes of black goo.

Ashley, still without a cloaking halo, stayed at Marilyn's side, hugging Pebbles close to her chest while pressing her hand on Marilyn's throat. One of the pendant dragons guarded them, spewing energy balls at any demon that dared to draw near.

Billy helped Sir Patrick hobble toward Ashley. Patrick sat down heavily, clutching his ankle. Billy pulled up his cuff and examined the wound. It was nasty, already swollen and dark red. "I'll be all right," Patrick said. "Tend to someone else."

Billy shifted to his mother and laid a hand on her cheek. "How is she?"

Ashley pressed harder on Marilyn's neck. "She's breathing, but now that her heart's pumping, she's losing more blood. I'm trying to slow it down, but it's pretty bad."

"Speaking of bad." He nodded toward the field where Morgan stood. Devin had flown to her side again, now a sparkling rusty color. Billy squinted at the glow. What was that stuff on his scales?

Morgan yelled a strange word, and the serpents drew back, flying and slithering into a mass around her and the dragon.

Billy clutched his mother's hand. "How did Devin get out?"

"I let him out." Ashley gazed at him through pitiful eyes. "Will you forgive me?"

"Forgive you?!" Billy leaned over and kissed Ashley on the forehead with a loud smack. "When this is over, I'm gonna knight you!" He braced Marilyn's back and pulled her forward, careful to keep her head from flopping, then lifted the pendant over her head. After leaning her back again, he pointed the rubellite, now as white as bleached wool, at her face. "Dad!" he yelled. "Since the Great Key opened the gates between the two worlds, I'm guessing you can probably hear me now." He drew the pendant back slightly to encompass his mom's slumped body. "This is Marilyn, your wife, and she needs you. Be ready to come out, but wait for my signal." Billy stood and draped the pendant around his neck, then marched quickly toward Walter, his muscles flexing as he steeled himself for battle.

Devin flew toward the professor, his mouth and nostrils blazing. The professor deflected his fire with Excalibur, then slashed across the dragon's body with the beam. The laser sizzled against his scales but immediately died away. With a mighty flap of his wings, Devin swooped low, but the professor ducked to the side.

Devin pulled up and made a sharp turn. He dove again, this time aiming straight for the group of girls. As the dragon leveled off, the professor leaped into the air, hooked his arm around Devin's neck, and swung himself to the top, losing Excalibur in the process.

Bonnie pushed Shiloh and Karen to the ground and lay on top of them, spreading her wings for cover. The professor wrenched the dragon's neck with both arms, forcing his scaly head back and making him fly blind.

Devin swerved away from the girls, roaring and spitting balls of flames. Billy ducked under one of the fireballs, grabbed the sword, and finally joined Walter. With Devin careening like a drunken driver only a few feet off the ground and the professor sitting on top, Billy couldn't get a clean shot at him. Would the beam work at all? Devin seemed unfazed by the professor's blasts.

The professor jerked the dragon's neck again. With a sudden heave, Devin slung him away, sending him tumbling across the ground. Devin soared into the air and banked full circle while Carl, Catherine, and the girls surrounded the fallen teacher.

Walter held out his fist toward Devin. "Dad gave me the candlestone. Let me take that critter out."

His muscles flexed, Billy shook his head and relit Excalibur's beam. "No! This is my fight. But stay close and keep it ready, just in case." He jumped up and down and screamed, "Devin, you mongrel coward! You yellow lizard! Come down here and fight!"

Walter shook his fist. "Yeah!" He pointed at Billy. "What he said!"

Devin zoomed toward the ground, looking like an armored battering ram ready to splinter the two teens like a pair of balsawood doors. Billy muttered, "He thinks that coat will protect him." He set his feet in a battle stance. "Gotta time this just right."

Walter held out his fist. "Just say the word."

The dragon spread his wings and streaked across the ground, no more than five feet in the air. Billy pushed Walter out of the way and yelled into the pendant. "Now, Dad! Now!" He dodged left, bent low, and thrust Excalibur upward into Devin's soft underbelly, driving the blade in to the hilt. The dragon fell, and they both tumbled over and over, finally coming to a stop with Billy prostrate on top, Excalibur still in his grip and the blade wedged deeply in the dragon's belly.

Devin lay on his back, his wings splayed underneath. Billy strangled the hilt of the sword, summoning every ounce of energy he could into the laser beam. Bright sparks spewed from the wound. The dragon's carcass flooded with light. Energy streamed back into Billy's quaking frame, shooting up his arms and covering his body with red arcs of electricity that swept up over his head and sizzled into the air.

A new stream erupted from the pendant, flowing down Billy's arms and back into the wound. Pain ripped through his chest like lightning bolts piercing his heart, each one worse than the plunge of Elaine's dagger. He shuddered, every bone rattling from head to toe. Fire shot out of his mouth and surged into the sky, a rushing torrent greater than any he had ever seen. After what felt like endless torture, the flames sputtered, and Excalibur's beam died away.

Dazed, he slowly climbed to his feet atop the dragon's belly. He grasped the hilt for balance, then, when the world stopped spinning, he withdrew the sword, bringing a flow of sparkling blood with it. He leaped off, bending his knees to soften his landing, then backed away, watching for signs of life.

319

A strange sound from above caught his attention, and he searched the sky. A narrow cylinder of red sparks hovered in the air, swirling like a crimson dust devil of pure energy. It glided to the ground, emitting a high-pitched squeal and a foul-smelling wind, then inched toward the people gathered around the professor, its lower end stirring up the soil.

Billy, with Walter on his heels, headed off the tornado. He halted in front of his friends and stood his ground. Carl knelt beside Professor Hamilton, his arms under the teacher's back, as if preparing to carry him to safety. Catherine and the girls jumped from place to place, stamping out demons.

As the twisting light drew closer to the professor, Walter crept closer to Billy, his head high. "Think it's Devin?" he shouted.

Billy raised Excalibur, the wind whipping his hair. "Yeah, it's Devin, and I'm through running from him."

Walter opened his hand, exposing the candlestone. "Want me to use the dragon slayer vacuum cleaner again?"

Billy tried not to wince, but the gem seemed to bite through his heart like the jaws of a pit bull. He ignited the sword's laser, but the light seemed dimmer than usual, flickering weakly. He could hardly catch his breath. "I don't know." As the cyclone drew within inches, the disgusting odor nearly made him retch. "Keeping him prisoner hasn't worked before."

Walter made a fist around the stone and retreated a single step, his heels touching the professor. "Better make up your mind. That tornado makes the Tasmanian devil look like Cupid doing the twist."

"Let's go for it." Billy nodded toward the ground. "Put it at the bottom of the swirl."

Walter stooped and placed the glittering candlestone just ahead of the swirl's funnel. The candlestone latched onto the light and drew it downward like a fisherman reeling in a prize marlin. The swirl struggled, stretching up and thinning out, its squeal growing louder.

Within seconds, the final stream of red slurped into the stone. Billy raised the sword and sliced through the gem with the bloody blade, splitting it cleanly in half. A dazzling explosion erupted from within, and a shower of sparks fell to the ground and twinkled into oblivion.

Billy stared down at the broken gem and took in a deep draft of air, now clean and fresh. Devin was finally gone for good. He marched back to the dragon's body and laid his palm on the scales. The body jerked. Billy backed away while the dragon rolled upright. It swung its head around and blinked at him, each blink revealing a red flare of nobility in its eyes. A low rumble sounded from its throat, stuttering, as if it were just learning to speak. Finally, it said, "Well done, Billy . . . my son."

The dragon rose to his haunches and lowered his head close to the ground. "We have work to do, so I bow my head to take a rider."

Billy shivered. He raised his hand and caressed his father's ruddy neck. Could it really be true? Was his father really in there now . . . and he remembered? "D—Dad? . . . I mean, Clefspeare? You're . . . You're bowing to me?"

A sort of chortling rumble emanated from the dragon's throat. "Call me 'Dad,' and yes, I am bowing to you, and to another king. But explanations must wait. I have been watching the battle, and I see that Morgan is ready to attack again."

A new foul breeze drifted through the air. Billy gazed windward. Morgan was huddling with Samyaza and one of the snake demons in the field not far from the forest edge. Across the field, the skirmish with the snake demons had almost ended. A few black wigglers remained, but the pendant dragons were

321

mopping them up with the help of the girls. Nearby, Walter knelt next to Carl as he tended to the professor.

Billy whistled a shrill note. "Walter! Get ready for an attack!"

Walter stood and spread his arms. "I was born ready!"

Billy straddled the base of Clefspeare's scaly neck and grabbed a spine. The dragon raised his wings, then drove them downward against the ground, sending out a wall of wind. Again and again he beat his wings, faster and faster, as if rejoicing in the glorious freedom. Billy felt the joy, warmth radiating from his father's glowing scales as his magnificent body lifted into the air.

As they rose, he saw Carl talking to Bonnie. She turned and gazed up at Billy, pain twisting her face.

A shiver crawled along Billy's skin. "Is Prof all right?"

"He's alive," Bonnie shouted. "That's about all I know."

322

Clefspeare spiraled upward, increasing the speed of his ascent. As the humans shrank below him, Billy cupped a hand to the side of his mouth. "Mr. Foley! Check on my mom and Ashley and Sir Patrick, okay?"

Carl flashed an "Okay" sign and ran toward Ashley.

As Clefspeare leveled off, Billy searched the skies for the other dragons. They had to be battling Watchers, but he couldn't find a trace of fiery jets anywhere. A cold breeze buffeted him, drying the blood on his sweater and making it stick to his chest wound. When he pulled it free, it smarted like bees stinging, but he didn't want to take the time to check for new bleeding. He tightened his grip on the sword. It was time for battle.

From the corner of his eye, he spotted another set of fluttering wings. Bonnie hovered close, holding Excalibur's scabbard and belt. ""You forgot something," she said, smiling.

Billy patted the spot behind him. "You up for another adventure?"

"I thought you'd never ask." She settled onto Clefspeare's back and strapped the scabbard around Billy.

Clefspeare's neck curled, and his head swung around to face his riders, a widening smile exposing a row of sharp teeth. "Hang on for the ride of your lives!"

The dragon widened his wings, slowing his body to a smooth glide. The sensation was like cresting the top of the first dip in a mile-high roller coaster. A snort of flames shot out of Clefspeare's nostrils, then another, like a steam engine stoking its furnace. Finally, from both his mouth and nostrils, a river of flames burst forth, and the great dragon angled his body downward.

Billy held his breath and grasped the spine with both hands. Bonnie's strong arms wrapped around his waist. Clefspeare pulled in his wings and dove, plummeting toward the enemy lines. The rush of wind stole Billy's breath away, but he didn't care. With the ground zooming toward his eyes, his drumming heart rising into his throat, and Clefspeare's fire singeing his eyebrows, it was a mind-numbing, hair-raising, gut-wrenching blast!

Like a video game played at triple speed, a hundred different images flashed by every second. First, the ground leveled off. Then, Samyaza came into view, as if Clefspeare had locked onto him, like a radar-equipped jet honing in on its target. Finally, Morgan's grotesque face appeared, shocked and horrified as she backed away from Samyaza.

Zooming ten feet off the surface, they careened toward the Watcher, Clefspeare's inferno-like breath even thicker and brighter than before. Samyaza leaped to one side. Clefspeare's blast missed, but another stream caught the demon, snaking around his body and riveting him in place.

Clefspeare shut off his jets and swerved, beating his wings furiously. Billy glanced back. Another dragon was diving from

323

above, her fiery salvo locked on Samyaza. Her rider waved his fist in the air and let out a Texas-style war whoop. "Yeehaw!"

"Sir Newman!" Billy called out. "And Hartanna!" He slapped Clefspeare's neck. "Dad, she's got the Watcher pinned. Let's circle back and blow him to smithereens!"

Bonnie trembled and pulled closer to Billy. "Mama's alive! Thank God!"

As Clefspeare and his riders made a wide turn, they zipped by their allies at the forest edge. With the help of several pendant dragons and their electricity balls, Walter and Carl fought off a new wave of snake demons encroaching on Professor Hamilton and the women.

"Walter!" Billy shouted. "Cut Morgan off! Careful, though. She might just be a ghost." That was all he could manage before Clefspeare zoomed out of range.

As Clefspeare realigned, Hartanna glided in a circle around her victim, bending her neck to keep her stream of flames on target. Her fire had already engorged Samyaza to twice his usual size. Lightning shot from his clawed fingertips, and darkness streaked from his eyes.

Morgan raised her arms as if preparing some new bit of sorcery, but she suddenly toppled to the ground. Walter stood over her like a conquering prizefighter, the broken broomstick in his hands and a foot planted on her wrist. A pendant dragon stood on the opposite side and pinned her other arm. "She's plenty physical right now," Walter yelled, "but I don't know if it'll last!"

Clefspeare shot out another volley of flames, slamming it into Samyaza's massive chest. The Watcher roared, spreading out his arms and aiming his lightning-charged fingers directly at Billy. He ducked under the first shot, but the second one caught Clefspeare just below Billy's foot. His dad groaned, but kept up his assault. Billy hunkered low. That blow wasn't Clefspeare's only wound. The deep gash in his belly must have been bleeding terribly. How could he keep flying with an injury like that?

Sir Newman rose on his mount, almost standing as he blew a shrill whistle into the sky. "Now!" he shouted.

Another dragon zoomed into the mix, nailing Samyaza's head with a volley of fire. Billy raised a fist. "Yes! Thigocia and Edmund!" In the distance, more dragons approached, diving toward the action with their wings folded in.

The Watcher's fingertip blasts suddenly stopped. Now at four times his original size, and with three dragons pumping energy into his body, he couldn't possibly hold out much longer. Less and less like an angel, he continued to bloat into a grotesque parade balloon.

The wind whipped against Billy's face, stinging his eyes. He shielded them as best he could and stared ahead. More Watchers zoomed up from the horizon. Pointing, he leaned back and shouted to Bonnie. "Things could really get dicey now!"

Suddenly, Samyaza exploded, sending flaming gobs of blackness hurtling through the air. One gob splattered across Sir Newman's face, knocking him off Hartanna. Another slapped the pendant dragon guarding Morgan and spread a coat of darkness across his sparkling body. Walter dodged a third gob, rolling away on the ground across three snake demons. With several lightning-fast swings of his broomstick, he smashed their slimy heads.

Hartanna shut off her flames and swerved back toward Newman, catching him with her claws as she passed. The pendant dragon teetered and fell across Morgan. She threw him off and leaped to a ghostly stance in a single motion. Walter jumped up and charged her with his broomstick, but she raised her hand and threw a swirling ball of blackness at him. It hit him square in the chest and sent him flying backwards.

Clefspeare fired cannonballs of flames at Morgan. She raised her hands and enveloped herself in a black shroud. Each fireball splashed against the shroud, coating it with a thin layer of glowing embers.

Six more dragons arrived and shot rivers of fire at her cloak, circling around her like scaly merry-go-round horses. With most of the snake-demons now destroyed, the pendant dragons joined the assault, but their energy blasts arced around her cocoon, making it look like an electrified dome of burnished coal.

As the dragons concentrated on their blitz, eight Watchers lined up several hundred feet in the air and attacked, hurling darkness in a barrage of sizzling black bombs. One smacked Legossi in the face and spread across her entire head. She hurtled into the ground near the forest edge, throwing Sir Barlow into the trees. The darkness swarmed across her body as she lay writhing on a patch of bare earth.

Firedda fell from the sky, covered in a blanket of black goo, then a third dragon and a fourth, their riders tumbling and sliding as their mounts crashed. A bolt nailed Hartanna's back, sending her spinning downward. Newman fell from her claws seconds before impact, slid to a stop in the tall grass, and lay deathly still.

Billy fumed. The scales under his backside radiated broiling heat. His biceps tightened into steel bands, and he slapped Clefspeare's neck and shouted, "Dad, we can't let them do that to Bonnie's mom! Let's end this fight here and now! You've been filled with energy from Excalibur's beam. I know you can do it!"

With a great flurry of his wings, Clefspeare vaulted higher into the air and charged directly at the eight flying Watchers, trumpeting an ear-splitting battle cry. Billy held on for dear life. Bonnie's grip squeezed his lungs. The torrent of fire that spewed from Clefspeare's mouth was like a volcanic eruption, so wide and powerful it engulfed the four closest Watchers in a flood of raging flames. Each demon clutched his chest, a brilliant light flashing from his eyes, as if he had swallowed Excalibur's beam and become engorged with energy. Like over-filled water balloons, they exploded in a dazzling eruption of black lava.

Clefspeare turned his body, and his momentum hurtled him sideways. He crashed through the other four Watchers, scattering them like humongous bowling pins. As they staggered in the sky, he blasted them one by one with his newly energized, volcano-like stream, bursting them into millions of black droplets.

Clefspeare glided slowly on a rising stream of air. Billy shook his head, trying to recover from the wildest ride in history. As he gazed at the empty sky all around, a chill of excitement ran up and down his spine. He pumped both fists and shouted, "Yes! You did it! Dad, you were awesome!"

Bonnie trembled against Billy's back, bringing his emotions to earth. He looked down at the scene below. Her mother had fallen, and there was no way to tell how badly she was hurt.

But something else was weird. As Clefspeare floated over the forest, a sparkling stream fell from his body to the trees. Billy gulped. Dad's blood! Had the wound opened wider?

Clefspeare sank lower. His wings faltered. The powerful canopies flailed aimlessly as he pitched downward. Seconds later, he dove straight for the ground.

"Hang on!" Billy shouted. The wind snatched his breath away. Every organ squeezed toward his throat. As they plunged, Clefspeare tried desperately to stop their descent, but he only managed to put them into a slow spin.

Suddenly, something tugged at Billy's waist. He glanced over his shoulder. Bonnie, holding onto him with a death grip, flapped her own wings, straining to keep the huge dragon in the air. Although the spiral smoothed out slightly, the forest still hurtled toward them.

327

Billy hung onto Clefspeare's spine with all his might. If he didn't come up with a new plan immediately, all three would be smashed to bits. Only one choice came to mind. His only choice. Clenching his teeth, he let go of the spine.

Bonnie's wings launched Billy upward. His body skimmed the needled tops of a stand of evergreen trees as she struggled to fly clear. Clefspeare crashed to the ground, twisting his frame into a huddled mass at the base of one of the largest evergreens.

Bonnie dove to where the dragon lay and set Billy down between the dragon and the tree trunk. Clefspeare sprawled in a pool of sparkling blood, another stream of red pouring from his mouth, his long neck angled fiercely back toward his body.

Billy and Bonnie knelt at his side. Billy put his arm around Bonnie and laid a hand on Clefspeare's back. His scales had cooled. Their sheen had vanished. The sun's setting rays cast beams of light through the trees, painting a golden mantle on the dragon's motionless body.

Billy's stomach tightened. A sob heaved from his chest, but he sucked it back. As he clung to Bonnie's shoulder, she shook under his hand, and a single tear trickled down her cheek.

Billy bit his lip. He didn't want to cry. No. It wouldn't be right. He had to have faith. There had to be a way to heal his dad. So many others had been healed. Why not Clefspeare?

Bonnie's tears turned into sobs, and she covered her face with her hands, her body rocking back and forth.

Billy finally let his own tears flow. Could this really be the end? After all the trials and tortures to save his dad, could this victory over the Watchers be his final mission? Could that be why God put him in Dragons' Rest, to prepare him to defend his family and the entire world?

Billy tightened his fingers into a fist. It wasn't enough. He knew there had to be more. Sure, the prophecies said the dragon must bow and die, and he had, but Billy's heart and mind screamed for justice. God couldn't let it all end here! His father had come too far to simply crash and die in the forest, to leave a widow suffering and grieving for years to come, to bring a tragic end to this story of renewed dragon faith.

Billy laid his head on his father's back. While he prayed for a miracle, the pendant hanging from his neck bumped against his arm. He grabbed hold of it to keep it still. A strange vibration shook the octagonal frame, increasing in strength by the second. Billy raised his head and released the pendant, letting it dangle against his chest. The rubellite suddenly flashed from white to red. A sunbeam struck its surface and cast a crimson reflection across Clefspeare's body. The red glow darkened and stretched away from Billy and Bonnie, like a shadow lengthening at the end of the day. The shadow took on a human form, a tall, masculine shape.

The shape congealed, amassing solid particles that seemed to flow from Clefspeare's body like a river of liquid flesh. As the human shape grew more solid, the dragon's body seemed to fade away. Tanned skin appeared on a man's face, then pinpoint eyes and a blob for a nose. Hair sprouted, a thick reddish brush that swayed in the breeze, and a pair of ears formed on the sides of his head.

The skin on his blurry torso thickened, transforming into a button-down white shirt with a huge red splotch in the middle of the chest. Shredded material formed on one of the shirt's long sleeves, and a dime-sized hole appeared on the breast pocket, the same hole the dragon slayer had drilled into his chest with a deadly bullet many months ago. While pants and shoes took shape on his lower body, the man patted his sides with his newly created hands.

At last, his face came into focus, the face Billy had seen in Dragons' Rest, a lost and lonely librarian who neither loved him nor even recognized him. But now, that face smiled. The man with the bloody shirt, the torn sleeve, and the bullet hole in his chest spread out his arms. "Billy," he said, "I'm home."

Billy leaped into his embrace, leaning his head against his father's powerful chest and wrapping his arms around him. All the bitterness, all the anger, all the fear that had built up in his soul through the months of fruitless searches, all the emotions he had pushed down in his gut while journeying through a literal hell and beyond, finally melted away, pouring out in hot tears on his father's shoulder. The dragon's body had completely vanished, and Jared Bannister really was finally home.

Time stood still. Every problem in the world dissolved. No Watcher or wraith or snake demon or dragon slayer or anything else could possibly separate him from his father's love. Not now or ever again.

A hand touched his shoulder. "Billy?"

He pulled back. Bonnie stood beside him with her hands folded in front of her. "Billy, I need to see about my mother."

Billy slapped his forehead. "Right! The black stuff nailed her!" He swiveled his head back and forth, then pointed toward a gap in the trees. "That way, Dad?"

Jared stooped and peered through the trees. "I think so, but I was in a mental fog on the way down, so I'm not sure."

Bonnie beat her wings and lifted into the air. "I'll find out," she said, already zooming upward. "You head that way on foot, and I'll let you know if it's right." She waved as she reached the treetops. "It's great to see you again, Mr. Bannister!"

As Billy and Jared ran across a bed of fallen needles, the worries of the battlefield stormed back into Billy's mind. The Watchers were gone, but Mom was still badly hurt, the professor seemed half dead, Sir Patrick was fighting snake venom,

Walter had been knocked for a loop, most of the dragons had been swallowed by the weird black goo, and last but not least, Morgan had to be finished off. Who could tell what she might be preparing in that weird cocoon of hers?

As they neared the forest edge, they could see Morgan's shroud still standing, its surface glowing with radiant heat.

Billy drew his sword and nodded toward his dad. With his face set like a granite cliff, his father returned the nod. Together they sprinted from the forest. It was time to go to war again, this time with his father at his side.

19

CHAPTER

The Return of the Prophet

S printing from the forest, Billy and Jared burst onto a scene that looked more like a movie disaster than a lakefront park. Bodies of humans and dragons littered the area, plumes of fire and smoke dotted the landscape, black goo smeared the grassy field, and the visitor center smoldered far in the background.

Thigocia, the only dragon still standing, shot a stream of fire at another dragon, burning away the oily darkness that had gripped her. The stricken dragon wriggled beneath Thigocia's superheated shower, her eyes bright and her scales glowing.

Walter pushed a shoulder under Sir Barlow's arm and helped the knight shuffle toward Ashley's makeshift infirmary, the huge oak tree where she tended Billy's mom and three knights. Ashley, pale and moving slowly, helped Marilyn shift her body to a more comfortable sitting position against the trunk of the oak. Marilyn grimaced with every move, but her eyes remained closed.

Billy dashed toward his mother, Jared at his heels. He slid to his knees beside her and gazed at her pallid face. Keeping his voice low, he called to her. "Mom?"

Jared knelt at her other side, his whisper barely audible. "Marilyn?"

Her eyes fluttered open. Seeing Billy first, she smiled weakly. "Ashley said the bleeding stopped. Looks like you're stuck with me a while longer."

Billy couldn't say a word. Too excited even to breathe, he glanced from his mother to his father. It would be perfect if she'd catch sight of him without being told he was there. If only she would look his way!

Finally, Jared took her hand in his, and her head swiveled toward him. She glanced back at Billy, her eyes wide, then, turning again to Jared, she let out a gasp. "Oh!" She boosted herself higher and whispered, "My husband!" She reached out for him with a trembling hand.

Jared swept her up in his powerful arms and cradled her, kissing her tenderly. He rubbed his cheek against hers, whispering, "I'm back, my love, and I'll never leave you again." He pulled her closer, his whole body quaking as he pushed his fingers through her hair. "Never!"

Billy pressed his lips together and wiped a tear. This scene was perfect—absolutely perfect.

Walter nudged him in the ribs. "Hey, Your Majesty. You and Ashley had better get with Prof and light him up with the sword. He's in pretty bad shape."

Billy rose to his feet, searching the field for the professor. Morgan's dark cocoon still smoldered in the grass, Thigocia standing nearby, keeping an eye on it as she swept black goo from another dragon. Bonnie knelt next to the victim's forelegs, cleaning her scales with a rag. "We'll be finished soon, Mama."

334

How are you feeling?" Hartanna gave Bonnie a hot kiss on the cheek, making her laugh.

Ashley hobbled to Billy's side, and they made their way to the circle of people surrounding the professor. In the center of the huddle, Sir Patrick sat cross-legged, propping Professor Hamilton up in his arms. His rolled-up pants cuff exposed his wound, pink and less swollen. Ashley's work.

Patrick looked up at Billy, dirt smearing one cheek on his grave face. "He is breathing, William, and his eyes are open, but if my old friend is in there, I cannot find him."

Billy crouched near the professor's head as it lay in the crook of Patrick's arm. He pushed a sweat-soaked strand of his teacher's white hair away from his brow. With his steely eyes staring into the sky and his mouth partly open, the professor seemed awestruck, as if gazing at a wonderful sight, or maybe a terrifying one.

Ashley knelt on the other side of Patrick. "I don't know how much healing energy I have left, but we'll both give it everything we've got."

Billy nodded. "You better believe we will." As he reached back to draw out Excalibur, the pendant vibrated again, flashing white and spewing a new burst of sparks. The energy swirled into a bright, cyclonic funnel and spun into the professor's body, disappearing in a twinkle.

The teacher's arms jerked. His hands grasped Patrick's arm. He blinked his eyes, then raised his head, turning to glance at each person in the huddle. When his gaze rested on Billy, his brow lifted. "Billy," he said, pushing himself out of Patrick's cradle, "I will need your sword."

Billy rose from his crouch. As the professor brushed off his clothes, Billy handed him the sword. What could have happened? How did Prof get healed without Ashley or the sword?

335

And why did he say "Billy" instead of "William"? Billy cleared his throat. "So . . . you're okay, Prof?"

"'Okay' is a relative term, Billy." The professor took the hilt and raised Excalibur to the sky. "But you might say that I am quite ready to end this conflict forever." He leaned toward Billy's chest and spoke to the pendant. "This will be over soon, my dears. Stay close to the screen, and we will soon pull you out."

The professor marched from the circle, Carl and Catherine parting to let him through, and the rest staring at him without a word. As he approached the black cocoon, humans and dragons gathered behind him. He energized the sword, shooting a brilliant laser into the sky, then halted a few feet from the smoldering black mass.

"Morgan!" he shouted, wielding Excalibur in one hand. "Come out and face me . . . if you dare!"

A fresh breeze blew across the field, fanning the rising gray smoke away from the cocoon. Sweat and blood dried under Billy's sweater, cooling his skin. He shivered.

"Morgan!" The professor angled the beam over the top of the black cylinder, bringing it within inches of the cocoon. "Are you now trembling in fear behind your own skirts? Has the queen been forced into the corner by a mere pawn?"

The cocoon trembled. A crack slowly formed, inching its way from top to bottom until the two sides fell away. The professor set his feet. Billy took a step toward him, but his teacher raised his hand. "No, Son. This is my battle alone."

Black smoke rose from inside the broken vessel, shrouding whatever lurked within. A sudden wind gust knocked down the two halves of the cocoon and swept away the fog. Morgan remained, standing fully erect and youthful. Only a scarred cheek blemished the smooth skin covering her beautiful, angular face.

Jet-black hair streamed past her waist. A devilish smile grew on her ruby lips. "Is it a tired, old professor who taunts me so bravely?"

"I am certainly tired and old," the professor replied, lifting the beam, "and I have been called a professor—of prophetic ballads, actually, a singing Elijah, if you will."

Morgan took a step closer and gazed into the professor's eyes as if trying to read his mind. "Elijah burned in a chariot of fire centuries ago," she said. "He is nothing but a flash of light in the sky."

"Elijah has returned, Morgan." He leaned closer to her. "Do you not recognize your old friend?"

Morgan's pupils burst into flames. "Merlin!" She floated backwards and thrust her hands in front of her. A swirling black ball shot out from her palms. Merlin vaporized it with the gleaming sword.

337

Morgan retreated farther, half floating, half stumbling. Fear glazed her eyes.

Merlin stalked toward her. "Defend yourself, you demonic sorceress, you murderer of innocent women and children. Your days of deceit and death have come to an end."

With a wave of her hands, ten enormous serpents sprouted from the ground, but Merlin whacked their heads off with a single swipe. Black smoke erupted at Morgan's feet, solidifying into narrow ropes that flew at Merlin and wrapped around his legs and waist.

"*Apoluson!*" Merlin shouted. The ropes ripped to shreds and fell to the ground. He continued his march forward.

Morgan swept a hand upward. Smoke shrouded her, then congealed into a six-foot-tall raven. With a flurry of wings, she vaulted into the air and sped toward the onlookers, her claws extended. She snatched Ashley by the hair and lifted her as high as the treetops. "Promise me safe passage to Avalon," the raven croaked, "or the girl dies."

Ashley, her feet kicking the air, grabbed the raven's legs. "Let me go, you ugly vulture, or I'll pluck you like a Christmas turkey!"

Bonnie and Thigocia launched into the sky after her. The raven dove away from the dragon, but Bonnie zoomed underneath and latched onto Ashley's waist. Flapping her dragon wings madly, she pulled the evil bird toward the ground. As they neared Merlin, the raven released her catch, but Ashley held on to the scrawny legs. When they glided within reach, Merlin grabbed the bird by the throat, and Ashley let go. Bonnie swept her safely away and set her down next to Walter.

The raven thrashed her wings and clawed at Merlin's chest, but the prophet didn't flinch. He raised his sword hand, and the raven suddenly stopped struggling. She opened her sharp beak and croaked again, her voice sounding thin and strangled. "You and I both know there is only one way to kill me with that sword."

Merlin relaxed his hold and nodded. "For a hell-bound wraith, you are well acquainted with God's ways, aren't you?"

Morgan's bird eyes flashed scarlet. "A wise man once said, 'Know thy enemy.' And I also know that your wife toils futilely where dragons once rested. The dragon savior has come, but there is no one to release the human spirits who still dwell there."

Merlin laughed. "Well, then, perhaps there are mysteries you have not yet learned." He nodded toward Billy. "Bring the Great Key."

Billy glanced at Bonnie and Walter. Both stared at Merlin and Morgan with wide eyes. Billy couldn't blame them. The whole scene was worse than the most twisted nightmare he could imagine. Too much evil. Too many deaths. And, worst of all, what happened to Prof? As Billy strode forward, he pulled the chain over his head and extended it to Merlin.

The old prophet dipped his head under the chain and let the pendant dangle at his chest. As he straightened, his eyebrows lifted. "Do you have a question, my son?"

A sob welled up in Billy's throat, but he swallowed it down. "Yeah . . . uh . . . where's Prof?"

Morgan flailed her wings and squawked, "He's—"

Merlin tightened his grip on her throat, freezing her in place. "He is in here with me, in this body." A gentle smile spread across his lips. "Don't worry, son. I have a final song to sing, and you must try to decipher its meaning. After that, you will see your professor again."

Clearing his throat, Merlin gazed into the sky, reddish sunlight illuminating his aged face. Then, raising Excalibur high, he began to sing in a sweet tenor.

339

The war of flesh and spirit raged,
Two soldiers red and white.
They fought with laws and codes of men,
A covenant of strife.

But laws will fail and codes will pass,
Like flowers in the field.
Then faith and hope and love will grow
In hearts that bow and yield.

A dragon bows and honors him
Who suffered wounds and died,
For scales and flesh have common needs
To cast out evil pride.

And now each soul must choose his way,
To walk on feet or claws.
Will flesh or scales become their guide
To follow grace or laws?

The Key unlocks the gates that hold
A mind and soul in place.
Its light transforms surrendered hearts
And changes them through grace.

Now anthrozils may use that light
To make their gems grow pale,
To humanize their dragon marks
And cast away their scales.

340

The words burned into Billy's mind, as though he could see a stone tablet chiseled with flaming letters, each word repeated in the prophet's voice as he read it silently in his thoughts.

Merlin heaved a deep sigh and turned to his audience. "And now I bid you farewell," he said, bowing politely, "but I trust that I will see you again someday." With the sword's beam blazing, he struck the raven's head. Her black feathers burst into flames, engulfing the huge bird in seconds. Merlin released her neck, and she attacked him, pecking and clawing his head furiously while tongues of fire lashed his shoulders and ignited his clothes. Before any of the onlookers could do anything, both prophet and wraith burst into millions of particles of light. Morgan's molecules dripped to the ground in a black stream, while Merlin's white light floated and danced in the sun's fading glow.

Billy leaped toward the dancing sparks. "No!" he yelled. "You can't! You didn't!" He dropped to his knees, holding out a palm as particles of light struck his skin and rolled to the ground. He could barely croak his nightmarish idea of what might be spilling from his hand. "Prof? Is that you?"

The sword and pendant lay in the midst of the shower, the rubellite flashing bright white. "Merlin?" Billy whispered, his voice cracking. "What have you done?"

The sparks of energy slowly piled up in two columns, each one taking a similar human shape—tall and lanky, with a broad forehead and flowing white hair. One of the shapes reached down and touched Billy's head. He spoke in a soft, familiar British tone. "William, can you see me?"

Billy stood, his heart thumping wildly. He searched the shining face, a young, radiant face, yet somehow still old and wise. The professor smiled. Billy raised a trembling hand to the shimmering arm and touched its tingly surface. "Prof?"

"Yes, William. It is I. My journey to find the king's star is over, and it is time for me to finally rest." He laid a hand on the shoulder of the identical shape standing next to him. "Merlin and I will fly to our reward."

"And Dorcas?" Billy asked.

The professor raised a finger. "Ah! I believe the answer is forthcoming." He bowed toward Merlin. "After you, my good fellow."

Merlin narrowed his sparkling hand to a thin line and reached into the pendant's stone. When he withdrew it, another hand grasped his. He stepped back, and a radiant body of energy, female in form, emerged from the gem and jumped into his embrace. She and Merlin whispered to each other, then she turned and hooked her arm around his elbow.

Billy nodded, giving her the best smile he could. "Good to see you again, Sarah."

She bent her knees into a half curtsy. "And you, young king."

The professor inserted his hand into the rubellite and with-drew another woman. Billy recognized Dorcas immediately as she flew into the professor's arms. "I remember!" she cried. "Charles, I remember!"

As Billy watched the emotion-packed reunion, a hand touched his back, then another. He spun around. His mom and dad stood behind him holding hands. On his father's finger, the rubellite ring shone whiter than a pearl.

Jared pulled off his ring and handed it to Billy. "Since I'm fully human now, I won't be needing this." He folded Billy into his arms and whispered, "You were right all along. Chains aren't so bad if you're in service to the true king. All the souls in Dragons' Rest saw that king . . . in you . . . in your sacrifice." His father's grip tightened. What was once a wrestling hold had become the luxurious embrace of a loving, human father who was home to stay. Billy grasped the ring tightly in his palm, unable to reply. He just patted his dad on the back and enjoyed the comfort of his strong arms.

Jared stepped toward Merlin and sank to one knee, bow-ing his head. His voice trembled. "My old friend . . ." He lifted his gaze, his eyes wet with tears. "You have watched over me . . . for a very long time." His voice strengthened. "From the day you gave me the wine of transformation, through all my years as a human, and even in the depths of Hades, you have delivered God's grace to me and my family." He spread out his empty hands. "I have nothing to give that could possibly repay you."

Merlin swept a glowing finger across Jared's cheek and picked up a sparkling tear. As it dangled from his fingertip, he knelt close to Jared. "Here is my reward, Jared Bannister. The tears of a dragon are rare indeed, but I prefer the tears of a father."

Jared and Marilyn stood and approached Professor Hamilton together. Marilyn reached her arms around the teacher and laughed when she passed through his body. She looked up at him, her face glowing in the light of his aura. "Thank you, Professor, for being a father to my son when Jared was unable to be here. Without you, Billy would never have found his true weapons, the sword and shield that come from the Light of the world."

Professor Hamilton folded his hands together and bowed. "It was my pleasure, Marilyn, but it was the Light who really guided his way."

Jared and Marilyn turned away, hand in hand. As they passed, Jared said softly, "Billy, Carl and I are going to start transporting the wounded to the hospital, so after you say your good-byes, we'll meet you and Walter and Bonnie at the parking lot."

343

His throat too tight to speak, Billy gave his parents a half-hearted nod. As they walked away, he slid the ring over his finger. Just after the band passed his knuckle, the rubellite flushed from white to red. He turned back to the four sparkling shapes and gazed at Professor Hamilton. Stooping low, Billy picked up the pendant, never taking his eyes off his teacher. After draping the chain around his neck, he gestured for Bonnie and Walter to join him.

They stepped to Billy's side. The professor floated to Walter and stood at attention in front of him, his hands behind his back. Walter copied his teacher's stance, a single tear trickling down his cheek.

"Mr. Foley," the professor said, "it has been an honor to serve with a warrior such as yourself. It is likely that neither William nor Bonnie would have survived their trials had you not stood by them with strength, courage, and unshakable faithfulness."

Walter firmed his chin and nodded. "None of us would've made it without you, Prof. You're . . ."—half laughing and half crying, he wiped away the tear—"you're the cat's pajamas!"

The professor smiled broadly and moved to Bonnie. With her wings spread fully behind her, she dipped to one knee and bowed her head. "I . . . I have a song for you, Professor." Her voice squeaking, she lifted her wet eyes toward her teacher and struggled past a series of sobs as she sang. "If I ascend . . . up into heaven, . . . thou art there. If I make my bed in hell, . . . behold, thou art there. If I take the wings of the morning, and dwell in the uttermost parts of the sea . . ." She couldn't go on. She lowered her head and wept.

The professor's glowing hand passed through Bonnie's halo and paused just above her head as he sang the end of her song. "Even there shall thy hand lead me, and thy right hand shall hold me." His fingers seemed to stroke her golden hair. "Miss Silver, the first day I met you, I saw a frightened orphan searching for acceptance and love. Now I see a valiant daughter of heaven, more deeply loved than you will ever know. I, for one, love you dearly, as do all who care to look beyond your dragon wings to find the heart of an angel."

As Walter and Bonnie backed away, the professor returned to Billy, hovering in front of him and casting a shining nimbus all around. Billy stepped forward and tried to embrace his beloved teacher. For a moment, he felt only tingles, like a mild electrical buzz, but when he closed his eyes, the pendant vibrated again, and the warm strong arms of his wise old mentor wrapped him up. Not daring to open his eyes again, he whispered, "I love you, Professor. And I'll miss you like crazy."

The professor's familiar voice whispered back. "And I love you, as well, William, as I have ever since the day I caught you flooding the water closet."

Billy's memory flashed back to an image of himself standing on a stool with Adam Lark, a shower of putrid water from
the ceiling sprinklers spraying all over him. When Professor
Hamilton entered the bathroom, his eyes gleamed with mirth,
the same kind of joy he expressed in everything he did. Yes, his
enthusiasm for life never wavered, even though, as Billy now
knew, he had suffered loneliness every day since his wife's death.

Billy felt a pat on his back as the voice continued. "I hope
our Lord allows me to watch you from heaven. I don't want to
miss your wedding for anything in the universe."

The pendant fell still. The embrace evaporated. Billy opened
his eyes and stepped back as the four dazzling people lifted off
the ground. As they rocketed into the heavens, the sky opened
up, a shining rift that captured their energy and pulled them
into paradise. Seconds after their souls disappeared, dozens of
pendant dragons lined up to enter into a true dragons' rest.
When the last one vanished, the rift closed and the sky dimmed.

Billy drooped his shoulders and slowly turned. He found
Excalibur on the ground next to a thick black puddle, the spot
where Morgan breathed her last. He kicked the oily mass, scattering sizzling droplets until they slowly sank into the dirt.

He stooped and wrapped his fingers around Excalibur's hilt,
the great sword that Professor Hamilton had searched so long
to find and now had left behind. He lifted the blade and
admired its detailed engraving, two dragons in the heat of battle. Finally, it all made sense. Every adventure undertaken, every
prophecy spoken or sung, every dangerous road pointed to this
simple truth—a battle between good and evil rages every day.

Billy gazed into the sky. He could almost see streams of fire
blazing again in the twilight extinguishing bolts of darkness.
Courageous dragons and knights stormed against myriad forces
of evil, no mater what the odds. He nodded at the images in his

345

mind. No doubt about it. Those battles symbolized his own. Sometimes he saw them with his eyes. Sometimes he felt them in his heart. And there came a time when the king had to come and fight the battle for him and end the conflict once and for all. For him . . . and all the dragons . . . that day had finally come, and the king had conquered their enemies.

Billy straightened his body and reverently slid Excalibur into his scabbard, then walked slowly toward his two best friends in the world.

Bonnie curled her arm around Billy's and walked at his side. "I heard the professor whispering. Can you tell me what he said to you?"

Billy finally found the strength to give a real smile. "Some of it. He said he loved me. I guess that's all that really matters." He lifted his head and gazed into her bright blue eyes. "How's your mom?"

346

"She'll be fine. After we cleaned off all the darkness stuff, she seemed as good as new, except for being exhausted. She and Newman had been searching for Edmund, but two Watchers found them and chased them for miles. She also cleaned the darkness from a couple of other dragons. That's why she was gone for so long."

Walter bounced along beside them, counting on his fingers as he talked. "Okay, we still have some business to take care of. All the ladies are safe, but your dad wants your mom to check into the hospital. Fiske and Woodrow are going, too. Fiske broke a leg, and Woodrow might have some broken ribs, but the rest of the knights are okay except for a few cuts and bruises. Sir Patrick's snakebite doesn't seem to be a problem anymore, thanks to Ashley. We have four wounded dragons, but they all made it to the parking lot, and Thigocia will work on them there, so they should be ready to hit the skies again soon."

Billy halted. Bonnie and Walter stopped with him, both staring at him curiously.

"The dragons," Billy said, staring straight ahead.

Walter waved his hand in front of Billy's eyes. "What about them?"

Billy grabbed Walter's wrist and held it in place. "Merlin's song. It said they have to choose."

"Choose what?"

Billy covered his ears. Merlin's song played again in his mind, and he wanted to get the words right. "Listen. It says they have to choose whether or not to walk on feet or claws." He lowered his hands and grasped the pendant. "That means they can become human, and the light from this is supposed to transform them if that's what they choose."

Walter passed his hand across the ray of white light flashing from the gem, highlighting a splotch of dirt on his palm. "Who would want to become human? I think it would be cool to be a dragon."

347

"That's for sure," Billy replied, "but wouldn't they want a human soul? They wouldn't want to end up back in Hades again."

Bonnie's eyes sparkled. Her halo had faded somewhat, but she still glowed with the countenance of an angel. "Did the song say anything else?" she asked.

"Yeah. It said anthrozils could make the choice too."

Bonnie laid a finger on her chest. "You mean *we* could make a choice? What kind of choice?"

Billy covered his ears again, this time closing his eyes as he concentrated on the lyrics. "The song says, 'To humanize their dragon marks and cast away their scales.'"

Bonnie's brow lifted. A lump moved up and down in her throat, and her wings shuddered. "But how?"

"Isn't that what happened to Sir Patrick?" Walter asked. "I mean, he was once Valcor, and now he says there isn't any dragon in him."

"And his rubellite turned white." Billy lifted his hand and showed his ring to Bonnie and Walter. "My dad's rubellite is red now, but when I was wearing it in the village, it was white."

"Mine too," Bonnie said, showing her borrowed red gem. "We didn't have our dragon traits there."

Billy slid his hands into his pockets and accelerated. Walter and Bonnie hurried to join him. "Well, there's only one way to figure out what to do," Billy said, his gaze fixed on the parking lot near the visitor center.

"The horse's mouth?" Walter asked.

"Yep. I think Sir Patrick knows a lot more than he's been telling us."

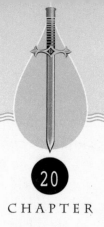

20

ORACLES OF FIRE

W hen Billy and his friends arrived, the parking lot looked like a triage facility. Carl's SUV was the only vehicle in sight, and several dragons and knights hobbled from place to place, as if testing their bodies for travel. Ashley wandered among the wounded, speaking to each one, but she looked half dead herself.

Billy hustled ahead in time to help his father and Carl slide Fiske into the SUV. As they propped him up next to Woodrow, the knight stifled a grunt, then smiled and nodded at Billy. "Thank you, young man. It was an honor to battle with you."

Billy patted him on the shoulder. "Likewise." He really didn't know what else to say, so he just nodded and stepped back.

Jared reached into a hatch in the door well. "Look what I found!" he said as he pulled out *Fama Regis*.

Billy looked over his shoulder as his father opened it near the middle. The familiar old runes covered both pages. "Have you ever thought about translating the whole thing?"

"Many times, but the stories always reminded me of how I lost my dragon life. The pain was just too much to bear." Jared closed the book and held it against his chest. "But now I think I'll finally do it."

Carl held the back car door open. "Anyone else need to go right away?"

Jared laid an arm over Marilyn's shoulders. "You should get checked out. At least get a tetanus shot."

She pulled him close. "I'm not leaving you, not for a second."

As Carl shut the door, Sir Barlow limped to the SUV and laid his hand on the hood. "If I may accompany my comrades, I would be most grateful. Perhaps they will need blood, or maybe even a song to lift their spirits."

Woodrow rolled his eyes, and Billy barely squelched a laugh.

Carl opened the passenger door. "Ride up front with me. We'll sing together."

While Barlow climbed in, Walter and Bonnie joined Billy at the driver's door. Billy nodded toward the group of dragons and humans assembled under a nearby light post. Ashley stood next to her mother, stretching on tiptoes to speak into her ear, while Shelly, Karen, and Shiloh went from dragon to dragon checking for remnants of the gooey darkness.

"Looks like Thigocia's got the dragons all patched up," Billy said.

Walter crossed his arms over his chest. "Yep. And here comes the man we need to talk to."

Sir Patrick hobbled toward the vehicle, Pebbles gripping his hand firmly.

"Did Alberta work on your leg yet?" she asked in her tiny voice.

Patrick leaned against the rear door. "Alberta? Who is Alberta?"

"That's Ashley," Bonnie explained. "Pebbles calls her Alberta."

Sir Patrick pulled his hand away and patted Pebbles on the head. "Alberta already drained the venom, young lady. I'll be fine." Pebbles ran back to the dragons and jumped into Ashley's arms.

Patrick sighed and extended his hand toward Billy. "Well done, young king."

Billy grasped Patrick's hand and shook it firmly. "I appreciate it, Sir Patrick, but, if you don't mind, I just want people to call me by my name from now on."

"Very well. Then I shall apply the label my departed friend used and simply call you William."

"I'd like that." Billy glanced around. His father was talking to Carl, so it looked like they weren't quite ready to leave yet. He gestured for Walter and Bonnie to gather close. "Listen, Sir Patrick. We have a question. Merlin's song said something about the dragons choosing to become human, and the pendant's gem could make it happen. Can you tell us anything about that?"

"Yes. I came over here for that very purpose." Patrick gazed into the dimming sky, his brow shading his eyes. "It's a long story you haven't heard yet, but the substance is fairly easy to grasp. When a dragon king dies and passes from a world of dragons to a world of men, the gateway from one existence to the other stays open for a time. The power to transform abides in the gateway's energy, but only for those who have the faith to completely deny their old lives and allow the energy to wash away the dragon within."

He pushed away from the SUV and faced Billy. "This happened to me years ago, when another son of Makaidos, an earlier dragon king, sacrificed his life to save me, and I chose to purge my remaining dragon essence. Being the son of Makaidos, he, of course, was my brother, though I didn't realize it for quite some time. I hope to tell you the whole story someday, but for now, we must focus on the decisions at hand. You and the dragons have the opportunity to become fully human in every aspect of your beings."

"But is the dragon essence evil?" Billy asked. "I mean, we already have human souls. Why would we want to change?"

Sir Patrick laid a hand on Billy's chest. "There is no good or evil except for what is in your heart and how that is expressed in your actions. Your dragon breath and your danger sensing abilities are mere physical manifestations. Your faith is what made you a new person."

He pointed at Billy and Bonnie in turn. "You two and Ashley must search your own hearts. Your physical traits are really nothing. It is the purity of your inner selves that makes all the difference in the world. So, in the end, it boils down to whether or not you want to continue to carry the marks of your heritage and possibly pass on dragon traits to any children you might beget. They come with both dangers and benefits."

"You know," Billy said, "I didn't use my fire breathing at all during that battle." He pulled Excalibur from its scabbard. "After I learned how to use this, I didn't even need the fire."

"There is so much more substance to what you said than you realize." Patrick reached for the pendant and drew the chain over Billy's head. "If you don't mind, I will take this and meet with each of you and with each dragon in private. Pray for guidance, and I advise you not to consult with one another. Then, when you meet with me, you can ask any questions you have and make your choice. But you must choose before we leave this place. If the gem's energy has the same endurance as it did when I was transformed, we have only an hour or so before it loses its power."

Billy returned the sword to its sheath. "So where do we meet, and who will go first?"

Patrick nodded toward the visitor center. "Behind the remains of the building. I believe privacy is crucial if you want to make your decisions without influencing each other." He pushed his head through the pendant chain and let it fall around his neck. "I will explain the situation to the dragons together, because they will likely wish to decide what to do as a group. After I am finished with them, I will take Ashley, then you, William, and Bonnie last."

Bonnie ran a hand through her hair, her voice quivering slightly. "Why me last?"

"Since one of your dragon traits is the most obvious, and perhaps even the most magnificent, your decision could be the most difficult." Patrick limped toward the dragons. "Walter, if you would, please come with me; I will likely need someone to ferry everyone back and forth."

Walter shrugged his shoulders. "I guess I'll see you guys soon." He trotted after Patrick.

Bonnie peered into the SUV. "Seen my backpack anywhere?"

Billy popped open the rear hatch. "Hey guys, you seen a backpack?"

Woodrow tossed it toward him. "Sorry. I was sitting on it."

"You three comfortable in there?" Billy asked. "I think it'll be a while before you get going."

"Oh, we're fine," Barlow said. "Woodrow and Fiske are having some trouble deciding which songs I should sing, but I am able to fill in the gaps."

Billy winked at Barlow. "Great. Don't wear out your voice." He closed the hatch and handed the backpack to Bonnie. "I knew my mom would never leave anything behind."

Billy helped Bonnie fold her wings into the pack. "So, this could be your last time to have to wear this."

She pulled a strap tight, her brow tightly furrowed. "I think we should take Patrick's advice and keep our thoughts private."

"Oh, yeah. Sorry. I was just thinking . . ."

She touched his arm with her fingertips. "It's okay. I was wondering the same thing, but I have to think about all the possibilities before I decide."

Billy kicked a pebble on the pavement. "I know what you mean. If it wasn't for our dragon traits, we couldn't have gone in and saved the dragons in the seventh circle. You couldn't have flown and rescued me when I needed you. And my danger-sensing saved my skin at least a hundred times."

Bonnie's lips thinned out, her brow still knit. "True," she said, nodding. "But now I might have to face billboards and TV ads looking for a dragon girl."

Billy laid a hand on her backpack. His fingers traced the indentation of one of the wing mainstays that bulged against the material. "Let's stop talking. I don't want to influence you one way or the other."

Bonnie walked to the front of the SUV and leaned back against the hood. She folded her arms and gazed toward the visitor center, her expression as lost and confused as that of a wandering orphan. Suddenly, she stood up straight, her hand over her mouth. Hartanna glided by with Walter riding on her back. She flew toward the center, and the two disappeared behind the building.

Bonnie glanced at Billy. Her chin quivered, but she said nothing and rested against the hood again. Billy settled back with her and crossed his arms over his chest. He let out a long sigh. Torture. That's what it was. He had endured the pain for months, the pain of not knowing who or what his father really was. Now it was Bonnie's turn. What would Hartanna decide? He slipped his hand into Bonnie's and gave her a gentle squeeze.

After a tense couple of minutes, Walter reappeared, walking side by side with a woman. Barefoot and wearing a bathrobe, the woman stopped at the edge of the parking lot. Walter laughed and pointed directly at Bonnie. Holding the robe's sash in place, the woman ran toward Bonnie, her blond hair flowing.

Bonnie's lips parted as if ready to speak, but she raised her hand and covered her mouth, her chest heaving. Finally, she lowered her hand and let out a pitiful cry. "Mama!" She leaped ahead and bolted across the parking lot, her arms outstretched. "Mama! You're back!"

Nearly colliding in the middle of the lot, the two embraced, wrapping each other up and kissing each other's cheeks while they spun in place.

Billy strolled up to the pair, tears welling in his eyes. When they stopped their dance, Bonnie pulled away. With an enormous smile, she looked up at her mother and gestured toward Billy. "Mama, now you can finally shake hands with Billy!"

Bonnie's mother extended her hand. A radiant smile decorated her beautiful face. "It's my pleasure," she said.

Billy shook her hand. "So you're back to being Irene . . . uh . . . Silver?"

Irene pulled Bonnie close again, her smile unabated. "I am Irene, but I think I'll keep my husband's last name. I am the widow of a man who died a hero."

A peal of laughter drew Billy's gaze toward the gathering under the light post. Jared, Marilyn, Carl, Catherine, and the girls greeted a new arrival, another dragon in her human form. A third woman emerged from the back of the visitor center, then, a minute or so later, a fourth. One by one, the former dragons paraded toward the group, each wearing clothing from a different time period and arriving to happy handshakes and warm embraces.

Walter ran out from behind the visitor center and laid his hand on Ashley's elbow. As he led her toward the ruins on one side of the building, another form appeared on the opposite side, out of Ashley's view. With wings of shimmering gold, Thigocia, still in dragon form, flew toward the parking lot.

Staying low to the ground, she landed near the SUV, then dipped her head and let out a mournful cry, much like a low note on a trombone. Irene approached her first and laid a hand on her neck as the other humans gathered around. "Thigocia, what happened?"

The dragon let her wings droop on the pavement. "I told Sir Patrick I would honor our group decision to become human, but he could tell that I was torn."

Irene stroked her scales. "I see. Because of your son."

Marilyn joined Irene at the dragon's side. "You have a son?" she asked.

Thigocia lowered her body to the ground. "I do. As I told my dragon friends when we gathered with Sir Patrick, my husband, Timothy, and I had a son named Gabriel almost fifty years before Ashley was born."

"Fifty years?" Marilyn clasped her hands together. "Seventy years isn't very old for an anthrozil, so he's probably still alive, right?"

"Yes—that is, if he kept away from the dragon slayers." Thigocia's ears rotated as she gazed into the sky. "But who knows where he might be? You see, Timothy and I moved to the U.S., while Gabriel stayed in Scotland. When it became clear that Devin was stalking me again, I stopped communicating with Gabriel, hoping to keep him safe. But when Ashley was born, I received an odd telegram from Glasgow. It said, 'Congratulations on the birth of your daughter. May she live in peace and learn the secret behind the Oracles of Fire.'"

"Oracles of Fire?" Irene tapped a finger on her chin. "Did you mention that before? It sounds familiar."

356

Billy gave Bonnie a quick look. She raised a shushing finger to her lips.

"It sounded familiar to me, as well," Thigocia continued, "but I was never able to track Gabriel down to find out." She let out a long, sparks-laden breath. "Soon after, while Ashley was out with Timothy 's father, Devin set our house on fire, murdering Timothy and sending my bones to the seventh circle."

Irene backed away and put her arm around Bonnie. "So now you want to find Gabriel, right?"

"Yes, and also my husband's spirit. It would take too long to explain, but Timothy has a very special origin himself. I can't believe he is gone forever." A large tear inched down Thigocia's scaly cheek. "Now you can see why I was so torn. By remaining a dragon, I would risk never having another chance to gain a human soul, but I would also be able to search more easily since I could probably sense Gabriel's presence." Thigocia lifted herself to her hind legs. "So Patrick told me to stand while he flashed the gem's light on me, just to see what would happen. He said the power behind the light is not blind to the desires of our hearts, and perhaps an eternal soul could be provided in the future."

357

"And?" Irene prodded.

The dragon stretched out her wings. "As you can see, nothing happened. I am still Thigocia."

"So you'll search for Gabriel right away?"

"Yes." She lifted her wings high. "I see no reason why I shouldn't begin immediately. I will—"

"Ahem!"

Everyone turned to see Walter standing next to Ashley. Bouncing on his toes, he rubbed his hands together. "That was a great story," he said, "but it's getting cold, so let's finish up this transformation thing and get going."

Ashley pushed him on the arm. "Oh, hush, Walter. Get a little backbone."

Bonnie laughed. "Well, I guess some things about Ashley haven't changed, but I can't tell if she lost her healing power and her smarts."

Walter looked inside Ashley's ear. "Hmmm. I think my life might be in danger if I tell you what I see."

Ashley set her hands on her hips and tapped her foot. "Walter, honestly, I . . ." She couldn't finish. Her scowl melted into a smile, then a laugh.

Walter squared his shoulders. "Okay, I survived that one." He turned to Billy and Bonnie and pointed over his shoulder with his thumb. "Patrick wants you two to come together."

"Why both of us?" Billy asked.

"He said what happened to Thigocia taught him something new about the gem. I guess you can ask him when you get there."

As Billy and Bonnie turned to leave, Ashley grabbed Bonnie's arm. "Wait! Aren't you going to say good-bye?"

"Good-bye?" Bonnie repeated. "Are you leaving?"

Ashley kissed Bonnie on the cheek, then hugged Billy. "I'm going with my mother." Taking two long steps, she leaped high onto Thigocia's back, then crawled up to the base of her neck. "Right, Mom?"

Thigocia curled her neck, bringing her head toward Ashley. "That would be—"

"Awesome!" Walter shouted, pumping his fist.

"Yes," Thigocia said, her huge maw widening into a grin. "Awesome."

Ashley rocked forward. "Mom, are you thinking what I'm thinking?"

"Almost certainly, my dear, and I say your idea is better than awesome. I am quite fond of that young man."

Ashley laid her hand on the space behind her and batted her eyelashes. "Walter," she said, speaking in a mock romantic tone, "we could use the help of a strong, brave, handsome knight in shining armor."

Walter's gaze darted all around. "Where you gonna find one of those?"

"Walter!" Ashley's hands flew to her hips again. "You promised me a dragon-riding trip. Are you coming with us or not?"

"Just kidding, just kidding." Walter tugged on his father's sleeve. "What do you say, Dad? We'd have a big, bad, scaly chaperone with danger sensing built in at no extra cost."

Catherine slid her hand behind Walter's head. "For how long, and what about school?"

Walter shrugged. "Who knows how long? I guess until we find this Gabriel guy. And if I can't learn from a dragon who's been around for thousands of years and a super genius who can calculate the square root of quantum physics, I'll never learn anything."

"But is she still a super genius?" Bonnie asked.

Ashley raised a finger. "Wait a minute. Larry wants something." She tapped her jaw. "What was that, Larry? . . . Well, you shouldn't be eavesdropping. . . . What news report? . . . Really? . . . Okay, that'll be our first stop. . . . No, you can't give me an IQ test. . . . What? Security reasons?" Ashley let out a low growl. "All right, just one question. . . . The square root of five thousand, two hundred, and six? How many digits do you want? . . . Okay, it's seventy-two point one, five, two, six. Satisfied? . . . Good!"

Walter lifted his hand toward Ashley and smiled at his parents. "And are you satisfied?"

Carl sighed. "If I were younger, I'd want to go myself." He glanced at Catherine, then nodded toward the dragon. "Sure. Go ahead."

"Now you're talkin'!" Walter crawled up Thigocia's scales and plopped down behind Ashley. "What was the news report Larry was talking about?"

Ashley laughed. "He heard that a mountain man and his dog were rescued in the flood waters."

"Arlo and Hambone? Cool! I guess he's okay, then."

"Yep. He claimed he was swimming to find help for two stranded boys, and he saw angels and dragons fighting in the sky. They're keeping him in the mental ward for observation."

Walter smirked. "Think we can spring him?"

Ashley patted Thigocia's scales. "I think Mom and I will be able to persuade them."

Walter laid his hands lightly on her shoulders. "Well, I'm ready if you're ready."

Karen reached up and pulled on Ashley's pant leg. "Ashley?"

360

"Yes?"

"I know Mrs. Bannister will take care of Stacey, Beck, Pebbles, and me, but who'll take care of Larry? I mean . . ." Karen pulled in her bottom lip, obviously trying not to cry. "Do you want me to do any work on Larry while you're gone?"

Ashley leaned forward and winked at Thigocia. The dragon wrapped her tail around Karen and lifted her into the air, then set her down behind Walter. Grinning from ear to ear, Karen threw her arms around Walter. "Tell Larry he's on his own!"

Ashley reached around Walter and patted Karen's red head. "You won't get airsick?"

Karen shook her head. "Not in the fresh air. I never get sick on regular roller coasters. Why would I get sick on a scaly one?"

Billy took off his scabbard and belt and tossed them up to Walter, sword and all. "You'll probably need this more than I will."

Walter caught the bundle and hugged it to his chest. He gazed at Billy, his eyes glinting red in the waning sunlight.

"Thanks." He gave Billy a thumbs up sign. "I'll do you proud."

Thigocia reared to her haunches. "Ready for liftoff?"

Ashley, Walter, and Karen all answered as one. "Ready!"

Thigocia flapped her mighty wings, sending a warm rush of wind over everyone. Billy's heart sank as he watched another friend lift into the sky. Half of him wanted to fly away to another great adventure, but the other half wanted to stay at home and rest for at least ten years. He let a smile break through. Okay, maybe nine years.

Thigocia made a sharp turn and flew by the crowd. Walter sat up high and waved at Billy. "Better get going! Sir Patrick's waiting for you." The dragon flew toward the lake, her winged frame becoming a shadow against the setting sun.

"Now that's a poetic sight," Bonnie said. "A boy, two girls, and a dragon flying into the sunset."

"Speaking of poetic . . ."—Billy held out his hand—"are you ready to see what Merlin's prophecy has in store?"

Bonnie slipped her hand into his, hesitating for a moment before looking into his eyes. "Will you like me no matter what I choose?"

Billy firmed his chin and answered slowly and clearly. "No matter what."

Without another word, the two walked hand in hand toward the visitor center. When they turned the corner they saw Sir Patrick standing next to a tall evergreen tree, the flashing pendant draped around his neck. With his straight and tall form, his deeply creased face, and scattered white hair, he could have been the professor's brother.

He pulled the pendant's chain over his head. "There's not much time left, so I'll explain this briefly. After seeing what the light did to Thigocia, it is clear that God uses the gem to transform according to something other than a spoken choice. In other words, no matter what you say you want, the light will only act according to what is true in your heart, and, I suppose, what his purposes for you are."

Billy let out a relieved sigh. Letting God read his mind took a huge burden off his shoulders. After all he had been through, after all the trials and torture that purged every trace of the old, faithless Billy Bannister, he knew he had nothing to hide. He tried to catch Bonnie's eye to guess what she was thinking, but her stoic expression gave him no clue.

"So," Patrick continued, "I will cast the gem's beam on both of you at once, and we shall see what God will decide. But first, you must pray, for your attachment with your maker is far more important than your relationship with one another."

Bonnie folded her hands over her chest, bowed her head, and closed her eyes.

Billy did the same, standing shoulder to shoulder with Bonnie, trying to put her out of his mind as he thought about all he had been through—surviving a plane crash in the West Virginia wilderness, fighting sword-to-sword with a dragon slayer, diving into a gem as a stream of energy, and wandering through the seven circles of Hades in search of long-lost prisoners. His dragon traits had been awesome . . . a pain, at times, but still awesome. He nodded slowly, breathing his thoughts in silent prayer. If God was finished using his fire-breathing and danger-sensing, he was ready to let them go.

Patrick's voice drifted into his thoughts. "I will now shine the light on your faces. You may look upon it if you wish."

Billy opened his eyes. As the light crossed his face, he was able to see through the rubellite's wide open gates, a brief flash, but the image inside the gem burned into his mind like a photograph. He saw an open book, an old book like *Fama Regis*, and two columns of fire leaped up from its pages, both shaped like humans, one male and one female. The image reminded him of what Thigocia had said. *Oracles of Fire.* Could this vision be like a prophecy? Could this flaming book be something that Walter and Ashley might have to deal with?

The flash of light crossed Bonnie's face, then flickered out completely. The gem suddenly shattered, and hundreds of sparks showered to the ground, twinkling briefly, then dying out.

"It is finished," Patrick said. "The light has completed its work, and I assume Dragons' Rest is no more."

Billy patted his body. Had he changed? He didn't feel any fire in his belly, but that wasn't so unusual, and he didn't sense any danger, but there probably wasn't any around.

He jerked his hand up and checked his ring. The gem was white! He quickly covered it with his other hand, hoping to surprise Bonnie at the right time, but as she turned to him, he forgot all about his own change. Her sparkling blue eyes filled with tears, and as the evening light faded, she gazed up at him with her hands behind her back. "Want to guess what color my ring is?" she asked.

Billy threw his arms around her shoulders and pulled her close. He didn't want to see her ring. He didn't want to see what was in her backpack, though he could have easily felt for a wing with his fingers. He laid his hand on the back of her head and cried. It didn't matter. It just didn't matter.

The Books:

The Books:
1. *Eye of the Oracle*
2. *Enoch's Ghost*
3. *Last of the Nephilim*
4. *The Bones of Makaidos*

For maximum enjoyment read all eight books in both series, starting with *Raising Dragons* and ending with *The Bones of Makaidos*.